WITHDRAWN

History of the Abderites

Sketch of Christoph Martin Wieland drawn by Anton Graff in 1794. Courtesy of the Schiller-Nationalmuseum and Deutsches Literaturarchiv in Marbach am Neckar, Germany. Reproduced by permission.

History of the Abderites
by Christoph Martin Wieland

Translated with an Introduction and Annotations
by Max Dufner

Bethlehem: Lehigh University Press
London and Toronto: Associated University Presses

Associated University Presses
440 Forsgate Drive
Cranbury, NJ 08512

Associated University Presses
25 Sicilian Avenue
London WC1A 2QH, England

Associated University Presses
P.O. Box 338, Port Credit
Mississauga, Ontario
Canada L5G 4L8

The paper used in this publication meets the requirements
of the American National Standard for Permanence of Paper
for Printed Library Materials Z39.48-1984.

Library of Congress Cataloging-in-Publication Data

Wieland, Christoph Martin, 1733–1813.
    [Abderites. English]
    History of the Abderites / by Christoph Martin Wieland ;
translated with an introduction and annotations by Max Dufner.
        p.   cm.
    Includes bibliographical references.
    ISBN 0-934223-25-4 (alk. paper)
    I. Dufner, Max, 1920–   . II. Title.
PT2563.A2E5   1993
833'.6—dc20   91-58966
                                                                                    CIP

PRINTED IN THE UNITED STATES OF AMERICA

For
MARGUERITE

Contents

Translator's Preface   9
Introduction   11
Chronology   35

Part One

Preface   41
First Book: Democritus among the Abderites   42
Second Book: Hippocrates in Abdera   104
Third Book: Euripides among the Abderites   136

Part Two

Fourth Book: The Trial Concerning the Ass's Shadow   191
Fifth Book: The Frogs of Latona   256

The Key to the History of the Abderites, 1781   301
Notes   308
Select Bibliography on Wieland and His Novel
    History of the Abderites   326

Translator's Preface

Christoph Martin Wieland's *History of the Abderites,* perhaps a greater literary work than his *Oberon* (Sengle) and one of the best German novels, has, so far as I know, appeared only once before in English, in the translation by Henry Christmas entitled *The Republic of Fools: being the History of the State and People of Abdera in Thrace.* It was published in two volumes without notes in 1861 by W. H. Allen in London. With my translation I wish to make this splendid novel available once again in English, and it is my hope that the Introduction and annotations will help make it accessible to a wide reading public so that I might, in some measure, repay this fascinating author for the many hours of enjoyment and delight I have found in his writings over the years.

To the version by Christmas I owe little or nothing, because I laid it aside until my own translation was finished. I differ basically with my predecessor about how Wieland should be translated. Wieland's style, as is well known, is the quintessence of his art and determines the character of his humor. The translation must therefore convey his manner as well as matter, and this is not possible if one changes his metaphors and imagery. These, however, are often bound, in turn, to his long, frequently very complex periods. Consequently, I have tried, wherever at all possible, to reproduce them in their entirety. (Cf., for example, the opening sentence of the Fourth Book.) Where I could not, I broke the construction into two or more parts and avoided scrupulously any summarizing of the original.

In translating dialogue I made such changes as were necessary to conform with current English style and punctuation. In almost all instances I left foreign expressions as they appear in Wieland's original. And so that the printed page of my version would at least somewhat resemble Wieland's, I retained as italics whatever words appear as *Sperrdruck* in German, but I dropped this device if it seemed to interfere with clarity.

Wieland's footnotes are indicated by asterisks and appear at the bottom of the page. My own annotations are given in back and are indicated by Arabic numerals in the text.

9

Grateful acknowledgement is made to the Weidmannsche Verlagsbuchhandlung in Hildesheim, Germany for permission to base my translation on the text of the *Geschichte der Abderiten* in Erste Abteilung: Werke, 10. Band, hrsg. von Ludwig Pfannmüller, in *Wielands Gesammelten Schriften,* hrsg. von der Deutschen Kommission der Königlich Preußischen Akademie der Wissenschaften (Berlin: Weidmann, 1913) and on the text of the preface [of 1796] in the same volume. My thanks, too, to the Oxford University Press for permission to quote a passage from Ian Jack's edition, 1968, of Laurence Sterne's *A Sentimental Journey through France and Italy.*

I am aware of how much I owe to the host of scholars who have written on Wieland. I also welcome this opportunity to acknowledge the help provided me by the notes in the Hanser edition of Wieland's selected works done by Fritz Martini and Hans Werner Seiffert, as well as those in the edition by Bernhard von Jacobi published by the Deutsches Verlagshaus Bong & Co. I also am under obligation for a number of valuable hints I found in William E. Yuill's textbook edition of *Der Prozeß um des Esels Schatten,* printed in 1964 by the Oxford University Press. I would like to add, too, that my students and I shed a tear when that book went out of print.

Professor Otto G. Graf of the Department of Germanic Languages and Literatures at The University of Michigan kindly read both the first version of my translation and the finished manuscript, and I am most grateful for his many invaluable suggestions.

To Professor Hansjörg Schelle, also of The University of Michigan, I wish to express my appreciation for his sustaining interest in this translation as well as for some important bibliographical data and for information that facilitated my securing the necessary copyright permissions.

Professors Richard C. Jensen and Thomas D. Worthen in the Classics Department at The University of Arizona gave me generous help in solving various problems posed by some of the Latin and Greek as well as classical themes and allusions in Wieland's novel.

I also am pleased to acknowledge gratefully the aid of William Sólyon-Fekete, senior legal specialist of the European Law Division in the Library of Congress, who translated a particularly obscure Latin legal phrase.

Most of all, however, I wish to thank my wife, who has, for so long and so patiently, borne up under being asked to listen to countless bits and pieces of translations, and with whom I discussed all aspects of this project. Her good advice, interest, and encouragement played a substantial part in bringing it to fruition.

Introduction

While the Golden Age of Spain, the classical period in France, and the Elizabethan Renaissance in England developed their great literatures, the Holy Roman Empire, of which the combined German nations formed the core, was gradually falling behind its western neighbors.

No single cause was responsible for this retardation. Perhaps it began with the decay of that union of commercial centers in the North known as the Hanseatic League, or with the opening of sea routes to the Orient, or with the discovery of the Americas. Surely the provincially oriented politics within the Empire, specifically the policies of the princes to weaken the emperor for their own profit, assured the cultural as well as the political decentralization of the country, and the establishment of a great German cultural center that would be the equivalent of Paris or London became an ever more remote possibility. Add to this the religious disorders leading to the Reformation, then the disruptions caused by the Reformation itself, and the almost simultaneous revolt of the peasants in 1525 with its awful aftermath, and it is not difficult to comprehend the extent of the dissipation and diversion of such energies as might otherwise have been directed toward more creative cultural ends. Then in the seventeenth century, the vast contest between France and Spain for hegemony in Europe was fought out in the Empire in the disastrous Thirty Years' War under the guise of a religious struggle. France emerged the overall victor. In the second half of that century, however, the recovery of the Empire was interrupted by French incursions from the west, and in the east the Turks unsuccessfully besieged Vienna.

Christoph Martin Wieland (1733–1813)

By the time of Wieland's birth on 5 September 1733, Paris, together with the French court at Versailles, was the hub of the world for many influential Germans. At most German courts, the aristocrats cultivated French manners and culture, but particularly

11

the French language. The members of the middle class with education used Latin for writing learned, technical, scientific, and legal
prose. German, consequently, was thought to lack the precision,
flexibility, subtlety, and refinement necessary for writing literature
comparable, let us say, to the works of Molière, Racine, and Pascal,
or of Milton and Dryden. If any really good new German literature
were to be written at all, therefore, it would have to be preceded,
or at least accompanied, by the development of a new medium of
expression—as is reflected in the title of Eric A. Blackall's book,
The Emergence of German as a Literary Language.[1] Among the
German authors who contributed to that effort, Wieland played a
substantial role both in his verse and prose. But good literature
needs not only to be written; somebody must also be interested in
reading it. Wieland was one of the writers acutely aware of this,
and he set out to create an enlightened readership that gradually
came to expect an ever higher quality of literature written in the
German language. He promoted those ends with his own literary
creations, by editing and publishing a long-lived journal, and by
translating into German a surprisingly large number of foreign
works. By using in his own works many forms, themes, and writing
techniques that he had encountered in his voluminous reading of
Latin, Greek, French, English, Italian, and Spanish authors and
others, he significantly expanded the possibilities for poetic and
literary expression in the German language.

Goethe, it has been said, stands last in a line that begins with
Homer and includes Sophocles, Dante, and Shakespeare. Wieland's name, on the other hand, may be similarly linked to those
of Aristophanes, Lucian of Samosata, Erasmus of Rotterdam, and
Voltaire, and he would surely merit that place if he had written
nothing but his *History of the Abderites.* However, he was incredibly prolific during his long life, and in his works we find in profu-
sion those qualities which combined to make him one of the great
German authors of his century: wit, grace, irony, humor, charm,
elegance of diction, and an artistic sprightliness and playful virtu-
osity comparable to that of his contemporary in music, Franz Joseph Haydn (1732–1809).

Much in his early writing reflected his background and education
as a preacher's son, for he was one of the many German authors of
the eighteenth century who, like Gotthold Ephraim Lessing (1729–
1781), the author of *Nathan der Weise (Nathan the Wise),* was
brought up in a parsonage. By the age of thirteen he had outgrown
the schooling available in his hometown, the little Free Imperial
City of Biberach on the river Riss in Swabia. He continued his

education at the boarding school at Klosterberge (near Magde-
burg), where he was also heavily influenced by pietistic ideas and
attitudes. But already at Klosterberge he was exposed to skepti-
cism and such modes of thinking that led to his writing an essay
on how the world could have been created without God. Here already, it seems, there were sown in his mind the germs of that
struggle between heart and head, idealism and materialism, the
ethereal and the human, and between pious enthusiasm and logic
that was to recur again and again in his writings. It became as
typical a theme for Wieland as that of the relationship between the
bourgeois and the artist for Thomas Mann.

In 1752 Wieland became the protégé of the Swiss critic and
author Johann Jakob Bodmer (1698–1783) in Zürich. Bodmer, who
in 1732 had completed a prose translation of Milton's *Paradise
Lost,* had previously been the host of the north German poet
Friedrich Gottlieb Klopstock (1724–1803), author of the religious
epic *Der Messias (The Messiah),* that Wieland admired very much
when its first three cantos appeared in 1748. Bodmer encouraged
the pious religiosity and zealous virtuousness he found in his young
guest. And the not altogether unexpected but nevertheless dis-
tressing news from home that Wieland's fiancée, Sophie Gutermann, was about to marry someone else only reinforced those
tendencies. But he left Bodmer's house and began to earn his living
by tutoring in Zürich.

On 20 July 1758 he had the satisfaction of seeing on the stage in
nearby Winterthur the blank-verse drama he had written in adaptation of *The Tragedy of Lady Jane Grey* by the English dramatist
Nicholas Rowe (1674–1718). In 1779 Lessing would complete his
own drama in blank verse, namely *Nathan the Wise,* and in the
decade after that both Goethe and Schiller would use this metrical
line in their classical dramas. Lessing, in his review of *Lady Jo-
hanna Gray,* noted a change in its author with the words: "Join me
in being pleased! Mr. Wieland has left the ethereal spheres and is
walking again among human beings."[2]

Some scholars believe, however, that the change in Wieland had
come much earlier and that it was the result of a kind of "negative
conversion," the sudden collapse of his former religious values and
attitudes.[3] But another view finds his early seraphic and pietistic
works more suffused with sensuality than has been commonly recognized and the so-called frivolous verse and prose of his later
years in Biberach informed with a more or less suppressed gravity
and seriousness. There was, accordingly, no real metamorphosis
in Wieland's mentality—much less a collapse—but rather just a

gradual shift in emphasis, with neither Platonic idealism nor sensuality being given up entirely.[4] This would seem to be an entirely reasonable assessment of Wieland's development in these early years of his career.

In June 1759 he left Zürich for Bern, where again he became a tutor but was soon disappointed with his new situation. Here, however, he met and was soon engaged to the brilliant but homely Julie Bondely, whose character and intellect were considerably stronger than his own. Later she became an admirer and friend of Jean-Jacques Rousseau. In Bern, Wieland wrote his prose drama *Clementina von Poretta,* based on an episode from Samuel Richardson's novel *Sir Charles Grandison* (1754).

His concern about the practical business of earning a living, especially in view of his engagement, caused him to consider bookselling and publishing, even the founding of a journal. Then suddenly he received word that he had been elected a senator of Biberach. As he was situated, that was most welcome news, and so at the end of May 1760 he was back in his hometown ready to take up his duties. He was also elected city clerk, but he immediately ran into such political complexities as would later serve him as models for the way municipal affairs are conducted in his novel about Abdera. Everything in Biberach was complicated by those provisions in the treaties concluding the Thirty Years' War in 1648 stipulating that this town, with a population divided almost equally between Catholics and Protestants, should—with some exceptions—fill each post in the city government with two people; that is, with one from each of the two religions. The office of the city clerk happened to be one exception, but that only caused him still greater difficulties. In point of fact, his first four years back home in Biberach were very likely the hardest and most trying times in his life.

Wieland himself, however, contributed to his own troubles. For example, his imprudent attentions to Sophie Gutermann's sister, Cateau von Hillern, the pretty wife of the mayor, aroused her husband's ire against him. This woman, incidentally, is thought to have been his model for Dame Salabanda in his *History of the Abderites.* Then he fell in love with a charming nineteen-year-old Catholic girl, Christine Hagel. She bore his illegitimate child, and he very much desired to make her his wife. But because neither her parents nor his would give up their adamant objections to a mixed marriage, and because such a marriage would have upset the town's delicate political equilibrium, he finally had to recognize that it would not be possible.[5]

This aspect of his existence was then settled on 21 October 1765 when he married Anna Dorothea von Hillenbrand, the daughter of an Augsburg merchant. She was neither pretty nor educated and intellectual, and it clearly was an arranged marriage. Despite that, it was more successful than most, because they came to care for one another like an ideal couple. When she died in 1801, they had been married for thirty-six years.

The diplomat and government official Count von Stadion had retired to Warthausen Castle on his estate just north of Biberach. Sophie La Roche, née Gutermann, Wieland's former fiancée and now the wife of the Count's illegitimate son, invited the Biberach poet to Warthausen. Soon the Count's fine library was available to him, and he was often asked to the castle to read from his newest creations. For the sophisticated and enlightened circle of friends here he wrote a series of four sensuous and rather racy verse narratives published in 1765 under the title *Comical Tales*. His audience was amazed that such things could be said in German as gracefully as they had been accustomed to hearing them said in French. Many of his countrymen, however, would object to these "lubricious verses," and with this criticism we see emerging the image of Wieland as an immoral writer. Others again would agree that he did indeed write like a Frenchman and, consequently, they thought he was not really a good *German* author.

One of the great accomplishments of his Biberach years is his translation of twenty-two of Shakespeare's plays—*A Midsummer Night's Dream* in verse, the rest in prose, and all based on the edition by Warburton. They were published between 1762 and 1766 in Zürich in eight volumes. While the last few plays may betray the translator's impatience to finish, and while the quality of his work is admittedly uneven, this version of Shakespeare was the one most often used as the basis of much of the theorizing about the great English playwright and of such German scripts as were used on the stages for much of the remainder of the eighteenth century.

As a kind of relaxation from translating Shakespeare, he wrote his first novel, published in 1764, *Der Sieg der Natur über die Schwärmerei, oder die Abenteuer des Don Sylvio von Rosalva (The Triumph of Nature over Fancy, or the Adventures of Don Sylvio of Rosalva)*, "in which everything marvelous happens naturally," to quote an early subtitle. It is a satirical work based very loosely on both *Gil Blas* by Lesage (1668–1747) and the *Don Quixote* of Cervantes (1547–1616). The setting, not surprisingly, is Spain, and Don Sylvio, the hero, accompanied by a Sancho Panza figure named Pedrillo, is to be cured of his belief in fairy tales—a meta-

phor for superstition. While this may sound a bit thin, the story is
told very cleverly and with much irony and an engaging light touch.
According to a recent evaluation, "Wieland's mastery of prose in
his first novel is such that *Don Sylvio* can stand as a stylistic accomplishment comparable to Cervantes', Fielding's, and Sterne's best
works."[6] And the intercalated fairy tale about Prince Biribinker,
sometimes published separately, is a rococo gem.

The most significant work he wrote in Biberach is the novel
Geschichte des Agathon (History of Agathon), the first version of
which was published in 1766 and 1767. It is considered the first
psychological novel in German, but also the first German *Bildungs-
roman* (novel of personal development), a type that has found much
favor in Germany and includes Goethe's *Wilhelm Meister,* for example, and Thomas Mann's *Zauberberg (The Magic Mountain).*
Much of Wieland's own experience is reflected in *Agathon,* and so
it is in a manner of speaking an autobiographical work. Here again
we find a young man having to choose repeatedly between idealism
and materialism, between the ethereal and the real. Heavily influenced by Henry Fielding's *Tom Jones* (1749), this novel is set, like
some earlier famous French novels such as Fénelon's *Télémaque*
(1699) and the *Voyage de Cyrus* (1727) by André Michel Ramsay,
in ancient Greece. Wieland, a highly gifted scholar of Greek, is
thoroughly at home in that milieu and writes about it with remarkable ease. He also has created some prepossessing and engaging
characters: Agathon, the naïve and almost incurable idealist; Hippias, the worldly and eloquent materialist; the lovely courtesan
Danae, whom Agathon loves and who tells her story in the second
version of the novel printed in 1773; and, finally, the attractive
philosopher Archytas, who, in the last expanded version of 1794,
leads Agathon to a harmonious, balanced view of life. No less a
critic than Lessing expressed his admiration for *Agathon* and said:
"It is the first and only novel for people who think, [it is] of classical
taste."[7]

Wieland's Biberach years close with two of his best works in
verse: *Idris,* later called *Idris und Zenide,* and *Musarion.* The first
poem, a romantic-comic epic, seems to have grown out of his attraction to the poetic works of the Italian Ludovico Ariosto (1474–
1533), author of the celebrated romantic epic *Orlando furioso.* Wieland set about adapting Ariosto's stanza form, the ottava rima, to
German and then composed a long poem of such sparkling color
and brilliance as will astonish any uninitiated reader. It is altogether
likely that this beautiful, resplendent creation, whose theme concerns the search for a love relationship that is balanced between

outright, uncontrolled sensuality and vapid Platonism, remained a fragment of five cantos because the poet found it impossible to maintain its intensity.

Musarion, oder die Philosophie der Grazien (Musarion, or the Philosophy of the Graces) is a comic narrative poem with a strongly didactic character, written in free verse, and divided into three parts. Neatly rounded off and far less intricate than *Idris und Zenide,* it is generally considered a high point of Wieland's rococo art. The plot, once again, concerns the hero's finding a golden mean between two extremes, here represented by two philosophers, Kleanth and Theophron. The loving Musarion leads Phanias to know and be himself. Goethe was one of those charmed by this poem when it first appeared in print.

In 1769 Wieland accepted a professorship of philosophy at the Catholic university in Erfurt. Since he lacked the academic degrees ordinarily required for such a position, and because he was a Protestant, the older faculty members were not overjoyed at his appointment. What had initially looked very promising did not turn out to be so favorable a position after all. Consequently, he did not stay there very long.

Nevertheless, he somehow found time enough in Erfurt for his writing in spite of having to prepare his lectures. Here he finished an intricate rococo poem of eighteen cantos written in especially devised ten-line stanzas, *Der neue Amadis (The new Amadis),* a comical and satirical work, in which he gave his capricious poetic spirit free rein.

Wieland, the philosopher in the Socratic sense, now turned his attention to other matters, and so he wrote the novel *Sokrates mainomenos oder die Dialogen des Diogenes von Sinope (The Mad Socrates or the Dialogues of Diogenes of Sinope).* This short work is a sort of vindication of Diogenes, the cynic, who lives in a barrel and wishes above all else to achieve an independent life without either burdensome expectations or obligations. The barrel of Wieland's Diogenes "is turned into the residence of an aristocrat of the spirit, a cosmopolitan and citizen of the world."[8] In the section bearing the title "Diogenes' Republic," Wieland has constructed a very amusingly impossible utopia with a playfulness of the imagination such as gave birth to the story of Prince Biribinker in *Don Sylvio* and to Democritus' story of the land of milk and honey in the *History of the Abderites.* All in all, it is a novel with many attractive ideas and very much worth reading. It was published in 1770 in Leipzig.

The second work of his Erfurt years is what Germans call a

Staatsroman, a novel concerned with politics and statecraft. It is entitled *Der goldene Spiegel oder Die Könige von Scheschian (The Golden Mirror or The Kings of Scheschian)* and was published in 1772, also in Leipzig. It is an excellent piece of storytelling that utilizes all the advantages of the narrative techniques afforded by its basic structure: stories told within a frame that is within a frame itself. In addition, Wieland uses a narrative device very popular in his century, namely the fiction that what is told has been translated from a translation of a translation, and so on, replete with notes and commentaries of the various translators. But the fundamental irony in *The Golden Mirror* is that the ruler Shah Gebal, listening to topics of the most serious import, appreciates what is being told him only for its soporific effect, for he wants to go to sleep.

When this novel was finished, its author sent a copy to the enlightened Emperor Joseph II in Vienna,[9] because Wieland was at this time in hopes of securing a position at the Imperial Court or some other post under its patronage. But these expectations came to nothing. Fortunately he was not long thereafter induced by the Dowager Duchess of Weimar, Anna Amalia, the niece of Frederick the Great, to leave his post at Erfurt so that he might participate as a philosopher in the education of her two sons, Karl August, the future duke, who was then but fifteen, and his brother Konstantin.[10] His novel had, after all, not failed to make an impression in high places. But Wieland's performance in this post was quite disappointing for several reasons.

Soon after his arrival in Weimar he began to be preoccupied with plans for his journal *Der teutsche Merkur (The German Mercury).* Its title, though not its format, was patterned after that of the *Mercure de France,* and its first issue was published in January 1773. While it was, first of all, a money-making venture that its editor and publisher needed to support his growing family, it did succeed in raising the level of its readers' taste and sophistication, and it appealed to a wide public for many years, from 1773 to 1810. Its issues contained a broad variety of contributions: original works, among them many of Wieland's own writings such as the *History of the Abderites,* that appeared serially, and his poem *Oberon;* essays, such as Wieland's on Erasmus; and reviews, critical articles, announcements of new publications, popular scientific articles, and Wieland's own observations on current events such as, later, the newest developments in the French Revolution. Although the number of subscribers tapered off after a few years—there were a mere 800 by 1798[11]—this journal outlasted many other similar enterprises.

It may be recalled that in 1773, too, there appeared the second, expanded version of his novel *Agathon*. Evidence of the social level of his readership and the extent and character of his popularity at this time is offered by the names of the subscribers to this novel that we find printed at the end of the fourth volume. Heading the list is Her Majesty, the Empress of Russia [Catherine the Great], who is down for twenty copies! Then come the King and Queen of Sweden, the Electors of Cologne, Trier, and the Palatinate, the Prince and Princess of Anhalt-Dessau, and so on for three more small octavo pages. After that comes the list—thirty-six pages long—of commoners from St. Petersburg, Utrecht, Milano, London, Prague, Rome, Paris, Stockholm, Copenhagen, Riga, and, of course, from numerous cities all over Germany.[12]

In that same year he also finished work on his operetta *Alceste,* after the *Alcestis* by Euripides, with music by Anton Schweitzer. Its initial success was ultimately eroded by the annoying criticisms of the younger generation, the quite unsympathetic "Storm and Stress" writers. Drama, musical or otherwise, was in fact not Wieland's forte, yet he wrote several other such *Singspiele,* as they are called in German, one of the last being *Rosamunde,* to the première of which in the theater at Mannheim he was invited in December 1777. But the Elector of Bavaria died, and so the performance was postponed until two years later, when Wieland, unfortunately, was not in the audience.

In the same year in which Goethe's novel *The Sorrows of Young Werther* was published, 1774, the pages of Wieland's *Geschichte der Abderiten (History of the Abderites)* first began appearing in *The German Mercury.* It is discussed fully in the second part of this introduction.

Then in 1775 there appeared the novel *Geschichte des weisen Danischmend (History of the Wise Danischmend),* his "appendage" to *The Golden Mirror.* The philosophical prime minister of the previous work is the principal character here. He learns the wisdom of staying as far as possible from the seats of the mighty and concentrating on the really important things in life, i.e., on cultivating one's garden.

That the twelve verse tales Wieland wrote in the seventies "are more than just preliminary steps toward mastery" in the celebrated *Oberon,*[13] which appeared in 1780, is certainly true; several of those poems, such as, perhaps, *Gandalin* (1776), *Geron der Adeliche (Geron the Noble,* 1777), and *Pervonte, oder die Wünsche (Pervonte, or the Wishes,* 1778–1779) are masterpieces of their kind and afford us an insight into this poet's remarkable abilities as a

writer of verse. Yet it is also true that the romantic epic *Oberon* is
the crown of this fruitful poetic decade, surely the most productive
period in his life.

Oberon consists of twelve cantos and is written in ottava rima,
as was *Idris und Zenide.* Invention was not one of Wieland's strong
points, but like Vergil in *The Aeneid,* he imposed his style on traditional materials. Indeed much of his art consisted of ingenious
combinations and reworking of themes and stories he had found—
we do not always know where. Here he took Oberon and Titania,
the king and queen of the fairies, from Shakespeare's *A Midsummer Night's Dream,* the story of "January and May" from Chau-
cer's "Merchant's Tale," probably via Alexander Pope, and the
character and adventures of Huon from a modern retelling of the
medieval romance *Huon de Bordeaux.* And some believe he used
still additional sources. In any event, themes, images, incidents,
and scenes from world literature that we find woven into the fabric
of *Oberon* include a desert isle, pirates who take slaves, and escape
and abduction from the seraglio.[14] The latter, as well as the magic
horn of Oberon together with a number of operatic elements, remind us how close this poem approaches the spirit of Mozart's
music, and so it is not surprising that this lively, poetic fairy tale
inspired an opera of the same name by Carl Maria von Weber
(1786–1826).

In the years 1786–1789, Wieland published *Dschinnistan,* a
three-volume collection of partly original, partly newly translated
and reworked fairy tales, and then, except for the work on his
various translations, he devoted most of his energies to the writing
of more novels.

His next novel was *Geheime Geschichte des Philosophen Peregrinus Proteus (Secret History of the Philosopher Peregrinus Proteus),* 1789–1791. The structure of this novel is particularly
interesting. It consists of a dialogue conducted in the hereafter
between Lucian of Samosata, the second-century satirist who had
written a very damaging life of Peregrinus, and his contemporary,
the now-deceased Peregrinus himself, who tells his biographer just
where and in what way his account is in error. Thus, and for Wieland typically, the author relates the life of his main character in
more than one perspective. Accordingly, the entire book has the
character of another vindication. In this one we are given the self-
corrected history of an honest and upright, but irrational, religious
enthusiast who, in the end, sets himself on fire under the illusion
that his example will somehow benefit mankind.

Apollonius of Tyana, a figure from the first century A.D. who was ostensibly a miracle worker, is the subject of the novel *Agatho-dämon* (1799), which means "good spirit," the name given him by the people who take his well-intended deceptions for miraculous deeds. He was regarded by various commentators as an unprincipled master deceiver, and Wieland wrote this novel to exonerate him. At the end of the book, the primitive Christians are discussed. Although he approves of them, Apollonius, who has retired to his mountain retreat, the setting for the novel, does not intend to join them. Again the narrative form is the dialogue, with the difference, however, that Hegesias, the narrator, conveys what is told by writing a letter about it to his friend.

Wieland's last major novel, *Aristipp und einige seiner Zeitgenossen (Aristipp and a Few of His Contemporaries)*, 1800–1801, is also his biggest and most complex. This four-volume account of the Greek world in the fourth century B.C. is written in epistolary form. Its title character is a philosopher from Cyrene in North Africa who was a pupil of Socrates and the predecessor of Epicurus. It is Wieland's purpose here to elucidate Aristippus's philosophy by contrasting it to the thought of other great thinkers of that age, among them Plato. Against the backdrop formed by these discussions and a huge panorama of the cultural life of those times, the author introduces Laïs, another famous courtesan, whose story is essentially tragic. She only superficially resembles Danae in the novel *Agathon*, and Wieland made the apparently unwitting error of allowing her to be killed at the end of the third volume. Because a great part of the fourth is taken up by a discussion of Plato's *Republic*, it was not likely to become as popular as its author had hoped.[15] He never did write the planned fifth volume, so it is actually an unfinished work.

The short epistolary novel *Menander and Glycerion* (1804) and its companion piece *Krates and Hipparchia* (1805) deal with the themes of love and marriage, and the *Hexameron of Rosenhain* (1805), a collection of six stories—three fairy tales and three novellas—bring to a close Wieland's career as an author.

After his work on Shakespeare in the sixties, Wieland did not return to translation until 1782, two years after the completion of *Oberon*, when his German version of the *Epistles* of Horace appeared in two parts. In 1786 his translation of Horace's *Satires* was published, that also in two parts. Then there followed in relatively quick succession: *The Complete Works of Lucian of Samosata* in six volumes (1788–1789); Aristophanes' *The Acharnians* (1794), *The Knights* (1797), *The Clouds* (1798), and *The Birds* (1805–1806); Isocrates's *Panegyricus* (1796); *Socratic Dialogues from Xeno-*

phon's "Memorabilia of Socrates" (1799–1800); Xenophon's Symposium (1802); Euripides' Ion (1802) and Helen (1805); and, finally, The Complete Letters of Cicero in five volumes (1808–1812)—the sixth completed and edited by Friedrich David Gräter and published in 1818. It is a formidable accomplishment.

In 1807, the year after the occupation of Weimar by Napoleon's troops following the Battle of Jena, Duchess Anna Amalia died, and Wieland, who had lost his wife six years earlier, felt the loss keenly, because in these last years she had been a close friend. In 1808, Napoleon expressed the wish to speak to both Goethe and Wieland, the two great German authors. Each was then later decorated with the Cross of the Legion of Honor, and from the Czar of Russia, Wieland also received the Order of St. Anne.[16]

Wieland died on 20 January 1813, and because he had joined the Lodge Amalia of the Weimar Freemasons in 1809, this group held a memorial service for him a month later. It was Goethe who delivered the eulogy which has been reprinted under the title In Fraternal Memory of Wieland.

During his own lifetime, Wieland had managed to survive the attacks made on him at his prime by writers of the younger generation. But posterity would probably have been much kinder to him if he had not been the object of a very malicious and defamatory accusation of plagiarism made in 1799 by a still younger generation, the group known as the early romanticists. His literary fame never really recovered from this attack.

Moreover, the times had changed, and an entirely different complex of literary sensibilities came into vogue. The young romanticists thought of Wieland as belonging to the time before the French Revolution. Dissatisfied with the realities of life in the Age of Napoleon, they sought escape in a yearning for unattainable ideals, or they fled into reveries about the Middle Ages, the era from which the enlightened thinkers of two centuries had worked so diligently to free themselves. In contrast to the earlier cosmopolitan attitudes, of which Wieland's History of the Abderites is such a fine example, the promotion of nationalism and indigenous culture became the fashion. In continuation of a trend begun in the "Storm and Stress" period, the folksong was elevated to the status of veritable paradigm of lyric poetry, and the simple speech of the peasant was thought to be aesthetically superior to the subtle and learned diction imitated from ancient models.

As was only natural, the Enlightenment, of which Wieland had been a leading German representative, generated its reaction and antithesis. The romanticists were consequently drawn not only to the irrational, but to the superrational as well; that is, to the supernatural, through which they hoped to transcend the "merely logical." Accordingly, they cultivated instinct, intuition, the fantastic and incomprehensible, the mystical and mysterious, "the nightside of science" (G. H. Schubert), the musical, the ethereal and, finally, a return to religious faith and values. Because the romantic canons of literary criticism were accepted in Germany until very recent times, and since the popularity of Schiller and Goethe grew to such proportions in the nineteenth century, Wieland was overshadowed and looked upon as an author of an epoch long outmoded.

Yet, in spite of his writings' being ill-suited for service in the interests of German nationalism, whether of the Bismarckian "blood and iron" variety or the saber-rattling kind in the reign of William II, enough literary scholars appreciated him to begin, before World War I, the Prussian Academy Edition of his works. It was intended to be definitive but continues to be far from complete. The era of National Socialism from 1933 to 1945 was, of course, an atmosphere hardly conducive to Wieland studies, but even then, surprisingly, scholarly interest did not cease.

Not long after World War II, new studies on Wieland by Fritz Martini appeared. Then in 1949 two important books were published: Friedrich Sengle's *Wieland* and Hans Wolffheim's *Wielands Begriff der Humanität (Wieland's Concept of Humanity)*. Since then, in the German-speaking lands as well as abroad, many valuable contributions have been made to Wieland scholarship, especially by some noteworthy doctoral dissertations. Moreover, just when the older out-of-print sets of his works had already become all too scarce, two new thin-paper editions of Wieland's selected works appeared: one in three volumes by Friedrich Beissner and published in 1964 by Winkler in Munich; and the other the five-volume annotated edition by Fritz Martini and Hans Werner Seiffert, also published in Munich, by Hanser in 1964–1968. In the course of the next two decades a surprising number of separate editions of single works were published. Then, in the later 1980s, a reprint of the "Prussian Academy Edition" appeared in fifteen volumes under the Weidmann imprint in Hildesheim. And, as the present translation goes to press, an entirely new edition of Wieland's works in twelve volumes (printed on thin paper and supplied with generous annotations) is in the process of publication by the Deutscher Klassiker Verlag in Frankfurt am Main. These editions should help to promote and maintain interest in Wieland. In any case, the newer literary historians give him such attention as would seem to assure his rightful place in the history of German and world literature. (See Select Bibliography, pp. 326–27.)

Let us now consider his novel.

History of the Abderites

Soon after he had completed the second version of his novel *Agathon,* Wieland began writing the *History of the Abderites,* which he then published in seventeen irregular installments from 1774 to 1780 in his journal *Der teutsche Merkur.* In doing so he also produced the first serialized novel in German.[17] When the "Key" was added, the entire work appeared in the next year, 1781, as a book.[18]

This satirical novel, in its author's own words, is a "work that was written to entertain all intelligent people and to admonish and chastise all fools."[19] It is thus in the tradition of European literature about fools that includes Sebastian Brant's *Das Narrenschiff (The Ship of Fools)* of 1494, the *Moriae Encomium (Praise of Folly)* of 1509 by Erasmus, and the two German chapbooks of the late sixteenth century: the *Lalenbuch* chronicling the deeds of the foolish inhabitants of Lalenburg, "situated in Misnopotamia behind Utopia," and *Die Schildbürger,* a reworking of the same material that relates the odd doings of the people living in the small backwoods town of Schilda.

It is not at all certain what initially impelled Wieland to write this novel. Could it have been suggested by the much-quoted words of Puck, "Lord, what fools these mortals be!" in act 3, scene ii of Shakespeare's *A Midsummer Night's Dream?* In the so-called "Key to the History of the Abderites," Wieland gives us a fictional account of how he came upon the idea. On a beautiful spring evening in the 1770s, he writes, he was bored and overcome with the consciousness that his creative spirit had deserted him. As he was looking out of his window, it seemed to him suddenly as if he were hearing a voice that said: "Sit down and write the history of the Abderites." Yes, this seemed a good idea, and right off he started looking things up, arranging his materials, and writing, and he was pleased with the rapid progress of his work (303–4).

However, in the posthumous papers of his friend Karl August Böttiger, we read a quite different version, for here Wieland is quoted as having said in 1796: "The Abderites had their origin in a period of ill humor while, as I was looking down from my dormer window, I saw the entire world full of excrement and ordure and decided to take my revenge on it."[20] This prepares us in part for the sharp edge on much of his humor and the misanthropic under-current apparent now and again throughout the novel. Obviously, however, he took the advice of Seneca, quoted in the first chapter of the Second Book, to the effect that we should strive to see the follies of the great multitude as ridiculous rather than odious, that we should not weep but laugh, rather, at human life (106), and so he criticizes with humor instead of invective. In other words, he takes his "revenge" through writing a satire. But his narration is generally developed in the capriciously humorous manner that he learned from the English author Laurence Sterne (1713–1768), whose novel *Tristram Shandy* he claimed to have read thirty times,[21] and the acerbity of his prose at the beginning is gradually relieved as the novel progresses.[22] We do find evidence of his sympathy with the Abderites, such as his assertion near the end of the Third Book: "By the way, the author of this history makes the comment here that: 'The pronounced disposition of the Abderites to allow the arts of the imagination and imitation to deceive them is not exactly what he likes least about them'" (181). Moreover, even as Democri-tus at the end of the Fourth Book is about to withdraw from Abdera permanently, he finds that his fellow citizens, like the Athenians,

> can laugh quite ingenuously at their own foolish tricks. For that reason they get no wiser. . . . but a lot has always been gained when a nation can bear to have honest people make fun of its follies, and when it laughs, too, instead of getting spiteful about it like the apes. (255)

The target of Wieland's wit and humor throughout is the igno-rance, backwardness, provinciality, bigotry, narrow-mindedness, pedantry, lack of taste, and the sodden contentment with things as they are that he had found all around him—in Biberach, at Erfurt, in Mannheim, Weimar, and elsewhere. But instead of attacking the follies of his contemporaries directly, he gives his novel an ancient Greek setting, the small Thracian city-state of Abdera in the fifth century B.C. And by allowing, indeed inviting his readers them-selves to draw whatever parallels they may wish or are able to perceive between the odd and foolish goings-on in this ancient backwater and life in contemporary Germany, he achieves the req-uisite degree of satirical indirection.

Yet no ancient Greek ever experienced anything quite like Wie-land's Abdera, for he has created some hilarious anachronisms, the source of much of the esoteric humor in the novel. Conse-quently, the more the readers know about ancient Greece, the more they find to laugh at. The free social life of the women in Abdera, for example, has little in common with that of their real ancient counterparts. The Abderite stage, orchestra, actors, and audience in the Third Book are almost entirely un-Greek. In addition, this sort of thing permits his indulging in little jokes such as his telling us in the Second Book that the physician Hippocrates could not appreciate the beauty of the Abderite women because he was short-sighted and had no lorgnette. In a footnote he then offers the ironic remark: "Those who might wonder a bit about this may be helped by the information that at that time lorgnettes—had not yet been invented" (124).

While some of the follies of the Abderites result from their drawing, like the chief priest Stilbon in the Fifth Book, the "correct conclusions from false premises" (269), most of the humor in this novel is generated by some kind of unsuitability, incongruities, disproportions, and discrepancies—between ends and means, cause and effect, ambition and accomplishment, duty and performance, the apparent and the real, what is and what should be, and between expectation and result.

The discrepancy between expectation and result is often expressed by Wieland through a humorous device found in many of his other works as well, and so it may be considered a typical element in his style. He uses it repeatedly and to especially good effect in the *History of the Abderites,* as is illustrated by the following example. In chapter 12 of the First Book, Democritus, playing a little joke on the good women of Abdera, tells them he knows a foolproof way to make any sleeping woman reveal in an audible voice whatever is on her mind. Since they know of no reason to disbelieve him, they blush in embarrassment and otherwise betray their uneasiness, all of them, that is, save one.

> Among the seven women present in the company there was only one whose face and bearing remained the same as before. It will be imagined that she was old, or ugly, or even virtuous; but she was none of these. She was—deaf. (96)

The important point, expressed in ironic humor after a dash, is in effect a deflation.[23] Readers are amused because they have been led to expect they know not what—and the author offers them nothing but the obvious.

Wieland often includes his readers in his narrative by discussing with them what is going on in the novel, by suggesting that they take part in filling in details of a description, anecdote, or story or, as in the Third Book, to cite a well-known example, by actually inviting them to participate directly in the action. There we read:

> We apologize to our readers if they have been detained too long with this general account of the Abderite theater. The time has meanwhile come for the play to begin, and so, without further ado, we now go into the amphitheater of this praiseworthy republic, where the reader will please take a seat, as he likes, either next to the small, fat councillor, or with the priest Strobylus, or next to the gossip Antistrepsiades, or next to any of those beautiful Abderite women with whom we have made him acquainted in the previous chapters. (151)

In the first three books the author provides his readers with a criterion in each by which to measure the foolishness and the shortcomings of the Abderites. In the first, it is the naturalist Democritus; in the second, the renowned Hippocrates; and in the third, the famous Athenian playwright Euripides. These three men resemble in their functions the figures with their backs to the viewers that we find in the foreground of many paintings by the artist Caspar David Friedrich (1774–1840). We are invited, as it were, to appreciate what appears in the rest of the pictures through their eyes. In much the same way we find ourselves submitting to the author's implied suggestions that we view the Abderites via the minds of these three aristocrats of the intellect. In a sense, however, each reader is himself an "Abderite," thus the ironic relationships among the author, characters, and reader sometimes achieve an unexpected subtlety.

In the second part of the work, consisting of the Fourth and Fifth Books, Wieland provides no further exemplary characters, perhaps because he believed his readers had, by this time, become sufficiently well oriented in Abdera. The leading Abderite characters are depicted vividly as well, for the author's deft touches give them what seems to be more than fictional reality.

His contrasting the high priest Strobylus with the archpriest Agathyrsus in chapter 6 of the Fourth Book turns out to be a very successful technique of character delineation, because each helps to define the other. Quite obviously we are to understand that the high priest of the cult of Latona, Strobylus, is the Abderite equivalent of an eighteenth-century Protestant clergyman. And, just as clearly, Agathyrsus, archpriest of the Jasonites, is supposed to suggest a corpulent Catholic prelate.

> In addition to so many reasons for the traditional jealousy and dislike between the two princes of the Abderite clergy there was, besides, a

personal antipathy which Strobylus and Agathyrsus felt toward one
another that was a natural result of the contrast in their mentality. (207)

Agathyrsus was the more worldly and the wealthier of the two.
He loved the arts, pleasure, and amusement. And in contrast to
Strobylus with his fanatic concern for the frogs of Latona, Agathyrsus "had the reputation of being one of those priests who have
little faith in their own gods" (207).

Dame Salabanda, the niece of Strobylus and formerly involved—
more or less—in a liaison with the archpriest, is the most interesting Abderite woman in the novel. It is she who was presumably
modeled on Cateau von Hillern, the mayor's wife in Biberach. Salabanda was considered a wise woman by her fellow citizens, and
she had immense influence on what went on in the Senate. Moreover, her house, "that belonged among the best in the city, was the
place where all affairs were prepared, all quarrels made up, and all
elections settled. In a word, Dame Salabanda did what she wanted
in Abdera" (168).

Guild master Pfriem, the cobbler, who emphasizes quite unnecessarily that he is "not an educated man" (213) and continually
proves it by stumbling over the learned or other polysyllabic words
he thinks are necessary to express himself adequately (89, 131,
177–78, 197–98), is a raucous professional democrat, rabble-rouser,
and the chief representative of hoi polloi in Abdera.

The gallery of Abderitic types would, of course, be incomplete
without the tittering women who, like a flock of nervous geese,
cackle and hiss from one scene into the next. Then there is that
ubiquitous busybody, the short, fat councillor, the very archetype
of the legislators of Abdera. Nor should we forget the poetic-musi-
cal-theatrical establishment led by Hyperbolus and his colleague,
that agile son of the Muses, Gryllus, the son of Cyniscus.

The *History of the Abderites* is not the usual sort of novel with
a plot developed from beginning to end. Its five divisions or
"Books" are variations on a theme, each of them conveying a dif-
ferent aspect of life in Abdera, and they respectively bear the titles
"Democritus among the Abderites," "Hippocrates in Abdera,"
"Euripides among the Abderites," "The Trial Concerning the Ass's
Shadow," and, finally, "The Frogs of Latona."

Democritus, the naturalist and philosopher in the First Book,
has just returned after many years on a journey abroad. He is
Abdera's most distinguished citizen, but he is so different from all
the other Abderites that they do not know what to make of him.
In fact, he seems to them to be a rather queer sort. As well he

might, for Democritus is actually a character combining the convictions and attitudes of an eighteenth-century empirical philosopher and scientist with the moral attributes of a "virtuoso," the ideal man in the *Characteristics of Men, Manners, Opinions, Times* of the Third Earl of Shaftesbury (1671–1713), an English philosopher greatly admired by Wieland. Such virtuosi, according to Shaftesbury include

> . . . the real fine gentlemen, the lovers of art and ingenuity, such as have seen the world, and informed themselves of the manners and customs of the several nations of Europe; searched into their antiquities and records; considered their police, laws, and constitutions; observed the situation, strength, and ornament of their cities, their principal arts, studies, and amusements; their architecture, sculpture, painting, music, and their taste in poetry, learning, language, and conversation.[24]

To state it briefly, it was Wieland's intention to make Democritus a completely enlightened individual. But as Yuill points out, the scene in chapter 5 of the First Book, in which Democritus induces paroxysms of laughter in the Abderite women with most embarrassing results, is a perversion of the legend of Democritus, "the laughing philosopher." Yuill adds that a man who does this "is no Shaftesbury—nor for that matter, is the poet who could invent such an episode."[25] This is, most certainly, a flaw in the novel, a kind of misanthropic excrescence, for Wieland here sacrificed the consistency of his most important character for the sake of a farcical scene that is itself entirely out of tune with the rest of the work.

Nevertheless, just how enlightened Democritus is otherwise becomes apparent when we see him rushing home to the "good, artless, tenderhearted Gulleru," "a well-groomed curly-haired black woman who hurried toward him with open arms . . ." (66). She is so beautiful "that the way she appeared, no prince of Senegal, Angola, Gambia, Kongo, and Loango could have looked at her with impunity" (67). When he returned from his travels abroad, Democritus brought Gulleru back to Abdera with him, and, in an inspired scene in chapter 4 of the First Book, he discusses her in a conversation with the Abderites about ideal beauty. They cannot understand how anyone who is all black could possibly be considered beautiful.

> "Oh, that is funny!" the Abderite women cried out. "Black all over their body, as if covered with pitch, and they let themselves dream of beauty! What stupid people they must be! Don't they have any painters who paint Apollo, Bacchus, the goddess of love, and the Graces for

them? Or could they not have learned from Homer that Juno has white arms, Thetis, feet of silver, and Aurora, rosy fingers?" (58)

With this Rousseauistic figure who is morally good because she is "in sympathy with all of nature" (66), Wieland castigates the rampant "Grecomania" of his time,[26] that is, the often ill-informed and mostly undiscriminating adulation of Greek art as an aesthetic ideal. In 1777 his essay *Gedanken über die Ideale der Alten (Thoughts on the Ideals of the Ancients),* in which he discusses this matter at some length, appeared in *Der teutsche Merkur.*

As we read on in the First Book, we become more and more aware that everything Democritus is, the Abderites are not. And even though they come out to visit him, he finds some refuge from these people who do not wish to be reasonable in his secluded little house in the forest some hours outside of Abdera.

The Second Book opens with a brief vindication of the historical Democritus of the kind Wieland would write later in his novels *Peregrinus Proteus* and *Agathodämon.* Then, in the next chapter, Thrasyllus, the presumable heir of Democritus, takes advantage of a ludicrous charge brought against the naturalist and conspires to have him locked up as a madman so as to gain control of his rich estate. The Senate decides it is necessary to get an outsider's medical opinion, and so a letter is sent inviting Hippocrates to come to Abdera. When he learns why they have had him come, he is stunned, but he keeps his opinions to himself and goes out to visit Democritus.

These two learned men immediately discern how much they have in common, that they are kindred spirits, for they belong, Wieland tells us, to the order of

> ... cosmopolites, who—without arrangement, without a badge, without maintaining a lodge, and without being bound by oaths—constitute a kind of brotherhood that hangs together more closely than any other order in the world. Two cosmopolites come, the one from the east, the other from the west, see one another for the first time, and are friends, not by virtue of a secret sympathy that is, perhaps, to be found only in novels; and not because sworn duties bind them to it, but rather *because they are cosmopolites.* (126)

This enlightened ideal of human relationships is certainly one of Wieland's most attractive creations. That he was quite conscious of its worth and significance is indicated by his returning to this subject once again in a *Merkur* article in 1788, *Das Geheimnis des Kosmopolitenordens (The Secret of the Order of Cosmopolites),* in which he tries to make clear that he means something infinitely superior to mere membership in a secret society.

Hippocrates returns to the Senate in Abdera and, with all due gravity and formality, declares that they, and not Democritus, are mad. Then he leaves.

In the Third Book we are introduced to the characteristically Abderite lack of taste and discrimination. Whatever play they see is *fine*, including the products of "their indigenous dramatic manufactories" (141). We also meet their playwrights and poets. This book is particularly rich in barbs aimed at the younger German authors.

When the *Andromeda* of Euripides is performed on the Abderite stage, it is really a parody of this drama that is put on. Then, after the play, a foreigner just leaving the theater is discovered to lack enthusiasm for the performance he has just witnessed. He turns out to be Euripides himself—to the delight of some and the consternation of others. After much urging, he agrees to stay and put on the same play, but with his own troupe and scenery. It is such a fantastic success that the town goes half crazy with enthusiasm. Some medicine provided by Hippocrates gets them back to normal, but they "were now one and all again—as wise as before" (187). In other words, being true Abderites, they had, once again, learned nothing from their experience.

The trial concerning the ass's shadow, which is the subject of the Fourth Book, involves an ancient Greek expression, *peri onou skias*, "about an ass's shadow," which is roughly equivalent to our "tempest in a tea cup." In Aristophanes' play *The Wasps*, we find the line: "He'll fight you over the donkey's shadow, like the man in the fable."[27] Apparently the fable to which this refers is that in Ben Perry's *Aesopica*,[28] which, in the translation by Daly, runs as follows:

> Once when Demosthenes was being interrupted by the Athenians in a speech he was making before the assembly, he said he had a little something he wanted to say to them. When they quieted down, he spoke: "On a summer day a young man hired an ass to take him from the city to Megara. About noontime, when the sun was blazing down, both the young man and the driver wanted to get into the shadow of the ass. They got in one another's way, and one said he had hired out the ass but not his shadow, and the other that he had hired all the rights to the ass."[29]

At this point in the fable, Demosthenes turned to leave the assembly, but the Athenians urged him to stay and finish his tale. He, however, replied that they, instead of listening to what he had to say about weightier matters, obviously preferred to hear about the shadow of an ass.

It is probable that Wieland knew some version of this fable. In his novel it is a dentist named Struthion who hires an ass from Anthrax, "the jackass man" (194), and he wishes to ride over to Gerania, in southern Thrace. Not so curiously, Wieland's dentist was born in Megara, he says (191), and that just happens to be the destination of the young man in the fable. With this touch he seems to be giving us the pedigree of his own story.

Now when Struthion sits down in the shadow of the rented ass to get some respite from the heat of the Thracian sun, Anthrax objects because the other had rented only the ass and not his shadow. What ensues is truly a quarrel over the shadow of an ass, and so they return to Abdera to settle the matter before a court. But this is Abdera, and what follows is not a simple trial but an affair that threatens to grow to the proportions of a civil war.

The trial that should finally settle the matter is interrupted by the unexpected appearance of the ass, and the entire affair ends with the Abderites' venting their anger on the poor animal and tearing him to shreds.

Over sixty years ago the literary historian Kuno Francke wrote: "There are few happier inventions in all comic literature than the lawsuit about the donkey's shadow. . . ."[30] It is not surprising then that this part of the novel also seems to have been found most attractive by later writers. From 1810 to the present at least eight authors have written plays, for the stage or radio, on "The Trial Concerning the Ass's Shadow": A. von Kotzebue, L. Fulda, S. Gronemann, R. Strauss et al., F. Dürrenmatt, H. Taner, K. Wassermann, and C. Gurzeler.[31]

The Fifth Book, "The Frogs of Latona," relates the history of the decline and fall of the Abderite Republic. A superficially pious fad leads to the city's being completely overrun with frogs. Desperate and at a loss about what should be done, the Senate, over the angry objections of the incredibly pedantic and fanatic high priest Stilbon, the third successor of the venerable Strobylus, finally asks the Academy of Sciences for an opinion about *what should be done.*

Korax, the freethinker charged with preparing the Academy's statement, raises the Senate's eager expectations ever higher—only to deflate them entirely with a suggestion for ridding the city of its frogs that is so obvious it is considered unacceptable.

The high priest answers the Academy with another thick book

but that does not hold back a sudden invasion of rats and mice that drives the Abderites from their city. They settle for some years at the borders of Macedonia and return when the animals have left. Then they disappear from history.

Wieland was surprised, he tells us, that his novel had offended a good number of readers who thought that he had attacked either them, their city, or their friends, and so, in order to make clear that he had singled no one out, he added in the book version of 1781 a "key" in explanation. Here he states that further researches revealed to him that the Abderites had not died out so entirely as he had imagined. They are "an indestructible, immortal tribe" (305) and live dispersed among all other peoples of the world. They are, in fact, to be encountered everywhere. This explains how, while he thought he was merely creating fools as he imagined them in ancient Thrace, some people got the impression he was actually describing his contemporaries. In his typically elaborate prose, Wieland ends by saying, in effect, to those of his readers who feel offended: "If the shoe fits, put it on!"

Chronology:
Wieland's Life and Work in Historical Context

1732	(Birth of Franz Joseph Haydn and George Washington)
1733	Christoph Martin Wieland born on 5 September in Oberholzheim near Biberach an der Riß.
1736	His father, a Protestant pastor, is appointed to a more favorable position in Biberach. Family moves there.
1747–49	Wieland at school in Klosterberge near Magdeburg.
1749	Stays for some months in Erfurt with J. W. Baumer, a relative, for private tutoring. (Birth of J. W. Goethe)
1750	Becomes engaged to Sophie Gutermann. Enrolls at University of Tübingen as law student. (Death of J. S. Bach)
1752	Accepts invitation to live with J. J. Bodmer, writer and critic in Zürich. *The Nature of Things,* long didactic poem.
1754	Leaves Bodmer's house and earns living by tutoring in Zürich.
1756	(Birth of W. A. Mozart; beginning of Seven Years' War)
1759	Goes to Bern and becomes engaged to Julie Bondely. (Death of G. F. Händel and birth of Friedrich Schiller)
1760	Elected senator of Biberach. Soon after he arrives there, he is appointed city clerk.
1762–66	Translation of twenty-two of Shakespeare's plays.
1764	*Don Sylvio of Rosalva,* Wieland's first novel.
1765	*Comical Tales,* narrative poems. Marries Anna Dorothea von Hillenbrand.
1766–67	*History of Agathon,* first version of the novel.
1768	*Musarion* and *Idris and Zenide,* two long poems.
1769	Appointed professor of philosophy at University of Erfurt.
1770	(Birth of Ludwig van Beethoven)
1771	*The New Amadis,* long narrative poem.
1772	*The Golden Mirror,* novel. He leaves Erfurt to accept

	position at court in Weimar as philosopher tutor of the sons of Dowager Duchess Anna Amalia.
1773	Founding of *The German Mercury,* a journal. Publication of the second version of *Agathon. Alceste,* an operetta.
1774	First installment of the *History of the Abderites,* satirical novel, in *The German Mercury.*
1775	*Danischmend,* novel. (Goethe comes to Weimar)
1776	(American Declaration of Independence)
1777	Goes to Mannheim to attend première of his *Rosamunde,* but it fails to materialize.
1779	(Lessing's play *Nathan the Wise*)
1780	*Oberon,* romantic epic poem in ottava rima.
1781	*History of the Abderites* appears as a book.
1788–89	*Complete Works of Lucian of Samosata,* one of Wieland's best translations.
1789	(Storming of the Bastille in Paris begins French Revolution)
1791	*Peregrinus Proteus,* novel. (Death of Mozart)
1794	Third version of *Agathon.* (End of Terror in Paris with the execution of Robespierre)
1799	*Agathodämon,* novel. (Death of George Washington)
1800–1	*Aristipp,* novel.
1808	(Publication of Goethe's dramatic poem *Faust, Part I*)
1808–12	Translation of five volumes of Cicero's letters.
1809	(Death of Franz Joseph Haydn; birth of Felix Mendelssohn-Bartholdy)
1813	Death of Wieland on 20 January. (Birth of Richard Wagner)
1815	(Congress of Vienna)

History of the Abderites

Part One

Preface

Those to whom it may be of importance to assure themselves of the truth of the facts and characteristic features underlying this history—provided that they do not wish to look them up in the sources themselves, namely in the works of Herodotus, Diogenes Laertius, Athenaeus, Aelian, Plutarch, Lucian, Palaephatus, Cicero, Horace, Petronius, Juvenal, Valerius, Gellius, Solinus, and others—can satisfy themselves from the articles "Abdera" and "Democritus" in Bayle's *Dictionary*[1] that these Abderites do not belong among the true histories in the manner of Lucian.[2] Both the Abderites and their learned fellow citizen Democritus appear here in their true light; and although the author, in filling out lacunae, in the clarification of obscure passages, in the cancelling out of real and in the unification of apparent contradictions which one finds in the aforementioned writers, appears to have used unknown sources, discerning readers will perceive, after all, that in all this he has made use of an informant whose reputation outweighs all the Aelians and Athenaeuses and against whose single voice the witness of a whole world and the decision of all Amphictyons,[3] Areopagites,[4] Decemviri,[5] Centumviri, and Ducentumviri,[6] as well as of all doctors, masters, and bachelors, all of them together, is without effect, namely of nature itself.

Should one wish to regard this small work as a contribution, although a modest one, to the history of human understanding, the author will very gladly suffer it, but he believes that even under such an elegant-sounding title it is neither more nor less than what all history books have to be if they are not to fall even below the beautiful Melusine[7] and to be cast into one and the same category as the most insipid of all of Madame d'Aulnoy's[8] fairy tales.

41

First Book:
Democritus among the Abderites

Chapter One

Introductory account of the origin of the city of Abdera and the character of its inhabitants.

Abdera in Thrace was a city so ancient its historical accounts disappear in the legendary heroic age. It can also very much be a matter of indifference to us whether it got its name from *Abdera,* a sister of the notorious Diomedes, king of the Bistonian Thracians—who was such a great fancier of horses and kept so many of them that he and his country were finally devoured by his horses*—or from *Abderus,* an equerry of this king, or from another *Abderus,* who is supposed to have been a favorite of Hercules.

A few centuries after its first founding, Abdera had collapsed again of old age, when, around the time of the thirty-first Olympiad, *Timesius of Clazomenae* undertook to rebuild it. The wild Thracians, who did not want any cities to arise in their proximity, left him no time to enjoy the fruits of his labor. They drove him away again, and Abdera remained uninhabited and unfinished until (approximately around the end of the fifty-ninth Olympiad) the inhabitants of the Ionian city of *Teos*—because they had no desire to submit to the conqueror Cyrus—took ship, sailed to Thrace and, since in one of its most fertile regions they found this Abdera already built, they took it over as an abandoned thing that belonged to nobody and also stood their ground in it against the Thracian barbarians so well that they and their descendants were called *Abderites* from that time on and constituted a small free state which (like most of the Greek cities) was an ambiguous cross between democracy and aristocracy and was governed—as small and great republics have been governed from time immemorial.

---

*Palaephatus in his book on *Incredible Things* explains in this way the story that this prince had fed his horses human flesh and was finally himself cast before them as fodder by Hercules.

42

"To what point (our readers shout) this account of the origin and the fortunes of the city of Abdera in Thrace? What do we care about Abdera? Of what concern is it to us to know or not know when, how, where, why, by whom, and to what end a city may have been built which long ago ceased to exist?"

Patience, gentle readers, patience. Before I continue my story, we have to come to some agreement on our conditions. Heaven forfend that you be asked to read *The Abderites* when you have something more pressing to do or something better to read!—"I have to prepare a sermon,"—"I must visit the sick,"—"I have a recommendation to write, a decision, a clarification, a report to prepare most humbly and obediently for higher authorities."—"I have to write a review."—"I still have sixteen sheets to get out for the four fascicles I have to send to my publisher within a week."—"I have bought a yoke of oxen."—"I have taken a wife." For Heaven's sake! Prepare, visit, report, review, translate, buy, and get married! Preoccupied readers are rarely *good* readers. Sometimes everything pleases them, sometimes nothing; now they half understand us, now not at all, and then (which is still worse) incorrectly. Whoever wishes to read with pleasure and profit must right then have nothing else to do nor to think of. And, if you are in this circumstance, why should you not want to spend two or three minutes on knowing something which cost a *Salmasius*,[1] a *Bayle*—and, to be honest, myself (because it did not occur to me in time to look up the article in Bayle)—just as many hours? You would, after all, have listened patiently to me if I had begun relating to you *The History of the King of Bohemia who had Seven Castles.*[2]

Hence the Abderites (according to what has already been reported about them) were supposed to be such a fine, lively, witty, and clever little nation as has ever existed under the sun.

"And why this?"

This question is presumably not being asked by the learned persons among our readers. However, who would want to write books anyway if all readers were as learned as the author? The question *why this?* is always a very reasonable question. In a discussion of human affairs it always deserves an answer (in divine matters things are different); and woe unto him who becomes ill at ease or gets embarrassed or annoyed when an answer is expected of him to the question *why this?* We, for our part, would have volunteered the answer if our readers had not been so hasty. Here it is!

Teos was an *Athenian* colony, one of the twelve or thirteen which, under the leadership of Neleus, the son of Codrus, were founded in *Ionia*.

The Athenians were from time immemorial a merry and ingenious people, and they still are, as people say. Athenians transferred
to Ionia improved under the beautiful sky over this land pampered
by nature just as Burgundian grapes do which have been transplanted to the Cape of Good Hope. More than any other people
on earth, the Ionian Greeks were the favorites of the Muses. Homer
himself most probably was an Ionian. Ionia was the fatherland of
the *erotic songs* and of the Milesian tales[3] (the models for our
novellas and novels). The Horace of the Greeks, *Alcaeus,* passion-
ate *Sappho, Anacreon* the singer—*Aspasia* the teacher—*Apelles,*
the painter of *the Graces,* were from Ionia; even Anacreon was
born in Teos. The latter was possibly a youth of eighteen (if Barnes[4]
otherwise made correct calculations) when his fellow citizens removed to Abdera. He went with them; and, as proof that he did
not leave behind his lyre dedicated to the gods of love, he sang
there the song *To a Thracian Girl*[5] (the sixty-first in Barnes' edition)
in which a certain wild Thracian tone contrasts in a very special
way with the Ionian grace characterizing his songs.

Now, who would not suppose that the Teians—*Athenians* originally—indigenous to *Ionia* for such a long time—fellow citizens of
an *Anacreon*—should also have asserted in Thrace the character
of an ingenious people? However (whatever the reason for it may
have been) the contrary is beyond any doubt. When the Teians had
barely turned into Abderites, they began to degenerate. Not that
they lost their former vivacity entirely and changed into *simpletons,* as *Juvenal* unjustly says of them. It's just that their liveliness
took a strange turn; for their imagination gained such a great advantage over their reason that the latter was never again able to
catch up. The Abderites never lacked ideas, but rarely were their
ideas suitable to the occasion where they were applied, or they did
not occur to them until the occasion was past. They talked a lot,
but always without considering for a moment what they wanted to
say or *how* they wanted to say it. The natural consequence of this
was that they rarely opened their mouths without saying something
silly. Unfortunately this bad habit also extended to their actions;
for generally they did not lock the cage until the bird had flown
away. This caused them to be reproached with rashness; but experience proved that they fared no better when they stopped to think.
If they did something especially foolish (which happened rather
often), that was always the result of their wanting to do things all
too well; and whenever they deliberated earnestly and at length
about matters concerning their community, one could with certainty count on their coming to the worst of all possible decisions.

They finally became a byword among the Greeks. An *Abderite inspiration,* an *Abderite trick* meant to them approximately what we mean with the expression *a Schildbürger imbecility* or the Swiss with *a Lalleburg foolishness,* and the good Abderites did not fail to provide abundantly people who scoffed and laughed with ingenious actions of this kind. For now a few examples thereof may serve as specimens.

One day they suddenly got the idea that a city like Abdera ought rightly to have a handsome fountain, too. It was to be set up in the middle of their great market place, and to defray the costs a new tax was levied. They had a famous sculptor come from Athens to fashion a group of statues that represented the god of the sea on a wagon drawn by four sea horses surrounded by nymphs, tritons, and dolphins. The sea horses and the dolphins were supposed to squirt lots of water out of their noses. But when the whole thing was completed it turned out that there was hardly enough water available to wet the nose of a single dolphin; and when they set the thing going one got the impression that all these sea horses and dolphins were suffering from a cold. So that they would not be laughed at, they had the entire group taken over to the Temple of Neptune; and as often as it was shown to a stranger, the sexton expressed his regret very earnestly, in the name of the laudable city of Abdera, that such a splendid work of art had to remain useless because of nature's parsimony.

Another time they purchased a very beautiful Venus of ivory which was considered to be one of Praxiteles' masterpieces. It was about five feet high and was to be set up on an altar of the goddess of love. When it had arrived, all of Abdera went into raptures over the beauty of its Venus; for the Abderites gave themselves the air of being fine connoisseurs and enthusiastic lovers of the arts. "She is too beautiful (they cried out unanimously) to be in such a low place; a masterpiece that does the city so much honor and has cost so much money cannot be set up in too high a place; it must be the first thing to attract the attention of strangers when they enter Abdera." In consequence of this fortunate idea they placed the small dainty statue on an eighty-foot obelisk; and although it was now impossible to discern whether it was supposed to represent a Venus or an oyster nymph, they nevertheless obliged all strangers to admit that nothing more perfect could be seen.

It strikes us that these examples already sufficiently prove that no injustice was done the Abderites if they were considered to suffer from an excess of fervor. But we doubt that a trait can be imagined which could delineate their character more strongly than the fact that (according to the report of Justinus[6]) they allowed the frogs in and around their city to spread to such an extent that finally they were themselves compelled to make room for their croaking fellow citizens and, until the matter was settled, go to a third site under the protection of King Kassander of Macedonia.

This misfortune did not happen to the Abderites without warning. A wise man among them had told them long before that things would finally turn out that way. In point of fact, their mistake consisted merely in the means by which they wanted to obviate the infestation, although they could never be induced to see this. What, all the same, should have opened their eyes was that they had hardly been away from Abdera for some months, when a large number of cranes came from the region of Gerania and finished off all their frogs so tidily that for a mile round about Abdera there was not one left who might have welcomed the returning spring with his brekekek koax koax.[7]

Chapter Two

Democritus of Abdera. Whether and to what extent his native town was justified in boasting about him.

No air is so dense, no people so stupid, no place so lacking in fame that now and then a great man might not spring therefrom, says Juvenal. Pindar and Epaminondas were born in *Boeotia,* Aristotle in *Stagira,* Cicero in *Arpinum,* Vergil in the little village of *Andes* near Mantua, Albertus Magnus in *Lauingen,* Martin Luther in *Eisleben,* Sixtus the Fifth in the village of *Montalto* in the march of Ancona, and one of the best of kings who ever lived at *Pau* in *Bearn.*[8] Small wonder if Abdera, too, happened to be honored by having the greatest naturalist of antiquity, Democritus, born within its walls.

I do not see how a place can avail itself of such a circumstance in order to lay claim to the fame of a great man. Whoever is to be born has to be born some place; nature bears the consequences for the rest. And I doubt very much whether, besides Lycurgus, there ever was a lawgiver who extended his welfare services to the homunculus[9] and took all possible precautions so that well-organized, handsome, and soulful children would be given to the state. We must admit that, in this regard, *Sparta* had some right to be proud of the virtues of its citizens. But in Abdera (as almost in the entire world), people gave chance and the guardian spirit of the place a free hand—natale comes qui temperat astrum[10]; and if a

*Protagoras** or *Democritus* sprang from their midst, the good city was certainly just as little to blame for that as Lycurgus and his laws if a blockhead or a coward was born in Sparta.

This negligence, although it concerns a matter of utmost importance to the state, might still be overlooked. Nature, if it is allowed to do its work undisturbed, mostly makes superfluous all further solicitude for the success of its works. However, although it seldom forgets to endow its favored creation with all the abilities through which a perfect man might be developed, it is nevertheless precisely this development that she leaves to art; and, therefore, enough opportunity is still left to every state to acquire a claim on the virtues and merits of its fellow citizens.

In this as well, however, the Abderites' good sense left a very great deal to be desired; and a place could hardly have been found where there was less concern for the development of the emotions, of the understanding, and of the heart of its future citizens.

The development of taste, that is, of a fine, correct, and learned feeling for everything beautiful, is the best foundation for that famous Socratic *kalokagathia*[11] or *inner beauty and goodness of soul* which make the kind, generous, charitable, and happy human being. And nothing is more suitable for developing this real feeling for the beautiful within us than—if everything we see and hear from childhood on is beautiful. To be born in an Athens, in a city where the arts of the muses are practiced in the greatest degree of perfection, in a city filled with the masterpieces of the fine arts, is certainly, therefore, no small advantage; and if the Athenians in the age of *Plato* and *Menander* had more taste than a thousand other nations, they indisputably owed this to their native country. In a Greek proverb (about whose meaning the scholars, as is their wont, are not in agreement), Abdera bore the sobriquet of which *Florence* boasts among the Italian cities—*the beautiful.* We have already observed that the Abderites were enthusiasts for the fine arts; and, as a matter of fact, at the time of their greatest flowering, that is, just at the time when, for a period, they had to make room for the frogs, their city was full of splendid buildings, rich in paintings and statues, furnished with a theater and a music hall (odeum), in short, *a second Athens*—except for its taste. For unfortunately, their odd frame of mind, of which we have spoken above, also extended to their concepts of the beautiful and the proper. *La-*

---

*A famous sophist of Abdera (somewhat older than Democritus) whom Cicero compares with Hippias, Prodicus, Gorgias, and, therefore, with the greatest men of his profession.

tona,[12] the tutelary goddess, had the most inferior temple; *Jason,* the leader of the *Argonauts,* on the other hand (whose Golden Fleece they asserted they possessed), had the most magnificent one. Their town hall resembled a warehouse, and right in front of the hall where the affairs of state were considered, stood the booths of all the women hawking herbs, fruit, and eggs in Abdera. However, the gymnasium in which its youth was getting practice in wrestling and swordplay rested on a triple row of columns. The fencing hall was decorated with nothing but paintings of conferences and statues in quiet and pensive attitudes.* But then the town hall constituted an all the more charming feast for the eyes of the nation's fathers. For, wherever they cast their eyes in the hall for their general meetings, they saw glistening at them the beautiful bodies of naked fighters or bathing Dianas and sleeping devotees of Bacchus; and Venus with her lover, exposed in the net of Vulcan to the gaze of all the inhabitants of Olympus (a large piece of which was hanging across from the archon's[13] seat), was shown to strangers with an attitude of triumph which would have compelled serious Phocion[14] himself to laugh for the first time in his life. *King Lysimachus* (they said) had offered them six cities and many miles of land for it; but they could not bring themselves to part with such a splendid piece, all the more since—it had just the height and width to take up one side of the council chamber; and moreover, one of their art critics had very cleverly set forth in an extensive work filled with great scholarship the relation of the allegorical sense of this picture to the place where it was situated.

We would never finish if we wished to touch upon all the improprieties with which this marvelous republic was teeming. But still there is one that we cannot pass over, because it concerns an essential feature of its constitution, and it had no small influence on the character of the Abderites. In the remotest times of the city, presumably according to an orphic precept, the *nomophylax* or *guardian of the laws* (one of the highest magistrates) was simultaneously leader of the religious choruses and superintendent of the musical life of the community. There was good reason for this in former times. However, with the passing of time, the reasons for having laws do change; these then become ludicrous when complied with literally and must, therefore, be recast according to the altered circumstances. But such a consideration did not enter the Abderites' pates. It had often happened that a nomophylax was

---

*What is told here about the Abderites other ancient authors relate about the city of Alabandus. Cf. Coel. Rhodog. Lect. Ant. L. XXVI. Cap. 25.

elected who guarded the laws quite tolerably, to be sure, but either sang badly or knew nothing at all about music. How did the Abderites deal with this? After frequent deliberations they finally decreed the ordinance that henceforth the best singer in Abdera should always at the same time be nomophylax; and that is the way things stayed as long as Abdera continued to exist. That the nomophylax and the leader of the choruses could be two different people had in twenty public conferences not occurred to a soul.

It is easy to see that under such circumstances music had to be highly esteemed in Abdera. Everybody in this city was musical; everybody sang, played the flute and the lyre. Their moral philosophy and politics, their theology and cosmology were based on musical principles; indeed, their physicians even cured illnesses by means of musical strains and melodies. To the extent that speculation is concerned, the reputation of the greatest wise men of antiquity, *Orpheus, Pythagoras,* and *Plato* appears to redound to their credit. But in practice they were all the further removed from the austerity of these philosophers. Plato bans all delicate and tender musical strains from his republic; music is to inspire his citizens with neither joy nor sadness; with the Ionic and Lydian harmonies he banishes all drinking songs and love songs; why, the very instruments themselves appear so little to be a matter of indifference to him that, on the contrary, he rejects the many-stringed ones and the Lydian flute as dangerous tools of voluptuousness and grants his citizens only the lyre and the cithara, and to the herdsmen and the peasantry only the reed pipe. The Abderites did not philosophize with such severity. No harmony, no instrument was excluded with them, and—in consequence of a principle that was very true but very often little understood by them—they maintained that all serious things should be treated *in a jolly way,* and all jolly things *seriously.* By extending this maxim to music they produced the most absurd effects. Their religious songs sounded like street ballads; on the other hand, however, nothing more solemn could be heard than the melodies for their dances. Generally, the music for a tragedy was comic; their war songs, on the contrary, sounded so melancholy that they were more appropriate for people going to the gallows. A lyre player was considered excellent in Abdera only if he knew how to touch the strings in such a way that his listeners thought they were hearing a flute; and a woman singer, in order to be admired, had to gurgle and trill like a nightingale. The Abderites did not understand that music is music only to the extent that it affects the heart; they were quite happy if only their ears were tickled or at least stuffed with meaningless but full and often varying harmonies. This absurdity extended to all matters of taste; or, to speak more correctly, with all their enthusiasm for the arts, the Abderites had no taste at all; and they did not even suspect that whatever was beautiful was so for a better reason than its merely pleasing them thus.

Nevertheless, however, nature, chance, and good fortune could, for once, accomplish so much that a native Abderite was endowed with human understanding. But at least it must be admitted that whenever something like that happened, Abdera had done nothing to help in the matter. For ordinarily an *Abderite* was intelligent only insofar as he was *no Abderite*—a circumstance that lets us comprehend without difficulty why the Abderites always thought least of that person among their fellow citizens who honored them most in the eyes of the world. This was not one of their common absurdities. They had a reason for it which is so natural that it would be unfair to reproach them with it.

This reason was not (as some imagine) because they had, for example, seen the naturalist *Democritus*—a long time before he was a great man—playing with his top or turning somersaults on a patch of grass—

Nor because from envy or jealousy they could not suffer that someone from their midst should be more intelligent than they. For—by the unfailing inscription over the entrance to the Temple at Delphi![15]—no single Abderite had enough wisdom to think this, or from that moment forth he would no longer have been an Abderite.

The real reason, my friends, why the Abderites didn't make much of their fellow citizen Democritus was this: because they— did not consider him a wise man.

"Why not?"

Because they couldn't.

"And why couldn't they?"

Because they would then have had to consider themselves blockheads. And to do that, however, they were not absurd enough. They could also just as easily have danced on their heads, have grasped the moon with their teeth, or have squared the circle as to consider a man wise who was their antipode in everything. This follows from a quality in human nature which must have been noticed as early as in Adam's times. And yet, since *Helvetius*[16] inferred from that—whatever follows therefrom, it seemed quite new to many people. However, from that time it was no longer new to anyone. Nevertheless, in life, it is—forgotten every moment.

Chapter Three

What kind of a man Democritus was. His journeys. He returns to Abdera. What he brings back, and how he is received. An examination to which they submit him, which is at the same time a sample of an Abderite conversation.

Democritus—I do not believe you will regret making his closer acquaintance—

Democritus was about twenty years old when he became the heir of his father, one of the richest citizens of Abdera. Now, instead of reflecting about how he would maintain or increase his wealth or squander it in the most agreeable or absurd way, the young man decided to make it the means—for the perfection of his soul.

"But what did the Abderites say about this decision of the youthful *Democritus*?"

These good people never had the foggiest notion that the soul might have an interest that differed from that of the stomach, the belly, and the remaining component parts of the visible human being. To be sure, therefore, this whim of their compatriot may have seemed strange enough. However, this was now the very thing he minded least. He went on his way and spent many years on educational journeys through all the continents and islands on which one could travel at that time. For, whoever in his age wished to become wise had to see things with his own eyes. There still were no printing shops, no journals, libraries, magazines, encyclopedias, handbooks, almanacs, and whatever all the tools are called with whose help one now, without knowing how, turns into a philosopher, a naturalist, an art critic, an author, a know-all. In those days wisdom was as costly and even more so than—*beautiful Laïs.*[17] Not everyone could *travel* to *Corinth.* The number of wise men was very small; but those who were, were so all the more.

Democritus did not merely travel to behold the customs and constitutions of men as did *Ulysses;* not merely to search out priests and visionaries as did Apollonius[18]; nor to look at temples, statues, paintings, and antiquities as did Pausanias[19]; nor to sketch plants and animals as did Doctor Solander.[20] His reason for traveling was to get acquainted with nature and art in all their effects and causes, with man in his nakedness and in all his garbs and disguises, crude and cultivated, painted and unpainted, whole and mutilated, and the remaining things in their relations to man. The caterpillars in Ethiopia (said *Democritus*) are, to be sure, only—caterpillars. Why would a caterpillar merit being the first, most urgent, sole object of man's study? But now since we just happen to be in Ethiopia, we will always keep on the lookout, incidentally, for Ethiopian caterpillars, too. There are caterpillars in the land of the Seres[21] which clothe and maintain millions of human beings; who knows whether or not there are also useful caterpillars on the *Niger River*?

With this way of thinking, *Democritus* had gathered on his journeys a treasure of knowledge which was, in his eyes, worth all the gold in the treasuries of the kings of India and all the pearls on the necks and arms of their women. He knew from the cedar of Lebanon down to the mold on an Arcadian cheese a host of trees, shrubs, herbs, grasses, and mosses; not just merely by their form and their name, genus, and species; he also knew their properties, efficacies, and virtues. But what he valued a thousand times more than all his other attainments was that in each place where he found it worth the trouble to stay, he had made the acquaintance of the wisest and the best. It had soon appeared that he was one of their kind. They had, therefore, become his friends, they opened their hearts to him and thereby spared him the effort of *seeking* through his own diligence for years and perhaps, after all, in vain what they had, fortunately, already found with an expenditure of resources and toil.

Enriched with all these treasures of the mind and heart, *Democritus,* after a journey of twenty years, returned to the Abderites who had almost forgotten him. He was a fine, handsome man, polite and refined as a man customarily is who has learned how to associate with divers kinds of mortals. His color was rather brownish yellow. He came from the ends of the world and had brought back a stuffed crocodile, a live monkey, and many other strange things. For some days the Abderites spoke of nothing else than of their fellow citizen *Democritus* who had returned and brought back monkeys and crocodiles. However, in a short time it turned out that they were very much mistaken in their opinion of such a widely traveled man.

By the honest men to whom he had in the interim entrusted the management of his estates, *Democritus* had been defrauded by half, and yet he signed their bills without objection. Naturally, this had to give the first blow to their good opinion of his intelligence. The lawyers and judges at least, who had had high hopes of profiting from a lucrative lawsuit, observed with a meaningful shrug that it would be risky to entrust the commonwealth to a man who managed his own house so badly. However, the Abderites did not doubt that he would present himself among the candidates for the most prominent posts of honor. They were already calculating how high they were willing to sell him their votes; they offered him a daughter, granddaughter, sister, niece, cousin, sister-in-law as a bride; they calculated the advantages that they wished to draw from his prestige for the attainment of this or that object when he would, at some future time, be archon or a priest of Latona, and so on. But *Democritus* spoke his mind to the effect that he wished to be neither a councillor of Abdera nor the husband of an Abderite woman, and thereby he once more thwarted all their designs. Now they hoped to be compensated at least a bit by his company. A man who had brought back monkeys, crocodiles, and tame dragons from his travels had to have a colossal number of wonderful things to tell. They expected him to talk about *giants twelve yards tall and of dwarfs six thumbs high, of men with the heads of dogs and donkeys, of green-haired mermaids, of white negroes and blue centaurs.* However, Democritus lied as little, and in fact less, than if he had never got farther than the Thracian Bosporus.

They asked him whether in the land of the *Garamantes*[22] he had not met with people without heads who had their eyes, nose, and mouth on their breast. And an Abderite scholar (who, without ever having gone beyond the walls of his city, acted as though there were no corner of the earth through which he had not crept) proved to him in a large group of people that he had either never been in *Ethiopia* or that he must necessarily have become acquainted with the *Agriophagae*, whose king has only one eye over his nose, with the *Sambers*, who always elect a dog to be their king, and with the *Artabatites*, who walk on all fours. "And if you penetrated into the farthest reaches of western Ethiopia," the learned man continued, "then I am certain that you came upon a people without noses and upon another with such small mouths that they have to sip their soup through straws."*

Democritus swore by Castor and Pollux that he did not remember having had this honor.

"At least," said the other man, "in India you met men who are born with only one leg but nevertheless because of the extraordinary width of their foot slide along on the ground so fast that one

---

*Solinus, C. XXX. also *Pliny, Mela,* and other old and newer authors who have no scruples about passing off all the human monsters mentioned here as real creatures of God.

can hardly keep up with them on horseback.* But what did you say to meeting at the source of the Ganges a nation whose people live, without any other food, on the mere fragrance of wild apples?"**

"Oh, do tell us about it," the beautiful Abderite women cried out, "tell us something, Mr. Democritus! What all, surely, you could tell us if only you had a mind to!"

In vain Democritus swore that he had neither seen nor heard anything about all these human monsters in Ethiopia and India.

"But then just *what* did you see?" asked a round, fat man who was, to be sure, neither one-eyed like the *Agriophagae,* nor did he have a dog's muzzle like the *Zymolgae,* nor have eyes on his shoulders like the *Omophthalmae,* nor like the birds of paradise did he live on mere odors, but nevertheless certainly had no more brains in his huge skull than a Mexican hummingbird, without on that account being any less a councillor of Abdera. —"But just *what* did you see then," asked *Paunch,* "you who have traveled around the world for twenty years, if you have seen nothing of all the astounding things that can be seen in distant lands?"

"Astounding things?" Democritus replied smiling. "I was so busy with my observations of the natural that I had no time left for astounding things."

"Now, that I admit," answered *Paunch,* "it is surely worth one's while to sail across all the seas and to climb over all the mountains to see nothing but what could just as well be seen at home!"

Democritus did not like to quarrel with people about their opinions, least of all with Abderites; and yet he did not want it to seem either as if he could tell about nothing. From among the beautiful Abderite women in the present company he selected one to whom he could address what he wished to say; and he found one with two great Junoesque eyes that enticed him to attribute to their owner somewhat more understanding or perception than to the rest in spite of his physiognomic competence. "What would you wish me to have done, for example," he said to her, "with a beauty who had eyes on her forehead or on her elbow? Or, of just what help would it be to me if I were ever so well trained in the art of touching the heart—of a female cannibal? I always felt too good when I abandoned myself to the gentle power of two beautiful eyes in their natural place ever to be tempted to look with fondness at the great ox eye on the forehead of a cyclops woman."

---

*Solinus from the Ktesias.
**Ibid.

The beauty with the large eyes, in doubt as to what she should make of this speech, looked with silent astonishment at the mouth of the man who spoke thus, displayed her beautiful teeth to him in a smile and looked about to the right and left as if she were looking for the sense of what he had said.

The rest of the Abderite women, indeed, had comprehended just as little; however, because, from the circumstance that it was the large-eyed woman to whom he had turned, they concluded that he had said something very nice to her, each one of them looked at the others with her own peculiar grimace. This one turned up her little snub nose, that one drew out her mouth, a third pursed her lips, a fourth opened her pair of small eyes wide, a fifth gave herself airs by throwing back her head, and so on.

Democritus saw and remembered that he was in Abdera—and fell silent.

Chapter Four

The examination is continued and is changed into a controversy about beauty, in the course of which things are made pretty hot for Democritus.

Keeping silent—is now and then an art, but all the same it is never such a great one as certain people would have us believe who are at their most intelligent when they keep still.

When a wise man sees that he is dealing with children, why should he consider himself too wise to talk to them the way they do?

"To be sure," Democritus said to his inquisitive company, "I have been honest enough to admit that I saw nothing of all that people want me to have seen; but do not, for that reason, imagine that on so many voyages by sea and land I did not come upon anything at all that could satisfy your curiosity. Believe me, among them are things that would perhaps seem even more fabulous to you than the ones just discussed."

At these words the beautiful Abderite women moved up closer and, with pursed lips, began to pay attention. "Now that was spoken like a much-traveled man," called out the short, *fat councillor.* The forehead of the learned man lost its wrinkles through the hope that he would get something to carp at and to correct, no matter what Democritus might say.

"Once I was in a land," our man began, "where I liked it so well that in the first three or four days I spent there I wished I had been immortal so that I could have lived there forever."

"I have never left Abdera," the councillor said, "but I always thought there was no place in the world where things could please me more than in Abdera. With me, it's just as it was with you in the country you liked so much; I'd be happy to do without the rest of the world if only I could live in Abdera forever! —But why did you like it so well in that country for only three days?"

"You will hear why right away. Imagine an immense country which has, wherever one looks, the appearance of the most splendid pleasure garden because of the very pleasant alternation of mountains, valleys, forests, hills, and meadows under the domination of an eternal spring and autumn; everything cultivated and irrigated, everything in bloom and fertile; everywhere an eternal green, and constantly refreshing shadows, and forests of the most beautiful fruit trees, dates, figs, lemons, and pomegranates that grow unattended as do the acorns in Thrace; groves of myrtle and jasmine; the favorite flowers of Amor and Cytherea, not on hedges, as in our country, but growing in dense clusters on big trees and in full blossom like the breasts of the beautiful women in this company of my fellow citizens—"

(*Democritus* had not brought this off at all well; and it can serve as a warning to future storytellers that one would do well to look about before one ventures making compliments of this kind, as courteous as they may sound in themselves. The beauties held their hands in front of their eyes and blushed. For, unfortunately, there wasn't any among those present who might have done honor to the flattering simile, although they did not fail to puff themselves up as much as they could.)

"—and these charming groves," he continued, "enlivened by the lovely singing of countless sorts of birds and filled with a thousand colorful parrots, whose hues in the sunlight dazzle the eyes. What a country! I did not comprehend why the goddess of love had chosen the rocky isle of Cythera for her place of residence since a country such as this was in the world. Where would it have been more pleasant for the Graces to dance than at the edge of brooks and springs where, in short thick grass of the liveliest green, lilies and hyacinths and ten thousand still more beautiful flowers for which there are no names in our language blossom forth spontaneously and fill the air with voluptuous fragrances?"

The beautiful Abderite women, as can easily be conceived, were endowed with no less lively an imagination than the men, and the picture that Democritus, without meaning any harm, presented to them was more than their little souls could stand. A few sighed aloud from a feeling of ease and comfort; others looked as if they wished to draw in through nose and mouth the voluptuous scents that in their fancy smelled so sweetly; the head of the beautiful *Juno* sank back onto a cushion on a couch, she half closed her eyes and found herself, without knowing how, at the flower-covered edge of one of these beautiful springs, shaded all around by rose bushes and lemon trees, from whose branches clouds of ambrosial fragrances wafted down upon her. In a gentle intoxication of sweet feelings she just began to fall asleep when she saw a youth, as beautiful as Bacchus and as insistent as Amor, lying at her feet. She sat up so that she could have a better look at him and found him so beautiful, so loving, that the words with which she wanted to chastise his boldness died on her lips. Hardly had she—

"And what do you think," *Democritus* continued, "this enchanting country is called of whose beauty everything I could say would scarcely give you the shadow of a concept? It is precisely this Ethiopia which my learned friend here peoples with monstrous human beings who are quite unworthy of such a beautiful fatherland. But one thing that he can repeat after me as true is that in all of Ethiopia and Libya (although these names comprise a number of different peoples) there is no human being who does not have a nose precisely where we do, who does not have just as many eyes and ears as we, and in brief—"

At this moment a great sigh of the kind with which a heart, burdened with either pain or pleasure, seeks to give vent to its feelings lifted the bosom of the beautiful woman who, while *Democritus* continued with his speech, had (so it appears) come upon a circumstance in her dream-vision, in which we hesitate to eavesdrop, that in one way or another attracted the very lively interest of her heart. Since the other people who were present could not know that the good lady was a few hundred miles from Abdera swimming in a sea of the sweetest fragrances under an Ethiopian rose tree, hearing a thousand new birds sing about the good fortune of love, seeing a thousand gay-colored parrots flutter about before her eyes and, to top it all off, with a youth with blond locks and coral lips lying at her feet—it was natural, then, that the aforementioned sigh was received with general surprise. No one realized that the last words *Democritus* had spoken could have been the cause of such an effect.

"What's wrong with you, Lysandra?" the Abderite women cried out as if out of one mouth while in their concern they crowded around her. Beautiful *Lysandra,* who at this moment was regaining consciousness of where she was, blushed and assured them that nothing was the matter. *Democritus,* who was now beginning to notice what this was about, affirmed that a bit of fresh air would make everything all right again; but in his heart he resolved that in the future he would paint his pictures with only one color, as did the painters in Thrace. "Just gods," he thought, "what an imagination these Abderite women have!"

"Now, my beautiful curious women," he continued, "what do you suppose the color of the inhabitants of such a beautiful country is?"

"The color? Why should they be of a different color than other human beings? Didn't you tell us that their nose was in the middle of their face and that in all respects they were human beings like us Greeks?"

"Human beings, without a doubt, but should they be less than human if they were black or olive?"

"What do you mean by that?"

"I mean that the most beautiful people among the Ethiopian nations (namely those who, according to our criteria, are the most beautiful, that is, are most similar to us) are olive like the Egyptians, and those who live farther in the interior and in the southernmost regions are from their head to the soles of their feet as black and still a bit blacker than the ravens in Abdera."

"Well, you don't say! —And aren't those people scared when they look at one another?"

"Scared? Why that? They like their being black as a raven very much and think nothing could be more beautiful."

"Oh, that is funny!" the Abderite women cried out. "Black all over their body, as if covered with pitch, and they let themselves dream of beauty! What stupid people they must be! Don't they have any painters who paint Apollo, Bacchus, the goddess of love, and the Graces for them? Or could they not have learned from *Homer* that *Juno* has white arms, Thetis, feet of silver, and *Aurora,* rosy fingers?"

"Alas," *Democritus* answered, "those good people have no *Homer;* or, if they have one, then we may rest assured that his *Juno* has coal-black arms. I heard nothing in Ethiopia about painters. But I saw a girl whose beauty caused just as much havoc among her countrymen as the daughter of *Leda* among the Greeks and Trojans; and this African Helen was blacker than ebony."

"Oh, do describe this beautiful monster for us," cried out the Abderite women, who, for the most natural reason in the world, tremendously enjoyed this conversation.

"You will have trouble in picturing her in your mind. Imagine the complete opposite of the *Greek* ideal of beauty: as tall as one of the Graces and with the abundant proportions of *Ceres;* black hair, but not flowing in long undulating locks about her shoulders, but short and as naturally curly as sheep's wool. Her forehead is broad and strongly arched; her nose is turned up with the middle of the cartilage pressed flat; her cheeks round as those of a trumpeter, her mouth large—"

Philinna smiled so that she could show how small hers was.

"Her lips very large and pursed up, and two rows of teeth like strings of pearls—"

The beauties all laughed even though they could have no other reason for doing so than to show their own teeth, for what was there to laugh about here otherwise?

"But her eyes?" *Lysandra* asked.

"Oh, as far as they are concerned, they were so small and of such a watery hue that for a long time I could not get myself to consider them beautiful—."

"Democritus is for Homer's cow's eyes, so it seems," said Myris while she cast a scornful side glance at the beauty with the great eyes.

"In fact," replied *Democritus* with a countenance from the looks of which a deaf person would have gathered that he was paying her the most flattering compliment, "beautiful eyes would have to be very big for me to consider them *too big;* and ugly eyes, it seems to me, can never be too small."

Beautiful Lysandra cast a triumphant glance at her sisters and then poured a whole effulgence of satisfaction out of her eyes over the fortunate Democritus.

"May we know what *you* think beautiful eyes look like?" asked little Myris while her nose became noticeably more pointed.

A glance from beautiful Lysandra appeared to say to him: you will not be at a loss for an answer to this question.

"I think they are eyes in which a beautiful soul is imaged," said *Democritus.*

Lysandra looked foolish like a person to whom something unexpected has been said and who cannot think of an answer. "A beautiful soul!" thought all the Abderite women at the same time. "What strange things this man has brought home from distant lands. A beautiful soul! That even beats his monkeys and parrots!"

"But with all these *subtleties,*" said *the fat councillor,* "we are drifting away from the main subject. It seems to me we were talking about the beautiful Helen from Ethiopia, and I would just like to hear what those honest folks could see in her that they found so beautiful."

"Everything," answered *Democritus.*

"Then they must have no idea of beauty at all," said the scholar.

"I beg your pardon," answered the narrator. "Because this Ethiopian Helen was the object of all wishes, one can safely infer that she resembled the *idea of beauty* which everyone found in his imagination."

"Are you of Parmenides'* school?" asked *the scholar* assuming a pugnacious stance.

"I am nothing—but myself, which is very little," answered *Democritus* half frightened. "If you have something against the word *idea,* allow me to express myself differently. Beautiful *Gulleru*— that is what the black woman we are talking about was called—"

"Gulleru?" the Abderite women cried as they broke out in laughter that seemed as if it were going to be endless. "Gulleru! What a name!"

"And how did things go with your beautiful Gulleru?" asked pointy-nosed *Myris* with a look and tone of voice three times more pointed than her nose.

"If you ever pay me the honor of a visit," answered the much-traveled man with the most unaffected civility, "you will learn how things went with beautiful *Gulleru.* Now I have to keep my promise to this gentleman. Well now, beautiful Gulleru's figure—"

(*"Beautiful Gulleru,"* the Abderite women repeated and laughed anew, but this time Democritus did not allow them to interrupt him.)

"—unfortunately for her, inspired the strongest passions in the young men of her country. This appears to prove that they thought her *beautiful;* and without a doubt, the reason she was thought to be beautiful lay in all the things because of which she was not considered *ugly.* These *Ethiopians,* therefore, perceived a difference between what seemed *beautiful* to them and what did not; and if ten different Ethiopians *agreed* in their judgment of this Helen, then that presumably happened because they had the same *concept* or *model* of beauty and ugliness."

"This does not follow!" said the Abderite scholar. "Could not each of the ten find something different in her to be charming?"

"That is not impossible; but it does not prove a thing against *me.*

Parmenides of *Elea* is considered the originator of the theory of *ideas* or essential primary forms that Plato included in his system and made so much his own that they are customarily identified with his name.

Suppose the one had found her *small eyes* admirable, another her *full lips,* a third her *large ears.* Then even this presupposes a comparison between her and other Ethiopian beauties. The rest had eyes, ears, and lips as did *Gulleru.* If hers then were thought to be more beautiful, there had to be a certain model of beauty with which, for example, *her* eyes and *other* eyes were compared; and that is all I wanted to say with my *ideal.*"

"Nevertheless," answered the *scholar,* "you will surely not wish to maintain that this *Gulleru* was absolutely *the most beautiful* among all the black girls before her, next to her, and after her? I mean, the most beautiful in comparison with the model you were talking about."

"I wouldn't know why I should maintain that," replied *Democritus.*

"Then there could, for example, be one with still smaller eyes, still thicker lips, still larger ears?"

"Possibly, so far as I know."

"And so far as she is concerned we can, no doubt, make the same assumption, and so on ad infinitum. The Ethiopians, therefore, had no *model of beauty;* it would then have to be said that infinitely small eyes, infinitely thick lips, and infinitely big ears can be imagined?"

"How subtle the Abderite scholars are!" *Democritus* thought. — "If I admitted," he said, "that there could be a black girl with smaller eyes or thicker lips than *Gulleru,* then that would still not be saying that this black girl would for that reason have had to seem *more beautiful* to the Ethiopians than *Gulleru.* The beautiful necessarily has a *definite proportion,* and whatever is in excess of that is just as far removed from it as whatever remains short thereof. Who—from the fact that the Greeks consider the largeness of the eyes and the smallness of the mouth a part of consummate beauty—would draw from this the conclusion that a woman whose eyeballs have a diameter as big as a thumb or whose mouth is so small as to make it difficult for her to put a straw between her lips would have to be considered so much the more beautiful by the Greeks?"

The Abderite was defeated, as is apparent, and he perceived that he was. However, an Abderite scholar would have preferred to be throttled rather than admit something like that. Were not Philinna and Lysandra and a short, fat councillor present by whose opinion of his intelligence he laid great store? And how little it cost him to get the Abderite men and women over to his side! As a matter of fact, he did not know right away what to say. But full of confidence that something would probably still occur to him, he answered, meanwhile, with a sneer that was at the same time supposed to suggest that he held his opponent's arguments in contempt and that he was about to strike the decisive blow. "Is it possible," he finally cried out in a tone as if this were his answer to Democritus's last speech,* "for you to carry your love of paradox so far as to maintain, in the presence of these beautiful women, that a creature such as you have described Gulleru to us is a beauty?"

"You appear to have forgotten," Democritus answered very calmly, "that we were not talking about me and these beauties, but rather about Ethiopians. I maintained nothing; I merely related what I had seen. I described for you a beauty in Ethiopian taste. It is not *my* fault if Greek ugliness is beauty in Ethiopia. I do not see either what would give me the justification to decide between the Greeks and Ethiopians. I presume that it is possible for both of them to be right."

Loud laughter, the like of which bursts out when someone has said something inconceivably preposterous, roared over toward the philosopher from the throats of all those present.

"Let's hear, let's just hear," called *the fat councillor* holding his paunch with both hands, "what our compatriot can say to prove that both are right. For the life of me, I like to hear somebody maintain something like that. To what other purpose would we have you learned gentlemen? —*The earth is round; the snow is black;* the moon is ten times as large as *the entire Peloponnesus; Achilles cannot catch up with a snail.*[23] Isn't that so, Mr. *Antistrepsiades*? —Isn't that so Mr. *Democritus*? You can see that I'm also a bit initiated in your mysteries. Ha, ha, ha!"

All the Abderite men and women relieved their lungs once more to indicate their sympathy, and Mr. *Antistrepsiades,* who had been aiming at an invitation to supper from the jovial councillor, obligingly supported the general laughter with loud applause.

Chapter Five

Unexpected denouement, with a few new examples of Abderite wit.

Democritus was in the mood to amuse himself with his *Abderites* and to have them divert one another. Too wise to take any of

---

*A very common dodge of Abderite scholars and art critics.

their national or individual bad habits amiss, he could quite easily tolerate their considering him a man too clever by half whose Abderite common sense had evaporated during his travels and who now was good for nothing but to arouse their laughter with his whims and capricious notions. Therefore, after the laughter at the witty idea of the fat councillor had finally subsided, he continued with his customary equanimity where the small jovial man had interrupted him.

"Didn't I say that, if Greek ugliness were beauty in Ethiopia, quite possibly both could be right?"

"Yes, yes, that's what you said, and a man stands by his word."

"If that's what I said, then that's what I have to maintain; that's understood, *Mr. Antistrepsiades.*"

"If you can."

"Am I, after all, not an *Abderite,* too? And besides, I need here prove only half of my statement in order to have proved the entire thing; for that the Greeks are right does not first need to be proved; this is a matter which long ago was settled in Greek minds. But that the Ethiopians are right *as well,* that's where the difficulty lies!—If I wished to fence with sophists or wished to be satisfied by forcing my opponents into silence without convincing them, then, as advocate of the Ethiopian Venus, I would have the entire dispute decided by *inner feeling.* Why, I would say, do people call this or that figure, this or that color beautiful?—Because they like it.—All right; but why do they like it? Because they find it agreeable. And why do they find it agreeable?—Oh, sir, I would say, you must finally stop asking, or—I will stop answering. Something is agreeable to us because it—makes an impression on us that is agreeable. I challenge all of your ponderers to give a better answer. Now it would be silly to deny that a person finds agreeable what is agreeable to him; or to prove to him that he is wrong in allowing a thing to please him that makes a pleasing impression on him. If, therefore, the figure of a *Gulleru* pleases his eyes, then he likes her, and if he likes her he calls her beautiful, or there would have to be no such word in his language."

"And *if*—and *if* a madman took horse droppings for apples and preferred eating them to peaches?" asked *Antistrepsiades.*

"Horse apples to peaches!—By my honor, that was well said, well said," exclaimed the *councillor.* "Take a crack at that, Mr. *Democritus!*"

"Why fie, fie, *Democritus,*" beautiful Myris whispered while holding her hand in front of her nose. "What's the idea of bringing up horse apples? You might at least spare our noses!"

Everybody knows that beautiful *Myris* should have directed her reprimand at witty *Antistrepsiades* who had first served up the horse apples and at the councillor who even expected Democritus to crack them open. But it was simply their intention to make the much-traveled man look ridiculous. In this among all those present, instinct took the place of conspiracy, and it was impossible for *Myris* to pass up this fine opportunity for a gibe that brought the laughs to her side. As things stood, Democritus, who had enough to swallow with the apples of Antistrepsiades, got a reprimand for it on top of everything else. Precisely this circumstance seemed so comical to the Abderites that they all began laughing at the same time and behaved entirely as if the philosopher had been struck on the head and were not at all able to get back on his feet.

Too much is too much. Good *Democritus* had, to be sure, traveled a lot in twenty years; but since he had left Abdera he had come upon no second Abdera; and now that he was back there again, he would now and then for a moment or two doubt *that he was anywhere at all.* How was it possible to deal with such people?

"Well, cousin,"—said the councillor, "can't you get Antistrepsiades's horse apples down? Ha, ha, ha!"

This notion was too Abderite not to overwhelm the tenderness of all the bent, blunt, square, and pointed noses in the company.

The ladies giggled a chirping "Hee, hee, hee" into the dull, thundering "Ha, ha, ha" of the men.

"You have won," cried *Democritus;* "and as a sign that I am laying down my weapon with good grace, you're going to see whether I merit the honor of being your countryman and cousin." And now, with a skill no Abderite could match and beginning with the lowest note and in a gradual crescendo rising to the *unisono* with the "Hee, hee, hee" of the beautiful Abderite women, he started to break out in laughter the like of which had not been heard as long as Abdera had been standing on Thracian soil.

At the beginning, the ladies looked as if they were going to resist; but it was impossible to endure against that confounded crescendo. They were finally swept along by it as if by a torrential stream; and since the force of contagion was added, things soon developed to the point that the matter got serious. The women, with tears in their eyes, begged for mercy. But *Democritus* could not hear, and the laughter increased. Finally he appeared to be moved to grant them a halt; however, he actually did this only so that they might endure so much the longer the torment he had in store for them. For they had hardly caught their breath a little again when he once more began to laugh through the same scale a third higher, but with so many trills and runs mixed in that even the wrinkled associate judges of the Court of Hell, Minos, Aeacus, and Rhadamanthus, in their infernal-judicial vestments, would have been disconcerted by it.

Unfortunately, two or three of our beauties had not thought of securing their persons against all possible consequences of such violent exercise. Modesty and nature had a life-and-death struggle in the poor girls. In vain did they implore pitiless Democritus for mercy with their voices and glances; in vain did they summon their sinews, completely slack from laughing, to make one last effort. Tyrannical nature came off victorious, and in a moment the room where the company was assembled could be seen g. . . . u. . . . w. . . . .

The consternation over such an unexpected natural phenomenon (which was so much the more marvelous since the general astonishment of the startled Abderite women appeared to prove that it was an effect without a cause) interrupted the laughers for several moments only to explode right away again with redoubled force. Naturally, the relieved beauties made every effort to hide the particular share they had in this event with grimaces of astonishment and loathing and to throw suspicion on their innocent neighbors who, through their ill-timed but involuntary blushes, strengthened the undeserved suspicion more than too much. The silly bickering about this that broke out among them—*Democritus* and *Antistrep-siades* who maliciously intervened and provoked still more through ironical remarks of consolation the anger of those who knew they were not guilty—and in the midst of them all the small, fat councillor who, bursting with laughter, called out over and over *that he wouldn't take half of Thrace for this evening*—all of this together made a scene that would have been worthy of the pencil of a Hogarth, if at that time there had been a Hogarth.

We cannot say how long it may have lasted, for it is one of the Abderites' virtues *that they cannot stop.* But *Democritus,* for whom everything had its time, was of the opinion that a comedy that does not come to an end was the most unamusing of all entertainments—a truth of which we (in passing) would like to be able to convince all of our writers of dramas and play directors—he, therefore, quite calmly packed up all the pretty things which he could have said in vindication of the Ethiopian Venus provided that he was dealing with reasonable creatures, wished the Abderites— what they did not have and went home, not without astonishment at *the good company* one ran the risk of meeting if one—visited a councillor of Abdera.

Chapter Six

An opportunity for the reader's brain to settle down after the rocking motion it suffered in the previous chapter.

"Good, artless, tenderhearted Gulleru"—said *Democritus,* when he had come home, to a well-groomed curly-haired black woman who hurried toward him with open arms—"let me embrace you, honest *Gulleru!* You are, indeed, as black as the goddess of the night. Your hair is woolly and your nose flat. Your eyes are small, your ears large, and your lips resemble a newly blossoming carnation. But your heart is pure and sincere and cheerful, and it is in sympathy with all of nature. You never have malicious thoughts, never say anything foolish, torment neither yourself nor others, and you do nothing that you might not wish to admit. Your soul is without guile as your face is unrouged. You know neither envy nor do you gloat over the misfortunes of others; and you never turned up your honest flat nose to mock or embarrass one of your fellow creatures. Unconcerned about whether you are liked or not, you live, enveloped in your purity of heart and mind, in peace with yourself and all of nature; always apt to delight and to receive pleasure and worthy of having the heart of a man rest on your breast. Good, tenderhearted Gulleru! I could give you another name, a beautiful, sonorous Greek name, one ending in *-ane* or *-ide, -arion* or *-erion;* but your name is beautiful enough because it is yours. And my name is not Democritus, or the time will yet come when every honest, good heart will beat with yearning at the mention of the name *Gulleru.*"

Gulleru did not comprehend all too well what *Democritus* wished to express with this sentimental address, but she saw that he was pouring out his heart, and so she understood exactly as much as was necessary.

"Was this *Gulleru* his wife?"

No.

"His concubine?"

No.

"His slave?"

To judge by what she was wearing, no.

"Just how was she dressed, anyway?"

So well that she could have passed as a maid of honor of the Queen of Sheba. Strings of fine, great pearls between the curls in her hair and about her neck and arms; a garment full of fine pleats of thin fire-colored satin with stripes of whatever color you wish, held together under her bosom with a richly embroidered girdle with a clasp of emeralds, and—what do I know what all—

"Her apparel was rich all right."

At least you can believe me when I tell you that the way she appeared, no prince of *Senegal, Angola, Gambia, Kongo,* and *Loango* could have looked at her with impunity.

"But—"

I see that you haven't yet come to the end of your questions.—

"Just who was this Gulleru, anyway? Was it really the same one discussed previously? How did *Democritus* meet her? On what footing was she living in his house?"—

I admit that these questions are fair enough, but for the present I see no possibility of answering them. Don't get the idea that I wish to act the part of a reticent person here or that some special secret lies behind the matter. The reason why I cannot answer them is the very simplest in the world. A thousand authors are in the same situation a thousand times; except that among a thousand hardly one will be honest enough to admit the real reason in such cases. Shall I tell you mine? You will admit that it is beyond any objection. For, in a word—I myself do not know a thing about all you want me to tell you; and since I am not writing the story of beautiful *Gulleru,* you will comprehend that with respect to this lady I have no obligations. Should the opportunity perhaps present itself (which I cannot foresee) to find out more about Democritus or about her herself in what follows, you may rest assured that you will be informed of everything in detail.

Chapter Seven

The Abderites' patriotism. Their partiality for Athens as their mother city. A few samples of their atticisms and of the embarrassing straightforwardness of the wise Democritus.

Democritus had not yet been living among the Abderites for a month when he became so unbearable to *them,* and at times they to *him,* as human beings have to be to one another whose notions and inclinations are constantly colliding.

The Abderites cherished a quite extraordinary opinion of themselves and of their city and republic. Their ignorance of everything worthy of note that happened to exist or to take place outside of their territory was a cause as well as a result of this ridiculous arrogance. That is why, through a natural consequence, they could not imagine how something could be decent or good if it was at any other place but Abdera or if nothing at all was known about it in Abdera. An idea that contradicted *their* ideas, a habit that deviated from *their own,* a way of thinking or of looking at things that was unknown to them, they regarded—without further examination—as absurd and ludicrous. For them, nature itself shrank to the narrow circle of their own activities. And although they did not carry things as far as the Japanese and imagine that outside of Abdera there were living nothing but devils, phantoms, and monsters, they nevertheless looked upon the rest of the earth and its inhabitants as an object unworthy of their attention; and whenever it happened that they got an opportunity to see or hear something foreign, they did not know what to make of it other than to criticize it and to congratulate themselves for not being like other people. This went so far that they did not consider anyone a *good citizen* who had found at some other place better institutions or customs than at home. Whoever wished to have the good fortune of pleasing them positively had to talk and act as if the city and republic of Abdera, with all its pertinent parts, attributes, and contingencies, was altogether without flaw and the ideal of all republics.

From this contempt for everything not called Abderite the city of Athens alone was exempted; but presumably even this was so only because, as former inhabitants of Teos, the Abderites honored it by regarding it as their mother city. They were proud of being considered *the Thracian Athens;* and although this name was never given them except in mockery, they nevertheless preferred to hear no flattery more than this. They strove to copy the Athenians in every respect and copied them exactly—as the ape the human being. When, intending to be vivacious and witty, they now and then dropped into drollery, dealt with important things in a frivolous way and seriously with trifles, assembled the people or their council twenty times for every petty matter in order to make long, silly speeches pro and contra about things which a man of every-day common sense would have settled better in a quarter of an hour, when they constantly were full of projects for beautification and enlargement and, as often as they undertook something, did not figure out until they got to the middle of their undertaking that it went beyond their means, when they interlarded their half-Thracian language with Attic idioms; affected, without having the least taste, an enormous passion for the arts and always prattled about painting and statues, and music and orators, and poets without ever having had a painter, sculptor, orator, or poet worthy of the name; when they built temples resembling baths and baths resembling temples;

when they had the story of Vulcan's net[24] painted in their council chamber and the Great Council of the Greeks concerning the return of the beautiful Chryseis[25] painted in their gymnastic school, when they attended comedies where they were made to weep and tragedies where they were made to laugh, and in twenty similar things these good people believed they were Athenians and were—*Abderites.*

"How sublime is the flight in this little poem which *Physignatus* has written about *my quail!*" said an Abderite woman.—"So much the worse!" said Democritus.

"Do you see," asked the first *archon of Abdera,* "the façade of this building which we intend to use as our arsenal? It is of the best Parian marble. Admit that you have never seen a work of greater taste!"

"It is surely costing the Republic a fine bit of money," answered Democritus.

"Whatever honors the Republic never costs too much," answered the *archon* who, at this moment, felt himself to be a second *Pericles.*[26] "I know you are a connoisseur, Democritus; for you always feel the need to find fault with everything. Now, if you please, find some flaw in this façade!"

"A thousand drachmas for one flaw, Mr. Democritus," a young man called out who had the honor of being a nephew of the archon and who had a short time before returned from Athens where, for half of his heritage, he managed to develop himself from a boorish Abderite rogue into an Attic coxcomb.

"The façade is beautiful," said Democritus quite modestly, "so much so that it would be beautiful in Athens or Corinth or Syracuse as well. If it be permitted to say something like that, I see only one flaw in this magnificent building."

"One flaw?"—said the archon with an expression which only an *Abderite* who was an archon could have.

"One flaw! One flaw!" the young coxcomb repeated while laughing out loud.

"May I ask, Democritus, what flaw you are talking about?"

"A trifle," the latter replied. "Nothing except that such a beautiful façade—cannot be seen."

"Can't be seen? And why not?"

"Well, by *Anubis!*[27] how do you expect somebody to see it with all the old badly built houses and barns that have been set down around here between people's eyes and your façade?"

"These houses were standing a long time before you and I were born," said the archon.

"Then you should have put your arsenal some place else," said *Democritus*.

There were dialogues of that sort as long as Democritus lived among them, every day, hour, and moment.

"What do you think of this purple, Democritus? You have been in Tyre, haven't you?"

"*I* certainly have, madam, but not this purple; this is *coccinus,* which the Syracusans bring you from Sardinia and charge you for it as if it were purple from Tyre."

"But you will at least admit that this veil is made of Indian linen of the finest sort?"

"Of the finest sort, beautiful *Atalanta,* made in *Memphis* and *Pelusium.*"[28]

The frank man had now made two enemies in one minute. But could anything be more aggravating anyway than such honesty?

Chapter Eight

Preliminary report on the state of the Abderite theater. Democritus is pressed to express his opinion about it.

The Abderites set great store by their theater. Their actors were ordinary citizens of Abdera who either could not earn a living from their craft or were too lazy to learn one. They had no learned concept of art, but for that reason an all the greater notion of their own cleverness; and they really could not be short on predisposition since the Abderites in general were born impostors, wags, and pantomimes, all the parts of whose bodies always helped them to speak, as little as what they said might have signified.

They possessed their own playwright, too, named Hyperbolus, who (if one were to believe them) had developed their stage to the point where it was hardly inferior to that of Athens. He was as strong in the comic vein as in the tragic, and, moreover, he composed the funniest satyr plays* in the world in which he parodied his own tragedies in such a funny way that, as the Abderites said, people had to laugh at them so hard they got hunchbacked. In their judgment, he united in his tragedy the high vitality and mighty imagination of *Aeschylus* with the eloquence and pathos of *Euripi-*

---

*Greek farces that had some similarity to the *Opera buffa* of the Italians and of which we can get some idea from the *Cyclops* of Euripides, the only extant piece of this sort.

des, as well as the temper and playful wit of *Aristophanes* with the fine taste and elegance of *Agathon*[29] in his comedies. The agility with which he gave birth to his works was the talent on which he most prided himself. Each month he provided his tragedy—with a little farcelet for an encore. "My best comedy," he said, "cost me no more than two weeks; and all the same it lasted four to five hours all told."

"For that may heaven have mercy!" thought *Democritus.*

Now the Abderites always pressed him from all sides to express his opinion about their theater; and, as much as he disliked entering into a dispute with them about their taste, he could, nevertheless, not get himself to flatter them either when, collectively, they wrenched his judgment out of him.

"How do you like this new tragedy?"

"A fortunate choice of subject. What an author he would have to be who would completely ruin such material."

"Didn't you think it was very moving?"

"A play could be very moving in a few places and still be a very wretched play," said *Democritus.* "I know a sculptor in Sicyon who has a mania for carving nothing but goddesses of love. In general they resemble very common trollops; but all of them have the most beautiful legs in the world. The whole secret of the matter is that the man uses his wife as his model who, luckily for his statues of Venus, at least can boast of very beautiful legs. Thus, the worst writer can now and then produce a moving passage if it just happens that he is in love or has lost a friend, or that some other sort of accident happened to him, putting his heart into a state which made it easy for him to put himself into the place of the person he is supposed to have speaking."

"So then you don't think the *Hecuba* of our poet is excellent?"

"I think the man probably did the best he could. But the many feathers plucked now from Aeschylus, now from Sophocles, and then from Euripides with which he seeks to cover up his shortcomings and which do him honor, perhaps, in the eyes of some people in his audience who do not know those poets as well as I do, are, in my own eyes, detrimental to him. A crow as created by God still seems to look prettier that way than if adorned with peacock and pheasant feathers. After all, I have the same right to ask the writer of a tragedy to give me a splendid tragedy *for my applause* as I have to ask my shoemaker to produce for me a pair of good boots *for my money;* and even though I gladly admit that it is more difficult to write a good tragedy than to make good boots, I am for that reason not less justified in demanding of every tragedy that it have *all* the attributes of a *good* tragedy than I am in asking of a boot to have all those things that belong to a good boot."

"And just what then, in your opinion, belongs to a *well-booted tragedy?*" asked a *young Abderite patrician* laughing heartily at the *bon mot* which had, in his opinion, escaped him.

Democritus was conversing about this subject with a small circle of people who *appeared* to be listening to him, and he continued without paying any attention to the question of the witty young gentleman. "The true rules of art works," he said, "can never be *arbitrary.* I demand nothing of a tragedy but *what Sophocles demands of his;* and that is neither more nor less than the nature and intention of the matter requires. A simple, well-reasoned plot in which the poet has foreseen everything, prepared everything, joined everything together naturally, brought everything to a point; wherein each part is an indispensable member, and the whole is a well-organized, beautiful body moving freely and nobly. No boring exposition, no episodes, no scenes for padding, no speeches the end of which one impatiently yawns for, no actions which do not contribute to the main end. Interesting characters taken from nature, ennobled, but in such a way that one might never fail to recognize the humanity in them; no superhuman virtues, no monsters of wickedness! Persons who always speak and act in a way suitable to their individuality and feelings, always in such a way that, according to all of their previous and present circumstances and the particulars about them, they must, in a given case, speak and act that way or cease to be what they are.

"I demand that the writer be acquainted not only with human nature inasmuch as it is *the model* for all his imitations; I demand that he also take *the members of his audience* into consideration and know exactly the ways by which one gains mastery over their hearts; that he prepare, without being noticed, every strong blow he wishes to give them; that he know *when it is enough,* and, before he tires us through one and the same kind of impressions or arouses in us one emotion to the point where he starts to be tormenting, that he know how to grant the heart small pauses to recover, and how to vary the emotions that he communicates to us without any disadvantage to the main effect.

"I demand fine language of him, polished with utmost assiduity and without timidity; expression that is always warm and robust, simple and sublime without ever *being inflated* nor *sagging,* strong and sinewy without getting *harsh* and *stiff;* sparkling without being dazzling; truly heroic language which is always the living expression of a great soul and inspired directly by the feeling of that moment and which never says too much nor too little, and, like a garment that fits the body perfectly, always allows the characteristic spirit of the speaker to become apparent.

"I demand that whoever ventures to have heroes speak must himself have a great soul and, since he has been transformed into his hero by the omnipotence of enthusiasm, that he find in his own heart everything he puts into his character's mouth. I demand—"

"Oh, Mr. Democritus," cried out the Abderites who did not know how to restrain themselves any longer, "you can, since you are making all these demands anyway, demand anything you like. In Abdera we put up with less. We are satisfied to have a writer move us. The man who makes us laugh or cry is a divine man in our eyes, and this he may do in whatever way he himself wishes. That is his concern, not ours! We like *Hyperbolus,* he moves us and amuses us; and granted, too, that he makes us yawn now and then, he will always remain a great writer nevertheless! Do we need further proof?"

"The blacks on the Gold Coast," said *Democritus,* "take delight in dancing to the din made on a mean hide of a sheep and with a few pieces of sheet metal which they beat together. Now give them a few cow bells and a bagpipe as well, and then they will think they are in Elysium. How much wit was needed by your nurse when you were still children to *move* you with her tales? The silliest fairy tale reeled off in a plaintive tone was good enough for that. Can we from that, however, draw the conclusion that the music of the blacks is splendid or that a nursery tale is right away a magnificent work?"

"You are very polite, Democritus!"

"I beg your pardon! I am so impolite as to call everything by its name, and so stubborn that I will never admit that everything is fine and splendid that people choose to designate as such."

"But the feelings of an entire people will, after all, count for more than the egotism of one individual?"

"Egotism? Precisely that is what I wish to see banned from the arts of the Muses. And of all the demands from which the Abderites so kindly except their favorite Hyperbolus, there is not a one that is not based on the strictest fairness. But the feeling of an entire people, if it is not an erudite feeling, can and must, in countless cases, be deceptive."

"What the deuce!" (called an Abderite who appeared very well satisfied with his feeling) "in the end you'll very likely even contest our right to have our five senses!"

"Heaven forfend!" answered Democritus. "If you are so modest as to have no further claims than to five senses, it would be the greatest injustice to wish to disturb your quiet possession of them. Five senses, to be sure, all the more if one takes all five of them together, are unexceptionable judges in all things where we are concerned with deciding what is white or black, smooth or rough, soft or hard, repellent or pleasant, bitter or sweet. A man who never goes any further than his five senses take him is always on the safe side; and indeed, if Hyperbolus will see to it that in his plays each sense is entertained and none offended, I will guarantee him a good reception, and even if they still were ten times worse than they are."

Had Democritus been nothing more in Abdera than what Diogenes was in Corinth, the freedom of his tongue might have got him into some trouble. For, as much as the Abderites liked to make fun of *important* matters, they could little bear anyone's poking fun at their dolls and hobbyhorses. But Democritus was of the best family in Abdera and, what is of still greater importance, he was rich. This double circumstance caused people to overlook in him what they scarcely would have pardoned in a philosopher in a ragged coat.

"You really are an insufferable man, Democritus!" the beautiful Abderite women said stridently and—suffered him nevertheless.

The poet *Hyperbolus* composed still that very evening a dreadful epigram on the philosopher. On the following morning it made the rounds of all the dressing tables, and on the third night it was being sung in all the streets of Abdera, for *Democritus had composed a melody for it.*

Chapter Nine

The good disposition of the Abderites and the way they know how to take revenge on Democritus because of his impoliteness. A sample of one of his admonitions. The Abderites pass a law against all journeys through which an Abderite human being could have become more intelligent. The curious way in which the nomophylax Gryllus[30] solves a difficulty that resulted from this law.

It is really a dangerous thing for a person to have more sense than his fellow citizens. *Socrates* had to pay for it with his life; and if *Aristotle* still came away unscathed when the high priest *Eurymedon* accused him of heresy in Athens, then that came about only because he decamped in good time. "I don't wish to give the

Athenians an opportunity," he said, "to sin against philosophy a second time."

The Abderites, with all their human weaknesses, were at least not very malicious people. Among them, *Socrates* could have become as old as Homer's *Nestor.*[31] They would have considered him a strange sort of fool and made fun of his alleged foolishness; but to carry the thing as far as the cup of poison, that was not in their character. *Democritus* assailed them so severely that a less jovial people would have lost its patience as a result. All the same, the revenge they took on him consisted in their saying just as bad things about him (for what reason was none of their concern) as he had about them, and they found fault with everything he undertook, thought everything he said silly, and did precisely the opposite of all he advised them to do. "We have to frustrate the philosopher's intentions," they said; "we must not make him believe that he knows everything better than we do." —And, according to this wise maxim, the good people did one foolish thing after another and thought they had gained ever so much by its vexing him. In this, however, they failed to attain their goal entirely. For Democritus laughed at this and his hair, on account of all their raillery, did not get grayer one moment earlier. "Oh the Abderites, the Abderites!" he cried out occasionally; "there they've again given themselves a box on the ear in the hope of hurting me!"

"But," the Abderites said, "can anybody be worse off with a man than with him? On everything in the world he has an opinion different from ours. He has some fault to find in everything we like. It is, after all, very unpleasant to have oneself constantly contradicted!"

"But if you are always wrong?" answered Democritus. "And let's just see how things could be otherwise. —You have your nurse to thank for all of your notions; you think about everything just as you did when you were children. Your bodies have grown, but your souls are still lying in your cradle. Just how many of you have taken the trouble to investigate the reason you call something true or good or beautiful? Like those who are not yet of age and like infants, you think everything is good and fine that tickles your senses, that pleases you. And on what trivial causes and circumstances that are often not at all pertinent does your liking something depend! How embarrassed you would often be if you were obliged to say *why* you like this and hate that! Whims, moods, obstinacy, the habit of letting other people lead you by the nose, of seeing with their eyes and hearing with their ears, and imitating the tune they have whistled for you—these are the mainsprings which take the place of *reason* with you. Should I tell you of what your error consists? You have taken *a false concept of freedom* into your head. To be sure, your children of three or four years of age have the same notion of it; but this does not make it more correct. 'We are a free people,' you say, and now you think that *reason* ought not to contradict you. 'Why should we not be permitted to think whatever we like, love and hate as we like, admire or despise what we like? Who has the right to call us to account or to pass judgment on our taste and our inclinations?' Well then, my dear Abderites, so think and rave, love and hate, admire and despise how, when, and whatever you like! Do silly things as often and as much as you like! Make yourselves as ridiculous as you like. Who, after all, cares? As long as only trifles, dolls, and hobby horses are concerned, it would be unreasonable to want to disturb you in your possession of the right to dress up your doll and ride your hobby horse as you please. Supposing, too, that your doll were ugly and the thing you call your hobby horse were to look from front and back like a little ox or donkey—what does it matter? If your follies make you happy and no one unhappy, what is it to other people that they are follies? Why should not the sapient council of Abdera in solemn procession, one member behind the other, from the town hall down to the Temple of Latona, be allowed—to turn somersaults, if that is what the council and the people of Abdera wanted to have them do. Why should you not be allowed to set your best building into a corner and your beautiful small Venus on an obelisk?—But my dear fellow countrymen, not all of your follies are as innocent as these; and when I see you doing yourselves harm with your whims and fits, I could not be your friend if I then kept silent. For example, your *frog-and-mouse war* with the *Lemnians*,[32] the most unnecessary and rashest that was ever begun—for the sake of a dancing girl! It was apparent that you were under the direct influence of your evil demon when you decided to wage it; all the protestations made to you against it were of no avail. The *Lemnians* were to be chastised, so people said; and, as you are a people with a lively imagination, nothing seemed easier to you than making yourselves masters of their entire island. For you customarily never weigh the difficulties in a matter until your *nose* reminds you to do so. Yet all this might still be overlooked if you had at least charged a competent man with the execution of your plans. But making young *Aphron*[33] commander-in-chief without anyone's having any possible reason other than that your women thought him as beautiful as Paris in his splendid new armor; and to forget, out of pleasure in seeing a great fire-colored tuft of feathers nodding on his brainless head, that you were not faced with a diverting bit of sport, this, do not deny it, this was a typical piece of *Abderite folly*! And now that you have paid for it with the loss of your honor, your galleys, and your best troops, of what help to you is it that the Athenians,* whom you have made the model for your follies, are accustomed to playing tricks that are just as ingenious and that now and then have just as fortunate an issue?"

Democritus spoke to the Abderites in this tone as often as they gave him the opportunity to do so; however, although this happened very often, it was nevertheless impossible for them to get accustomed to finding this tone pleasant.

"That's the way things go," they said, "when young men are allowed to travel about in the wide world to learn how to be ashamed of their fatherland and, with their head full of foreign ideas, to return after ten or twenty years as *cosmopolitans* who know everything better than their grandfathers and have seen everything elsewhere better than at home. The old Egyptians who allowed nobody to travel before he bore fifty years on his back were wise people."

And the Abderites quickly passed a law to the effect that no son of an Abderite was henceforth to be permitted to travel *farther* than to the Isthmus of Corinth, *longer* than one year, and *in any other manner* than under the supervision of an aged tutor of old Abderite origin, way of thinking, and manners.

"To be sure, young people must see the world," said the decree, "but precisely for that reason they are not to stop any longer at each place than it takes them to see what is to be seen with their eyes. The tutor is to take especially exact notice of the kinds of inns they visit, how they eat, and how much they spend, so that their fellow citizens can in the future make use of this profitable secret information. Further (as the decree continues), with a view to saving the expenses of an all too long sojourn in one place, the tutor is to see to the young Abderite's not getting involved in any unnecessary acquaintanceships. At an inn, either the proprietor or a servant, as natives of the place and as ingenuous persons, can

---

*The Athenians had no better reason for their war with Megara (if Aristophanes might be believed) than that a few young gentlemen of Megara, in order to avenge the abduction of a Megarian courtesan, had kidnapped a few young girls of the same profession from the nursery of Aspasia. Pericles was completely under the influence of Aspasia, Athens under that of Pericles, and so war was declared against the Megarians.

best tell him what noteworthy things can be seen there, what the names of the local scholars and artists are, where they live, and at what time one can see them—this the tutor notes in his diary; and so, if one husbands one's time properly, a lot can be seen."

It was unfortunate for this wise decree that, just when it was drawn up and then (in keeping with an old custom) announced to the city by being *sung* in the principal squares, a couple of very important young Abderite gentlemen were out of the country. The one was the son of a shopkeeper who had over a period of some forty years, through avarice and dirty tricks, scratched together a considerable fortune by virtue of which he had just recently married his daughter (the ugliest and most stupid little creature in all of Abdera) to a nephew of the *short fat councillor,* who was mentioned with praise above. The other was the *nomophylax's* only son. He was to travel to Athens and there get more familiar with the art of music in order, the sooner the better, to become his father's assistant, while the heir of the shopkeeper, who wanted to accompany him, was minded to become better acquainted with the girls who made finery or those who sold flowers. The decree now had not taken into consideration the special case that these young men represented. The point was whether a modification of the law ought to be proposed or whether the Senate should merely be requested to make a dispensation for this case.

"Neither," said the *nomophylax,* who had just finished composing a dance for the Feast of Latona and was extraordinarily satisfied with himself. "In order to change something in the law the people would have to be convoked for that purpose; and this would only give those citizens who are dissatisfied the opportunity to rant. So far as the dispensation is concerned, it is indeed true that laws are mostly made for the sake of the dispensations; and I have no doubt that the Senate would grant us without difficulty whatever anyone in similar situations wishes to be able to demand by operation of a contravening law. However, every exemption has, after all, the appearance of a bestowed favor; and for what reason do we find it necessary to saddle ourselves with obligations? The law is a *sleeping lion* past whom, as long as he is not awakened, one can creep as securely as past a lamb. And who is going to have the impudence or the audacity to wake him up to oppose the son of the nomophylax?"

This *protector of the laws* was, as we see, a man who had very refined notions about the laws and about his office and knew how to make skillful use of the advantages that the latter gave him. His name deserves to be remembered. He was called *Gryllus,* the son of *Cyniscus.*[34]

Chapter Ten

Democritus withdraws to the country and is assiduously visited by the Abderites. All kinds of curiosities, and a conversation about the moral philosophers' land of milk and honey.
When Democritus returned to his fatherland, he had buoyed himself up with the idea of being able to be of service to it by means of the betterment that had taken place in his understanding and in his heart. He had not imagined that the Abderites' brains were in such a bad way as he now found them to be. But when he had been living among them for some time, it was apparent to him that it would have been a vain project to wish to improve them. Everything about them was so askew that it was not possible to know where the improvement was to commence. Each of their abuses was connected to twenty others; it was impossible to put a stop to one of them without transforming the entire state. "A good epidemic" (he thought) "that would wipe them from the face of the earth—down to a few dozen children just big enough to be able to get along without a nurse—would be the only means to help the *city of Abdera; the Abderites* cannot be helped!"
He decided, therefore, to move away from them in good humor and to live on a small estate that he owned in their vicinity and with the utilization and beautification of which he employed the hours left him by his favorite study, the investigation of the workings of nature. But unfortunately for him, this property was situated too close to Abdera. For, because its site was uncommonly beautiful and the way there was one of the most pleasant walks, he saw himself plagued on every one of God's days by a swarm of Abderites (nothing but cousins) who used the fine weather and the pleasant walk as a pretext to disturb him in his happy solitude.
Although the Abderites liked Democritus at least no better than he liked them, the effect of that was nevertheless very different. He *fled* from them because they bored him; and they *sought* him because they passed the time this way. He knew how to use his; they, on the other hand, had nothing better to do.
"We are coming to help you pass the time in your solitude," the Abderites said.

"I am used to finding entertainment in my own company," said Democritus.

"But how is it possible for anybody to be alone all the time that way?" lovely *Pithoeca* cried. "I would expire of boredom if I were to live a single day without *seeing* people."

"That was a slip of the tongue, Pithoeca; you meant to say *being seen by people.*"

"But," someone blurted out, "what makes you think that our friend is bored? His whole house is filled with rare things. By your leave, Democritus—do let us see the beautiful things which, as people say, you collected on your journey."

Now, more than ever, did the suffering of the poor recluse begin. He had indeed brought back a fine collection of natural curiosities from all the realms of nature: stuffed animals and birds, dried fish, rare butterflies, shells, petrified objects, ores, and so on. Everything was new to the Abderites, everything aroused their astonishment. The good naturalist was in a minute so deafened with questions that he would have had, like *Fama,* to be constituted of nothing but ears and tongues in order to be able to answer everything.

"Do explain to us what this is, what is it called, where it comes from, how you close it, why it is that way."

Democritus explained as well as his knowledge allowed; but nothing was for that reason any clearer to the Abderites; to them it appeared rather as if they comprehended less and less about the matter the more he explained it to them. It was not *his* fault!

"Wonderful! Inconceivable! Very wonderful!"—was their incessant response.

"As natural as anything in the world!" he answered quite frostily.

"You are very much too modest, cousin! or, I suppose, you only want to have people pay you all the more compliments on your good taste and on your great journeys?"

"Don't go to any expense on that account, ladies and gentlemen! I'll regard everything as a gift."

"But it may, after all be a pleasant thing to travel that far into the world, isn't that so?" said the Abderite.

"And I would think just the opposite," answered another. "—Take all the dangers and difficulties to which one is exposed daily, the bad roads, the wretched inns, the sandbanks, the shipwrecks, the wild animals, crocodiles, unicorns, griffins, and winged lions with which all parts of barbarian lands are teeming!"

"And then what good does it do you in the end," a *matador* of Abdera chimed in, "to have seen how big the world is? I would think that the piece of it that I own myself would then seem so small to me that I couldn't be pleased with it any more."

"But don't you think seeing so many people is worth something?" answered the first.

"And so what do you see anyway? People! You could see them at home. Things are everywhere as they are here."

"Ah, there's even a bird here without feet!" called a young woman.

"Without any feet?—And the entire bird only one single feather! That's amazing!" said another woman. "Do you grasp that?"

"Please, dear Democritus, explain to us how it can walk seeing that it hasn't got any feet!"

"And how does it fly with just one feather?"

"Oh, what I would like to see best," said one of the cousins, a woman, "would be a living sphinx! You must surely have found many of them in Egypt!"

"But please tell us, is it possible that the wives and daughters of the gymnosophists in India—as people say—you do understand what I am asking you about, don't you?"

"Not I, madam *Salabanda*!"

"Oh, you surely do understand me! Weren't you in India? Didn't you see the women of the gymnosophists?"

"Oh yes, and you can take it from me that the women of the gymnosophists are neither more nor less women than the women of Abdera."

"You do us much honor. But that's not what I wanted to know. I'm asking if it isn't true that they—." Here madam *Salabanda* held one hand in front of her bosom and the other—in short, she assumed the posture of the *Medicean Venus* in order to make comprehensible to the philosopher what she wanted to know. "You do understand me now, don't you?" she asked.

"Yes, madam, nature wasn't more parsimonious with them than with others. What a question that is!"

"You simply do not want to understand me, you licentious man! I would have thought, after all, that I had told you plainly enough that I'd like to know whether it was true that they—because you do want me to tell it to you plain—walk about as *naked* as when they were born."

"Naked!"—the Abderite women cried all at the same time. "Why, then they'd be even more impudent than the girls in *Lacedaemon*! Now really, who's going to believe something like that?"

"You are right," said the naturalist, "the gymnosophists are less naked than the women of the Greeks in their most complete apparel; from head to foot they are enveloped in their innocence and in public respectability."

"How do you mean that?"

"Can I put it more plainly?"

"Oh, now I get your meaning! That's supposed to be a gibe! But you are surely joking about their respectability and innocence. If the women of the gymnosophists aren't more substantially dressed, then—they either have to be very ugly or the men in their country are very frigid."

"Neither. Their women are well formed, and their children healthy and full of life, an unexceptionable testimony in favor of their fathers, it seems to me!"

"You are a lover of paradoxes, Democritus," said the *matador.* "But in all eternity you're not going to persuade me that the morals of a people are the purer the more naked its women are."

"If I were such a great lover of paradoxes as people accuse me of being, then perhaps I would not find it difficult to convince you of that by means of examples and arguments. But I am not so favorably inclined to the custom of the gymnosophists' women as to set myself up as its defender. It was not my intention either to say what sagacious *Kratylus* says that I said. The women of the gymnosophists merely appear to me to prove that habit and circumstances determine everything in customs of this kind. The Spartan daughters because they wear short skirts, and those on the banks of the Indus because they wear no skirts at all, are for that reason neither more indecent nor exposed to greater danger than those who wrap up their virtue in seven veils. Not the objects, but rather *our opinions* about them are the cause of dissolute passions. The *gymnosophists,* who consider no part of the human body less noble than another, regard their women, although they are clothed only with the skin in which they were born, as just as much dressed as the Scythians do theirs when they have a tiger-cat skin hanging about their loins."

"I wouldn't like to have Democritus with his philosophy get so much influence on our women that they would take up such ideas," said an upright, strait-laced Abderite who dealt in furs.

"Neither would I," a linen dealer agreed.

"Nor I, in truth," said Democritus, "even though I deal neither in furs nor in linen."

"But allow me still to ask," whispered his cousin who would so very much have liked to see live sphinxes, "you got around in the whole world; and there are said to be many wonderful countries where everything is different from ours."

"I don't believe a word of it," the councillor murmured while, like Homer's Jupiter, he shook the ambrosial hair on his head that was pregnant with wisdom.

"Do tell me," the cousin went on, "which of all these countries did you like best?"

"Where could anybody like things better than—in Abdera?"

"Oh, we already know that you don't really mean that. Without compliments! Answer the young lady according to your views," said the councillor.

"You'll laugh at me," answered Democritus, "but because you desire it, beautiful *Klonarion,* I will tell you the unvarnished truth. Have you never heard about a country where nature is so complaisant as to take upon itself not only its own functions but the work of human beings as well? About a country where eternal peace prevails? Where no one is servant and no one master, nobody poor and everyone rich; where the thirst for gold forces nobody to commit crimes because the gold cannot be used for anything; where a sickle is an object that is just as unknown as a sword; where the industrious man doesn't have to work for the idler; where there are no physicians because nobody gets ill, no judges because there are no disputes, no disputes because everyone is content, and everyone is content because everyone has everything he could possibly wish—in a word, about a country where all human beings are as pious as lambs and as happy as gods? Haven't you ever heard about such a country?"

"Not that I remember."

"That's what I call some country, Klonarion! There it is never too warm and never too cold, never too wet and never too dry; spring and autumn do not prevail there alternately, but rather, as in the Gardens of Alcinous,[35] simultaneously, in eternal concord. Hills and valleys, forests and meadows are filled with everything a human heart can crave. But it's not as if people would have to take the trouble to hunt the hares, to catch the birds or fish, and to pick the fruit that they want to eat; or that they would have to pay first with much hardship for the comforts they are enjoying. No! Everything comes about by itself there. The partridges and woodcocks fly larded and roasted about one's mouth and beg humbly to be eaten; fishes of all kinds swim cooked in ponds of all possible sorts of sauces the banks of which are ever covered with oysters, crayfish, pastries, hams, and ox tongue. Hares and roebucks come running of their own accord, strip their hides over their ears, impale themselves on the spit, and lay themselves, when they are done, into the dish. Everywhere there are tables that set themselves; and softly padded little couches invite people on all sides to rest from—doing nothing and to enjoy pleasant weariness. Next to them murmur small brooks of milk and honey, of Cyprian wine, lemonade, and other pleasant beverages; and up and over them there are arching, mingled with roses and jasmine, shrubs full of goblets and glasses which, as often as someone drains them, fill themselves up again right away. There are also trees there which, instead of fruit, bear little pastries, fried sausages, almond fritters, and buttered rolls; and there are others all the branches of which are decked out with violins, harps, zithers, theorbos, flutes, and horns, and they all produce the most pleasant concert that can be heard. The happy human beings, after they have slept through the warmer part of the day and have spent the evening in dancing, singing, and joking, refresh themselves then in cool marble baths, where they are given a gentle massage by invisible hands, dried off with fine byssus that has spun and woven itself, and perfumed with the costliest essences that drop down as dew from the evening clouds. Then they lie down on swelling cushions round about full tables and eat and drink and laugh, sing, dally, and kiss the whole night through, which an eternal full moon makes into a softer day; and—what is still the most pleasant thing of all—"

"Oh, go on, Mr. Democritus, you're pulling my leg! Why, what you are telling me here is the fairy tale about the land of milk and honey that I heard a thousand times from my nurse when I was still a little girl."

"But you do find, too, don't you, Klonarion, that life would have to be good in that country?"

"Don't you notice then that there is a hidden meaning concealed under all of this?" said the *wise man of the council,* "presumably a satire on certain philosophers who seek the highest good in sensual pleasure?"

"A bad guess, Mr. Councillor!" Democritus thought to himself.

"I remember having read a similar description of the Golden Age in the *Amphictyons of Telecleides,*" said *madam Salabanda.**

"The country I was describing to beautiful Klonarion," said the

---

*Madam Salabanda told the truth. A long time before the *Wether* of Madame *D'Aulnoy,* Lucian in his *True Story* and, long before *Lucian,* the Greek writers of comedy *Metagenes, Pherecrates, Telecleides, Crates,* and *Cratinus,* wrote descriptions of the land of milk and honey and of what it was like to live there, and they competed with one another in leaving nothing to the most extravagant imagination of a more modern writer of fairy tales. The boldest strokes in the picture of it given by Democritus are taken from fragments which *Athenaeus* has preserved for us in the sixth book of his *Deipnosophistae.*

naturalist, "is no satire. It is the land to which twelve out of every dozen of you wise people secretly wish to go, and as far as possible you work toward that end, and your *Abderite moral philosophers wish to talk us into going there, if their declamations otherwise make any sense at all.*"

"I'd really like to know how you see this!" said the councillor, who, by virtue of a many-years-old habit of half listening and of voting in the council when he was dozing, did not like to take the trouble to reflect a long time about something.

"You like strong illumination, as I see, Mr. Master of the Council," Democritus replied. "But too much light is just as inconvenient for seeing as too little. The twilight of chiaroscuro, it seems to me, is just as much light as one needs in order to see in such things neither too much nor too little. I am taking for granted that you are really able to see. For if this were not the case, you surely comprehend that we would see no better by the light of ten thousand suns than by the gleam of a firefly."

"You're taking about fireflies?" said the councillor as, on hearing the word firefly, he awoke out of a kind of mental slumber into which he had fallen upon gaping at Salabanda's bosom while Democritus was talking. "I thought we were talking about moralists."

"About moralists or fireflies, as you like," replied Democritus. "What I mean to say in order to clarify what we were talking about was this. A country where there is eternal peace and where all men are in the same measure free and happy, where the good is not mixed with the bad, pain not with pleasure, and virtue not with vice, where there is nothing but beauty, nothing but order, nothing but harmony—in a word, a country *such as your moralists wish the entire earth to be,* is either a country where the people have *no stomach and no abdomen,* or it must positively be the country that *Telecleides* describes for us, from whose *Amphictyons* I (as beautiful Salabanda quite rightly observed) have taken my description. *Complete equality, complete satisfaction with the present state of things, everlasting concord*—in short, *the Saturnian Age* when there is no need for kings, priests, soldiers, councillors, moralists, tailors, cooks, physicians, and executioners is only possible in that country where the partridges fly roasted into one's mouth or, what amounts to about the same thing, *where one has no wants.* This is so clear, it seems to me, that to him who cannot understand it, all the light in the empyrean would be of no avail. Nevertheless, your moralists are vexed that the world is as it is; and when the honest philosopher who knows the reasons why it can be no different finds the vexation of these gentlemen to be silly, they treat him as if he were an enemy of gods and men—which is, indeed, in itself still sillier, but now and then, where these splenetic gentlemen play the masters, turns out rather tragically."

"But what, after all, do you want to have the moralists do?"

"First get a little bit acquainted with nature before getting the idea that they know better than it does; be sociable and tolerant of the follies and bad habits of human beings who have to suffer theirs; to effect improvements through examples instead of making people tired with their frosty nonsense or embitter them with their invective; to demand no effects of which the causes do not yet exist, and not require us to reach the summit of a mountain before we have climbed it."

"Surely no one is going to be that foolish?" said one of the Abderites.

"Just as foolish as that are nine-tenths of the lawgivers, schemers, schoolmasters, and social reformers on the entire earth every day!" said *Democritus*.

The entertaining company, which began to find the mood of the naturalist unbearable, now began to go home again and, on the way, by the radiance of the evening star and a beautiful twilight, talked all sorts of fiddle-faddle about sphinxes, unicorns, gymnosophists, and milk-and-honey-lands; and however great the diversity among all the silly things that were said, they nevertheless all agreed that *Democritus* was a strange, conceited, overwise, faultfinding, *eccentric fellow,* although withal a quite entertaining one.

"His wine is the best thing you find at his house," said the *councillor.*

"Gracious Anubis!" Democritus thought when he was alone again. "What all you don't have to say to these Abderites—to get them to pass your time for you!"

Chapter Eleven

Something about Abderite philosophers and how Democritus has the misfortune of bringing himself very badly into discredit with a few well-meant words.

All the same, one ought not, however, to think that all Abderites without exception had been bound by a vow or by their civic oath to have no more understanding than their grandmothers, nurses, and councillors! Abdera, the rival of Athens, also had *philosophers,* that is, they had philosophers—as they had *painters* and *poets.* The famous sophist *Protagoras* had been an Abderite and left behind a crowd of pupils who, to be sure, did not equal their master in wit and eloquence but, to make up for that, they were so much the more his superiors in self-conceit and silliness.

These gentlemen had concocted for themselves a convenient kind of philosophy by means of which they found an answer to every question without any difficulty and chatted so fluently about everything under and over the sun that—inasmuch as they always had only Abderites as an audience—the good listeners firmly believed that their philosophers knew very much more about it than they themselves; although, when all is said and done, the difference was not so great that a reasonable man would have given a fig for it. For the result always finally was, after all, that the Abderite philosopher knew just as much about the matter, except for a few long words signifying nothing, as that person among all the Abderites—who thought he knew least about it.

The philosophers, presumably because they considered it too petty to descend into the details of Nature, concerned themselves with nothing but problems lying beyond the limits of human understanding. "As far as this region," they thought, "no one will follow us, except for—for somebody who is the like of us; and whatever we say to the Abderites, we are in any case at least certain that no one can accuse us of telling lies."

For example, one of their favorite subjects was the question: "*How, why,* and *from what* did the world come into being?"

"It emerged from an egg," said *one,* "the ether was the white, chaos the yolk, and night hatched it."*

"It sprang from fire and water," said *another.*

"It did not come into existence at all," spoke a *third.* "Everything always was as it is and will always stay as it was."

This view met with much approval in Abdera because of its convenience. "It explains everything," they said, "without your having first to cudgel your brains a long time."

"Things have always been like this," was the common answer of an Abderite whenever he was asked about the cause or origin of a thing; and whoever was not satisfied with it was considered stupid.

"What you call *the world,*" said a *fourth,* "is really an eternal

---

*In order to spare those readers erroneous conjectures who have read neither *Diogenes Laertius* nor *Delandes'* or *Brucker's* Critical History of Philosophy nor the compendia of *Mr. Formey* or those of *D. Busching,* the author calls attention to the fact that all the hypotheses appearing here can boast of a very venerable antiquity and a host of defenders and adherents. The opinion of our Democritus is the only one which, presumably only because it is the most reasonable one, has had no following.

series of worlds which, like the layers of an onion, lie on top of
one another and gradually peel off."

"Very clearly presented," called the Abderites, "very clearly!"
They thought that they had understood that philosopher *because
they knew very well what an onion was.*

"A chimera!" spoke the *fifth.* "To be sure, there are countless
worlds; but they originate from the chance motion of indivisible
motes, and it is very fortunate if, after ten thousand times a thousand have turned out badly, one finally emerges that still looks as
passably reasonable as does ours."

"I'll admit atoms," spoke a *sixth;* "but no motions by chance
and without direction. Atoms are nothing, or they have definite
forces and properties and, according to whether they are similar
to one another or not, they attract or repel one another. For that
reason wise *Empedocles* (the man who, in order to discover the
nature of Mount Etna, is said to have wisely thrown himself into
its abyss) made *hatred* and *love* the first causes of all combinations;
and Empedocles is right."

"Forgive me, gentlemen, you are all wrong," spoke the philosopher *Sisamis.* "No world will emerge in all eternity from your *mystical egg,* nor from your *alliance of fire and water,* nor from your
atoms, nor from your *homoeomeries,* if you don't get help from a
spirit. The world (like every other animal) is a combination of matter and spirit. It is the spirit that gives the matter *form;* both have
eternally been unified. And, just as individual bodies are decom-
posed as soon as the spirit that holds together its parts withdraws,
so, if the general world-spirit could cease embracing and animating
the whole, heaven and earth would in the same moment collapse
into a single, colossal, formless, dark, and dead lump."

"May Jupiter and Latona preserve us from that!" the Abderites
cried, not without taking fright when they heard that man utter
such a terrible threat.

"There's no danger," said the priest *Strobylus;* "as long as we
have *the frogs of Latona* within our walls, the *world-spirit of Sisamis* had better keep from doing such mischief in the world."

"My friends," spoke the *eighth,* "the world-spirit of wise *Sisamis*
is of the same stamp as the atoms, homoeomeries, onions, and
eggs of my colleagues. A *demiurge* is what we must assume if we
wish to have a world; for a building presupposes a master builder,
or at least a master carpenter; and *nothing makes itself,* as we all
know."

"But every day people say: '*this will come all by itself or get
along by itself,*'" said the *Abderites.*

"It's true people talk like that," the man answered. "However, where did you ever see something really happening like that? Indeed, I have heard our *archons* say surely a thousand times: 'the problem will solve itself, it will come along, this or that will turn out all right by itself!' But we could wait in vain: it did not solve itself, did not come along, and did not turn out all right."

"Only too true so far as *the deeds of our archons are concerned,*" said an old *cobbler* who had the reputation among the people of being a man of insight and had great hopes of becoming master of the guild in the next election, "but with *the works of Nature,* as the world is, things may be quite different, don't you see? Why shouldn't the world be able to grow out of chaos just as readily as a mushroom out of the ground?"

"Master Pfriem,"[36] replied the philosopher, "you will get my vote and the votes of my cousins when you are a candidate for the post of guild master, but no objections to my system, if you please! Mushrooms do indeed grow out of the ground by themselves because—because—because they are mushrooms. But a world doesn't grow by itself because it isn't a mushroom. Do you understand me now, Master *Pfriem*?"

All those present laughed heartily that Master *Pfriem* was checked this way. "The world is no mushroom; that's as clear as daylight," the *Abderites* cried. "You can't object to that, Master Pfriem!"

"Confound it!" murmured the future guild master. "But that's the way things go when a person has to do with those gentlemen who can prove that snow is white."

"'Is black' is what you wanted to say, neighbor."

"I know what I said and what I wanted to say," answered Master Pfriem, "and I only wish that the Republic—"

"Don't forget the fourteen votes I'll get for you, Master Pfriem!" cried the philosopher.

"Right, right! all right! But *demiurge*—that sounds to me almost like *demagogue;* and I want to have neither demagogues nor demiurges, I'm for *freedom,* and whoever is a good Abderite, let him wave his hat and follow me!"

And with that Master *Pfriem* went off (for the reader will perceive on his own that all this was said in a *hall* of Abdera), and a few idle louts who used to accompany him everywhere followed him.

But the philosopher, without letting on that he was aware of it, continued: "Without an *architect,* a *demiurge,* or whatever you want to call him, no world can be rationally constructed. But mark well, it depended on the demiurge *whether* and *how* he wished to construct. And let us see how he undertook this. Imagine matter as a huge lump of completely dense crystal and how the demiurge with a great hammer out of diamond smashes this lump with one blow into so many infinitesimally small bits that they scatter about for many millions of cubic miles through empty space. Naturally, these infinitesimally little pieces of crystal broke in various ways; and while they collided in a thousand different ways with the entire violence of motion imparted to them by the blow of the diamond hammer and rubbed, hit, and bumped together from all sides, there necessarily came into being a countless number of little bodies in all kinds of shapes: triangular, rectangular, octangular, polyangular, and round. The round ones turned into *water* and *air,* which is nothing but rarefied water; the triangular ones turned into *fire;* and the rest became *earth;* and out of these four elements, as you know, nature composes all the bodies in the world."

"That is *wonderful,* very wonderful! But that you can comprehend," said the *Abderites.* "A lump of crystal, a diamond hammer, and a demiurge who so masterfully smashes the crystal to bits that a world comes into being out of the splinters without his being any further concerned about it! The shrewdest hypothesis, one can see, and yet so simple that one might believe he himself could have hit upon it at any moment."

"By means of this simple presupposition I explain all the possible workings of nature," the philosopher said with a self-satisfied grin.

"Not a nest of wasps," cried a *ninth* called Daemonax who, up until now, had been listening to the assertions of his fellows with silent scorn. "Other forces and measures are necessary for creating a work as big, as beautiful, as wonderful as this world. Only a most *perfect understanding* could invent its plan; although I'll gladly admit that lesser foremen were adequate for its *execution.* It left this for various classes of subaltern gods to do, assigned to each class its special working sphere, and was satisfied with having general supervision over the whole. It is ridiculous to wish to explain the origin of heavenly bodies, of the earth, of plants, of animals, and of everything in the air and water with atoms or sympathies, or accidental motion, or with a single hammer blow. It is demons that dominate in the elements, turn the spheres of the heavens, form organic bodies, embroider the vernal raiment of nature with flowers, pour the fruits of autumn out into their lap. Can anything be more easily understood and more agreeable than this theory? It explains everything; it deduces every effect from an appropriate cause; and through it one comprehends the *art of nature,* inexplicable in any other system, just as easily as one comprehends how a Zeuxis[37] or Parrhasius[38] can with a little colored earth create an enchanting landscape or a bath of Diana."

"What a fine thing philosophy is," said the *Abderites*. "The only fault one might find in it is *that it gets hard to make a choice from among so many fine theories.*"

Nevertheless, the *Pythagorean*[39] who accomplished everything through demons had the most success. The *poets,* the *painters,* and all the *others enjoying the protection of the Muses* with all *the women of Abdera* at their head, declared themselves for—the demons; under the condition, however, that it would have to be allowed them to endue them with forms so pleasant as might be agreeable to everyone.

"I have never been an especial friend of philosophy," said the *priest Strobylus,* "and with reason! But because the Abderites once and for all cannot refrain from their brooding about the *how* and the *why* of things, I still have the fewest objections to the physics of Daemonax; with the proper restrictions it is still passably compatible with—"

"Oh, it is compatible with everything in the world," said Daemonax; "that is precisely the beauty of it."

Finally Democritus spoke up: "Shall I, after all the fine and amusing things you have already heard, now give you *my* humble opinion, too? If you should perhaps be genuinely concerned about becoming acquainted with the things surrounding you, it seems to me you are taking an enormous detour. The world is very big, and from where we are looking into it the principal provinces and capitals are so far away that I cannot really grasp how any of us could get the idea of picking up the map of a country of which (his native village excepted) everything else, even the boundaries, is unknown to him. I would think that before we dreamt of *cosmogonies* and *cosmologies,* we might sit down and observe, for example, *the origin of a cobweb, and this so long until we had found out as much as five human minds with their intelligence straining* could discover in it. You will have enough to do, you can take my word for it. But in return you will also learn that this single cobweb will give you more *information about the great system of nature* and *more estimable concepts of its creator* than all the fine systems of the universe that you have spun out of your own brain."

Democritus was entirely serious when he said this; but the philosophers of Abdera thought he wanted to make fun of them. "He doesn't understand anything about *pneumatics*," said the one. "Still less about *physics*," said the other. "He is a *skeptic—he doesn't believe in any primary instincts—in any spirit of the universe—in any demiurge—in any god!"* said the third, fourth, fifth, sixth, and seventh. *"We ought not to put up with such people in the community at all,"* said the *priest Strobylus.*

Chapter Twelve

Democritus withdraws farther from Abdera. How he occupies himself in his solitude. He arouses in the Abderites the suspicion that he is practicing magic. An experiment he conducts on this occasion with the Abderite ladies and how it turned out.

With all that, *Democritus* was a *philanthropist* in the truest sense of the word. For he was well disposed toward mankind and enjoyed nothing so much as preventing something evil or being able to do, cause, or promote something good. And although he believed that the character of a cosmopolitan involved relations to which all others, in case of a conflict, would have to yield, he nevertheless considered himself no less bound to take an interest, as *a citizen of Abdera,* in the condition of his native land and to contribute as much as he could to its improvement. However, since one can do people only as much good as they can take, he found his capacity enclosed within such narrow limits by the countless obstacles the Abderites put in his way that he thought he had cause to regard himself as one of the most superfluous persons in this little republic. "What they need most," he thought, "and the best thing I could do for them would be to make them reasonable. But the Abderites are free people. If they do not wish to be reasonable, who can compel them to be?"

Since in such circumstances he could do little or nothing for the Abderites as Abderites, he considered himself sufficiently justified if he attempted at least to secure the safety of his own person and saved as large a part as at all possible of the time he thought he owed to the fulfilling of his *cosmopolitan duties.*

Because his place of refuge until now was either not far enough away from Abdera or had so much attraction for the Abderites on account of its site and other amenities that, in spite of his residing in the country, he nevertheless always found himself in their midst, he withdrew a few hours farther into a forest that belonged to his estate, and in its wildest tract he built himself a little house, where he devoted most of his time—in the secluded peace and quiet that is the special element of the philosopher and poet—to the study of nature and to contemplation.

A few newer scholars—whether *Abderite* or *not* we will leave undecided here—got strange, although on their side very natural, notions about the pursuits of this Greek Bacon[40] in his solitude. "He was working *on the philosopher's stone*," says *Borrichius*,[41] "and he found it and made gold." As proof of it he adduces Democritus's having written a book about *stones and metals*.

The Abderites, his contemporaries and fellow citizens, went still further, and their conjectures—that quite soon became certainties in Abderite heads—were based on conclusions just as good as that drawn by *Borrichius*. Democritus *had been reared by Persian magi;** he had traveled around for twenty years in oriental countries, had cultivated the company of *Egyptian priests, Chaldeans, Brahmans*, and *gymnosophists*, and was initiated in all their mysteries; he had brought back with him a thousand *arcana* from his travels and knew ten thousand things of which nothing ever came into the mind of an Abderite. Did not all this together constitute the most complete proof that he had to be an experienced master of magic and of all the arts depending upon it? The reverend Father Delrio[42] would have had Spain, Portugal, and Algarve[43] burned to ashes with but half a proof like this one.

But the good Abderites had a hold of still *more cogent* evidence that their learned compatriot—could practice a bit of witchcraft. He *predicted eclipses of the sun and moon, crop failure, epidemics, and other things in the future*. He had foretold—just like that—to an amorous girl that she would—have a fall, and to a councillor of Abdera whose entire life was divided between sleeping and feasting that he—would die of indigestion. And both came true exactly. Moreover, people had seen books with *strange signs* in his room; they had come upon him when he was performing all kinds of *presumably* magic operations with the blood of birds and animals. He had been seen boiling *suspect* herbs. And a few young people even claimed they had sneaked up on him late at night—in very pale moonlight—when he was sitting between *tombs*. In order to frighten him "we had disguised ourselves with the most hideous masks," they said, "horns, goats' hooves, dragon tails, nothing was missing for us to look just like real devils of the field and ghosts of the night. We even blew smoke from our noses and ears and raised such a hubbub round about him that a Hercules would out of fright have wished to turn into a woman. But Democritus paid us no heed

---

*Xerxes who, on his military expedition against the Greeks had his headquarters in the house of Democritus's father for a few days, had taken a liking to Democritus, who was at that time still very young, and for the latter's better education left behind a few of the magi he had along.

and, since he finally thought we were carrying on too long, he merely said, 'Well, is this childish game going to go on much longer?'"

"There you plainly see," the Abderites said, "that he's really not quite right in the upper story! Ghosts are nothing new to him; he surely knows how he stands with them!"

"He's a magician; nothing can be more certain," said the priest *Strobylus;* "we'll have to watch him a bit more closely."

It must be admitted that Democritus, either out of imprudence or (what is more believable) because he cared little about the opinion of his compatriots, gave some occasion for these and other wicked rumors. It was indeed impossible to live for long among the Abderites without succumbing to the temptation of palming something off on them. Their meddlesomeness and their gullibility on the one hand, and the conceited notion they had of their own sagacity on the other, presented one with a challenge, as it were. And there were, moreover, no other means, in any case, to compensate for their boring ways. Democritus was not seldom in this situation. And since the Abderites were foolish enough to take everything literally that he said to them ironically, there came into being many absurd opinions and fairy tales that circulated in the world at his expense and, for many centuries after his death, were taken by other Abderites at face value or, at the very least, laid unfairly to his charge.

He had, among other things, occupied himself with physiognomics[44] and, partly from his own observations and partly on the basis of what others had told him about theirs, fashioned a theory about it, concerning the use of which he judged (very reasonably, it seems to us) that here matters stood just *as they did in the theory of poetry or of any other art.* For just as no one has yet become a good poet or artist by means of the mere knowledge of the rules and only he, whom inborn genius, assiduous study, obstinate diligence, and long practice have made into a poet or an artist, is skilled in rightly understanding and applying the rules of his art, so also the theory of the *art of drawing conclusions about the interior of a human being on the basis of his exterior* is useful only for people of great skill in observation and differentiation; for anyone else, on the other hand, it is a most uncertain and deceptive matter, and just for that reason it must always be reserved, as one of the *secret sciences* or *great mysteries* of philosophy, only to the small number of *Epóptai.**

Epóptai (watchers) was the name of those who, after having undergone a test, were admitted to watch the *great mysteries* at *Eleusis.*

This way of thinking about the matter proved that Democritus was no charlatan, but to the Abderites it proved merely that he was making a secret of his science. For that reason they did not cease, as often as the subject was brought up, provoking and pestering him to reveal something to them about it. This inquisitiveness was especially tormenting the *Abderite women*. They wanted to know from him—what exterior traits would reveal a faithful lover? Whether *Milon of Crotona** had a very large nose? Whether a pale color were a necessary sign of a person in love?—and a hundred other questions of this kind with which they so wore out his patience that finally, to get rid of them, he got the idea of frightening them a little.

"But you probably did not imagine," Democritus said, "that virginity could have an infallible distinctive mark in the eyes?"

"In the *eyes*?" cried the Abderite women. "Oh, that is not possible! Just why in the eyes?"

"It is not otherwise," he replied. "And you can certainly believe me when I tell you that this sign has often revealed to me more of the secrets of young and old beauties than they would have desired to confide in me of their own accord."**

The confident tone in which he said this caused some to grow pale, although the Abderite women (who in all cases where the common security of their sex was concerned were accustomed to stand by one another faithfully) insisted quite heatedly that his ostensible secret was a chimera.

"By your disbelief you force me to tell you more," the philosopher continued. "Nature is full of such secrets, my beautiful ladies. And why should I have traveled all the way to Ethiopia and India if it was not worth the trouble? The gymnosophists, whose women—as you know—walk around naked, revealed very nice things to me."

"For example?" said the Abderite women.

"Among other things, a secret which I, if I were a married man, would rather not wish to know."

"Ah, now we have the reason why Democritus doesn't want to get married," cried beautiful *Thryallis*.

"As if we had not known for a long time," *Salabanda* said, "that

---

*A man about whose marvelous physical strength and voracity the mythical Graeculi[45] can tell us astonishing things; for example, that he bore a well-fed ox three hundred paces on his shoulders and, after killing the animal with one blow of his fist, ate it up in one day.

**A piece of sagacity odious to half of humanity—is what Joh. Chrysostomus *Magnenus*[46] calls this in his life of Democritus.

it is his Ethiopian Venus who is making him so indifferent to our Greek goddess. But your secret, Democritus, if it may be confided to chaste ears?"

"As proof that it may, I will confide it to the ears of all the present beauties," the natural scientist answered. "I know an infallible means for causing a woman to say in her sleep in a clear voice everything that she has on her mind."

"Oh, go on," cried the Abderite women, "you want to frighten us; but—we don't allow people to scare us so easily."

"Now who is thinking about *frightening* someone," Democritus said, "when we are talking about a means with which every honorable woman is given the opportunity of showing that she has no secrets that her husband would not be allowed to know?"

"Does your means work with unmarried women, too?" asked an Abderite woman who appeared to be neither young nor charming enough to ask such a question.

"It works from the tenth year on to the eightieth," he replied, "without regard to any other circumstances in which a woman can be."

The matter began to get serious. "But you're only joking, Democritus?" said the spouse of a *Thesmothetes*[47] not without a secret fear of being assured of the contrary.

"Do you want to take the test, *Lysistrata*?"

"The test?—Why not?—With the stipulation that no magic is going to be used. For with the help of your talismans and spirits you could make a poor woman say what you wished."

"Neither spirits nor talismans are involved. Everything goes on naturally. The means I use is the simplest thing in the world."

The ladies began, with all their grimaces of courage to which they attempted to force themselves, to betray an anxiety that much amused the philosopher.

"If one didn't know that you are a sarcastic man who is making fun of the whole world—But may we ask of what your means consists?"

"As I told you, the most natural thing in the world. A quite small, innocuous thing, laid in the cleavage near the heart of a sleeping woman, that is the entire secret; but it performs miracles, you can take my word for it! It causes her to speak as long as there is still something to be discovered in the innermost corner of her heart."

Among the seven women present in the company there was only one whose face and bearing remained the same as before. It will be imagined that she was old, or ugly, or even virtuous; but she was none of all these. She was—deaf.

"If you want us to believe you, Democritus, then tell us what your means is."

"I will whisper it to the husband of beautiful Thryallis," the mischievous natural philosopher said.

The husband of beautiful Thryallis was, without being blind, as happy as *Hagedorn*[48] considers a blind man whose wife is *beautiful*. In his house he always had good company, or at least what was called that in Abdera. The good man believed people found ever so much pleasure in his company and in the verses he was in the habit of reciting to his visitors. In fact, he did have the talent of not reading badly the bad verses he made; and because he read with much enthusiasm, he did not become aware that his listeners, instead of paying attention to his verses, were flirting with beautiful Thryallis. In brief, the councillor *Smilax* was a man who had a much too good opinion of himself to entertain a bad one of his spouse's virtue.

He did not deliberate for a moment, therefore, about lending his ear to the secret.

"It is nothing more," the philosopher whispered into his ear, "than the tongue of a live frog that one has to lay on the lady's left breast. But when you tear it out you have to be careful that none of the other parts connected with it comes out as well, and the frog has to be put back into the water."

"The means may not be bad," *Smilax* said softly, "it's only too bad that it's a little risky! What would the priest *Strobylus* say about it?"

"Don't worry about that," *Democritus* replied, "a frog is, after all, no Latona, the priest Strobylus may say whatever he wishes. And besides, it doesn't cost the frog's life, you know."

"So I may pass it on?" Smilax asked.

"With all my heart! All the men in the company may know about it; and everyone may without fear reveal it to all of his acquaintances; only with the stipulation that no one is to repeat it to his wife or his sweetheart."

The good Abderite women did not know what they should think of the matter. It did not seem impossible to them; and what, after all, should appear impossible to Abderites? Their husbands or lovers, who were present as well, were not much more composed; each one secretly resolved to try the expedient without delay, and each one (except for happy *Smilax*) feared that he would thereby learn more than he wished.

"Isn't that so, my dear husband," said Thryallis to her spouse while tapping him amiably on the cheeks, "you know me too well to be in need of such a test?"

"Mine should not allow himself to get such an idea," said *Lagisca*. "A test presupposes doubt, and a husband who doubts the virtue of his wife—"

"—Is a man who runs the danger of seeing his doubt changed into certainty," *Democritus* added, since he saw that she paused. "Surely that is what you wanted to say, beautiful Lagisca?"

"You're a woman-hater," the Abderite women all cried at the same time, "but do not forget that we are in Thrace, and beware the fate of Orpheus!"[49]

Although this was said in jest, there was earnestness in it nevertheless. Naturally one does not allow people needlessly to give one sleepless nights; a purpose of which we can absolve the philosopher all the less since he had necessarily to foresee the results of his jest. Actually, this matter gave the seven ladies so much to think about that they did not close an eye all night. And since the ostensible secret went the rounds in all Abdera on the following day, he thereby caused a general sleeplessness several nights running.

Meanwhile the women made up again during the day what they lost at night; and because the thought did not occur to various ones that the *arcanum* could just as well be applied to them when they were sleeping in the daytime as at night and, therefore, forgot to lock their bedrooms, the men unexpectedly got the opportunity of making use of their frogs' tongues. *Lysistrata, Thryallis,* and a few others who had the most to risk in this, were the first to be tested, with the result that one can easily foresee.

But precisely this soon again restored peace and quiet to Abdera. The husbands of these ladies, after they had used the expedient unsuccessfully, came running at full tilt to our philosopher to find out what this might mean.

"So?" he called to them, "was the frog's tongue effective? Did your wives confess?"

"Not a word, not one syllable," the *Abderites* said.

"All the better," cried *Democritus,* "be triumphant about it! Whenever a sleeping woman with a frog's tongue on her heart says nothing, it is a sign that she—has nothing to say. I wish you luck, gentlemen! Each of you can boast of possessing the phoenix of women in his house."

Who was happier than our Abderites! They ran back again as fast as they had come, embraced their astonished wives, suffocated them with kisses and hugs, and now voluntarily confessed what they had done in order to make themselves still more certain of the virtue of their better halves ("although we were already certain of it," they said).

The good women did not know whether they should trust their senses. However, although they were Abderite women, they had

enough sense to pull themselves together immediately and to repre-
hend their husbands vigorously for the rude mistrust of which they
were accusing themselves. Some of them carried on to the point
of tears; but they all had trouble in concealing the joy caused them
by such an unexpected confirmation of their virtue; and although
they had to scold against Democritus for the sake of propriety,
there was not one who would not have liked to embrace him for
having done them such a good turn. To be sure, this was not what
he had wanted. But the consequences of this single innocent jest
possibly taught him *that one cannot jest cautiously enough with
Abderites.*

However (as all things of this world have more than one side), it
turned out that from the mischief our philosopher had done the
Abderites, contrary to his intention, there nevertheless sprang
more good than could presumably have been expected if the frogs'
tongues had had their effect. The men made their wives happy
through their unlimited *confidence,* and the women, their husbands
through their *complaisance* and *good spirits.* Nowhere in the world
were more contented marriages to be seen than in Abdera. And
with all that the Abderites' *brows* were as *smooth*—and the *ears*
and *tongues* of the Abderite women as *chaste* as among other
people.

Chapter Thirteen

*Democritus is supposed to teach the language of the birds to
the Abderite women. In passing, a sample of how they educated
their daughters.*

At another time it happened that on a fine spring evening our
philosopher was with a group of people in one of the pleasure
gardens with which the Abderites had embellished the area around
their city.

"Really embellished?"

"Well now, not exactly. For where should the Abderites have
learned that nature is more beautiful than art and that there is a
difference between the *artificial* and the *artistic*? However, that is
not what is going to be discussed now."

The company was lying about in a circle on a soft lawn bestrewn
with flowers under a high bower. In the branches of a neighboring
tree a nightingale was singing. And that appeared to cause a four-
teen-year-old Abderite girl to feel something that the others did
not. *Democritus* noticed it. The girl had soft features and soulful

eyes. "Too bad you are an Abderite!" he thought. "What is a sensitive soul going to get you in Abdera? It would only make you unhappy. There is no danger though. Whatever the education of your mother and grandmother has left unspoiled, the youngsters of our archons and councillors will ruin, and whatever they will spare, that will be destroyed by the example of your girl friends. In less than four years you are going to be an Abderite woman just like the others. And only when you learn that a frog's tongue in the cleavage near your heart means nothing—"

"Of what are you thinking, beautiful *Nannion*?" Democritus asked the girl.

"I think I would like to sit down under those trees to be able to listen to the nightingale quite undisturbed."

"That silly thing!" said the girl's mother. "Haven't you ever heard a nightingale?"

Little *Nannion* lowered her eyes blushing and kept silent.

"*Nannion* is right," said beautiful *Thryallis; I myself am very fond of listening to nightingales. They sing with such fire, and there is something so special in their modulations that I have often wished I understood what it is they are saying. I am certain we would hear the most beautiful things in the world. But you, Democritus, who knows everything, ought you not to understand the language of the nightingales, too?"

"Why not?" the philosopher answered with his customary equanimity; "and the language of all other birds as well!"

"Seriously?"

"You know, of course, that I always speak seriously."

"Oh, that is most charming! Quickly, translate something for us from the language of the nightingales! What was the meaning of what that one over there was singing when *Nannion* was so moved by it?"

"That cannot so easily be translated into Greek as you think, beautiful *Thryallis*. There are no expressions in our language that would be tender and fiery enough for that."

"But how then can you understand the language of the birds if you can't repeat in Greek what you have heard?"

"The birds do not know Greek either and understand one another all the same."

"But you're not a bird, although you're a waggish man who's always making fun of us."

"How depressing it is that people in Abdera, when everything is said and done, like to think bad things about their neighbors. However, your answer deserves a more detailed explanation from me.

The birds understand one another by means of a certain sympathy which ordinarily only takes place among creatures of the same kind. Each tone of a singing nightingale is the living expression of a feeling and arouses directly in the one listening the unison of this feeling. It therefore understands, by means of its own inner feeling, what the other wished to tell it; and in the same way exactly I understand it, too."

"But just how do you do that?" several Abderite women asked.

This question, after Democritus had already given such a clear explanation, was quite too Abderite for him to be able to let it pass unenjoyed. He reflected a moment.

"I understand him," said little *Nannion* softly.

"You understand him, you cheeky thing?" her mother snarled at the poor girl. "Well, let's hear, doll, what you understand about it!"

"I can't put it into words, but I feel it, it seems to me," *Nannion* replied.

"She is, as you hear, still a child," the mother said, "although she shot up so fast that a lot of people have taken her for my younger sister. But let us not dwell on the chatter of a silly girl who doesn't yet know what she is saying."

"*Nannion* has feeling," Democritus said. "She finds the key to the universal language of nature in her heart, and maybe she understands more of it than—"

"Oh, Sir, please don't make the foolish little girl still more conceited! She's impertinent and flippant enough as it is—"

"Bravo," Democritus thought, "just keep on that way! On this path there might still be hope for little *Nannion's* head and heart."

"Let's stay on the subject!" (continued the Abderite woman who, without ever having rightly known how and why, had the *unrecognized honor* of being Nannion's mother) "you were about to explain to us, you know, how you managed to understand the language of the birds."

We owe the Abderite women the justice of not concealing that they considered everything Democritus had said about his knowledge of bird language to be mere *boasting*. But this did not prevent the continuation of this conversation from having something very entertaining for them; for they liked hearing nothing more than about things they did *not* believe and yet believed *nevertheless;* than about sphinxes, mermen, sibyls, kobolds, bugbears, ghosts, and everything belonging in this category. And the language of the birds belonged there, too, they thought.

"It is a secret," Democritus replied, "that I learned from the high priest at Memphis when I had myself initiated into the Egyptian mysteries. He was a tall, lean man and had a very long name and a still longer hoary beard that reached down to his belt. You would have considered him a man from the other world, so solemn and mysterious did he appear in his pointed cap and in his trailing cloak."

The attention of the Abderite women increased noticeably. *Nannion,* who had seated herself a little farther back, listened with her left ear in the direction of the nightingale. But from time to time she shot a grateful side-glance at the philosopher which he, as often as her mother looked at her bosom or kissed her dog, answered with an encouraging smile.

"The entire secret," he continued, "consists in one's cutting, under a certain constellation, the throats of seven different birds (whose names I am not permitted to reveal), letting their blood flow together into a small cavity that is made in the earth for this purpose, covering the pit with laurel branches, and—going one's way. After twenty-one days have passed, one returns, uncovers the pit, and finds a little strangely shaped dragon that has come into being from the putrefaction of that mingled blood."*

"A dragon!"—cried the Abderite women with all the symptoms of astonishment.

"A dragon, although not much larger than an ordinary bat. Take this dragon, cut it into small pieces, and eat it with some vinegar, oil, and pepper without leaving the least part of it. Go to bed thereafter, cover up well, and sleep straight through for twenty-one hours. After that you wake up, get dressed, walk in your garden or a little forest and are not a little astonished in being instantaneously surrounded and greeted on all sides by birds whose language and

---

*Pliny,[50] who in his History of Nature and Art has compiled the true and false indiscriminately, relates in the forty-ninth chapter of his tenth book in all seriousness that Democritus had in his writings named certain birds from the mixed blood of which a snake originates that has the property that whoever eats it (whether with vinegar and oil he does not say) will immediately understand everything the birds say to one another. Because of this and similar absurdities with which (as he says) the writings of Democritus abound, at another place in his work he reads him a very schoolmasterly lecture. But Gellius[51] (Noct. Atticae. L. X., chapter 12) defends our philosopher with better reason than Pliny condemns him. What could Democritus do about the Abderites' being dumb enough to take everything he said in earnest as irony and everything he said as a joke as something serious? Or how, not long after his death, could he prevent Abderites from selling to other Abderites under his name and authority a thousand absurdities he had never thought of? What sorry stuff was *Magnenus* having him say no earlier than 1646 in his *Democritus Revived?* And what do the people in the other world not have to allow people to say of them!

song you understand as well as if all the days of your life you had been nothing but magpies, geese, and turkeys."*

Democritus related all this with such calm gravity that they were all the less able to restrain themselves from believing him, since he (in their opinion) would have been unable to tell the entire business with so many particulars if it had not been true. However, now they only knew as much about it, after all, as was necessary to become all the more impatient to know everything.

"But," they asked, "what kind of birds is it anyway that you need for this purpose? Is the sparrow, the finch, the nightingale, the magpie, the quail, the raven, the pewit, the night-owl, etc. also among them? What does the dragon look like? Does it have wings? How many of them does it have? Is it yellow, or green, or blue, or rosy? Does it spit fire? Doesn't it bite or sting when you want to touch it? Is it *good* to eat? How does it taste? How is it to digest? What do you drink with it?"—All of these questions with which the naturalist was assailed from all sides made things so unpleasant for him that he finally thought he could most easily get out of the affair if he confessed to them that he had invented the entire story only for fun.

"Oh, you're not going to tell us that!" the Abderite women cried. "You only want us not to discover your secrets. But we're not going to leave you any peace and quiet, you can count on that! We want to see the dragon, touch it, smell it, taste it, and eat it all up, or— you're going to tell us why not."

---

*This is probably an error of the translator. For who does not know that turkeys were unknown even to Aristotle and had to be unknown because they only came to us and to the rest of our hemisphere from the West Indies! See Buffon, *The Natural History of Birds,* vol. 3, p. 187 ff.

Second Book:
Hippocrates in Abdera

Chapter One

A digression on the character and the philosophy of Democritus that we ask the reader not to skip.

We do not know how Democritus set about getting rid of the inquisitive women. It is enough that these examples make comprehensible for us how a mere chance idea could offer the occasion for giving the innocent naturalist the reputation of being sufficiently Abderite to believe all the fairy tales himself that he palmed off on his foolish compatriots. Those who have said this about him in reproach refer to his *writings*. But long before the times of *Vitruvius*[1] and *Pliny* a great many spurious little books with very weighty titles under his name were being carried around. It is known how common this kind of fraud was for the idle Graeculis[2] of later times. The names *Hermes Trismegistus, Zoroaster, Orpheus, Pythagoras,*[3] and *Democritus* were venerable enough to make the most wretched creations of insipid minds saleable, especially after the Alexandrine school of philosophers[4] had given *magic* a kind of general respectability and the scholars a taste for persuading the unlearned that they were powerful miracle-workers who had found the key to the spirit world and for whom there was now nothing secret in all of nature. The Abderites had given Democritus the reputation of being a magician because they could not comprehend how, without being a sorcerer, one could know as much *as they— did not know;* and later impostors fabricated conjuring books in his name to take advantage of that reputation among the blockheads of their time.

The Greeks in general liked to make their philosophers look foolish. The *Athenians* laughed heartily when the witty jester *Aristophanes* made them believe that *Socrates* considered the clouds goddesses, that he measured how many flea-feet high a flea could jump,* that he had himself hung up in a basket when he wanted to meditate so that the attractive force of the earth would not suck in his thoughts, etc., and it seemed to them extremely entertaining to hear the man who had always told them the truth, and often, therefore, unpleasant things, saying, at least on the stage, trite pedantries. And how did not *Diogenes* (who among the imitators of Socrates still had more than any other the mien of his original) have to allow himself to be abused by this people that liked so much to laugh! Even the inspired *Plato* and the profound *Aristotle* did not escape the charges with which people attempted to degrade them to hoi polloi. Is it, therefore, any wonder that things did not go better for the man who was so bold as to have good sense in the midst of the Abderites?

Democritus laughed now and then, as we all do, and maybe, if he had lived in Corinth, or Smyrna, or Syracuse, or in any other place in the world, he would not have laughed *more* than any other honest man who, for good reason or because of his temperament, feels more inclined to laugh at the follies of human beings than to bewail them. But he lived among *Abderites*. It was, once and for all, the nature of these good people always to do something about which one had either to laugh, or cry, or get angry. And *Democritus* laughed where *Phocion*[5] would have wrinkled his brow, a *Cato*[6] scolded, and *Swift* laid on his whip. It is possible that during a rather long sojourn in Abdera an ironic grimace, therefore, very likely became characteristic of him. But that he always, in the

---

*Nothing is more possible than that Socrates could at some time really have said something that gave occasion for this aristophanic joke. He might, in a social gathering where the conversation was about bigness and smallness, only have commented on the error that is commonly made by talking about big and little as if they were essential properties and not considering that it depends merely on the criterion whether exactly the same thing is supposed to be big or little. He could have said in his jocular manner: it is a mistake to measure the jump of a flea with the Attic ell; in order to compare the jumping ability of a flea with that of a gymnast one would have to take as a criterion not the human foot, but the foot of a flea if one wished otherwise to give the fleas their due—and the like. Now is was only necessary for an Abderite to be in that company for us to be able to count with certainty on his having related it in his own way as a great absurdity that had escaped the philosopher. And although Aristophanes was intelligent enough to comprehend that Socrates probably said something intelligent, it was, after all, enough for a man of his profession and in accord with his purpose of making the philosopher ridiculous, so that one could give this idea a turn whereby it became fit for splitting for a moment the sides of the Athenians, who (if we make allowances for their taste and wit) were fairly Abderite.

literal sense, roared with laughter, as a poet who likes to exaggerate says about him,* no one, at least, should have said in prose. This gossip, however, might still pass, all the more since a philosopher as celebrated as *Seneca*[7] justifies our friend Democritus on this point and even finds him worthy of imitation. "We must strive to attain the attitude," *Seneca* says, "that the follies and foibles of the great multitude do not appear odious one and all, but ridiculous rather; and we will be doing better if in this we take *Democritus* as our model rather than *Heraclitus*.[8] The *latter* was accustomed to *weep* as often as he went among the people, the *former,* to *laugh.* The *latter* saw in all our activities vain *want and misery;* the *former,* vain *baubles and trifles.* Now it is *friendlier,* however, *to laugh* at human kind than to sneer at it; and it can be said that he who laughs at the human race is more deserving than he who laments over it. For the former, after all, still leaves us a little hope; the latter, to the contrary, weeps foolishly about things that he *despairs* of being able to improve. Also, he who cannot restrain himself from laughter when he surveys the whole displays a *greater soul* than the person who cannot keep from tears; for thereby he indicates that everything that seems *great* and important enough to others to arouse in them the most vehement passions is in his eyes so small that in him it can stir up only the lightest and calmest of all emotions."**

In passing, it seems to me the decision of the *sophist Seneca* makes sense, although he would perhaps have done better neither to adduce such far-fetched reasons nor to couch them in such artificial antitheses. Nevertheless, as I have said, the mere circumstance that Democritus was living among *Abderites* and laughed

---

*Perpetuo risu pulmonem agitare solebat *Democritus. Juvenal, Sat.* 10. 33. (*Democritus* was accustomed to exercise his lungs in constant laughter.)

**With all that, *Seneca* nevertheless explains soon thereafter that it is still better and more suitable for a wise man to put up with the prevailing customs and defects of human beings placidly and with equanimity than to laugh or weep about them. It seems to me he could with little difficulty have found that there—is something still better than this *better.* Why *always* laugh, *always* weep, *always* be angry, or *always* be indifferent? There are follies that deserve to be laughed at; there are others that are grave enough to squeeze a sigh out of the philanthropist; others that could provoke a saint to indignation; finally, still others that one ought to make allowance for, chalking them up to human weakness. A wise and good man (*nisi pituita molesta est,* as Horace[9] wisely stipulates) laughs or smiles, regrets or bewails, excuses or pardons, according as persons and things, time and place are involved. For laughing and weeping, loving and hating, chastising and setting free have their time, says Solomon, who was older, more intelligent, and better than Seneca with all his antitheses.

about Abderites made the reproach in question (however exaggerated it may also be) the most tolerable of all those imposed upon our wise man. *Homer,* after all, has the gods burst out in *inextinguishable laughter* about a far less ridiculous subject—at the limping Vulcan who, with the good-hearted intention of bringing about peace among the Olympians, acts as cup-bearer.[10] But the allegation that Democritus had *voluntarily deprived himself of his sight* and *the reason why he is supposed to have done so* presupposes an inclination on the part of those receptive to it that does little honor at least to their minds.

"And what sort of an inclination, then, may that be?"

I will tell you, dear friends, and may the favorable heavens grant that this may not have been entirely spoken to the winds.

It is the wretched inclination to allow any blockhead, any malicious knave to pass for an unexceptionable witness as soon as he tells some extravagant absurdity or other about a great man which even the ordinary man with five sound senses would be incapable of committing.

I would not like to believe that this inclination is as common as the detractors of human nature maintain. Experience, however, at least teaches that the little anecdotes that are customarily circulated about great men at the expense of their good sense very readily meet with the approval of most people. Yet, is this bent basically perhaps no more censurable than the pleasure with which astronomers discovered spots in the sun? Is it perhaps merely the unexpected and the incomprehensible that makes the discovery of such spots so pleasant? Moreover, it also does not seldom occur that the poor people, while imputing absurdities to a great man, believe (in their way of thinking) that they are even doing him much honor. And this may well have been the case, so far as the voluntary blindness of our philosopher is concerned, with more than one Abderite brain.

"Democritus deprived himself of his sight," they say, "so that he could *think all the more deeply.* What is so unbelievable in this? Don't we have examples of voluntary mutilations of a similar kind? Combabus—Origenes—"[11]

Good! Combabus and Origenes discarded a part of their person, and indeed a part that probably most men (in the event of danger) would rather pay dearly for with all of their eyes, and even if they had as many of them as *Argus.* However, they also had a great motive for doing it. What does a man not give for his life! And what is not done or suffered *to remain the favorite of a prince* or even *to become a pagod!*[12]—Democritus, on the contrary, could have no motive of this potency. It might still pass if he had been a *metaphysician* or a *poet*. There are people who, in pursuing their occupation, can do without sight. They mostly work with their imagination, and this even improves through blindness. But when did anybody ever hear that an observer of nature, a dissector, an astronomer had put out his eyes the better to observe, to dissect, and to look at the stars?

The absurdity is so palpable that *Tertullian* deduces the alleged deed of our philosopher from another cause, which, however, should have seemed at least just as absurd to him if he had not right then stood in need of changing into *straw men* the philosophers he wished to strike down. "He deprived himself of his eyes," Tertullian says,* *"because he could not look at a woman without desiring her."*[13] A fine reason for a Greek philosopher from the age of Pericles![14] Democritus, to whom it certainly did not occur to wish to be wiser than Solon, Anaxagoras,[15] and Socrates, also stood in need of taking refuge in such an expedient! It is true, the advice of the latter** (that certainly was not unknown to Democritus, because he had sense enough to give it to himself) avails little against the power of love; and to a philosopher who wished to devote his entire life to discovering truth, it was, to be sure, very important to be on his guard against such a tyrannical passion. However, Democritus, at least in Abdera, had nothing to fear from this either. The Abderite women were beautiful, to be sure; but benevolent nature had given them *stupidity as an antidote for their physical charms*. An Abderite woman was beautiful only until she—opened her mouth or until one saw her in her housedress. Passions lasting three days were the utmost they could inspire in an honorable man who was no Abderite. And a three-day love is such a small impediment to a *Democritus* engaged in philosophizing that we would rather humbly advise all naturalists, dissectors, surveyors, and astronomers to make frequent use of this remedy as a splendid prescription for trouble with the spleen, if we could not expect that these gentlemen are too wise to be in need of advice. Whether Democritus himself might by chance have tried this remedy with one or the other of the Abderite beauties with whom we have already become acquainted, we can neither affirm nor deny for lack of authentic information. But that he—in order *not* to become infatuated *at all* or not *too much* with such harmless creatures, and because he was in any case certain that they would

---

*Apolog. C. 46.
**Memorab. Socrat. Lib. I. Cap. 3. Num. 14.

not scratch out his eyes—was weak enough to scratch them out himself, this *Tertullian* may believe as long as he likes. We very much doubt that anyone will share his belief.

But all these absurdities become insignificant when we compare them with what a collector of materials for a history of the human understanding, a very deserving scholar of his kind otherwise, calls *the philosophy of Democritus.* It would be difficult to say with certainty about a pile of odd fragments, stones, and smashed columns that have been collected from innumerable places as ostensible relics of the great Temple at Olympia that they really are ruins of this temple. But what would you think of a man who—when he had laid these fragments on top of one another, as well as was possible for him to do in a hurry, and patched them together with some mud and straw—wished to pass off such miserable bungled work, without plan, without foundation, without greatness, without symmetry and beauty for the *Temple at Olympia?*

It is not at all probable that Democritus produced a system. A man who spends his life on *journeys, observations,* and *experiments* seldom lives long enough to fit together what he has seen and experienced into an artistically and technically correct philosophical system. And in this regard, Democritus, too, although he is said to have lived longer than a century, could still have been surprised too early by death. But that such a man, with the penetrating intellect and with the burning thirst for truth with which antiquity unanimously credits him, was capable of maintaining palpable nonsense is something still less than improbable. "According to Democritus (they tell us) the atoms, empty space, and necessity or fate account solely for the existence of the world. He *questioned nature for eighty years* and *it told him not a word* about *its creator,* about *his plan,* and *his purpose?* To all the *atoms* he ascribed the *same motion* and *did not perceive** that from elements moving in *parallel lines* no bodies could originate in all eternity? He denied that the combination of the atoms takes place according *to the laws of similarity;* according to him an infinitely rapid but *blind* motion accounted for everything in the world, and he maintained, nevertheless, that the world was a *whole?*" etc. This and other similar nonsense is charged to his account. *Stobaeus, Sextus,* and *Censorinus*[16] are cited, and there is little concern about whether it is possible for a man of intelligence (as Democritus is nevertheless represented) to reason so very wretchedly. To be sure, great minds are no freer than little ones from the possibility of erring or of

---

*Brucker, Histor. Crit. Philos. T. I. p. 1190

drawing incorrect conclusions, although it must be admitted that they commit these errors infinitely less often than the *Lilliputians* would like. But there are absurdities that only a blockhead is capable of thinking or saying, just as there are outrages that only a scoundrel can perpetrate. The best people have their *anomalies,* and the wisest now and then suffer a *passing eclipse.* But this does not prevent our being able to maintain with sufficient certainty about a rational man that he will generally proceed like a man of intelligence, and especially on such occasions when even the most stupid will pull all of theirs together.

This maxim, if it were properly applied, could help spare us in life from many a rash judgment, from many a confusion of illusion and truth with the attendant important consequences. But it did not help the Abderites. For, to apply a maxim, precisely that thing is required—which they did not have. These good people resorted to a logic quite different from that of rational human beings; and in their heads ideas were *associated* that, if there were no Abderites, would otherwise never come together in all eternity. *Democritus* inquired into the nature of things and observed causes of certain natural occurrences a little earlier than the Abderites: *therefore, he was a sorcerer.* He thought about everything differently from the way they did, lived according to other principles, spent his time by himself in a manner incomprehensible to them:— *therefore, things were not quite right* in his head. The man had overexerted himself in studying, and it was feared that he would come to an unfortunate end. Such inferences are drawn by the Abderites of all times and places.

Chapter Two

Democritus is accused of a serious crime and is exculpated by one of his relatives with the allegation that he is not really in the possession of his senses. How he manages in time to turn aside the violent storm that the priest Strobylus wanted to prepare for him.

"What do you hear about Democritus?" the Abderites asked one another. "It has been six whole weeks since anyone has claimed seeing him. You can never get a hold of him; or, if you finally do meet him, he's sitting deep in thought, and you'll have been standing in front of him for half an hour, have been talking to him, and have left again without his being aware of it. Sometimes he is probing around in the entrails of dogs and cats; sometimes he is boiling herbs or is standing in front of a magician's stove with a bellows in his hand making gold or doing something even worse. By day he scampers like an ibex up the steepest crags of Mt. Haemus to— look for herbs, as if there were not enough of them around here. And at night, when even dumb creatures are used to rest, he wraps himself in a Scythian fur piece and looks, by Castor, through a blowpipe at the stars."

"Ha, ha, ha! You couldn't dream up anything crazier than that! Ha, ha, ha!" laughed the short, fat councillor.

"With all that, it is a pity about that man," the *archon of Abdera* said. "Nevertheless, you have to admit that he knows a lot."

"But what does the Republic get out of it?" replied a councillor who, with projects, proposals for improvements, and deductions of superannuated claims, had earned a good round sum from the Republic and, by virtue of which, he always boasted with full cheeks about the services he had rendered the Abderite state, although the Abderite state through all his projects, deductions, and improvements was not by a hundred drachmas in a better condition.

"It is true," said another, "his science comes to nothing but playthings; nothing solid! In minimis maximus!"[17]

"And then his insufferable arrogance, his mania for contradicting people, his everlasting hairsplitting, and faultfinding, and sneering!"

"And his bad taste!"

"About music, at least, he doesn't know beans," the *nomophylax*[18] said.

"Still less about the theater," shouted *Hyperbolus*.

"And nothing at all about the high ode," *Physignatus* said.

"He is a charlatan, a windbag—"

"And a freethinker on top of that," cried the priest *Strobylus,* "an out-and-out freethinker, a man who believes nothing, to whom nothing is holy! It can be proved that he tore the tongues out of a great many living frogs."

"There's a lot of talk going around of his having even dissected some of them alive," somebody said.

"Is it possible?" Strobylus shouted with all the signs of extreme horror. "Would it be possible to prove this? Just Latona! To what consequences this accursed philosophy cannot lead a man! But would it really be possible to prove it?"

"I'm passing it on as I heard it," the other answered.

"It has to be investigated," Strobylus cried. "Most praiseworthy archon! Most wise gentlemen! I call upon you herewith *in the name of Latona*! This matter has to be investigated!"

"Why an investigation?" asked *Thrasyllus,* one of the leaders of the Republic, a close relative and the presumable heir of the philosopher. "This thing is quite true. But it proves nothing more than what I, unfortunately, have noticed in my poor cousin for a long time—that *his brains* are not in as good a condition as might be wished. Democritus is not a bad man; he doesn't scorn the gods; but there are times when he is not himself. When he dissected a frog, I would swear for him that he took the frog for a cat."

"All the worse," Strobylus said.

"All the worse, indeed—for his head and for his household!" *Thrasyllus* continued. "The poor man is in a condition that no longer permits us to remain indifferent. The family will find itself compelled to call for help from the Republic. He is in no regard capable of administering his property himself. He will have to be put in the charge of a guardian."

"If this is so—" the *archon* said with a serious countenance— and paused.

"I will have the honor of informing you, Your Magnificence, of particulars about this affair," the councillor *Thrasyllus* replied.

"How is that? Democritus is not supposed to be in his right mind?" one of those present shouted. "Gentlemen of Abdera, think over well what you are doing! You are in danger of preparing a great laughing matter for all of Greece. May I lose my ears if you find a more intelligent man on this side of the *Hebrus River*[19] and on the other than this same Democritus! Beware, gentlemen! This business is more ticklish than you perhaps think."

Our readers are astonished—but we will help them out of this miracle right away. The man who said this was *no Abderite.* He was a foreigner from Syracuse[20] and, what maintained the respect of the councillors of Abdera, he was a close relative of the elder Dionysius,[21] who shortly before had set himself up as the prince of this republic.

"You can be assured," the archon answered the Syracusan, "that we will proceed no further in this matter than we find reason for doing so."

"I share too much in the honor the illustrious Syracusan renders my cousin by his good opinion," *Thrasyllus* said, "not to wish to be able to corroborate it. It is true, Democritus does have his *lucid* moments—and probably the Prince spoke with him in one of them. But unfortunately, they are only moments!"

"Then the moments in Abdera must be very long," the Syracusan retorted.

"Noble and very wise gentlemen," the priest Strobylus said, "the circumstances may be as they wish. Do consider that we are talking about a frog dissected alive! This is an important matter, and I insist on an investigation. For Latona and Apollo forefend that I should fear—"

"Calm yourself, High Priest," said the archon, cutting him short—who (between us) was himself a little under suspicion of not thinking as *soundly* about the frogs of Latona as people in Abdera had to think about them. "As soon as the *Directors of the Hallowed Pond* introduce a new measure in the Senate, the frogs are going to get all the satisfaction due them."

The *Syracusan* informed Democritus immediately of everything that had been said in this gathering.

"Have the neck of the fattest young peacock* wrung in the poultry yard and the bird put on the spit," Democritus said to his housekeeper, "and let me know when it's ready."

On the same evening, when *Strobylus* sat down at his table, the roasted peacock was served in a silver dish as a present from Democritus. When it was opened, behold, it was filled with a hundred golden *darics.***

"That man's mind must not be in such a bad condition after all," thought Strobylus.

The expedient had the immediate effect that it was supposed to have. The High Priest enjoyed eating the peacock very much, drank Greek wine with it, swept the hundred darics into his purse, and gave thanks to Latona for the satisfaction that she had obtained for her frogs.

---

*An inaccuracy seems to have crept into the text here. The peacock was an unknown bird in Greece *before Alexander's conquest of the Persian Empire.* And when it subsequently went from Asia to Europe, it was in the beginning so rare that in Athens it was exhibited for money. However, in a short time it became (to use the expression of *Antiphanes,* the author of comedies) as common as quail. In the opulent epoch of Rome, a vast quantity of them was raised there, and the peacock constituted a choice dish on Roman tables. Where *monsieur de Buffon*[22] got the idea that the Greeks ate no peacocks I do not know; a passage from the poet *Alexis*[23] in *Athenaeus*[24] could have proved the contrary to him. However, if there had been no peacocks in Europe *before Alexander,* it would, after all, be certain that Democritus could not have sent a roasted peacock to the priest Strobylus; one would then have to assume that this naturalist had brought peacocks back with him from India among other curiosities. And why should one not be able to assume this? If necessary, the old Samian coins, on which one sees a peacock depicted next to Juno, could help us out of our difficulty—if it were worth the trouble.
**A Persian gold coin that is supposed to have been minted first by Cyaxares II or Darius of Media after the conquest of Babylon.

"We all have our shortcomings," *Strobylus* said the next day in a large gathering. "*Democritus* is a philosopher, to be sure; but yet I find that his intentions are not as bad as his enemies say. The world is evil; people have related strange things about him. But I like to think the best of everybody. I hope his heart is better than his head! Things are not supposed to be at all right in the latter, and I think so myself. You have to make allowances for a lot with a man in such circumstances. I am certain he would be the finest man in all of Abdera if philosophy hadn't ruined his brains!"

With this speech, Strobylus killed two birds with one stone. He got rid of his obligation to our philosopher, since he spoke of him as a good man, and he deserved well of the councillor *Thrasyllus,* since he did it at the expense of Democritus's brains. From which it can be seen that the venerable priest Strobylus, with all of his naïveté or stupidity (if that is what you wish to call it), was a sly customer.

Chapter Three

A small digression into the reign of Shah Baham the Wise. The Character of the Councillor Thrasyllus.

There is a sort of people that you can know and observe for many years without being able to make up your mind about whether to put them into the class of *weak* or of *bad* people. No sooner have they played a trick of which no person of some consideration appears capable, than they surprise us by means of a malicious act so well thought out that we, with every good will of thinking the best of their *heart,* find it impossible to impute blame to their head. Yesterday we considered it settled that Mr. *Quidam*[25] had such a weak mind that it would be a sin to make crimes out of his absurdities. Today we are convinced by what we see that the man does too much evil to be a mere blockhead. We see no way of absolving him from the guilt of having an evil will. But hardly have we taken our stand in this matter when he says or does something that throws us back into our previous hypothesis, or at least into one of the most disagreeable psychological states, embarrassment, for not knowing what we are to think of the man or, if our evil star wills us to have to deal with him—what we should do with him.

The secret history of *Agra*[26] tells us that the famous *Shah Baham*[27] once found himself in this situation with one of his omrahs.[28] The omrah was accused of having committed some injustices.

"Then he is to be hanged," said Shah Baham.

"But Sire," they objected, "poor Kurli has such a weak mind that there is still the question of whether he understands clearly enough the difference between right and left in order *to know* whether he is committing an injustice or not."

"If this is so," Shah Baham said, "then send him to the hospital for the mad!"

"However, Sire, since he has enough sense to dodge a wagon filled with hay and to pass by a pillar against which he could smash his head because he very likely perceives that the pillar is not going to pass by him—"

"Does he perceive that?" the Sultan cried; "by the beard of the Prophet, then tell me nothing more. We'll see tomorrow whether there is any justice in Agra."

"Nevertheless, there are people who will assure Your Majesty that the omrah—except for his stupidity that occasionally makes him malicious—is the most honest man in the world."

"Pardon!" (another of the courtiers present interrupted) "precisely the opposite! Kurli has his stupidity to thank for everything that is still good in him. He would be ten times worse than he is if he had enough sense to know how to set about being so."

"Do you know, too, my friends, that there's no common sense in everything you're telling me here?" Shah Baham replied. "Compare yourselves with yourselves first, if you please. *'Kurli,'* says this one, 'is a bad man because he is *slow-witted.'* 'No,' says that one, 'he is slow-witted because he is *malicious.'* 'Off the mark,' says the third; 'he would be a worse man if he were *not so stupid.'* How do you want a man like me to make head or tail of this gibberish? Now just let somebody decide for me what I'm supposed to do with him! For he is either too malicious for the hospital, or too stupid for the gallows."

"This is just it," said the Sultana *Darejan.* "Kurli is too obtuse to be very malicious; and yet Kurli would be still less malicious than he is, if he were less stupid."

"The devil take the enigmatic fellow," shouted *Shah Baham.* "Here we sit and rack our brains to discover whether he is an ass or a scoundrel; and in the end you're going to see that he's both. Everything considered, do you know what I'm going to do? I'm going to let him go! His maliciousness and his stupidity will counterbalance each other. He will not do much damage through the one or the other *only in so far as he is no omrah.* The world is wide; let him go, *Itimaddulet!*[29] But before going he is to come and thank the Sultana. Not longer than three minutes ago I wouldn't have wished to give him a fig for his neck."

For a long time people could not discover *why Shah Baham* is given the epithet *the Wise* in the history books of Hindustan. But after this decision there can no longer by any doubt. All the Seven Sages of Greece[30] could not have undone the knot better than Shah Baham—cut it asunder.

The councillor *Thrasyllus* had the misfortune of being one of these, fortunately, not quite so common people in whose head and heart stupidity and malice, to use the Sultan's expression, counterbalance each other. His designs on his relative's property were not simpleminded. He had counted on Democritus's not returning at all after such a long absence, and on this assumption he had gone to the trouble of making a plan which the return of the same thwarted in a very disagreeable way. Thrasyllus, whose imagination was already accustomed to regarding the ancestral estate of Democritus as a part of his own property, could now not so easily get used to thinking otherwise. He looked upon him, therefore, as a robber who was withholding what was his. But unfortunately this robber had—the laws on his side.

Poor Thrasyllus thoroughly searched all the corners of his head to find some means of opposing this unfavorable circumstance, and he searched in vain for a long time. Finally he thought he had found in his cousin's mode of living a foundation on which he could build. The Abderites were already prepared, Thrasyllus thought, for in Abdera it was a foregone conclusion that Democritus was a fool. Therefore, it all still depended merely on demonstrating legally to the Great Council that his foolishness was of the sort that makes the person afflicted with it incapable of being his own master. Now a few difficulties were involved in this. With his own intelligence, Thrasyllus would hardly have managed to succeed. But in such cases, the likes of him will always find a rogue for their money who will lend them his brains; and then that amounts to the same thing as if they themselves had some.

Chapter Four

Brief, although adequate, information about the Abderite syco-phants.[31] A fragment from the speech in which Thrasyllus petitions for having his cousin placed under guardianship.

At that time in Abdera there was a sort of people who supported themselves by the art of so adjusting *bad quarrels that they appeared to be good.* For that they used only two principal artifices: either *they falsified the facts* or *they perverted the law.* Because this way of life was very lucrative, such a great number of idle people gradually devoted themselves to it that finally the bunglers displaced the masters. Through this the profession suffered a loss of repute. Those who occupied themselves with it were called *sycophants,* presumably because most of them were such poor wretches that for a fig they *said* everything one wished.*

Nevertheless, since the sycophants constituted at least the twentieth part of the inhabitants of Abdera, and since these people, moreover, could not live from figs alone, the ordinary occasions in which lawsuits used to arise consequently no longer sufficed. The sycophants' ancestors had waited until their counsel was solicited. But with this method their successors would have had to starve or dig; for *begging* was not allowed in Abdera, which (let it be said in passing) was the only thing that foreigners found praiseworthy in the Abderite policies of government. Now the sycophants were too lazy for digging; accordingly, for most of them, there was nothing left but—to *instigate themselves* the legal actions that they wished to prosecute.

Because the Abderites were people of such a hot temper and of little circumspection, opportunity for this was never lacking. Every trifle, therefore, resulted in a lawsuit; each Abderite had his sycophant. And thus a kind of equilibrium was again produced, through which the profession gained all the more in repute because emulation developed great talents.

Thereby Abdera earned the renown that the art of *falsifying facts* and *perverting laws* had not been developed so highly in Athens itself; and subsequently this renown became profitable for the state. For whoever had an unusually serious lawsuit of some importance engaged the services of an Abderite sycophant. And things would not have taken place naturally if the sycophant had left such a client alone before there was nothing left on him to gnaw off.

However, this was not yet the greatest advantage the Abderites derived from their sycophants. What made these people most superior in their eyes was—the convenience of being able to carry out any villainy without having to trouble themselves about it or to fall out with the law. The affair needed only to be turned over to a sycophant, then one could generally be calm about the way it would turn out. I say generally, for, to be sure, now and then there were

---

*A learned annotation could be adduced here on the difference between the *Athenian* and the Abderite sycophants; but it does not belong here. It is enough that we are now not in *Athens,* but in *Abdera.*

also cases where the sycophant, after he first had the client pay him a stiff fee, nevertheless secretly helped the *opponent* get justice. But this never happened either except when the latter paid at least two-thirds more than the client.

Moreover, it was not possible to see anything more edifying than the good understanding that the sycophants in Abdera had with the magistrates. The only people who fared badly in this concord were—*the clients.* In all other enterprises, however dangerous and risky they may be, there at least remains, after all, a *possibility* of getting off unharmed. But an Abderite client was always certain to lose his money whether he won his suit or lost it. Now, to be sure, the people got into disputes neither more nor less for that reason; however, their administration of justice therewith acquired a reputation towards which only Abderites could be indifferent. For it became a proverb in Greece *to wish* the person whom one wanted to saddle with the worst *a lawsuit in Abdera.*

But, on account of the sycophants, we would almost have forgotten that we were talking about the designs of the councillor Thrasyllus on the property of our philosopher and the means by which he wanted to try committing his intended robbery under the protection of the laws.

In order not to detain the gentle reader with any boring complicated particulars, we are satisfied with saying that Thrasyllus turned the affair over to his sycophant. It was one of the most clever ones in all of Abdera, a man who disdained the common ruses of his colleagues and who was very proud that, in all the time he had been engaged in his noble calling, he had won a few hundred serious lawsuits without ever telling a single *direct lie.* He relied on nothing but *undeniable facts;* but his strength lay in *synthesis* and in *chiaroscuro.* Democritus could have fallen into no better hands. We only regret that, because the records of the entire trial have long ago been devoured by mice, we are not able to impart for the benefit of young, incipient sycophants the entire speech in which this master of the art proved to the Great Council of Abdera that Democritus would have to be relieved of his property. All that has remained of this speech is a small fragment that appears sufficiently remarkable for us to include in this history a few sheets as a sample of how these gentlemen were accustomed to twist a matter.

"The greatest, the most dangerous, the most intolerable of all fools," he said, "are the *reasoning* fools. Without being less fools than others, they conceal the derangement of their head from the unthinking crowd through the fluency of their tongue and are considered wise because they rave *more coherently* than their colleagues in the madhouse. An *unlearned* fool is lost as soon as things have gone so far with him *that he talks nonsense.* With the *learned* fool, on the other hand, we see precisely the contrary. His fortune is made and his fame established as soon as he begins to speak or write nonsense. For most people, although they are really quite aware *that they comprehend none of it,* are either too *distrustful* of their own intelligence to perceive that it is not they who are at fault, are too *stupid* to notice, or too *vain* to admit that they have understood nothing. The more, therefore, the *learned fool* talks nonsense, the louder the *stupid fools* cry out about marvels, the more busily they turn their heads in order to find some sense in that high-flown rubbish. The former, like a gymnast refreshed by the public's applause, performs more and more daring leaps the more he is applauded; the latter clap more and more to see the charlatan perform still greater marvels. And thus it often happens that the vertiginous spirit of an individual seizes an entire people and that, as long as the *vogue of nonsense* lasts, altars are erected to the same man who, at another time, would have been rather unceremoniously put in the care of a hospital.

"Fortunately for our good city of Abdera, things have not gone this far with us yet. We all recognize and admit as with one voice that *Democritus* is an eccentric, a visionary, a crank. But we are satisfied with *laughing* at him; and it is just this in which we are making a mistake. Now we are laughing at him; but how long will it take for us to find something extraordinary in his foolishness? From amazement to admiration is but a step; and when we once have taken it—Ye gods! Who will be able to tell us where we will stop? Democritus is a visionary we now say and laugh. But what kind of a visionary is Democritus? A conceited, clever spirit, a mocker of our ancient customs and institutions; an idler whose occupations profit the state no more than if he did nothing at all; a man who dismembers cats, who understands the language of the birds and is seeking the philosopher's stone, a necromancer, a chaser after butterflies, a stargazer! And we can still be in doubt about whether he deserves to be locked up? What would become of Abdera if finally his foolishness became contagious? Will we prefer to await the consequences of such a great evil rather than make use of the only remedy with which we could ward it off? We are fortunate that the laws provide this remedy. It is simple, it is lawful, it is infallible. A dark little chamber, High and Wise Fathers, a dank little chamber! Then all at once we will be out of danger, and Democritus may rave all he pleases.

120 SECOND BOOK: HIPPOCRATES IN ABDERA

"'However,' say his friends—for things have already come so far with us that a man we all consider mad has friends among us— 'however,' they say, 'where is the evidence that his madness has already reached the stage that the laws require for putting him away?'—My word! If, after all we already know, we are still going to ask for *evidence*! Then he will have to take glowing coals for coins or to search for the sun with a lantern at noon, if we are to be convinced. Did he not maintain that the goddess of love in Ethiopia was black? Did he not try to persuade our wives to walk about naked like the wives of the gymnosophists? Did he not recently give his assurance in a large gathering that the sun stands still and that the earth revolves three hundred sixty-five times a year through the zodiac; and the reason why we do not fall out into space when it is turning its somersaults is that a great magnet is lying at the center of the earth which attracts us like just so many filings, although we are not made of iron?

"Nevertheless, I will gladly admit that these are all trifles. You can *say foolish* things and *do intelligent* ones. Would *Latona* that this were the philosopher's case. However, and I am sorry I have to say so, his actions presuppose such an uncommon degree of madness that all the hellebore[32] in the world would be too little to clean out the brain where they are hatched. In order not to wear out the illustrious Senate's patience, I will cite from among countless examples only two, whose certainty can be proved judicially, in case they should be doubted.

"Some time ago some figs were served up to our philosopher which, so it seemed to him, had a quite special taste of honey. This matter appeared to him to be important. He got up from the table, went into the garden, had someone show him the tree from which the figs had been gathered, examined the tree from bottom to top, had it dug up together with the roots, investigated the soil in which it stood and (as I have no doubt) also the constellation in which it had been planted. In short, he cudgeled his brain for some days about how and in what way the atoms had to adjust to one another if a fig was to taste of honey. He devised a hypothesis, rejected it again, found another, then the third and fourth, and rejected all of them again because none appeared to him to be ingenious and learned enough. The matter was so much on his mind that he lost sleep and his appetite over it. Finally his cook felt sorry for him. 'Master,' the cook said, 'if you were not so learned, it would surely have had to occur to you long ago why the figs tasted of honey.' 'Well, why then?'Democritus asked. 'To keep them fresher I put them in a pot in which there had been honey,' the cook said. 'This is the whole secret, and there's nothing more to investigate, I would think.' 'You are a stupid soul,' cried the moonstruck philosopher. 'A fine explanation you are giving me here. For creatures like you it may be good enough perhaps. But do you think that we allow ourselves to be satisfied with such simple explanations? Supposing the matter were as you say. What concern is that of *mine*? Your honey pot is indeed not going to keep me from inquiring into how the same natural occurrence could have resulted without a honey pot.' And thus the wise man continued, in spite of reason and his cook, to seek in the unfathomable fountain, in which (according to his allegation) truth lies hidden, a cause that lay no deeper than in a honey pot—until another whim that came across his fancy led him astray to other perhaps still more absurd investigations.

"However, as ridiculous as even this anecdote is, it is, nevertheless, nothing compared with the proof of intelligence he gave when last year the olive crop in Thrace and all the adjacent regions had failed. The year before, Democritus had found out, whether through geomancy or other magic arts, I do not know, that the olives, which at that time were very cheap, would in the following year fail entirely. Such foreknowledge would be sufficient to make the good fortune of a reasonable man for his entire life. At the beginning it also appeared as if he did not wish to let this opportunity escape, for he bought up all the oil in the entire country. A year after that the price of oil, partly because of the crop failure and partly because the entire stock was in Democritus's hands, rose four times as high as it had cost him. Now, I will let all the people who know that four is four times more than one guess what this man did. Can you imagine that he was irrational enough to give back the oil at the same price to those who had sold it to him as he had bought it from them?* We also know how far generosity can go in a person who is in control of his senses. But this deed lay so far beyond the bounds of credibility that the very people who drew profit from it shook their heads and doubted the intelli-

---

*How differently the same thing can be told! Of precisely this deed, which our sycophant considers the complete proof of a deranged brain, *Pliny* speaks as of a most noble action doing honor to philosophy. Democritus was much too good-hearted to wish to enrich himself at the expense of others who could not spare as much as he. He was touched by their anxious alarm and despair about having missed such a large profit. He gave them back their oil, or the money made from the sale of it, and was satisfied with having shown the Abderites that it depended only upon him to acquire wealth, if he thought it worth the trouble. *Pliny* looks upon the matter in this light, and one has indeed to be an Abderite, a sycophant, and a knave at the same time in order to speak of it as does our sycophant.

gence of the man who looked upon a pile of gold as if it were a heap of nutshells, a doubt that, to the misfortune of his heirs, was only too well founded."

Chapter Five

A medical opinion is sought on the matter. The Senate has a letter sent to Hippocrates.[33] The physician arrives in Abdera, appears before the Council, is invited by the Councillor Thrasyllus to a feast, and is—bored. An example that a moneybag full of darics does not have an effect on all people.

That is how far the fragment goes; and if one could draw conclusions about the whole on the basis of such a small part, then the sycophant certainly would have earned more than a basket full of figs from the councillor *Thrasyllus*. It was at least not *his* fault when the Great Council of Abdera did not condemn our philosopher to confinement. But there were people in the Senate who held a grudge against Thrasyllus; and *Master Pfriem*, who had meanwhile become Guild Master, maintained with great zeal that it would run *contrary to the freedoms of Abdera* to declare a citizen mad before he was found to be so by an impartial physician.

"All right," *Thrasyllus* cried, "for all I care *Hippocrates* himself can be asked to give his opinion. I'll be satisfied with that, to be sure."

Did we not say above that Councillor Thrasyllus's stupidity counterbalanced his malice? It was a stupid trick on his part to appeal to the testimony of Hippocrates in such a ticklish affair. But, of course, it also did not occur to him that he would be taken at his word.

"Hippocrates," the archon said, "is, to be sure, the man who could best get us out of this dubious dispute. Fortunately, he is just now over on the Island of Thasos[34]; maybe he can be persuaded to come over to us if we have him invited in the name of the Republic."

Thrasyllus blanched a little when he heard that this business was going to be treated seriously. But the majority of the votes supported the archon. Immediately deputies were sent off to the physician with a letter of invitation,* and the rest of the session was

---

*There is something under this head in the editions of the works of Hippocrates. But it doubtless has been falsely attributed to him and is the work of a shallow *Graeculus* of later times just as the entire story about the meeting of this physician with Democritus in one of the spurious letters that bear the name of the former.

spent in deliberating about the honors with which they intended to receive him.

"This, however, was not so Abderite, after all," those physicians who are among our readers will think. But where did we say anyway that the Abderites had done nothing at all that would befit a reasonable people, too? Yet, the true reason, after all, why they wished to show Hippocrates so much honor was by no means the esteem that they felt for him, but rather only the vanity of being considered people who knew how to appreciate a great man. And moreover, did we not note on another occasion that they were from time immemorial extraordinarily fond of ceremonies?

The deputies were instructed to say nothing further to Hippocrates than that the Senate of Abdera had need of his presence and his verdict in a very important matter; and Hippocrates could not imagine, with all of his philosophy, what kind of important business this could be. "For, why do they," he thought, "deem it necessary to make a secret of it? After all, the Senate of Abdera can hardly have been attacked in a body by a disease that they do not wish to come to light."

Nevertheless, he made up his mind the more readily to go on this journey because he had been wishing for a long time to become acquainted personally with *Democritus*. But how great was his astonishment when, after he had been fetched with great pomp and led before the assembled Council, he was informed by the ruling archon in a well-worded speech that he had been summoned to Abdera only to investigate the madness of their fellow citizen, Democritus, and to give his expert opinion on whether he could still be helped or whether things had not already gone so far with him that he might, without compunction, be declared legally dead.

"This must be some other Democritus," the physician thought initially. But the gentlemen of Abdera did not leave him with this doubt for long. "Good, good," he said to himself, "am I not in Abdera? Just how can anyone forget something like that?"

Hippocrates revealed nothing of his astonishment to them. He contented himself with praising the Senate and people of Abdera for having such a great feeling for the worth of such a fellow citizen as to regard his health as a matter of consequence to the community. "Madness," he said with great seriousness, "is a point at which the greatest minds and the greatest simpletons now and then meet. We shall see!"

Thrasyllus invited the physician to dinner and had the courtesy of offering him as company the finest gentlemen and the most beautiful women in the city. But *Hippocrates,* who was shortsighted and had no *lorgnette,** was not conscious of the fact that the ladies were *beautiful.* And thus it happened then through no fault of the good creatures, who had needlessly vied with one another in getting dressed up, that they did not completely make on him the impression that they could otherwise hope for. It really was a pity that he could not see any better. For a man of intelligence, the sight of a beautiful woman is always something very entertaining. And if the beautiful woman says something stupid, which is said to happen to beautiful women now and then as well as to ugly ones, it makes a perceptible difference whether she is only heard or whether she is seen at the same time. For in the latter case, one is always inclined to find everything she can say reasonable, or pleasing, or at least bearable. Since the Abderite women had lost this advantage with the shortsighted foreigner, as he was compelled to judge their beauty through the impression they made on his ears, there was thus nothing more natural than that the idea he thereby got of them was rather similar to what a deaf person might get of a concert by means of a pair of sound *eyes.*

"Who is the lady who was just now talking with the witty gentleman?" he asked Thrasyllus softly. He was given the name of the wife of a leader of the Republic. He looked at her now with new attention. "Confound it!" he thought to himself. "I cannot get that damned oyster woman out of my head whom I recently heard joking in front of my house in Larissa[35] with a Molossian[36] donkey driver."

Thrasyllus had secret designs on our Asclepius.[37] His table was good, his wine tempting, and he needlessly sent for Milesian dancing girls.[38] But Hippocrates ate little, drank water, and in Aspasia's[39] house in Athens had seen much more beautiful dancing girls. Nothing would take effect. Something happened to the wise man that probably had not happened to him for many years: *he was bored,* and it did not seem worth the trouble to him to conceal it from the Abderites.

The Abderite women, therefore, noticed—without a great expenditure of their powers of observation—what he allowed them to see plainly enough, and, naturally, the glosses they made about it were not to his advantage.

"He is supposed to be very learned," they whispered to one another.

"It's a pity that he doesn't have better breeding!"

---

*Those who might wonder a bit about this may be helped by the information that at that time lorgnettes—had not yet been invented.

"What I know for certain is that I will never get the notion of getting sick to please him," said beautiful *Thryallis.*

Thrasyllus, meanwhile, was engaged in reflections of another kind. "As great a man as this Hippocrates may be," he thought, "he has to have a weak side, after all. He didn't seem to make much of the marks of esteem with which the Senate overwhelmed him. He doesn't love pleasure either. But I bet that a purse full of new shiny darics is going to drive away this peevish face."

As soon as they rose from the table, Thrasyllus got to work. He took the physician aside and, with a show of the great sympathy he had for the unfortunate condition of his relative, endeavored to convince him that the derangement of his cousin's brain was such a well-known and settled affair that nothing but the duty of satisfying the formalities of the laws had induced the Senate to have a fact, about which nobody has any doubts, confirmed, though unnecessarily, by the verdict of a foreign physician. "Since, however, you have been put to the trouble of making a journey to us which you presumably would not have undertaken without this occasion, nothing is fairer, therefore, than that the person most concerned with this affair repay you in some measure because of the loss you are the while suffering by neglecting your affairs. Take this trifle as a pledge of my gratitude, of which I hope to give you stronger proofs.—"

A rather round purse that Thrasyllus pressed with these words into the physician's hand brought the latter back out of the distraction with which he had been listening to the councillor's speech.

"What do you want me to do with this purse?" *Hippocrates* asked with an apathy that completely disconcerted the Abderite. "You intended, probably, to give it to your steward. Are you commonly so distracted? If this should be the case, I would like to advise you to discuss it with your physician. But a short while ago you reminded me of the reason why I am here. I thank you for that. My stay can only be brief, and I may no longer delay the visit that, as you know, I owe Democritus." With these words this Asclepius made his bow and disappeared.

In his entire life the councillor had never looked so stupid as at this moment. But just how should an Abderite councillor ever have dreamt that he would encounter something like that? These are, after all, not contingencies for which a person is prepared.

Chapter Six

Hippocrates pays Democritus a visit. Secret information about the ancient Order of Cosmopolites.

As history tells us, *Hippocrates* met our naturalist as he was engaged in dissecting various animals, the inner structure and natural economy of which he wished to examine in order, perhaps, to come upon the reasons for certain differences in their attributes and inclinations. This occupation offered them abundant material for a conversation that did not leave *Democritus* uncertain about the character of the stranger. Their mutual pleasure over such an unexpected meeting was equal to the greatness of their worth on both sides, but it was so much the livelier on Democritus's side, since, for so long in his seclusion from the world, he had had to do without association with a being of his kind.

There is a kind of mortal already mentioned here and there by the ancients under the name of *cosmopolites*,[40] who—without arrangement, without a badge, without maintaining a lodge, and without being bound by oaths—constitute a kind of brotherhood that hangs together more closely than any other order in the world. Two *cosmopolites* come, the one from the east, the other from the west, see one another for the first time, and are friends, not by virtue of a secret sympathy that is, perhaps, to be found only in novels; not because sworn duties bind them to it, but rather *because they are cosmopolites*. In any other order there are also false or at least unworthy brothers. In this one, on the contrary, that is a complete impossibility. And that is, it seems to us, no small advantage of the *cosmopolites* over all other societies, communities, guilds, orders, and fraternities in the world. For where is one of all these that could boast that in its midst there never was a seeker of honors, a person filled with envy, a miser, a usurer, a slanderer, a braggart, a hypocrite, a dissembler, a secret accuser, an ingrate, a procurer, a flatterer, a parasite, a slave, a man without a head or without a heart, a pedant, a hairsplitter,[41] a persecutor, a false prophet, a charlatan, a financial schemer, and a court fool? The *cosmopolites* are the only ones who can boast of that. Their society has no need of excluding the *unclean* from their number as the Egyptian priests did in former times by means of secret ceremonies and forbidding customs. These exclude themselves; and one can no more *appear to be* a cosmopolite if one is not than one can pass oneself off without any talent as a good singer or violinist. The deception would come to light as soon as we would have to let people hear us. *It is not possible to imitate* the way the cosmopolites think, their principles, their convictions, their language, their equanimity, their warmth, even their moods, weaknesses, and mistakes, because, for all who do not belong to their order, they are a true mystery. Not a mystery that depends upon the reticence of their members or upon their precautions against being overheard; but rather a mystery over which nature itself has draped its veil. For the cosmopolites could without hesitation have it made known with trumpets sounding throughout the entire world and might safely count on no one's understanding anything about it except themselves. The circumstances of this matter being as they are, nothing is more natural than the cordial understanding and mutual trust that establish themselves between two cosmopolites at once in the first hour of their acquaintance. *Pylades* and *Orestes*,[42] after a twenty-year duration of their friendship tried by all kinds of tests and sacrifices, were not friends more than are these two from the moment they recognize one another. Their friendship has no need of being matured by time; it requires no tests; it is based on the most necessary of all natural laws, on the necessity of loving ourselves in the one who is most similar to us.

It would be demanding something, if not impossible, yet certainly absurd, of us, if it were expected that we ought *still more plainly* to express ourselves on the mystery of the cosmopolites. For it belongs, as we have plainly enough explained, to the *nature of the matter* that everything that can be said about it is an enigma to which only the members of this order have the key. The only thing that we can still add is that their number has at all times been *very small* and that they, the *invisibility* of their society notwithstanding, have maintained from time immemorial an influence in the things of this world whose effects are the more certain and more lasting because they make no noise and are mostly attained by means whose *apparent* direction confuses the eyes of the multitude. We entreat the person to whom this is a *new riddle* to read on rather than rack his brains needlessly about something that concerns him so little.

Democritus and *Hippocrates* both belonged to this wonderful and rare kind of human being. They had, therefore, been the most intimate friends for a long time although they did not know one another personally, and their meeting resembled a reunion after a long separation rather than a new incipient association. Their conversations, for which the reader is perhaps eager, were presumably interesting enough to be worth passing on. But they would take us too far away from the Abderites, who are the real subject of this history. All we have to say about them is that our cosmopolites spent the entire evening and the greatest part of the night in talking with one another, in the course of which the time passed very quickly, and that, while doing this, they so entirely forgot their *antipodes,* the Abderites and their Senate, and the reason why they had sent for Hippocrates, as if such a place and such people had never existed.

Not until the following morning when, after a light sleep of a few hours, they met again in order to enjoy the morning air on a hill adjoining Democritus's gardens, did the view of the city lying below them in the splendor of the sun remind Hippocrates that he had business in Abdera. "Can you possibly guess," he said to his friend, "for what purpose the Abderites invited me?"

"The Abderites invited you?" Democritus cried. "In all this time I've not heard anything about an epidemic raging among them. Indeed, it is a certain hereditary disease with which from olden times they have been afflicted, one and all, down to a very few; however—"

"Bull's-eye, bull's-eye, good Democritus; that's the way it is."

"You're joking," replied our man. "You mean the Abderites have come to feel *what has been wrong with them?* I know them too well. Their disease consists precisely in their not feeling that."

"Nevertheless," the other said, "nothing is more certain than that I would not be in Abdera now if the Abderites were not plagued by the very malady of which you are speaking. Those poor people!"

"Ah, now I understand you. Your being summoned could be an effect of their disease without their knowing it themselves. Now, let's see!—Ha! There we have it. I'll bet they had you come to prescribe so many bleedings and so much hellebore for honest Democritus as he might be in need of to become like one of them! Isn't that so?"

"You know your people splendidly, as I see, Democritus; but to talk so cold-bloodedly about their foolishness one has to be used to it like you."

"As if there were not Abderites everywhere."

"But Abderites to *this degree!* Forgive me if I cannot grant as much forbearance to your fatherland as you. I assure you, meanwhile, that they are not going to have sent for me in vain!"

Chapter Seven

Hippocrates gives the Abderites his expert advice. Great and dangerous commotions that arise over it in the Senate, and how, fortunately for the Abderite commonwealth, the crier suddenly gets everything back in order.

The time was approaching when this Asclepius was to make his report to the Senate of Abdera. He came, walked in the midst of the assembled fathers and spoke with an eloquence that amazed all those present.

"Peace be with Abdera! Noble, steadfast, prudent, and wise sires, dear gentlemen and Abderites! Yesterday I praised you because of your concern for the brain of your fellow citizen Democritus. Today, with good intentions, I advise you to extend this concern to your entire city and republic. To be sound of body and mind is the highest good that you can obtain for yourselves, your children, and your citizens. And really to do this is the first of your magisterial duties. As short as my stay among you is, it is, nevertheless, long enough indeed to convince me that the Abderites are not as well as might be wished. To be sure, I was born on the Island of Cos, and I live now in Athens, now in Larissa, now elsewhere, at present in Abdera, and maybe tomorrow I will be on the way to Byzantium. But I am neither a Coan nor an Athenian, neither a Larissan nor an Abderite; I am a *physician*. As long as there are sick people on the earth, it is my duty to restore as many to health as I can. The most dangerous sick persons are those who *do not know that they are ill;* and this is, as I find, the case with the Abderites. The malady is too deep-seated for my skill; but what I can advise in preparation for the cure is this: with the first good wind, send six large ships to Anticyra.[43] So far as I am concerned, they can carry there whatever cargo the Abderites wish. But at Anticyra have the six ships loaded with as much hellebore as they can carry without sinking. To be sure, hellebore can also be obtained in Galatia,[44] and it is somewhat cheaper; but that from Anticyra is the best. When the ships will have arrived, gather all the people on your great market place, and arrange, with your entire priesthood at its head, a solemn procession to all the temples in Abdera, and ask of the gods that they might grant to the Senate and to the people of Abdera what the Senate and the people of Abdera *are lacking*. Then return to the market place and, at the city's public expense, distribute among all the citizens your entire supply of hellebore; *seven pounds per person*. And do not forget to give the councillors, who have, in addition, to think for so many others, a double portion besides what they need for themselves! The portions are large, I grant you; but deeply rooted ailments are obstinate and can be cured only by means of long, continuous use of the medicine. Now, when you will have made use of this preparatory remedy for the requisite period of time according to the prescription I will give you, then I will leave you to *another physician*. For, as I have said, the malady of the Abderites is too deep-seated for *my* skill. For fifty miles around Abdera I know only one single man who could help you fundamentally if, patiently and obediently, you wanted to take his course of treatments. That man's name is *Democritus,* the son of Damasippus. Do not take amiss the circumstance that he was born in Abdera. He is on that account no Abderite, you can take my word for it. Or, if you do not wish to believe me, ask the god at Delphi.[45] He is a kindhearted man, who will find pleasure in rendering you his services. And herewith, gentlemen and citizens of Abdera, I commend you and your city to the gods. Do not be contemptuous of my advice because I am giving it gratis; it is the best I have ever given a sick person who considers himself healthy."

When *Hippocrates* had said this, he made a polite bow to the Senate and went his way.

"Never,"—said the historian Hecataeus,[46] a witness all the more credible because he was an Abderite himself*—"never were two hundred people, all at the same time, seen in a posture as odd as was that of the Senate of Abdera at this moment; unless it was the two hundred Phoenicians whom *Perseus*[47] transformed suddenly into just as many statues with the sight of the Medusa's head when their leader wanted to retrieve his hard-won Andromeda from him."

As a matter of fact, they had all possible reasons in the world to be petrified for some minutes. To wish to describe what went on in their minds would be wasted effort. *Nothing* went on in them; their minds were as petrified as their bodies. With stupid, speechless astonishment, they all looked over to the door through which the physician had withdrawn; and on each face there was expressed at the same time the strained effort and the entire incapacity to comprehend something of this event.

Finally, they gradually appeared to recover their senses, some earlier, some later. They looked at one another with wide-open eyes; fifty mouths opened at the same time to ask the same question and fell shut again, because they had been opened before anyone knew *what* to ask.

"Hang it all, gentlemen," guild master Pfriem finally cried, "I quite believe that the quack is making fools of us with his double portion of hellebore!"

---

*Unfortunately, all of his works have been lost. S. Recherches sur Hecatée de Milet, Tom. IX des Mém. de Litterat.

"Right from the start I didn't expect anything good from him," *Thrasyllus* said.

"My wife didn't see anything in him last night at all," the councillor *Smilax* said.

"I thought things would turn out bad right away when he talked about the six ships that we ought to send to Anticyras," said another.

"And the damned seriousness with which he declaimed all of that before us," cried a fifth; "I confess I could not at all imagine what his point was going to be."

"Ha, ha, ha! an amusing incident, as sure as I'm honest!" the small, fat councillor bleated while holding his sides with laughter. "Let's admit that we've really been had! A dreadful prank! That shouldn't have happened to us! Ha, ha, ha!"

"But who could expect something like that from such a man?" the *nomophylax* cried.

"Quite surely he's one of your philosophers, too," master *Pfriem* said. "The priest *Strobylus* is truly not so wrong! If it were not contrary to our freedoms, I would be the first to make a motion that all these pointed heads be chased out of the country."

"Gentlemen," the archon now began, "the honor of the City of Abdera has been impugned, and instead of our sitting here and wondering, or making comments, we should earnestly be pondering what is appropriate for us to do in such a ticklish matter. First of all, take a look and see what has become of Hippocrates!"

A summoner, who was sent off for this purpose, returned after a considerable space of time with the information that he was not to be found anywhere.

"A damned trick!" the councillors shouted with one voice. "Now what if he has escaped from us?"

"He's probably no wizard," guild master Pfriem said while looking for an *amulet* that he was accustomed to carry on his person to guard him against evil spirits and evil eyes.

Soon after that, it was reported the foreign gentleman had been seen on his donkey trotting off quite calmly behind the Temple of the Dioscuri[48] in the direction of Democritus's estate.

"What is to be done now, gentlemen?" asked the archon.

"Yes—certainly!—what's to be done now—what's to be done now?—Just this is the question!" the councillors cried while they looked at one another. After a long interval, it turned out that the gentlemen did not know what was to be done now.

"That man is held in great esteem by the King of Macedonia,

the archon continued. "He is revered in all of Greece like a second Asclepius. We could easily get entangled in real trouble if we wanted to give hearing to such touchiness, just though it may be. With all that, the honor of Abdera is for me—"

"Without meaning to interrupt you, sir archon," the guild master *Pfriem* interrupted him. "The honor and freedom of Abdera can be closer to no one's heart than to my own. But, all this considered, I truly do not see what the honor of the city can have to do with this incident. This *Harpocrates* or *Hypocritus,* whatever he calls himself, is a physician; and in my time I heard that a physician considers the whole world a big infirmary and all people his patients. Everybody talks and acts as he thinks right; and whatever a person desires, that he likes to believe. *Hypocritus,* I think, would like us all to be sick so that he would have all the more people to heal. Now, he thinks, if only I can get them to take my medicine, then they'll get sick enough for me. My name isn't master Pfriem if this isn't the whole secret."

"Upon my soul! You've hit it!" cried the small, fat councillor; "neither more nor less. That fellow isn't all that foolish! I'll bet, whenever he can, he's going to send down on us all possible fluxes and fevers only so that he'll have the fun of restoring us to health for our money! Ha, ha, ha!"

"But fourteen pounds of hellebore for each councillor!" cried one of the eldest whose brain, to judge by his face, was possibly already completely dried up. "By all the frogs of Latona, that is too much! You almost have to suspect that there is more behind it."

"Fourteen pounds of hellebore for every councillor!" master Pfriem repeated and laughed loudly.

"And for every guild master," *Smilax* added with a tone full of meaning.

"I must insist," cried master *Pfriem,* "that he said not a word about *guild masters.*"

"But that surely goes without saying," replied the former. "Councillors and guild masters, guild masters and councillors; I don't see why the guild masters ought to have something special in this."

"How's that, what?" shouted master *Pfriem* with great zeal. "You can't see what puts the guild masters ahead of the councillors? Gentlemen, you heard it! City clerk, I ask that that be put in the minutes!"

The guild masters all got up from their seats with much grumbling.

"Didn't I say," cried the *old hypochondriac councillor,* "that there was something more behind the affair? A secret plot against the *aristocracy.* But these gentlemen have betrayed themselves a little too early."

"Against the aristocracy?" shouted *Pfriem* in a doubly loud voice. "Against which aristocracy? Confound it, Mr. Chairman, since when is Abdera an aristocracy? Are *we guild masters* only painted on the wall perhaps? Do we not represent the people? Do we not have to defend their rights and freedoms? City clerk, put in the minutes that I am protesting against everything contrary and reserving the rights of the praiseworthy institution of the guild masters as well as of the City of Abdera."

"We protest, we protest!" shouted all of the guild masters together.

"We protest back! we protest back!" shouted the councillors. The noise increased.

"Gentlemen," the ruling archon called out as loudly as he could. "What kind of dizziness has taken hold of you? I beg you, do consider *who* you are and *where* you are! What will the women selling eggs and those selling fruit down there think of us when they hear us bawling like the toothbreakers?"[49]

But the voice of wisdom was lost unheard in the deafening uproar. Nobody heard his own voice.

Very fortunately it had from time immemorial been the custom everywhere in the entire city to eat the midday meal at twelve o'clock sharp. And, by dint of a council regulation, as soon as an hour had expired, a kind of herald had to step in front of the council chamber and call out the hour.

"Sirs," the herald called out with the voice of the Homeric *Stentor,*[50] "the twelfth hour has passed."[51]

"Quiet! the crier is calling out the hour!"

"What did he call?"

"Twelve, gentlemen, past twelve!"

"Twelve already?"

"Already past?"

"Then it's high time!"

Most of the gentlemen had been invited by someone. The happy word *twelve,* therefore, suddenly aroused in them a series of pleasant images that had not the slightest connection with the subject of their quarrel. More quickly than the figures of a peep show are transformed, a great table, covered with lots of pretty dishes, appeared before their mind; their noses delighted by anticipation in aromas of most favorable augury. Their ears heard the clatter of plates. Their tongues were already tasting the dainty sauces, in the concoction of which the Abderite cooks vied with one another. In short, the *immaterial banquet* occupied all the power of their souls, and all at once the peace and quiet of the Abderite state were restored.

"Where are you going to eat today?"

"At the house of Polyphontus."

"I've been invited there, too."

"I'm pleased to have the honor of your company!"

"The honor is all mine!"

"What comedy is going to be presented tonight?"

"The *Andromeda* of Euripides."

"A tragedy then!"

"Oh, it's my favorite! And what music! Between us, the nomophylax composed some of the choruses himself. You're going to hear marvels!"

Engaged in such gentle conversations, the fathers of Abdera left the city hall in a hasty, but peaceable, throng, to the great astonishment of the women selling eggs and others selling fruit who, a short while before, had heard the walls of the council chamber reverberating with genuine Thracian hue and cry.

All this they owed to you, beneficent crier. Without your fortunate intervention, the quarrel between the councillors and the guild masters would probably, like the anger of Achilles, as ridiculous as its cause was, have broken out into a fire that could have caused the most terrible disorder if not even the overthrow of the Republic.

If ever an Abderite had earned being rewarded with a public monument, then it was certainly this crier. To be sure, it must be admitted that the great service he rendered his native city at that moment loses its entire meritoriousness through the sole circumstance that it became useful only *by chance.* For when the honest man automatically called out "twelve" at the appointed time, he thought of nothing less than of the incalculable evils that he averted from the commonwealth. But, on the contrary, it must also be considered that from time immemorial no Abderite deserved well of his country in *any other way.* Therefore, if it happened that they did something that became of use to the city *through some happy accident,* they thanked the gods for it, for they very likely felt that they had collaborated as mere instruments or as incidental causes. Nevertheless, they had themselves paid for this *merit of chance* all the same just as well as if it had been their own; or, to speak more correctly, precisely because they were at the same time conscious of no merit of their own, they had themselves paid for the good that chance had done under their name on the same terms as a muleteer collects the daily earnings of his animal.

It goes without saying that we are talking here only of archons, councillors, and guild masters. For the honest crier could render as many or as few services to the Republic as he wished. He received his six pennies a day in good Abderite coin, and—goodbye!

Third Book:
Euripides Among the Abderites

Chapter One

The Abderites get ready to go to the comic theater.

Among the councillors of Abdera it was an old, traditional habit and custom, whether they had company or dined alone with their family, to recapitulate immediately thereafter at table the matters deliberated upon before the council and to make them into a rich source of either witty quips and amusing comments or of patriotic groans, laments, wishes, dreams, prospects, and more of the same—all the more whenever, perchance, secrecy had been explicitly recommended in the resolution drawn up by the council.

But this time—although the adventure of the Abderites with the prince of physicians was strange enough to merit a place in the annals of their republic—at all the tables where a councillor or guild master sat at the head, *Hippocrates* and *Democritus* were thought about no more than if men with these names had never existed. In this respect the Abderites had a quite exceptional public spirit and a finer feeling than one should have given them credit for, in view of their usual conceit. In point of fact, their affair with Hippocrates, however one might have wished to twist or color it, could be told in no way that was a credit to them. The safest thing was to let the matter rest and to keep silent.

Today's comedy, therefore, constituted, this time as usual, the chief topic of coversation. For, ever since the Abderites, following the example of their great model, the Athenians, had provided themselves with their own theater and, according to their custom, had carried the thing so far that, throughout the greater part of the year, some kind of play was to be seen in their theater every day, just as soon as the other commonplaces, weather, attire, and local news were exhausted in social gatherings, their talk turned unfailingly either to the drama that had been played *yesterday* or to the drama that was to be played *today*—and the gentlemen of Abdera were rather conceited, especially in the presence of foreigners, about the fact that they had provided their fellow citizens with such inexhaustible material for harmless conversations in social gatherings, and, especially for the beautiful sex, such a splendid remedy for what is so ruinous to body and soul—boredom.

We do not say it to find fault, but rather in well-deserved praise of the Abderites, that they considered their theater important enough to turn over its supervision to a special committee of the Council whose chairman was always the man who was then the *nomophylax,* consequently one of the most august fathers of the country. This was incontestably very commendable. All that one could in justice criticize about such a nice institution was that their theater was, for all that, no better by a hair. Because the choice of plays now depended on the committee of the Council, and because the devising of the playbill belongs among the imposing multitude of inventions that puts the superiority of the *moderns* over the *ancients*[1] beyond the remotest contradiction, the public seldom knew beforehand, except when a new original Abderite play was being staged, what would be playing. For, although the gentlemen on the committee did not exactly make a secret of the matter, before it became public it had to pass through many a wry mouth and through so many insensitive ears, that almost always a *qui pro quo*[2] resulted, and the members of the audience, when, for example, they expected the *Antigone* of Sophocles, had to be content with the *Erigone* of Physignatus,[3] which they then hardly ever or never failed to do.

"What play is going to be given for us today?" was now, therefore, the general question in Abdera—a question that was, in itself, the most innocent question in the world, but, through a single little circumstance, it became arch-Abderite, namely *that the answer could be of absolutely no practical usefulness.* For the people went to the theater whether an old or a new, good or bad play was being given.

Properly speaking, for the Abderites there were no *bad* plays *at all;* for they accepted everything as good, and a natural consequence of this unbounded good nature was that for them there were also *no good* plays. Bad or good, whatever passed the time for them was all right with them; and anything that looked like a play passed the time for them.

Every play, therefore, however miserable it was, and however miserably it might have been performed, concluded with clapping that would not at all cease. Then, through the entire parterre there suddenly resounded a general: "How did you like today's play?" and this was directly answered just as generally with: "Very well!"

As much inclined as our worthy readers may be not to be easily surprised about what we can tell them about the idiocies of our Thracian Athens, this aforementioned trait is, nevertheless, something so entirely peculiar that we must fear not being believed if we do not make comprehensible to them how it happened that the Abderites, with such a great liking for plays, could yet achieve such a high, boundless *dramatic apathy,* or rather *hedypathy,*[4] that a wretched play not only caused them no distress, but even pleased them just, or at least nearly just, as much as a good one.

We must, if we are to solve this riddle, be permitted a little digression on the entire Abderite stage.

We see ourselves compelled, however, to ask beforehand of the well-disposed and fair-minded reader a little favor, in the magnanimous granting of which he will, perhaps, be more interested than we. And this is: all the hostile inspirations of his *cacodaemon*[5] notwithstanding, to be sure not to get the notion that, under hidden names, the dramatic poets, the actors, and the audience of his dear native city are being discussed here. We are, to be sure, not denying that the entire history of the Abderites has, from a certain view, a double meaning. But without the key for unlocking the hidden import, which our readers are to obtain from us ourselves, they would run the risk of making incorrect interpretations. Until then, therefore, we request them

Per genium, dextramque, Deosque Penates[6]

to refrain from all unneighborly and unfriendly interpretations and to read all that follows, as also this entire book, in no other frame of mind than that in which they would read any other ancient or modern impartial historical narrative.

Chapter Two

More detailed information about the Abderite National Theater. The taste of the Abderites. The character of the nomophylax Gryllus.

When the Abderites had decided to have a regular theater, it was at the same time stipulated that it should be a *National Theater.*[7] Since the nation now, at least for the greatest part, consisted of Abderites, their theater had perforce to become *Abderitic.* This, naturally, was the first and irreparable source of all evil.

The respect the Abderites had for the holy city of *Minerva*[8] as their alleged mother resulted, to be sure, in the fact that the plays of all the *Athenian poets* enjoyed a great reputation among them, not because they were *good,* for that was certainly not always the case, but rather because they came from *Athens.* And in the beginning, from a lack of a sufficient number of *indigenous* plays, almost nothing else could be given either. However, for that very reason it was considered necessary, in honor of the City and the Republic of Abdera, as well as because of divers other advantages, to establish in their own midst a *factory for making comedies and tragedies,* and this new dramatic manufactory—in which Abderite wit, Abderite feelings, Abderite customs and follies, as well as an equal number of *national raw products*[9] were to be *wrought dramatically* for their own use—was to be encouraged in every possible way, as is incumbent upon good and wise regents and patriots.

To bring this about *at the expense of the public purse* would not really do for two reasons: first, because this purse, by virtue of how it was administered, almost always contained less than one wished to take out of it; and second, because at that time it was still not the fashion to have the spectators pay, but rather the *aerarium*[10] had to bear the expenses of the theater, and therefore, already had enough to spend anyhow with this new item. For there could be no thought of a new tax on the citizenry for the present and until it was known how much it would get to like this new entertainment. No other means remained but *to encourage* the Abderite poets *at the expense of the city's public fancy,* i.e., to accept as *good* all wares that they would deliver *gratis*—according to the old adage: *don't look a gift horse in the mouth;* or, as the Abderites rendered it: *wherever you can eat for nothing, the cooking is always good.*

What *Horace* says of his time in Rome:

Scribimus indocti doctique poemata passim,[11]

held good now for Abdera to the most superlative degree. Because it redounded to a person's *credit* when he wrote a play, and because absolutely nothing was thereby to be risked, whoever had enough breath to blow up a few dozen hastily collected thoughts into an equal number of periods filled to bursting with *bombast* wrote tragedies; and every shallow buffoon attempted now to belabor from the stage, too, the sides of the Abderites, on which he had formerly been drumming in social gatherings or in taverns.

This patriotic forbearance towards the national products had a natural consequence that at the same time increased the evil and made it lasting. However barren of ideas, windy, inflated, and ignorant *the young patricians* of Abdera were, a set incapable of any effort, one of them, nevertheless, quite soon allowed himself to be persuaded, we do not know whether by his girl or by one of his toadies, or also by his own inherited conceit, that it was only up to him to garner dramatic laurels as readily as anyone else. This first attempt was crowned with such splendid success that *Blemmias,* a nephew of the archon *Onolaus,*[12] a seventeen-year-old boy and, what was nothing unusual in the family of *Onolaus,* a *notorius dunce,* felt an irresistible itching in his fingers to write a goat-play,[13] as the thing was called at that time which we are now accustomed to speak of as a tragedy. Never, since Abdera had stood on Thracian soil, had a more stupid national product been seen. But the author was the nephew of the archon, and so he could not miss. The theater was so full that the young gentlemen had to sit on the laps of the beautiful Abderite women.[14] The common people stood on each others' shoulders. All five acts were heard in stony, mutely expectant silence. People yawned, sighed, wiped their brow, rubbed their eyes, were monstrously bored—and listened. And as the long-sighed-for ending now finally came, people clapped so dreadfully that several mother's darlings with delicate nerves lost their hearing.

Now it was clear that making a tragedy must not take such great skill because even young Blemmias had made one. Everybody, without any great lack of modesty, could believe himself capable of just as much. It became a point of honor that every good family had to be able to boast at least of a son, nephew, brother-in-law, or cousin who had presented the national stage with a comedy or a goat-play, or at least with a little operetta. No one considered how great the intrinsic value of this contribution might be; good plays, mediocre and wretched ones ran along pell-mell in one herd. No intrigue was necessary to defend a poor play. One courtesy deserved another. And because the gentlemen on all sides had ass's ears, it could occur to none to whisper to the other the famous words: Auriculas asini Mida rex habet.[15]

One can easily imagine that with this toleration art did not gain a great deal. But what did the Abderites care about the interests of art? It was enough that it was more advantageous for the peace and quiet of the city and for the diversion of all concerned to dispose of things of that sort amicably.

"There one can see," the archon *Onolaus* was accustomed to

say, "how much depends on getting hold of a thing by the right end. The dramatic stage, that in Athens is at any moment the cause of the nastiest quarrels, is in *Abdera* a bond of general good understanding and the most innocent pastime in the world. People go to the theater, are amused one way or other, either by listening, or by the woman in the next seat, or by dreaming and sleeping, however each one likes; and then there is clapping, everybody goes home satisfied, and good night!"

We said a while ago that the Abderites were so preoccupied with their theater that in social gatherings people talked about almost nothing but drama, and that is the way things really were, too. But when they talked about plays, performances, and actors, they did not do this to examine perhaps what was, in fact, worthy of approbation or not. For, whether they wished to take pleasure in a thing or not, that, in their opinion, depended solely upon *their free will;* and, as I have said, they simply had made a kind of silent agreement with one another *to encourage* their indigenous dramatic manufactories. "It is really obvious, isn't it," they said, "what it means when the arts in a place are encouraged. Twenty years ago we still had hardly two or three poets, of whom nobody took any notice, except perhaps on birthdays or at weddings. Now, since the ten or twelve years that we have had our own theater, we can already boast, counting the big ones and little ones together, of over six hundred plays, all of which have grown on Abderite soil."

When, therefore, they chatted about their plays, it was only to ask one another if, for example, yesterday's play had not been *fine* and to answer one another: yes, it had been *very fine*—and what a beautiful new dress the actress had on who played Iphigenia[16] or Andromache,[17] for in Abdera the female roles were played by real women[18]; and that certainly was not so Abderitic. And this then offered the occasion for a thousand little interesting comments, statements, and replies about the attire, voice, demeanor, carriage, the bearing of the head and arms, and twenty other things of this sort about the actors and actresses. Now and then the play itself was possibly discussed, too, and music as well as the *words,* as they called its poetry; that is, everyone said what had pleased him most or least. The predominantly *sentimental* and *sublime* passages were emphasized. It was also likely that, here and there, an *expression* or *a much too vulgar word,* or an idea that was considered exaggerated or offensive, was criticized adversely. But the criticism always ended with the eternal Abderite refrain: *it ever remains, after all, a fine play—and there's a lot of moral philosophy in it.* "Fine moral philosophy!" the short, fat councillor used to add—and it always happened that the plays he extolled to the skies because of their fine moral were just the most wretched.

You will perhaps think: since the special reasons that they had in Abdera for encouraging all indigenous plays without regard to merit and worth did not apply to those from abroad, the great diversity of the Athenian playwrights and the difference between an *Astydamas*[19] and a *Sophocles* should, after all, have at least contributed something to the improvement of their taste and to making clear for them the difference between good and inferior, excellent and mediocre—especially the mighty difference between natural vocation and mere pretension and mimicry, between the lively, even, sustained stride of the true master, and the stilted gait or the panting, hobbling, or creeping along of the imitators. However, in the first place, taste is a thing that cannot be acquired without a natural bent, without *a certain refinement of that organ of the mind with which one is supposed to taste,* nor by means of any art or education. And we noted right at the beginning of this history that nature appeared to have denied this bent to the Abderites entirely. They liked *everything.* On their tables the masterpieces of genius and wit could be found lying mixed together with the discharge of the shallowest minds, the casual labor of the sorriest bunglers. In such things one could make them believe whatever one wished; and nothing was easier than to pass off to an Abderite the most sublime ode by Pindar as the first try of a beginner, and conversely, the most senseless scrawl, if only it had the arrangement of a song in strophes and antistrophes,[20] as a work of Pindar. Therefore, with every new play they caught sight of, their first question was always: "by whom?"; and there were a hundred examples that they had remained indifferent toward the most splendid work until they had learned that it belonged to a famous name.

To this was added the circumstance that the nomophylax *Gryllus,* the son of Cyniscus,[21] who had played the most influential role in the establishment of the Abderite National Theater and who was the superintendent over all their theatrical activities, claimed to be a great expert on music and the first composer of his time—a claim against which the complaisant Abderites had the fewer objections because he was a very popular gentleman and because the entire art of his composing consisted of a number of *melodic forms or lasts* which he knew how to adapt to all kinds of libretti, so that nothing was easier than to sing and memorize his melodies.

The quality of which Gryllus was most proud was his *agility* in composing. "Well now! How do you like my *Iphigenia, Hecuba, Alceste*[22] (or whatever it was otherwise), eh?"

"Oh, quite excellent, Sir Nomophylax!"

"Don't you agree? The phrasing is neat there! the melody flowing, heh, heh, heh! And how long do you think I was working on it? Count it up! Today is the thirteenth—on the fourth at five o'clock in the morning—as you know, I get up early—I sat down at my desk and began—and yesterday morning at ten o'clock sharp I wrote the last line. Now count it up: 4, 5, 6, 7, 8, 9, 10, 11, 12—amounts, as you see to not nine full days, and among them two days of council meetings, and two or three when I was invited out, not counting other business—Hm! What do you say? Isn't that what you call working quickly? I'm not saying it to be boastful, don't you see; but, if I were making a bet, I dare say that no composer in all of European and Asiatic Greece[23] would be finishing a piece sooner than I! It's nothing! But yet, you know, it's a sort of special gift I have, heh, heh, heh!"

We hope our readers now see this man before them, and if they have some talent for music, it must seem to them as if they had already heard him grinding out all of his *Iphigenia, Hecuba,* and *Alceste.*

Now this great man had besides, incidentally, the little weakness that he could find no music any good except—his own. None of the best composers at Athens, Thebes, Corinth, and so on, could give him satisfaction. Among his intimate friends he called even the famous *Damon,*[24] whose pleasing, ingenious way of composing always appealed to the heart and enchanted everyone outside of Abdera who had a soul, the composer merely of low popular ballads. With this way of thinking and by virtue of the infinite ease with which he emitted his musical spawn, he now had, within a few years, written the music for more than sixty plays by renowned and unrenowned Athenian playwrights. For he mostly left the Abderite national products to his pupils and imitators and was satisfied with the mere revision of their work. Of course, as one can imagine, he did not always choose the best plays. Half of them at least were unsuccessful bombastic imitations of *Aeschylus* or tasteless farcical comedies, low entertainments that were intended by their authors themselves for the amusement of the lowest rabble at annual fairs. But enough, *the nomophylax,* a leader of the City *had composed them;* they were, therefore, endlessly applauded; and if, when they were repeated, they then also induced people to yawn now and then, and even to yawn outrageously to the point at which their jaw came near to slipping out of its joints, the members of the audience nevertheless assured one another in a very comforting way upon leaving: it was quite a fine play and quite fine music.

And so among these Thracians imitating the Greeks then, everything united to produce that *mechanical indifference* not only towards the kinds and degrees of the beautiful, but also towards the inner difference between the excellent and the wretched itself, an indifference through which they distinguished themselves, as with a fixed national trait of character, from all the rest of the civilized peoples of the earth; and this indifference became all the more peculiar by the fact that it nevertheless left them the capacity to be affected occasionally by the truly beautiful in a quite strange way—as will shortly be seen from a remarkable example.

Chapter Three

Contributions to the history of Abderite literature. Information about their most prominent playwrights, Hyperbolus, Paraspasmus, Antiphilus, and Thlaps.

With all of this apparent indifference, tolerance, apathy, hedypathy, or however one wishes to call it, we must, nevertheless, not imagine the *Abderites* as people without any taste. For they had counted their five senses correctly and completely. And although under the circumstances indicated, they liked everything well enough, it did seem to them, however, that they liked this or that *better* than something else. And thus they, as well as other people, had their *favorite plays* and favorite *playwrights*.

At the time when the little annoyance with the physician *Hippocrates* befell them, principally two playwrights were in possession of the highest favor of the Abderite public among a considerable number who made a trade out of it (not counting *the volunteers*). One of them wrote tragedies and a kind of play that we now call *comic opera*. The other named *Thlaps*,[25] fabricated a sort of intermediate thing that caused one to feel neither *joy* nor *grief.* He was the originator of these, and for that reason they were named *Thlapsodies* after him.

The first was none other than *Hyperbolus*, who was already mentioned at the beginning of this true as well as plausible history as the most famous among the Abderite poets. He had indeed distinguished himself in the other genres, too. The extraordinary partiality of his countrymen resulted in his being awarded the prize in all of them;

and precisely this preference gained him the grandiloquent surname *Hyperbolus,* for originally his name was *Hegesias.*

The reason why this man succeeded so especially well with the Abderites was the most natural in the world—namely, just for the reason why *he* and *his works* would have been hissed off the stage in any other place in the world. Among all their poets, he was the one in whom resided most truly the real *spirit of Abdera* with all of its idiocies and deviations from the beautiful forms, proportions, and lineaments of humanity, the one with whom all the rest sympathized most, who always did everything exactly as they would also have done it, who always took the words out of their mouths and always hit just the spot where they wished to be tickled—in a word, the poet after their mind and heart. And that not by virtue, perhaps, of an extraordinary sagacity, and it was not as if he had made a special study out of it, but solely because he, among all his *brothers in Marsyas,*[26] was the most—Abderitic. With him, one could rely on the fact that the point of view from which he looked at a thing was always the most distorted one from which it could be seen, that he always found the similarity between two things exactly where their essential difference lay, that he would ever and always look solemn where a reasonable person laughs, and would laugh where it can occur only to an Abderite to laugh, and so on. A man who was so full of the Abderite genius could, naturally, be anything in Abdera he wanted. He was also their *Anacreon,* their *Alcaeus,* their *Pindar,* their *Aeschylus,* their *Aristophanes,*[27] and for a brief while now he had been working on a great *national epic* in forty-eight cantos entitled the *Abderiad*—to the great joy of the entire Abderite people. "For," they said, "a *Homer* is the only thing we are still lacking; and, when *Hyperbolus* will be finished with his *Abderiad,* we will have the *Iliad* and *Odyssey* together in one piece. And then let the other Greeks come and still look at us over their shoulder, if they have the heart! Let them then suggest a *man* for us, whom we would not be willing to oppose with one of ours."

Tragedy, however, was the real province of *Hyperbolus.* He had made one hundred twenty of them (presumably also *big* and *little* taken together)—a circumstance which already by itself had to give him an extraordinary advantage with a people who in all things consider only *quantity* and *physical bulk.* For, of all his rivals, none had been able to achieve even the third part only of this figure. In spite of the Abderites' being accustomed to calling him their *Aeschylus* because of his bombastic style, he was, nevertheless, not just a little proud of his *originality.* "Just let anybody show me," he said, "a character, an idea, a feeling, an expression in all of my work that I have taken from somebody else!"

"Or from nature," added *Democritus.*

"Oh," cried Hyperbolus, "so far as that is concerned, I can grant you that without losing much thereby. Nature, nature! You gentlemen are always raising a clatter with your nature, and in the end you don't know what you want. Ordinary nature—and that is what you mean, after all—belongs in the *comedy,* in the *farce,* in the *Thlapsody,* if you wish! But tragedy must rise *above nature,* or I'll not give you a hollow nut for it."

This held good for his own to the highest degree. No human being ever looked, ever felt, thought, talked, nor acted like his characters. But that is exactly what the Abderites wanted—and that is also the reason why they cared least for *Sophocles* among all of the poets from elsewhere.

"If I am to say frankly what I think," Hyperbolus once said in a distinguished gathering where people were arguing about this subject in good Abderite, "I have never been able to comprehend what is supposed to be so extraordinary about the *Oedipus* or the *Electra,* and especially about the *Philoctetes,* of Sophocles. As a successor of such a sublime poet as *Aeschylus,* he truly falls far short. *Well yes,* Attic urbanity, that I do not deny him. Urbanity as much as you wish! But the stream of fire, the ideas charged with lightning, the crashes of thunder, the overpowering whirlwind—in short, the gigantic strength, the eagle's flight, the lion's fury, the storm and stress that make the true tragic poet—where is that?"

"That's what I call talking about the matter like a master," a member of the company said.

"Oh, do rely on the judgment of Hyperbolus about such things," another cried, "if *he* didn't know what's what there!"

"He has made one hundred twenty tragedies," an Abderite woman whispered into the ear of a stranger, "he's the foremost playwright in Abdera!"

However, among all of his rivals, pupils, and *trainbearers,* two of them were successful, after all, in making him totter on the throne to which general approbation had raised him. The one by means of a play in which the *hero murders his father* right away in the first scene of the first act, *marries his own sister* in the second, discovers in the third *that he had begotten her with his mother,* *cuts off his own ears and nose* in the fourth, and in the fifth, after he *poisons his mother* and *strangles his sister,* is taken by the Furies amid lightning and thunder down to Hell. The other by means of a *Niobe,*[28] in which, except for a lot of Ω! Ω! Αι, Αι! Φεῦ

Φεῦ, Φεῦ, Ελελελελεῦ[29] and a few blasphemies, because of which the audience's hair stood on end, the entire play was composed of nothing but *action* and *pantomime*. Both plays had had the most astonishing effect. Never, since an Abdera had existed, had so many handkerchiefs been wept full of tears within three hours.

"No, it is unbearable," the beautiful Abderite women sobbed. "That poor prince! How he moaned! How he rolled about!"

"And the speech he gave after he had cut off his nose," cried another.

"And the Furies, the Furies!" a third shouted, "with them in my mind, I'll not be able to close an eye in four weeks!"

"It was dreadful, I must admit," said the fourth. "But *oh, poor Niobe*, how she stands there in the midst of her dead children piled up one on top of the others, and tears her hair out and strews it over the steaming corpses, then throws herself upon them, would like to bring them back to life, then jumps up again in despair, rolls her eyes like fiery wheels, then tears her breast open with her own nails and tosses handfuls of blood toward Heaven while she shouts terrible curses! No, something so moving was probably never seen. What a man he must be, that *Paraspasmus,* who had enough strength to put such a scene on the stage!"

"Well now, as far as strength is concerned," said beautiful *Salabanda*, "you can't always draw such certain conclusions about that, I'm afraid. I doubt that *Paraspasmus* would live up to what he appears to promise; big braggarts, poor swordsmen."

Beautiful Salabanda was known as a woman who did not say something like that without a reason. And this insignificant circumstance succeeded in doing so much that the second performance of the *Niobe* of Paraspasmus no longer had half of its former effect. The poet himself, indeed, could not in the future recover from the blow that Salabanda had given him in the imagination of the Abderite women with a single word.

However, he and his friend *Antiphilus* still retained the honor of having given new impetus to tragedy in Abdera, and of being the inventors of two new genres, the *morose drama* and the *pantomimic drama,* in which there was opened to the Abderite poets a career where reaping laurels was so much more certain, since nothing is basically easier than—frightening children and, through sheer emotion, having the heroes—say nothing at all.

As human inconstancy, however, is quite soon satiated with all that is ever so pleasant because of its novelty, the Abderites, too, already began to weary of having, always and every day, to find very fine what for a long time had, in point of fact, been giving them little pleasure at all, when young *Thlaps* got the idea of putting on plays that were neither comedy, nor tragedy, nor farce, but rather a kind of living Abderite picture of family life, where neither heroes nor fools, but good, honest, homemade Abderites were to appear, pursue their daily business in the town, the market place, their house, and their family, and act and speak on the stage before a laudable audience exactly as if they were at home, and as if there were no other people in the world than they. It can be seen that this was approximately the same genre through which Menander[30] subsequently gained so much fame. The difference consisted merely in his putting *Athenians,* and the other *Abderites,* on the stage, and in his being *Menander,* and the other *Thlaps.* But since this difference did not matter to the Abderites, or rather just because of that, it turned out to Thlaps's advantage, and his first play* in this genre was received with a delight, of which no one up to that time had seen an example. The honest Abderites saw themselves for the first time on a stage in *puris naturalibus,*[31] without stilts, without lions' skins, without a club, scepter and diadem, in their everyday clothes, speaking their ordinary language, being their very selves in accord with their inherent Abderite way of doing things, eating and drinking, wooing and being wooed, and so on, and just that was what they so much enjoyed. They felt like a girl looking in a mirror for the first time; they could not get enough of it at all. *The fourfold Bride* was played twenty-four times in a row, and for a long time the Abderites wanted to see nothing but *Thlapsodies. Thlaps,* who was not so nimble an author as the great *Hyperbolus* and the nomophylax *Gryllus,* could not get as many ready as they wished to have from him. But since he once had set the fashion for his colleagues, he was not lacking in imitators. Everybody went over to the new genre. And in less than three years, all possible subjects and titles of Thlapsodies were so exhausted that it really was a pity to see the distress of the poor poets, the way they wavered and sweated, in order to squeeze out of the sponge that so many had wrung out before them one more drop of murky water.

The natural consequence of this was that everything imperceptibly returned to the proper equilibrium. The Abderites, who, as human beings are rather generally wont to do, initially took an exclusive

---

*It was entitle *Eugamia, or the fourfold Bride.* Eugamia had been promised by her father to one man, by her mother to another, and by her aunt, in whose inheritance she was interested, to a third man. In the end, it came out that the rash girl had already given herself secretly to a fourth.

fancy for each genre, found in the end that it is only all the better
if they could ward off satiety through alternation and diversity. The
tragedies, ordinary ones, the morose and the pantomimic kind, the
comedies, operettas, and farces came back into circulation. The *nomophylax* wrote music for the tragedies of Euripides. And *Hyperbolus* (all the more since he had in his head the project of becoming the
Abderite Homer) finally acquiesced, since it could not be changed
anyway, in sharing the highest favor of the Abderite audience with
Thlaps, especially since the latter, by marrying the niece of a chief
guild master, had recently become an important person.

Chapter Four

*A remarkable example of the good political economy of the Ab-
derites. Conclusion of the digression on their theater.*

Before we return from this digression to the course of our history, it might be necessary to remove from the gentle reader's mind
a small doubt that might have arisen during the preceding brief
adumbration of the Abderite stage.

It is, I dare say, not comprehensible, one will say, how the *aerarium*[32] of Abdera, whose revenues could not exactly be so very
considerable, could have in the long run defrayed such a large
additional expense as a daily play with all its properties, supposing,
too, that the poets served for neither pay nor reward, out of pure
patriotism or for the mere honor. If it was the latter, however, it will
hardly be found credible that there were a number of professional
playwrights in Abdera, and that the great Hyperbolus, with all his
patriotism and selfishness, was said to have gone as far as to write
one hundred twenty dramas.

Now in order not to detain the kind reader needlessly, we will admit
to him frankly that their playwrights by no means worked for nothing
(for the great law, "Thou shalt not muzzle the ox when he treadeth
out the corn,"[33] is a law of nature whose binding force even the Abderites felt, too) and that by virtue of a special financial operation,
the City Treasury did not really have to defray any new expenditure
on account of the theater, but rather this expense was spared, for the
greater part, from other more *necessary* and *useful* items.

The matter stood as follows. As soon as the patrons of the theater
saw that the Abderites had caught fire and that plays had become
a necessity for them, they did not fail to have it explained to the
people by the guild masters that the Treasury was not up to such
a great increase of expenditures without new sources of revenue

or reducing the expenditures. This occasioned the setting up of a committee which, after more than sixty paid sessions, finally laid before the Council a draft for the establishment of a public Abderite stage that was found to be so thorough and well thought out that, in a general assembly of the citizenry, it was immediately styled a fundamental law.

We would take pleasure in laying this Abderite masterpiece before our readers, too, if we might expect them to have enough patience to read it. If, however, any community within or without the Holy Roman Empire[34] would like to have a copy of it, we are willing, after receiving the request, to send it free of charge except for the mere costs of having the copy made. All we can say about it here is that, by virtue of this arrangement, *sine aggravio publici,*[35] through mere economizing on a lot of other expenses that in any other state would certainly have been regarded as more necessary and more useful than the support of a national theater, sufficient funds were agreed upon to *treat* "the Abderites four times a week to plays, to remunerate properly poets, actors, and orchestra as well as the members of the committee and the nomophylax, and, still beyond that, to present to the two lowest classes of spectators at each performance one penny roll and two dried figs *viritim.*[36] The only defect in this fine arrangement was that the gentlemen of the committee made a mistake in their calculating the revenue and expenditure (for the correctness of which calculation their well-known dextrousness was relied on) of such magnitude that the Treasury had to pay out eighteen thousand drachmae (about three thousand talers in specie) more than the amount of the funds allotted. Now that was certainly no entirely casual error in computation. However, the gentlemen of Abdera were so accustomed to going about their governmental business without much ado and in good faith that some years elapsed before they perceived the reason why every year there turned out to be a deficit of three thousand talers in the general account. When finally, after much effort, they found out, the leaders considered it necessary to bring the matter before the whole people and *pro forma* to propose closing the theater. However, the Abderites reacted to this proposal as if one wished to deprive them of fire and water. In short, a plebiscite resulted in the decree that the three talents[37] missing every year were to be obtained from the public treasure that was stored in the Temple of Latona; and whoever would in the future presume to propose abolishing the theater should be regarded as an *enemy of the City of Abdera.*

The Abderites now believed that they had acquitted themselves quite intelligently, and to strangers they were in the habit of boasting that their theater cost eighty talents (eighty thousand talers) a year and yet cost the citizenry of Abdera not a penny.

"Everything depends upon a good constitution," they said. "But in return, we also have a National Theater like no other in the world!"

"That is certainly true," *Democritus* said, "such actors, such music, and four times a week for eighty talents! I, at least, have not met with that in any other place in the world."

What they had to be given credit for was that their theater could rate as one of the most sumptuous in Greece. Of course, they had to put their best jurisdiction into pledge to the King of Macedonia in order to build it. But since the King had conceded to them that the administrator, the clerk, and the treasurer should always be Abderites, nobody could really have any objections to make.

We apologize to our readers if they have been detained too long with this general account of the Abderite theater. The time has meanwhile come for the play to begin, and so, without further ado, we now go into the amphitheater of this praiseworthy republic, where the gentle reader will please take a seat, as he likes, either next to the small, fat councillor, or with the priest Strobylus, or next to the gossip Antistrepsiades, or next to any of those beautiful Abderite women with whom we have made him acquainted in the previous chapters.

Chapter Five

The Andromeda of Euripides is performed. Great success of the nomophylax, and what the singer Eukolpis contributed to it. A few comments on the rest of the actors, the choruses, and the scenery.

The play that was performed this evening was the *Andromeda*[38] of Euripides, one of the sixty or seventy works of this poet of which only a few little shavings and splinters have escaped destruction. The Abderites, without even knowing very well why, held the name Euripides and everything that bore his name in high respect. Various ones of his tragedies or lyrical dramas (as we should really call them) had already been often performed and always been found to be *very fine*. The *Andromeda*, one of the newest, was now being put on the Abderite stage for the first time. The *nomophylax* had written the music for it and (as he said rather loudly into the ears of his friends) this time he surpassed himself; that is, this man had resolved to display all of his skills at the same time, and while he was engaged in doing that, without his noticing it, he lost sight of good Euripides completely. In short, Mr. *Gryllus* had set music to himself, without any concern for whether his music was making nonsense of the libretto, or the libretto of his music, which then was exactly the point about which the Abderites were the least concerned. In a word, it made a great din, had very *sublime* and *moving* passages (as his brothers, cousins, brothers-in-law, clients, and servants all, as connoisseurs, assured him), and was received with the loudest, most resolute applause. It was not as if, not even in Abdera, there were not people still here and there who—because they might perhaps have brought somewhat thinner ears into the world than their fellow citizens, or because they might have heard something better elsewhere—admitted to one another that the no-mophylax, with all of his presuming to be an Orpheus,[39] was only an organ grinder, and the best of his works a rhapsody without *taste* and mostly without *sense* as well. These few had formerly even ventured to express some of their heterodoxies in public. But the reception they got each time from the devotees of the *Gryllian muse* was so ugly that they, to escape unscathed, considered it a good idea to submit to the majority while there was still time. And now these gentlemen were always the ones who clapped first and loudest at the most wretched passages.

The orchestra did its best this time to show itself worthy of its leader. "But I gave them enough to do to keep their hands full, too," *Gryllus* said and appeared to be very proud of the fact that already in the second act the poor people had not a dry thread on their bodies.

Let it be said in passing that the orchestra was one of the institutions in which the Abderites vied with all the cities in the world. The first thing they told a foreigner about it was that it had one hundred twenty members. "The Athenian one," they were in the habit of adding with an accent full of meaning, "is supposed to have only eighty; but, to be sure, with one hundred twenty men you can really accomplish something!"

Among so many there was no lack of capable people, at least out of some of whom a director such as—did not nor could not exist in Abdera—could have made something. But how did that help their music? It had simply been decided in the council of the gods that in Thracian Athens nothing was to be in its place, nothing to be appropriate to its purpose, nothing *fitting* and nothing *whole*. Because the people got little for their effort, it was not believed possible to demand much of them. And because they were satisfied with everybody who did *his best* (as they called it), *nobody* did his best. The apt people became careless, and whoever still performed halfway decently, lost the courage and, finally, the ability to advance. Why, in the end, should they have made the effort to achieve *perfection,* since they were working for Abderite ears? To be sure, the *tiresome foreigners* had ears, too; but, after all, they had no vote, and they did not find it worth the trouble either, or were too polite or too political to wish to assault the taste of Abdera. The nomophylax, as stupid as he was, noticed as well as anyone else, of course, that things were not going as well as they should. But besides his having no taste or (what amounted to the same thing) that nothing tasted good to him that he had not cooked himself and that he, therefore, always lacked the right means whereby it could be better—he was also too sluggish and too inflexible to associate with others in the proper way. Perhaps in the end he also liked, when the din he created (as probably happened now and then) would not even really appeal to the Abderites' ears, to lay the blame on the orchestra and could assure the ladies and gentlemen who, for honor's sake paid him their compliment on that account, that not a note had been performed as he had conceived and written it. However, that was only an emergency exit in case of fire. For, from the sneering tone in which he was given to talk about all other orchestras, and from the merit in the service of the Abderite one that he attributed to himself, it could only be concluded that he was as well satisfied with it—as was proper for a *patriotic* nomophylax of Abdera.

But, however the music of this *Andromeda* and its performance were constituted, it is certain that the audience had not so generally liked any play for a long time. The singer who played *Perseus* was so violently applauded that, in the middle of the finest scene, he sang off key and went astray into a passage from the *Cyclops.* *Andromeda*—in the scene where she is chained to the rock, abandoned by all of her friends and given up to the anger of the Nereïds, and fearfully awaits the surfacing of the monster—had to repeat her monologue three times. The nomophylax could not restrain his joy at such a brilliant success. He went around from row to row to collect the tribute of praise that rang out to him from all lips. And in the middle of his assurance that too much honor was being done him, he admitted that he was himself as satisfied with none of his playthings (as he chose to call his operas with a great deal of modesty) as he was with this *Andromeda.*

However, in order to render justice to himself and the Abderites, he should have charged at least half of this fortunate success to the account of the singer *Eukolpis,*[40] who, to be sure, had already possessed the means to please before, but found the opportunity as Andromache to show herself in such a favorable light that the young and old gentlemen of Abdera could not—see enough of her. For there was so much to *see* that there was no thought at all of *hearing. Eukolpis* had a large, well-turned figure—considerably more materialistic, indeed, than what was required of beauty in Athens—but in this respect (as in many others) the Abderites were confirmed *Thracians;* and a girl, out of which the sculptors in Sicyon[41] would have made two, was, according to their accepted due proportions, a marvelous figure of a nymph. Since Andromeda was required to be dressed only in something very thin, *Eukolpis,* who was very conscious of where the real power of her magic lay, had invented a drapery out of rose-colored Coan fabric, under which, without propriety's being all too greatly offended, little or nothing of the beautiful forms she was admired for was lost on the spectators. Now it was easy for her to sing. Even if the composition could possibly have been in even worse taste and her execution ten times more full of mistakes, she would always have had to repeat her *monologue* because that was still, after all, the most honest pretext for being able all the longer to touch her with concupiscent glances.

"In truth, by Jupiter, a splended specimen," one said to the other with half-closed eyes, "an incomparable specimen!"

"But don't you, too, find that Eukolpis is singing like a goddess today?"

"Oh, beyond all expression! By *Anubis,*[42] it's exactly as if Euripides had written the entire play just for her sake!" The young gentleman who said this was in the habit of always swearing "by Anubis" to show that he had been in Egypt.

The ladies, as is easy to imagine, did not find the new Andromeda quite as wonderful as did the men. "Not bad! Quite pretty!" they said. "But how come the roles were handed out so unfortunately this time? The play was the worse for it. They should have exchanged the roles and given that of the mother to *fat Eukolpis.* She would have been admirably suited to play a Cassiopeia."[43]

There was a lot to bring up, too, against her costume, coiffure, and so on. "She was not got up to her advantage"—"the belt was too high and drawn up too tight"—and especially annoying was found to be the affectation of always displaying her foot, "on the *disproportionate smallness* of which she prided herself a bit too much"—said the ladies who were accustomed to hide their own for the opposite reason.

Nevertheless, the women and men all did agree that she sang exceedingly well and that nothing could be prettier than the *aria* in which she lamented her fate. *Eukolpis,* although her performance was inferior, had a good, resonant, and supple voice. But what really had made her the favorite singer of the Abderites was the effort she had made with considerable success to learn certain runs and cadences from the nightingales, in which she and her listeners took such delight that she mixed these in everywhere, at the right time and at the wrong time, and they were always well received. Whatever her role required of her, to laugh or to cry, to lament or be angry, to hope or to fear, she always found an opportunity to get in her nightingales and was always certain of being applauded, even though she had spoiled the best passages with them.

About the remaining actors, who played *Perseus* as the first lover, *Agenor,* the former lover of Andromeda, the *father,* the *mother,* and a *priest of Neptune,* we find not much more to say than that people found a lot of fault with details; on the whole, however, they were thought to have performed very satisfactorily. *Perseus* was a man with a good build, and he had a great talent—for playing an *Abderite* buffoon. The previously mentioned *Cyclops* in the satyr play of this name[44] was his master role. "He plays Perseus quite well," said the Abderite women. "Only it's a pity that, without his noticing it, Cyclops keeps *getting in his way.*"

Cassiopeia, a little dressed-up doll, full of pretentious charm, had not a single natural tone. But she was a great favorite of the second archon's wife, had a quite odd manner of singing little songs, and *did her best.*

The priest of Neptune bellowed in a monstrous sailor's bass. And *Agenor*—sang as wretchedly as is proper *for a second lover.* To be sure, he did not sing any better either when he played the first; but, because he danced very well, he had received a kind of license allowing him to sing that much worse. *"He dances very well,"* was always the answer of the Abderite women whenever anybody commented that his cawing was intolerable. However, *Agenor* only seldom danced, but he sang in all the lyrical dramas and operettas.

In order to survey the beauty of this *Andromeda* entirely, one still has to imagine two choruses, one composed of Nereïds, and the other of the playmates of Andromeda, both of them made up of *disguised schoolboys,* who set about performing their roles in such an unruly way that the Abderites (to their great consolation) got enough and their fill of laughing. Especially the *Chorus of Nereïds,* by means of the inventions the nomophylax added, had the drollest effect in the world. The Nereïds appeared with half of their bodies rising up out of the water, with artificial yellow hair, and with huge artificial breasts that, from afar, looked quite naturally like—padded balls and, therefore, entirely what they really were.

The symphony, to the accompaniment of which these mermaids came swimming up, was an imitation of the celebrated wreckeckeck koax koax in *The Frogs of Aristophanes*. And, in order to make the illusion more complete, Mr. *Gryllus* had added several cows' horns that joined in, from time to time, to imitate the *Tritons* blowing on their conches.

For the sake of proper brevity, we will say nothing further about the scenery than that it was found to be *very fine* by the Abderites. A *sunset* was especially admired that they brought about by means of a windmill wheel on which long lucifers were stuck. "It would have produced a good effect," they said, "if it had only been turned a little faster." With the way Perseus came flying onto the stage in his Mercury boots, the *Abderite connoisseurs* wished that the cords with which he was suspended had been painted the *color of air* so that they could not have been seen quite so plainly.

Chapter Six

Strange sequel that the Abderites played with an unknown foreigner, and its most unexpected development.

As soon as the play had ended and the deafening applause had abated a little, they asked one another, as usual, "Well, how did you like the play?" and received everywhere the answer: "Very well!" One of the young gentlemen who was considered a first-rate connoisseur also directed this great question at a somewhat elderly *foreigner* who sat in one of the middle rows and, to judge by his appearance, seemed to be no ordinary man. The foreigner, who perhaps had already made a mental note of what answer had to be given in Abdera to such a question, got off his "very well" rather quickly; but, because his face made this approbation somewhat suspect, and even an involuntary, although quite weak movement of the shoulders that he made at the same time could be interpreted as a shrug, the young Abderite gentleman did not allow him to slip past so cheaply. "It seems," he said, "that you didn't like the play? After all, it passes as one of the best pieces of Euripides!"

"The play may not be so bad," the foreigner answered.

"So you have some fault to find with the music, perhaps?"

"With the music? Oh, so far as the music is concerned, that is music—such as is heard only in Abdera."

"You are very polite! Indeed, our nomophylax is a great man in his way."

"Quite certainly!"

"So you are presumably not content with the actors?"

"I am content with the whole world."

"I would think, though, that Andromeda played her role charmingly?"

"Oh, very charmingly!"

"She's very effective, isn't she?"

"You probably know that best; for that I'm not young enough any more."

"At least you'll admit that Perseus is a great actor?"

"Indeed, a handsome, well-built man!"

"And the *choruses?* Those were surely choruses that did honor to the master! Didn't you, for example, find the idea of getting the Nereïds onto the stage that way uncommonly successful?"

The foreigner appeared to have had enough of the Abderites. "I find," he answered with some impatience, "that the Abderites are fortunate in enjoying all these things so much."

"Sir," the young peacock said in a derisive tone, "just admit that the play did not have the honor and good fortune of getting your approval."

"What interest do you have in my approval? The *majority decides.*"

"You're right there. But, I would for the sake of the gods though, like to hear what you could say against our music or against our actors."

"Could say?" the foreigner said somewhat quickly, but immediately checked himself again. "Pardon me, I don't wish to argue with anyone about his amusements. The play, as it was performed here, was generally liked in Abdera. What more do you want?"

"Not so generally, since you didn't like it!"

"I am a foreigner—"

"Foreign or not, I would like to hear your reasons! Hee, hee, hee! Your reasons, sir, your reasons. But they, at least, will not be foreign? Hee, hee, hee, hee!"

The foreigner began to lose his patience. "Young sir," he said, "I *paid* for my share of your play, for I *clapped* like the others. Let it go at that. I am about to depart again. I have to go about my business."

"Indeed, indeed," said another Abderite young man who had been listening to the conversation, "you surely don't want to leave us already? You appear to be a great expert. You've aroused our curiosity, our eagerness to have you teach us" (he said this with a stupidly impertinent sneer). "We really will not let you go until you've told us what fault you find with today's lyrical drama. I don't want to say anything about *the words,* because I'm no expert. But the music, I would think, was, after all, incomparable."

"That, surely the *words,* as you call them, would have to decide," the foreigner said.

"How do you mean that? I think music is music, and you only need to have ears to hear what's beautiful."

"I admit, if you wish," the former answered, "that there are beautiful passages in this music. It may in general be erudite music composed in due style according to all the academic rules of art; I have nothing against it. I only say that *it is not the music for the Andromeda of Euripides!"*

"You mean that the words should be better expressed?"

"Oh, *the words* are occasionally expressed *all too well;* but on the whole, gentlemen, on the whole, the *sense* and *tone of the poet* have been missed. The *character* of the roles, truth of the emotions and feelings, the *inherent decorum* of the situations—what the music can and ought to be in order to be the language of nature, the language of emotion—what it has to be for the poet to swim on it as if in his element, and not drown—all that is absolutely unsuccessful—in short, *the whole thing is no good!* There you have my confession in a few words."

"The whole thing," shouted both Abderites, *"the whole thing is no good?* Now that's saying a lot! We'd just like to hear how you'd go about proving that!"

The liveliness with which our two defenders of their national taste vigorously attacked the graybearded foreigner had already attracted various other Abderites. Everybody's attention was called to a quarrel that appeared to concern the honor of the National Theater. Everyone crowded around, and the foreigner, although he was a tall, imposing man, found it necessary to withdraw to a pillar in order to keep at least his back free.

"How I would go about proving that?" he answered quite composed. "I will *not* prove it! If you have read the play, seen the performance, heard the music, and can still demand that I should prove my opinion of it to you, then I would lose my time and breath if I had anything further to do with you."

"This gentleman, as I hear, is a little hard to satisfy," a councillor said who wished to join in the conversation and for whom the two young Abderites respectfully made way. "We here in Abdera have ears, too, after all! To be sure, everyone is allowed his freedom; but yet—"

"How is that? What? What's going on here?" shouted *the short, fat councillor,* who also came waddling up. "Does this man have some fault to find with the play? That I'd like to hear, ha, ha, ha! One of the best plays, upon my honor, on our stage for a long time! A lot of action. A lot of —ah—ah. What I'm saying. A fine play. And a fine moral!"

"Gentlemen," the foreigner said, "I must attend to my own business. I came here to rest up a little. I clapped the way your country's custom demands and would have proceeded on my way, quietly and peacefully, if these young men here had not compelled me in the most obtrusive way to give them my opinion."

"You also have a perfect right to it," answered the other councillor, who was at bottom no great admirer of the nomophylax and for political reasons had for some time been waiting for an opportunity to cause him distress in a harmless way. "You are a connoisseur of music, as it appears, and—"

"I speak in accordance with my convictions," the foreigner said.

The Abderites round about him were getting louder and louder.

Finally, Mr. Gryllus in person came, too, who, from a distance, had heard that his music was being discussed. He had a quite peculiar way of drawing his eyes together, turning up his nose, shrugging his shoulders, grinning, and speaking in a tremulous voice whenever he wished to have someone with whom he was engaged in a dispute feel his contempt beforehand. "So?" he said, "Did my composition not have the good fortune to please the gentleman? So he's an expert? Heh, heh, heh! Understands the art of composition, no doubt? Ha?"

"It is the nomophylax!" somebody spoke into the foreigner's ear—in order to knock him down suddenly through the discovery of the high rank of the man whose works he had judged so unfavorably.

The foreigner bowed to the nomophylax, as was the custom in Abdera, and said nothing.

"Well, I would just like to hear what the gentleman might have to bring up against the composition! I will not defend the mistakes made by the *orchestra;* but a hundred drachmae for *one* mistake in the *composition!* Heh, heh, heh! Well! Let's hear!"

"I don't know what you call *mistakes,*" the foreigner said; "to my way of thinking, all the music we are talking about has only one flaw."

"And that is?" grinned the nomophylax sneering.

"That the sense and spirit of the poet have been missed entirely."

"So? Nothing more? Heh, heh, heh, heh! So I'm supposed to

have failed to *understand* the poet? And *you know that?* Do you think that we here don't also understand Greek? Or is it, perhaps the case that you've been sitting in the poet's head? Hee, hee, hee!"

"I know what I am talking about," the foreigner replied. "And if, then, it has to be that way, I offer to prove my opinion, line by line through the entire play, at Olympia[45] before all of Greece."

"That might entail too much trouble," said the political councillor.

"It's not necessary either," the nomophylax cried. "There's a ship leaving for Athens tomorrow. I will write to *Euripides,* to the *poet himself.* I'll send him the entire score! You will surely not claim to understand the play, sir, better than the poet himself. All of you here will sign your names as *witnesses. Euripides* himself shall pronounce his opinion."

"You can spare yourself this effort," the foreigner said smiling, "for in order to put an end to this dispute with a word, *I myself am* that Euripides to whom you are appealing."

Among all the possible nasty tricks which Euripides could have played on the nomophylax of Abdera, the nastiest was certainly that, at the moment when they appealed to him as to someone absent, he stood there in person. But who could ever foresee a trick like that? What business, by Anubis!, did he have being in Abdera? And precisely at the moment at which they would have preferred to see the Lernaean Hydra[46] to seeing him. If, as they naturally had to believe, after all, he had been in Athens, where he belonged—well, then everything would have gone its regular way. The nomophylax would have sent a nice letter along with his score and added all of his titles and honors to his name. That should have made an impression, surely. Euripides would have given an urbane Attic answer; *Gryllus* would have had it read in all of Abdera; and who, then, would have wanted to dispute his victory over the foreigner? But that the *foreigner,* that impertinent, critical foreigner who had spoken right up and said to his face what no one in Abdera was allowed to say to a nomophylax's face, was Euripides himself; that was one of those coincidences for which a man like him had not been prepared and that would be capable of defeating anyone else but—an Abderite.

The nomophylax could take care of himself; however, the initial blow did bewilder him for a moment. "Euripides!" he cried and recoiled three paces; and at the same moment the political councillor, the short, fat councillor, the two young men, and all the persons standing about cried "Euripides!" while they looked around quite astonished, as if they wanted to see from which cloud Euripides had so suddenly fallen down into their midst.

A human being is never more disinclined to believe than whenever he is surprised by an event that he had not thought about at all as something possible. What? That was supposed to be Euripides? The same Euripides they had been talking about? Who had written the *Andromeda?* To whom the nomophlax threatened to write? How was that possible?

The *political councillor* was the first to recover from the general amazement. "A fortunate coincidence, truly," he cried, "by Castor, a fortunate coincidence, Sir Nomophylax! So you don't need to have a copy of your music written, and you will be spared writing a letter."

The nomophylax felt the entire importance of the moment, and if he is a great man who, in such a decisive moment, immediately takes the only side that can draw him out of the difficulty, then it must be admitted that Gryllus had a great natural tendency to be a great man. "Euripides!" he cried—"how's that? The gentleman is so *suddenly* supposed to have become Euripides? Heh, heh, heh! That's a good one! But here in Abdera we don't so easily allow people to give us black for white."

"That would be comical," said the foreigner, "if in Abdera I had to allow the right to my name to be disputed."

"Pardon me, sir," the *sycophant of Thrasyllus* interrupted him, "not the right to your name, but the right to pass yourself off as the Euripides to whom the nomophylax was going to appeal. Your name can be Euripides; however, whether you *are* Euripides, that is a different question."

"Gentlemen," the foreigner said, "I will be whatever you like, if only you permit me to leave. I promise you that with this step I will follow the straightest path I can find through your gate, and the nomophylax is—*to write a composition* on me if I ever return in my life!"

"Nay, nay, nay," cried the nomophylax, "it won't go as swiftly as that! The gentleman has passed himself off as Euripides, and now that he sees that matters are getting serious, he's getting up on his hind legs. Nay! that's not what we agreed upon. Go ahead and prove you are Euripides, or—as truly as my name is *Gryllus*—"

"Don't get excited, colleague," said the *political councillor.* "I am, indeed, no physiognomist,[47] but to me the foreigner seems entirely to look as if he could be Euripides; and, in my humble opinion, it would be advisable to proceed with caution."

"I am astonished," one of the bystanders began, "that you are wasting so many words here, since the entire dispute could be decided with yes and no. There, up over the portal, stands the bust of Euripides, you know, as large as life. Nothing further is needed, don't you see, than to find out whether the foreigner looks like the bust."

"Bravo, bravo," cried the small, fat councillor, "now that is a shrewd man talking! Ha, ha, ha! The bust. There's no question at all, the bust will have to give the verdict—although it cannot talk, ha, ha, ha, ha, ha!"

The Abderites standing about all laughed loudly at the small, round little man's flash of wit, and now everything with feet ran towards the portal. The foreigner resigned himself good-naturedly to his fate, allowed people to look at him from in front and behind, and to compare him, detail by detail, with his *bust* as long as they wished. But unfortunately, it was impossible for the comparison to turn out to his advantage, for the aforesaid bust resembled any other human being or animal more than *him*.

"Now," the nomoplax shouted triumphant, "what can the gentleman say now to what is standing before him?"

"I can say something," replied the foreigner, whom the comedy by now began to amuse, "of which none of you all seems to be thinking, although it is just as true as that you—are Abderites and I am Euripides."

"Say it, say it," smirked the nomophylax, "a lot can certainly be said when the day is long, heh, heh, heh! And what can the gentleman say?"

"I say that this bust bears no resemblance at all to Euripides."

"No sir," cried *the fat councillor,* "you must not say that! The bust is a fine bust; it is of white marble, as you see, of Parian marble, may Jupiter strike me down, and cost us one hundred darics cash in specie, you can say that I said so! It is a fine piece by our *municipal sculptor.* A clever, famous man! Calls himself *Moschion.* You've probably heard of him? A famous man! And, as I have said, all of the foreigners who have ever come to us have admired that bust. It is genuine. You can repeat that. You yourself see, don't you that at the bottom of it there is inscribed with large golden letters ΕΥΡΙΠΙΔΗΣ.[48]

"Gentlemen," said the foreigner, who had to collect all of his inborn gravity so as not to burst out, "may I ask only one single question?"

"By all means do so," cried the Abderites.

"In case," the former continued, "a dispute should arise between *me* and *my bust* over who resembles me—whom will you wish to believe, the *bust* or *me?*"

"That is a *curious* question," said one of the Abderites scratching himself behind the ears. "A *captious* question, by Jupiter," cried another, "be careful, highly esteemed Councillor, how you answer!"

"Is the corpulent gentleman a councillor of this famous Republic?" the foreigner asked with a bow, "then I very much beg your pardon! I admit that the bust is a handsome, sleek work, of beautiful Parian marble. And if it does not resemble me, that is probably only because your famous municipal sculptor has made the bust better looking than nature made—me. It is, in any case, evidence of his good will, and it deserves all of my gratitude."

This compliment was very effective, for the Abderites liked overmuch to be spoken to in a nice and polite way.

"It must be Euripides after all," one murmured into the other's ear. And the fat councillor himself observed, after once again comparing the bust with the foreigner, that *the beards* were perfectly similar to one another.

By good fortune, the archon *Onolaus* arrived and with him his nephew Onobulus, who had seen Euripides in Athens a hundred times and spoken to him often. The joy of young *Onobulus* at such an unexpected meeting, and his positive assertion that the foreigner really was the famous Euripides, suddenly cut through the knot. The Abderites now assured one another that *they could tell who he was right off with the first glance.*

The nomophylax, as he saw that Euripides turned out to be right about his bust, went to one side and took to his heels. "A damned trick!" he muttered to himself through his teeth. "But why did he ever need to keep us in the dark that way? If he knew that he was Euripides, why didn't he have himself presented to me? Then everything would have turned out quite differently!"

The archon *Onolaus,* who in such cases generally was accustomed to doing the honors of the City of Abdera, invited the poet with great courtesy to be his guest at his home, and at the same time he insisted on having the honor of the political and the fat councillors' company that evening, and both accepted with much pleasure.

"Didn't I think so right away?" the fat councillor said to one of the bystanders. "Euripides in person. Beard, nose, forehead, the lobes of his ears, eyebrows, everything down to a hair! Something more similar can't be seen! I just wonder where the nomophylax kept his senses! But—yes, yes, he might just have had a little bit too much—Hm! You get what I mean?—*Cantores amant hu-*

mores[49]—Ha, ha, ha, ha! Enough! All the better that we have Euripides with us. I tell you, he's a fine man, by Jupiter! and he's going to give us a lot of fun! Ha, ha, ha!"

Chapter Seven

What led Euripides to Abdera, along with some secret information about the court at Pella.

As possible as it was in itself that Euripides could be in Abdera, and just as well at the moment when the nomophylax Gryllus appealed to him, as in any other place—and as accustomed as one is to such unexpected apparitions *on the stage,* we do, indeed, understand that it is quite a different matter when such an apparition shows up in real life. And in such a case, it is in conformity with *the majesty of history** to inform the reader how it happened. We wish to report faithfully everything we know about it. And if the sagacious reader should, in spite of this, still have some doubts, they would concern only the general question that can be raised about any event under and over the moon, to wit: *why,* for example, precisely by a *gnat,* and precisely by *this* individual *gnat,* at precisely this second—of this tenth minute—of this sixth hour in the afternoon, of this tenth of August of this 1778th year of our common chronology, was precisely this very Mrs. or Miss ∗ ∗ ∗ stung—not in the face, not in the nape of the neck, elbow, or bosom, not on the hand nor in the heel, and so on, but rather precisely four thumbs high above her left kneecap, and so on—and here we are not timid in admitting that we not know how to answer this *why. Ask the gods!* we could say in any event, to quote a great man. But because this would obviously be a *heroic* answer, we consider it more seemly merely to let the matter rest. Now then—what we know.

King Archelaus[50] of Macedonia, a great lover of the fine arts and of beaux-esprits (as at that time certain pampered children of nature were *not* called and as these days everybody is called of whom one cannot say what he is)—this King Archelaus had got the idea of having his own court theater. And by virtue of a concatenation of circumstances, reasons, means, and purposes, which cannot matter much to anybody any longer, he had prevailed upon Euripi-

---

*An expression that was recently used by a French writer on such an occasion that it can now be regarded as irreparably ruined and can still be tolerated only in a farce.

des to come to Pella to his court, under very advantageous conditions, with a company of select actors, musicians, architects, painters, and a stage crew, in short, with everything that belongs to a complete stage, and to take over the supervision of the new court theater.

Euripides was now on this journey with his entire company; and although the way via Abdera was neither the only one nor the shortest, he took it, nevertheless, because he wanted to see with his own eyes a republic so famous because of the wit of its inhabitants. But how it happened that he just arrived on the same day when the nomophylax gave his *Andromeda* for the first time, of that we can, as I have said, give no account. Coincidences of that sort happen more frequently than one thinks. And it is at least no greater miracle than that, for example, the young gentleman * * was just at the point of pulling up his breeches, when unexpectedly his seamstress entered the room to bring the silk stockings he had sent her to darn—which, as you know, was the occason of an accidental occurrence that in his prominent family produced commotions just as great as the unprepared appearance of Euripides in the Abderite theater audience. Whoever can be surprised about something like that must not understand the ΔΑΙΜΟΝΙΑ[51] well, as just this Euripides says.

By the way, when we said that *King Archelaus* was a great lover of the fine arts and beaux-esprits, this must not be taken quite so exactly and in the strictest sense of the words, for it is only a manner of speaking, and this lord was at bottom nothing less than a lover of the fine arts and beaux-esprits. The truth of the matter was that the aforesaid King Archelaus had for some time often been bored—because all of his former amusements, for example F * *, G * *, H * *, J * *, K * *, L * *, M * *, and so on, would no longer amuse him. Moreover, he was a gentleman of great *ambition*, who had allowed his Lord High Chamberlain to persuade him that it had absolutely belonged among the responsibilities of a great prince to put the arts and sciences under his protection. "For," the Lord High Chamberlain said, "your Majesty probably has observed that one never sees a statue or a half-length portrait of a great man on a medal, and so on, at the right hand of which there is not standing a *Minerva* next to a trophy of armor, banners, spears, and maces—to the left there are always kneeling some winged boys or half-naked girls, with paintbrush and palette, a square, a flute, a lyre, and a paper scroll in their hands, representing the arts, that commend themselves, as it were, to the great lord for his protection; at the top above it, however, there hovers a woman representing fame, with a trumpet raised to her lips to intimate that kings and princes earn immortal fame, and so on, through the protection they bestow on the arts."

King Archelaus, therefore, had put the arts *under* his *protection,* and the historians can, accordingly, relate at length and in detail how much building he had done and how much he spent on paintings and statuary, on beautiful tapestries and other beautiful furnishings; and how he required that everything down to the toilet had to be in Etruscan style; and how he had summoned famous artists, musicians, and beaux-esprits and so on, to his court, all of which he did so much the more (they say) to extinghish the memory of the misdeeds by which he had forced his way to the throne, to which he was not born—as, your worships, you can learn from your Bayle[52] along with other things.

After this small digression, we return to our Attic poet, whom we will meet in a glittering circle of Abderite men and women of the first rank under a green pavilion in the garden of the *archon Onolaus.*

Chapter Eight

How Euripides conducts himself with the Abderites. They mount a conspiracy against him, in connection with which their political hustle and bustle appears in a strong light, and which must succeed all the more certainly because all the difficulties they see involved in it are merely imagined.

It has already been observed above that Euripides, although he was not known to them personally, had been enjoying the Abderites' great esteem for a long time. Now, as soon as word got out that he was present in person, the entire city was in commotion. People talked about nothing but Euripides.

"Have you already seen Euripides?"

"How does he look?"

"Does he have a big nose?"

"How does he hold his head?"

"What sort of eyes does he have?"

"He probably talks in nothing but poetry!"

"Is he proud?"—and they asked one another a hundred such questions more rapidly than it was possible to answer one.

The curiosity to see Euripides attracted, in addition to such people as the archon had asked, others who had not been invited. They all crowded around the good, baldheaded poet in order to see with their own eyes whether he really looked like what they imagined he would have to look like. Various ones, particularly among the ladies, appeared to be surprised that, in the end, he looked, after all, like any other human being. Others observed that he had a lot of fire in his eyes. And beautiful *Thryallis* whispered into her neighbor's ear that one could very clearly see that he was a confirmed woman-hater.* She made this remark with an expression of anticipated pleasure over the triumph that she was promising herself when such a professed enemy of her sex would have to admit the power of her charms.

Stupidity has its sublime degree as does intelligence, and he who can go as far as the absurd in it has achieved the sublime of this sort, which is always a source of amusement for sensible people. The Abderites had the good fortune of being in possession of this perfection. In the beginning, to be sure, their absurdity made a foreigner impatient now and then, but as soon as one saw that they were so all of one piece and (just for that reason) had in them so much trust and good nature, one immediately reconciled oneself with them and often amused oneself more with their foolishness than with the wit of others.

Never in his life had Euripides been in such a good mood as at this Abderite feast. He answered all of their questions with the greatest complaisance, laughed at all their trite notions, let each person pass as being no less worthy than he rated himself, and even talked about their theater and music in such a reasonable way that everyone was content with him.

"A fine fellow to have as a guest!" the political councillor whispered into the ear of Dame Salabanda, who sat closer to the guest than he, "he treads lightly!"

"And is so polite, so modest, as if he didn't have a great mind!" Salabanda answered.

"The most amusing man in the world, by Jupiter!" the short, fat councillor said as he got up from the table, "a really diverting man! I wouldn't have expected it of him, my soul!"

The ladies he had found to be *beautiful* were, in return, so polite and acted as if they thought him twenty years younger than he was. In short, people were completely enchanted with him and only regretted that they were not to have the *honor* and *pleasure* of seeing him in Abdera for a longer time. For Euripides persisted in saying that he could not stay.

---

*It is well known that Euripides was accused, although undeservedly, of having this odious vice.

Finally, Dame Salabanda took the political councillor and young Onobulus aside. "What do you think," she asked, "couldn't we persuade him to put on *Andromeda* for us? He has his own troupe with him. They're said to be extraordinary performers."

Onobulus thought the idea was *divine.*

"Why, I had the same idea myself," the political councillor said, "and was about to suggest it to you. But there are going to be difficulties. The nomophylax—"

"Oh, let me take care of that," Salabanda interrupted him. "I'll make things hot for him, all right!"

"I can easily believe, madam, that you'll be able to do that," the councillor replied with a sly glance. "However, before anything else we have to sound out the archon."

"I vouch for my uncle," *Onobulus* said, "and still before morning I'll drum up a party from among us young people that will make enough of a racket all over town."

"Not too rash," muttered *the political councillor* shaking his head. "We don't want to betray our intentions! First, get the lay of the land, then proceed very gently. That's what I always say."

"But we have no time to lose, Sir Frog-Guardian!* Euripides is leaving—"

"We'll make him stay longer, all right," Salabanda answered. He's supposed to be *at my house* tomorrow! Let's have a garden party and invite all of our fine people to it. Let *me* go ahead. It will work, I'm sure."

Dame Salabanda was considered in Abdera to be a very wise woman. She was very politically minded and had much influence on the archon Onolaus. The chief priest was her uncle, and five or six councillors, whom she counted among her friends, rarely expressed any opinion in the Council other than the one she had put in their head the evening before. Moreover, the lovers of beautiful *Thryallis,* with whom she lived on terms of closest confidence, were entirely at her beck and call, to say nothing of her own, of which she always had a few who served in expectation and were, therefore, as pliable as gloves. Her house, that belonged among the best in the city, was the place where all affairs were prepared, all quarrels made up, and all elections settled. In a word, Dame Salabanda did what she wanted in Abdera.

---

*The councillor was one of those who cared for the hallowed Frog Pond, which, in Abdera, was a very considerable position. Such people were called *Batrachotropheis,* which can very appropriately be rendered in German with *Froschpfleger* (Frog-Guardian).

Euripides, without the slightest intention of making use of the importance of this woman, had on this evening insinuated himself so well with her as if, at the very least, he had been aiming at the position of a Frog-Guardian. If she uttered a political platitude as an idea, he found it to be a very sagacious remark. If she quoted Simonides[53] or Homer, he admired her talent in declaiming verses. She had teased him with a few passages from his works that in Athens had given him the bad reputation of being a misogynist. And he had, while he was bowing to her and to beautiful Thryallis, given his assurance that it was his misfortune not to have come to Abdera any sooner. In short, he had so conducted himself that Dame Salabanda was ready to raise a revolt in case her project devised with the political councillor could not be accomplished by any more gentle means.

They did not delay in assuring themselves, before anything else, of the *archon,* who was, generally, soon won over, if he was told that a thing would redound to the great glory of the Republic of Abdera and that the people would find it very pleasant. But, because he was a gentleman who loved his peace and quiet, he declared that he was leaving it to them to get everything started on the right road. He, for his part, would not like to have a falling out with anyone about it, least of all with the nomophylax, who was a rude fellow and had a strong following among the populace.

"Don't worry about the people, your Excellency," the councillor whispered to him. "I'll have somebody take care of that, have no fear, as well as we could wish."

"And I," Salabanda said, "will be responsible for the councillors."

"We'll see," the archon said and went back to the company.

"Do be calm," the lady said to the political councillor while taking him aside. "I know the archon. If you wish to have him on your side, you only have to talk about a thing in the evening to him, and, if he's said *no,* come back the next morning, and, with a straight face, talk just as if he had said *yes,* and at the same time show him that you're certain of success. Then you can rely on him as on gold. It is not the first time that I've brought him around in this way."

"You are a sly woman," the Frog-Guardian replied while gently tapping her on her round arm. "How gently you tread! But people will notice that we're planning something—and that would be to our disadvantage. We must proceed cautiously!"

At this moment a few Abderite women came tripping up, whom all the rest of the company soon followed in order to hear what they were talking about. The political councillor stole away.

"Well, how do you like Euripides?" asked Dame Salabanda, "that is a real man, don't you agree?"

"Oh, a charming man," the Abderite women cried.

"But it's too bad that he's so bald," one of them added, "and that he's missing a few teeth," the other said.

"You little fool, the harder for him to bite you," the third said, and because this was a witty remark, they all laughed heartily about it.

"Is he already married?" a young thing asked that looked as if, like a mushroom, she had sprung up out of the ground in one single night.

"Would you like to have him, maybe?" another young woman answered sarcastically. "I think he already has great-grandsons to give in marriage."

"Oh, I'll let you have them," the former said pertly. And the sting of her remark was all the more like that of a wasp because the other young woman, even though she acted as young as a girl of eighteen, was burdened with at least a full thirty-five years.

"Girls," Dame Salabanda interrupted them, "all that is now off the subject. We're talking about something quite different. How would you like to have me persuade the foreign gentleman to stay here for a few days and to put on one of his plays for us with the troupe he has brought with him?"

"Oh, that is splendid!" cried all the Abderite women hopping gleefully, "oh yes, if only you could get him to!"

"I'll get him to, all right," Salabanda replied, "but you're all go-ling to have to help."

"Oh yes, oh yes!" the women chattered. And now they ran in a large group up to Euripides, and all shouted at the same time: "Oh yes, Mr. Euripides, you must put on a play for us! We will not let you go until you've put on a play for us. You will, won't you? Give us your promise?"

The poor man, who was struck by this suggestion as if someone had thrown a bucket of water on his head, retreated a few steps and assured them it had never occurred to him to put on a play in Abdera, that he had to resume his journey with all haste, and so on. But all that did not help.

"Oh, but you *must*," the women cried. "We will not leave you alone. You're much too gallant to refuse us anything. We're asking you so nicely—"

"Seriously," Dame Salabanda said, "we've mounted a plot against you."

"And it's not going to fail," Onobulus interrupted her, "or my name's not Onobulus."

"What's going on, what's going on?" asked the political councillor, who acted as if he knew nothing about all this, while slowly and with a shifting gaze he stole up to the group. "What are you asking of the gentleman?"

The short, fat councillor came waddling up, too. "I'm ready to believe, strike me, you all want to lay hold of his heart at the same time, ha, ha, ha!" he shouted and laughed so hard he had to hold his sides.

They informed him what they were talking about.

"Ha, ha, ha! A fine idea, may Jupiter strike me down! I'll certainly be coming to that, too, I promise you that! The master himself! That's got to be worth the trouble! Will be a really great honor for Abdera, Mr. Euripides, a great honor! We have to consider ourselves lucky that our people will get to profit from such a skillful man!"

A few other important men paid him approximately the same compliment.

Euripides, although he did not find the idea so bad of having this fun with the Abderites, kept acting as if he were astonished and used as his excuse the promise he had made to King Archelaus to hasten his journey.

"Oh come now!" Onobulus said, "you are a republican, and a republic has a prior claim on you."

"Just tell the King," said beautiful Myris stridently, "that we did ask you so very nicely. He is said to be a gallant gentleman. He will not be offended with you for not being able to refuse something to six women at once."

"Oh you, Love, tyrant over gods and men!" cried Euripides in the tone of the tragedy, while at the same time he was looking at beautiful *Thryallis*.

"If you're serious about that," said Thryallis with the countenance of a person who is not used to refusing nor to being refused, "if you're serious about that, then prove it by agreeing to do what I want."

This "I want" vexed the other Abderite women. "We don't wish to be immodest," one of them said while she drew in her lips and looked aside.

"We must not demand of the gentleman what is impossible for him," another said.

"To amuse you, my beautiful ladies," the poet said, "the impossible could become possible for me."

Because this was nonsense, they all liked it. Onobulus whipped out his writing tablet in order to note the idea down. The women and girls cast a glance at Thryallis as if they wanted to say: "So there! He called us beautiful, too! You don't need to be so conceited about your Atalanta[54] figure, madam! He's going to stay on as much because of us as because of you."

Salabanda finally put an end to the dispute by only asking for the favor that he might still grant her and her friends, who were all great admirers of his, no more than the next day. Because Euripides, after all, was not in a hurry and enjoyed being in Abdera very much, he did not let them ask him a long time to accept their invitation that promised him fine material for—farcical comedies for the Court at Pella. And so then, with everyone feeling pleased and looking forward to the honor of meeting one another again the following day at Dame Salabanda's house, the social gathering dispersed toward midnight.

Chapter Nine

Euripides views the city, becomes acquainted with the priest Strobylus and hears from him the history of the Frogs of Latona. Remarkable conversation which takes place on this occasion between Democritus, the priest, and the poet.

Meanwhile Onobulus, accompanied by some young men of his sort, conducted his guest around the city in order to show him everything that might be worth seeing in it. On the way they met *Democritus*, with whom Euripides had already been acquainted for a long time. So they walked together. And since the city of Abdera was rather extensive, the two old men had opportunity enough to profit from the young gentlemen, who always had their mouths open, gave judgments on everything, knew everything, and did not at all allow it to enter their heads that, in the presence of men, it was more befitting for the likes of them to listen than to make themselves heard.

So Euripides had enough to hear and see on this morning. The young Abderites, who had never got farther than to the toll bars at the edge of their native city, talked about all the things they showed him as if they were marvels that did not at all have their equals in the world. Onobulus, who, to the contrary, had made the grand tour, compared everything with what he had seen of just this sort in Athens, Corinth, and Syracuse,[55] and brought up, in a silly tone of apology, a lot of ridiculous reasons why these things in Athens, Corinth, and Syracuse were finer and more splendid than in Abdera.

"Young man," *Democritus* said, "it is nice that you honor the city of your father and mother; but if you wish to give us proof of that, then leave out your references to Athens, Corinth, and Syracuse. Let us take each thing as it is, and no comparison. Then no apology is necessary either."

Euripides found everything he was shown to be very remarkable, and it was, too. For he was shown a library with many useless and unread books; a coin collection with many worn-down coins; a rich hospital with badly nursed poor people; an arsenal with few weapons; and a fountain in which there was even less water. He was also shown the meeting house of the Council, the city hall, where the good city of Abdera was so well counseled; the Temple of *Jason* and a gilt ram's skin which, although there was little gold to be seen on it any more, they passed off for the famous Golden Fleece. They also viewed the old smoky Temple of *Latona,* the tomb of *Abderus,* who was said to have first built the city, and the gallery, where all the archons of Abdera stood painted in life-size portraits, and all of them so resembled one another as if the next one had always been the copy of the one preceding. Finally, when they had seen everything, they were also taken to the Hallowed Pond, in which, at public expense, the biggest and fattest frogs ever seen were fed and which, as the *chief priest Strobylus* very earnestly assured them, were descended in a straight line from the Lycian peasants who would not permit *Latona,* wandering about, finding no rest anywhere, and dying of thirst, to drink from a pond that belonged to them, and for that were transformed into frogs by Jupiter in punishment of their uncivilized behavior.

"Oh, Sir Chief Priest," Democritus said, "why don't you relate to the foreign gentleman the history of these frogs and how it happened that the Hallowed Pond was transferred from Lycia across the Ionian Sea[56] over to Abdera—which, as you know, amounts to a pretty considerable distance overland and sea and (if one may say so) is almost a greater miracle itself than the Lycian peasants' transformation into frogs."

Strobylus looked Democritus and the foreigner in the eye. However, because he could see nothing therein that would have justified his declaring them mockers who did not deserve being admitted to such venerable mysteries, he asked them to sit down under a large wild fig tree that shaded one side of the little Temple of Latona and thereupon related to them, with the very same ingenuousness with which one can tell about the most ordinary occurrence, everything he thought he knew about the matter.

"The history of the service of Latona in Abdera," he said, "is lost in the mist of grayest antiquity. Our forefathers, the Teians, who had made themselves masters of Abdera about a hundred forty years ago, found it had already been introduced from time immemorial; and this temple here is, perhaps, one of the oldest in the world, as you can already conclude from its style and other signs of its high antiquity. It is, as you know, not allowed out of culpable inquisitiveness to lift the holy veil that time has thrown about the origin of the gods and their service. Everything disappears in times when the art of writing had not yet been invented. However, oral tradition, that was transmitted from father to son through so many centuries, compensates more than adequately for the loss of written records and constitutes, so to speak, a living record, that is reasonably still to be preferred to the dead letter. This tradition says: when the aforementioned transformation of the Lycian peasants occurred, the neighboring inhabitants and a few of the aforesaid peasants themselves who had had no part in the crime of the rest had, as witnesses of the miracle that had taken place, recognized Latona with her twins, Apollo and Diana, still at her breast, as deities, erected an altar to them at the pond where the transformation had happened, and also hallowed the tract of land and the bushes that surrounded the pond. The country was at that time still called *Milia,* and the peasants transformed into frogs were, properly speaking, therefore *Milians.* When, however, a long time thereafter, *Lycus,* the son of Pandion II,[57] seized an Attic colony in the country, it received the name *Lycia* from him, and the older name disappeard entirely. On this occasion the inhabitants of the region where the altar and grove of Latona were situated left their native land because they did not wish to submit to the rule of the aforesaid Lycus, boarded ship, wandered about for a time on the Aegean Sea, and finally settled in Abdera, that had a short time before been almost entirely depopulated by the plague. At their departure, nothing pained them so much as that they had to leave the hallowed grove and pond of Latona behind. They pondered this and that and finally found that it would be best to take along a few young trees from the aforesaid grove, with roots and earth, and a number of frogs from the aforesaid pond in a tun full of hallowed water. As soon as they arrived in Abdera, their first concern was to dig a new pond, which is precisely this one that you see before you.

"They diverted a tributary of the *Nestus River*[58] into it and stocked it with the descendants of the Lycians or Milians that had been transformed into frogs that they had brought along with them in the holy water. Round about the pond, to which they carefully gave the complete form and size of the old one, they planted the holy trees they brought with them, consecrated them anew as the grove of Latona, built her this temple, and appointed a priest, who was in charge of its service and was to look after the grove and the pond, which in this way, without such a great miracle as Mr. Democritus considered necessary, were transplanted from Lycia to Abdera. This temple, grove, and pond were maintained, by virtue of the respect that even the neighboring wild Thracians entertained for them, through all the vicissitudes and disasters to which Abdera was subsequently subjected, until the city, at the time of the great Cyrus,[59] was reestablished by the Teians, our ancestors, and, as may be said without boastfulness, was brought to such a splendor that it has no reason to envy any other in the world."

"You speak like a true patriot, Sir Chief Priest," *Euripides* said. "But if I were allowed to ask a modest question—"

"Ask whatever you wish," Strobylus interrupted him. "I will never, praise be to God, be at a loss for an answer."

"With the permission of your reverence, then," Euripides continued, "the whole world is acquaintd with the noble turn of mind and the love of magnificence and of the fine arts that is characteristic of the Teian Abderites and of which their city displays everywhere the most remarkable proofs. So how does it happen, all the more since the Teians, even from olden times, enjoy the reputation of having a special reverence for Latona, that the Abderites did not get the idea of building her a more imposing temple?"

"I was expecting this objection," Strobylus said with a smile while he drew up his eyebrows and wished to appear mightily wise.

"It's not supposed to be an objection," Euripides replied, "but rather a modest question merely."

"I will give you my answer," the priest said. "Without a doubt, it would have been easy for the Republic to erect just as magnificent a temple to Latona, as a *goddess of the first rank,* as it has built for Jason, who is, after all, *only a hero.* But it justly believed that it was more suitable to the reverence we owe the mother of Apollo and Diana, to leave her ancient temple as it had been found. And it is and remains, in spite of that, the chief and holiest temple in Abdera, whatever objections the priest of Jason may have about it."

Strobylus said this last with such zeal and such a *crescendo il forte* that Democritus found it necessary to assure him that this, at least among all soundly thinking people, was a foregone conclusion.

"Meanwhile," the chief priest continued, "the Republic has, however, given such proofs of its special devotion for the Temple of

Latona and its appurtenances that there can remain not the slightest doubt about the sincerity of its intentions. For performing the service it has not only appointed a staff of six priests, whose head I have the honor to be, although I am unworthy, but also three Guardians of the Hallowed Frog Pond from the midst of the Senate, of which the first is always one of the city's leaders. Indeed, from motives, to dispute the correctness of which is no longer permitted, it has extended the inviolability of the frogs in the Pond of Latona to all the animals of this species in its entire territory, and to this end has banished from its borders the entire race of storks, cranes, and all other enemies of frogs."

"If the assurance that it is no longer permitted to doubt the correctness of this policy did not bind my tongue," Democritus said, "then I would take the liberty of reminding you that it appears to be based rather on a *deisidaemonia,** praiseworthy in itself, to be sure, but driven to extremes nevertheless, than on the nature of the thing or on the reverence we owe to Latona. For, as a matter of fact, nothing is more certain than that the frogs in Abdera and in the region around it, that are already very troublesome to the inhabitants, will, under such protection, with time increase so superabundantly that I do not comprehend how our descendants will be able to come to terms with them. I am speaking here merely *from the human point of view* and submit my opinion to the judgment of the authorities, as is proper for a right-minded Abderite."

"In that you do well," Strobylus said, "whether you are serious or not; and you would, do not take offense at my saying so, be doing better still if you did not express opinions of that sort at all. Moreover, nothing can be more ridiculous than to be afraid of frogs; and under the protection of Latona, we can, I think, scorn enemies more dangerous than these good, innocent little animals could ever be, even if they should become our enemies."

"I should think so, too," Euripides said. "I'm surprised how such a great naturalist like Democritus can be ignorant of the fact that frogs, that feed on insects and little snails, are much more useful to man than harmful."

The priest Strobylus received this comment so well that from this moment on he became a high patron and promoter of our poet. The gentlemen had hardly taken their leave of him, when he went

---

*The Apostle Paul uses the adjective derived from this word when he appears, ironically or at least ambiguously, to be praising the Athenians because of their boundless religiosity. Acts xvii. 22. It could be translated as *Götterfurcht* (fear of the gods) or *Dämonenfurcht* (fear of demons).[60]

to a few of the best houses and gave his assurance that Euripides was a man of great merit. "I noticed very well," he said, "that he is not on the best of terms with Democritus; he gave him one or two good ones on the noggin. He is really a nice, intelligent man—for a poet."

Chapter Ten

The Senate of Abdera gives Euripides, without his having requested it, permission to put on one of his plays in the Abderite Theater. Stratagem by means of which the Abderite Secretariat was accustomed to help in such cases. Sly behavior of the nomophylax. Remarkable way the Abderites had of giving all help to someone who stood in their way.

After Euripides had viewed all the *landmarks* of *Abdera,* he was led to Salabanda's garden, where he found the councillor, her husband, a man who was noticed only because of his wife, and a large company of fashionable Abderite society, all of them very eager to see *what a person did to be Euripides.*

Euripides saw only one way to get out of the affair with honor; and that was—not to be Euripides in such good Abderite society—but rather so very much an Abderite as was ever possible for him. The good people were surprised at finding him so similar to themselves. "He is a charming man," they said; you might think that he had been living in Abdera all his life.

Dame Salabanda's cabal, meanwhile, took its course dauntlessly, and the following morning the city was already full of the rumor that the foreign poet would put on a play with his people such as had not yet been seen in Abdera.

It was a meeting day for the Council. The gentlemen were assembling, and one asked the other when Euripides would be giving his play. None wished to admit his knowing anything about it, although everyone gave his positive assurance that the preparations for it were already under way.

When the archon introduced the matter for discussion, the friends of the nomophylax were not a little indignant about it. "Why," they asked, "is it necessary still to ask whether we will permit what has already been decided and about which everyone is talking as of a foregone conclusion?"

One of the most excited maintained that the Senate should just for that reason say no to it and show thereby that *it* was the master.

"I think that would be a nice participle,"[61] cried guild master

Pfriem. "Because the whole city is in favor of the matter and wishes to hear the foreign players, the Senate is supposed to say no to it? I maintain just the opposite. Just because the people wish to hear them, let them go ahead and play! *Fox populus, fox Deus!*[62] That has always been my *simplum*[63] and will remain so as long as my name's going to be guild master Pfriem!"

Most of them went over to the guild master's side. The political councillor shrugged his shoulders, spoke for and against it, and resolved finally that, if the nomophylax had no objections to make, then he believed that one could this time *connivendo*[64] allow the foreigners to play in the Municipal Theater.

Up until now the nomophylax had merely turned up his nose, grinned, stroked his moustache, and spoken a few abrupt words in a trembling voice with intermixed "heh, heh, heh." He did not want to have people think that he considered it desirable to thwart the affair. However, the more he wished to conceal it, the more obvious it became. He visibly became as puffed up as a turkey facing a red cloth; and finally, since he either had to burst or talk, he said: "The gentlemen may now believe what they wish—but I am really the first who wishes to hear the new play. Without a doubt, the poet wrote the text and the music himself, and that being the case, it must indeed be a real marvel. However, because he cannot stay, as people are saying, I don't see how they're going to manage with the scenery. And if we are to lend them our people for the choruses, as can be supposed, I am sorry to have to say we can't think of it any earlier than two weeks from now."

"We'll let Euripides take care of that," said one of the fathers, out of whose mouth the voice of Dame Salabanda spoke. "For honor's sake, we are going to have to leave the entire direction of his play to him anyhow."

"Without prejudice in any way to the rights of the nomophylax at any given time and to the theater committee," the archon added.

"Well and good," *Gryllus* said. "The gentlemen want to have something new—good! I hope you take joy in it. I'm eager to hear the thing myself, as I've said. Everything, of course, merely depends on whether one has faith in the people—you understand me. Meanwhile justice will remain justice, and music, music; and I'll bet whatever you gentlemen wish, the thirds, fifths, and octaves of the Athenian gentlemen will sound like ours, heh, heh, heh, heh!"

So it passed with a large majority: "That the foreign players should be allowed, once and for all and without anyone's being able to use this case as a precedent, to perform a tragedy on the National Stage and that all possible support should be given them for this on the part of the theater committee, and the costs defrayed by the treasury."

However, because the expression "should be allowed" could have been offensive to Euripides, who had asked for nothing but rather had merely acceded to requests, *Dame Salabanda* arranged for the Secretary of the Council, who was her special friend and servant, to change the words "should be allowed" in the *decree* to "should be requested" and "the foreign players" to "the famous Euripides." Everything, moreover, without prejudice to the decision of the Council and to the Secretariat, and *citra consequentiam*.[65]

As soon as the Senate meeting broke up, the nomophylax went to Euripides, overwhelmed him with compliments, offered him his services, and assured him that he would be given all possible assistance to enable him to perform his play very soon. The effect of this assurance was that, without anyone's being willing to shoulder the responsibility for it, all possible obstacles were put in his way, and everything he needed was always lacking. If he complained, then the one person always directed him to another, and each averred his innocence and his good will by explaining to him quite clearly that this person or that one was merely at fault, who a quarter of an hour ago had averred his good will just as strongly.

Euripides found the Abderite way of giving all possible assistance so onerous that he was not able to refrain from declaring to Dame Salabanda on the morning of the third day that he had a good mind to board ship again with the first wind, no matter from which direction it might blow, if she could not get the Council to order the gentlemen on the committee *to give him no assistance*. Since the archon, although really all *executive* power depended on him, was not a man to get things done, the only way in this predicament was to get guild master Pfriem and the priest Strobylus to do something, for they had much influence on the people. Salabanda took over this task with such good effect that, within a day and a night, everything that had to be provided on the part of the theater committee was finished and ready; which could happen so much more easily since Euripides had his own scenery along, and thus there was almost nothing more to do than adapt it to the Abderite stage.

Chapter Eleven

The Andromeda of Euripides is finally performed by his own actors in spite of all obstacles. The extraordinary sentimentality of the Abderites, with a digression that belongs among the most instructive in this entire work and will, consequently, be of no use at all.

The Abderites had been expecting a *new* play and were, therefore, rather disinclined to be satisfied when they heard that it was precisely the *Andromeda* that they believed they had already seen a few days before. They were even less satisfied at the beginning with the foreign actors, whose tone and action were so natural that the good people—accustomed to seeing their heroes and heroines rush about like people possessed and to hearing them shout like wounded Mars in the *Iliad*[66]—did not know at all what they should make of it. "That is a strange way to act," they whispered to one another; "you don't notice at all that you're in the theater. Why, it sounds downright as if those people were playing themselves."

Nevertheless, they did express their astonishment at the scenery that was painted in Athens by a famous master in theater perspective.[67] And since most of them had not seen anything good of this sort in their lives, they thought they were enchanted when they saw before them the seashore, the rock to which Andromeda was chained, and the grove of the Nereïds on a little bay on the one side, and the palace of King Cepheus in the distance on the other, so natural that they would have sworn that everything were really and truly just as it presented itself. Now, since the music was perfectly in accord with the poet's meaning and was, therefore, everything that the music of the nomophylax Gryllus—was not, and since it always affected the heart directly and, in spite of its great simplicity and singability, was ever new and surprising, so all of this, combined with the liveliness and truth of the declamation and pantomime and with the beauty of the voices and the execution, produced a degree of illusion in the Abderites such as they had not yet experienced in any play. They forgot entirely that they were sitting in their National Theater, believed unawares that they were in the middle of the real scene of the action, sympathized with the fortune and misfortune of the *dramatis personae* as if they had been their closest kinsmen, grieved and became uneasy, hoped and feared, loved and hated, wept and laughed, as it pleased the wizard in whose power they were. In short, *Andromeda* had such an extraordinary effect on them that Euripides himself admitted that the play had never yet been received with such complete sensibility.

Parenthetically, we very much beg pardon of the young ladies and gentlemen of our sentimental—most unsentimental—age.* But

---

*It should not be forgotten that this was written in the year 1777.

it was, as a matter of fact, not our intention by means of this touch of the extraordinary *sentimentality* of the Abderites to give them a thrust and, as it were, arouse thereby some doubt about their own good sense, either within themselves or in other people. In all seriousness, we are relating the matter merely as it took place. And, whoever finds such a strong sentimentality *in Abderites* odd, him we ask most politely to consider that, with all their *Abderidity*, in the end they were, after all, human beings like other people; indeed, in a certain sense, they were *all the more only human beings—the more they were Abderites.* For precisely their Abderidity caused them to be deceived just as easily *as the birds that picked at the grapes painted by Zeuxis*[68]—by giving themselves up to every impression, especially to the illusions of art, much more heedlessly and naively than more refined and reserved, consequently also more sensible, people are accustomed to do, who are not so easily to be hindered from seeing through any magic mist raised round about them.

By the way, the author of this history makes the comment here that: "The pronounced disposition of the Abderites to allow the arts of the imagination and of imitation to deceive them is not exactly what he likes least about them." However, he may well have had his special reasons for this.

In point of fact, poets, musicians, and painters have no easy task vis-à-vis an enlightened and refined public. And just the *conceited connoisseurs,* who always constitute the largest crowd in such a public, are most difficult to satisfy. Instead of holding still for the impression, they do all they can to prevent it. Instead of enjoying what *is there,* they argue about what *could* be there. Instead of submitting to the illusion,* where destroying the enchantment can serve only to rob us of pleasure, they make a point of I know not what sort of childish honor to play the philosopher out of season, force themselves to laugh where people who give themselves up to their natural feelings have tears in their eyes, and, where the latter laugh, turn up their nose in order to give themselves the appearance of being *too strong,* or *too refined,* or *too learned* to allow *something like that* to upset their equipoise.

But the real connoisseurs, too, spoil the enjoyment that they could get from a thousand things that are good *in their way* by

---

*It goes without saying that the poet must have done his part to bring about the illusion and sustain it; otherwise, of course, he has no right to ask us, *as a favor to him,* to act as if we were seeing what he does not show us and feeling what he does not cause us to feel, and so on.

making *comparison* of the same with things of another sort, comparisons that are mostly unjust and always to our own disadvantage. For what our vanity gains by *disdaining a pleasure* is always, after all, but a shadow that we try to snatch, while the real thing eludes us.

We find, therefore, that at all times it was among still uncultured human beings where the sons of Apollo, god of the Muses, performed those great miracles of which one still speaks without rightly knowing what one is saying. The forests in Thrace danced to the lyre of Orpheus, and the wild animals nestled against his feet, not because *he*—was a *demigod,* but rather because *the Thracians* were—bears; not because *he* sang *like someone more than human,* but because those listening heard him with the ears of mere human beings in the state of nature; in short, for just the reason why (according to Forster's report[69]) a Scottish bagpipe enraptured the good souls of Tahiti.

The gentle reader himself, whenever he thinks proper, will apply this not very new but very practical observation that has so often been heard but yet almost always disregarded. Our own conscience may tell us whether and to what extent we are in other things more or less Thracians and Abderites. But if we were so in this single respect, it might be all the better for us—and, of course, for the greater part of our poetical bagpipers, too.

Chapter Twelve

How all of Abdera turned into fools because of their admiration for and delight in Euripides' Andromeda. Philosophical-critical essay on this strange kind of frenzy that is secretly called among the ancients the Abderite sickness—dedicated most respectfully to the historians.

After the curtain had come down, the Abderites, with open eyes and open-mouthed, continued looking at the stage; and their ecstasy was so great that they not only forgot their usual question: "How did you like the play?" but would even have forgotten to clap, had not *Salabanda* and *Onolaus,* who, in the general stillness, were the first to recover their senses, hastily remedied this lack and thereby spared their fellow citizens the shame of not having applauded for the first time just when they really had a reason for doing so.

But then they made up with interest for what they had omitted doing. For, as soon as they started, they applauded so loudly and so long until nobody any longer felt his hands. Those who could not go on took a rest for a moment and then began again all the more loudly until they, in turn, were again relieved by others who had, meanwhile, been resting.

The matter did not rest with this uproarious outbreak of their applause. The good Abderites were so full of what they had heard and seen that they found themselves compelled to give vent to their repletion in still another matter. Various ones, while on their way home, stopped on the public strcet and *declaimed* too loudly those passages of the play that had moved them most. Others, whose passion had risen to the point that they had to *sing*, began singing and repeated, come what may, what they had remembered of the most beautiful arias. Imperceptibly, as customarily happens on such occasions, the *paroxysm* became general; a fairy appeared to have raised her wand over Abdera and to have transformed all of its inhabitants into actors and singers. Everybody with a breath spoke, sang, hummed, droned, and whistled, waking and sleeping, for many days nothing but passages from the *Andromeda* of Euripides. Wherever one went, one heard the great aria "Oh you, Love, ruler of gods and men," and so on, and it was sung so long until there was nothing left of the original melody; and the itinerant journeymen, to whose level it finally sank, bellowed it on the street at night to their own melody.

If the advice, like so much other counsel given us by the wise, did not have the sole flaw—of not being practicable, we would hasten as much as we could to give all people the advice: "never believe a word of what someone relates to you about an event." For the wide experience we have had in this matter for more than thirty years has convinced us that in such accounts there is ordinarily not a word of truth; and we cannot remember, in all seriousness, a single case where a thing, although it had happened only a few hours before, had not been recounted differently by each person who gave an account of it, and, therefore, because a thing is true, after all, in only one way, had been falsely reported by everyone.

Since this is the case with things that occurred in our time, at the place we happened to be, and almost before our seeing eyes, one can easily imagine how things must stand with regard to the historical accuracy and reliability of such happenings as occurred a long time ago and for which we have no other testimony than what is misrepresented to us about it in written or printed books. God knows how they play havoc with the poor, honest truth and what can remain of it when, for a few thousand years, it has been sifted, filtered, and strained through all the falsifying means of transmission such as traditions, chronicles, annals, pragmatical histories, short epitomes, historical dictionaries, collections of anecdotes, and so on, and through so many washed or unwashed hands of scribes, copyists, compositors, translators, censors, and proofreaders, and so on! I, for my part, by the rather exact observation of these circumstances, have long ago been induced to take a vow to write no other history but that of persons whose existence—and of events whose authenticity—cannot matter to anyone in the world.

What brings me to this little *expectoration* is exactly the event that we have before us and which has been so strangely treated and mistreated by the various writers that mention it as can hardly be imagined by a kind and unsuspecting reader.

There is now, for example, this *Yorick,*[70] this inventor, father, *protoplast,* and *prototype* of all sentimental journeys and sentimentalizing travelers, who, without purse and bag, indeed without having worn down just one pair of shoe soles because of it, have taken sentimental journeys to who knows where merely with the intention of paying with a description of them their bills for beer and tobacco—I say, there is now this Yorick who, in order to make a nice little chapter out of it in his famous *Sentimental Journey,* has so prepared this same event that it has become as amazing and fantastic as a fairy tale, but has, because of that, lost all of its *individual truth* and even all family resemblance to the Abderites.

Just listen to this! "The town of Abdera (he says) . . . was the *vilest* and most *profligate* town in all Thrace. What for poisons, conspiracies, and assassinations—libels, pasquinades and tumults, there was no going there by day—'twas worse by night.

"Now [he continues] when things were at their worst, it came to pass, that the Andromeda of Euripides being represented at Abdera, the whole orchestra was delighted with it: but of all the passages which delighted them, nothing operated more upon their imaginations, than the tender strokes of nature which the poet had wrought up in that pathetic speech of Perseus,

O Cupid, prince of God and men, and so on.

"Every man almost spoke pure iambics the next day, and talk'd of nothing but Perseus his pathetic address—'O Cupid! prince of God and men'—* in every street of Abdera, in every house—'O Cupid! Cupid!'—in every mouth, etc. . . . nothing but 'Cupid! Cupid! prince of God and men'—The fire caught—and the whole city, like the heart of one man, open'd itself to Love.

"No pharmacopolist could sell one grain of helebore—not a single armourer had a heart to forge one instrument of death—Friendship and Virtue met together . . . in the street—the golden age return'd, and hung o'er the town of Abdera—every Abderite took his oaten pipe, and every Abderitish woman left her purple web, and chastly sat her down and listen'd to the song—"[71]

A very nice little chapter, indeed! All boys and girls found it delicious—"Oh Cupid, Cupid! prince of God and men, Cupid!"— And that single line from Euripides—a line such as, truly, by both ears of King Midas![72] the least among your oaten pipe singers can venture at any moment to make twenty while standing on one leg— is supposed to have performed a miracle that all of the priests, prophets, and wise men of the whole world were not capable, with all their efforts combined, of bringing about a single time—the miracle of transforming such a vile, wicked, and godforsaken city and republic as Abdera is supposed to have been, all at once into an innocent, loving Arcadia, that, of course, pleases the downy-bearded, sentimental, saucy, young turtle doves of both sexes! Only it's a pity, as I have said, that in the entire little anecdote, as brother *Yorick* relates it, there is not a word of truth.

The entire secret is that the strange man was *enamored* when he imagined all that; and so he wrote down (as things usually go with every honest *lover* and *virtuoso,* hobby-horse rider and moonstruck cavalier) everything that he imagined for the truth. Only it isn't very nice of him—just in order to pay his *favorite idol* and *fetish, Amor,* all the greater a compliment—to say the worst things about the poor Abderites that can be thought and said about human beings. But let all of Greek and Roman antiquity come forward and testify whether anything of the sort had ever been brought down on these good people. As we know, of course, they had their moods

---

*To speak candidly, this line is the only moving one in the entire fragment of Perseus's speech that still happens to be extant, as our readers who know Greek may judge for themselves—for the words run thus:

'Αλλ' ὦ τύραννε θεῶν τε κ' ἀνθρώπων, "Ερως,
"Ημὴ δίδασκε τὰ κακὰ φαίνεσθαι καλά,
"Η τοῖς 'ερῶσιν, ὧν συ δημιοῦργος εἶ,
Μοχθοῦσι μόχθους εὐτυχῶς συνεκπονεῖ, κ.τ.λ.[73]

and whims, and what we properly call intelligence and wisdom had never been their forte. But for that reason to turn their city into a den of cutthroats, that goes a little beyond the limits of notorious poetic license, which, after all, however great an arena one wishes to concede to it, must in the end have its bounds like all other things in the world.

Lucian of Samosata,[74] in the introduction of his famous little book *The way to write history—if one could,* tells the thing quite differently, although, with his leave, not much more correctly than *Yorick.* He must, as it appears, have heard something about King Archelaus, and about the *Andromeda* of Euripides, and about the curious enthusiasm that seized the Abderites, and that at last Hippocrates had to be summoned to help so that he could put everything in Abdera back on the beaten track. And now, just take a look and see how this man gets everything all mixed up!

"The actor *Archelaus* (who was at that time as much as if among us one spoke of *Brockmann* or *Schröter,* or of the *German Garrick*[75])—this Archelaus came to Abdera in the days of King Lysimachus[76] and gave the *Andromeda* of Euripides. It was then an extraordinarily hot summer day. The sun was burning down on the heads of the Abderites, who were truly warm enough anyhow. The whole city took a strong fever home with them from the theater. On the seventh day, the sickness became less severe among most of them either through a heavy bleeding from the nose or a severe perspiration; on the other hand, they were left with an odd sort of paroxysm. For when the fever was gone, they were all overcome with an irresistible urge to declaim tragic verses. They spoke in nothing but iambs, shouted in a loud voice, where they stood and walked, entire tirades from the *Andromeda,* sang the monologue of Perseus," and so on.

Lucian, in accordance with his mocking way, has a lot of fun with the idea of how silly it must have looked to see all the streets in Abdera teeming with pale tragic actors, emaciated by the sevenday fever, singing with all their might "Oh you, Love, ruler of gods and men!" And he assures us that this epidemic lasted until winter, and a sudden great frost finally put an end to these excesses.

It must be admitted that *Lucian's* way of telling the course of events is much better than Yorick's. For, as odd as this Abderite fever may seem, all physicians will surely admit that it is at least possible, and all poets, that it is *in character.* We can, therefore, assert about it what the Italians are accustomed to say: "Se non è vero, è ben trovato."[77] But *true,* to be sure, it is not, as already becomes clear from the single circumstance that, around the time when this event is supposed to have happened in Abdera, there was really no Abdera any longer because, a few years before this, the Abderites had already emigrated and had left their city to the frogs and rats.

In short, the thing happened—as we have related it. And if one wishes to call the seizure that came over the Abderites after the *Andromeda* of Euripides a fever, then it was at least no other sort than the theater fever, with which up until this day we see some cities of our worthy German fatherland afflicted. The malady was not so much in their blood as in the Abderidity of the good people in general.

Nevertheless, it is not to be denied that with some, in whom it could find more tinder and sustenance than in others, it became serious enough to require a physician; from which, presumably, Lucian's error of considering the entire matter a kind of hot fever may subsequently have arisen. Fortunately, Hippocrates was still in the vicinity, and since he had already become rather well acquainted with the nature of the Abderites, a few hundredweight of hellebore put everything back in its old condition within a short time—that is, the Abderites ceased singing: "Oh you, Love, ruler of gods and men!" and were now one and all again—as wise as before.

End of Part One

Part Two

Fourth Book:
The Trial Concerning the Ass's Shadow

Chapter One

What brought on the trial and facti species.[1]

The good citizens of Abdera had barely recovered a bit from that wondrous stage fever with which they had been afflicted by that *ruler of gods and men, Amor,* created by the honorable and guileless Euripides, hardly did they speak again with one another on the streets in prose, hardly were the druggists selling again their hellebore, the armorers again at work fashioning their rapiers and carving knives, the women of Abdera acting chaste and busy at their purple fabric, and hardly had the Abderites thrown away their tiresome oaten pipes[2] in order once again to devote themselves to their several occupations with their customary good sense, when the Fates quite secretly drew forth from the dullest, thinnest, flimsiest material ever spun by gods or men such a tangled web of misadventures, squabbles, exacerbations, goadings, intrigues, factions, and other rubbish, that finally all of Abdera was enmeshed by it and, since the terrible stuff burst into flames through the impetuous zeal of assistants and accomplices, this famous republic would almost, and perhaps entirely, have gone to ruin, if, according to the resolution of fate, it could have been destroyed by a lesser cause than—*frogs and rats.*[3]

The affair began (as do all great historical events) with a very insignificant cause. A certain dentist named *Struthion,* born in *Megara*[4] of citizens of that town, had many years ago established his residence in Abdera. And because he was perhaps in the whole country the only one of his profession, his practice extended over a considerable part of southern Thrace. This he exploited by traveling to the fairs in all the small towns and hamlets for more than thirty miles around, where, besides his toothpowder and his dental tinctures, he occasionally also sold to considerable advantage various *arcana,* good for complaints about the spleen and uterus, pursiness, maligant fluxes, and so on. For this purpose he had in his stable a fat she-ass which was loaded down on such occasions at the same time with his own short, stocky person and with a great bag full of medicines and victuals.

Now it once happened that, when he was supposed to go to the fair in *Gerania,* his she-ass had foaled the previous evening and as a result was not capable of coming along on the trip. Struthion, therefore, rented another ass to ride as far as the locality where he intended to stay the night, and the owner accompanied him on foot in order to look after this beast of burden and to ride it home again. The way led across a large heath. It was in the middle of summer, and the heat of the day was very great. The dentist, for whom it got to be unbearable, looked about, parched with thirst, for a shady spot where he could dismount for a moment and breathe some fresh air. But far and wide there was to be seen neither tree nor shrub, nor yet any other object that cast a shadow. Finally, when he could find no other expedient, he dismounted and sat down in the shadow of the ass.

"Well now, sir, what are you doing there," said the donkey driver, "what's the meaning of that?"

"I'm sitting down a bit in the shade," replied Struthion, "for the sun has been beating down on my head so, it's unbearable."

"Oh no, my good sir," replied the other, "that was not a part of our deal! I hired the *jackass* out to you, but nobody had anything in mind about the *shadow.*"

"You're joking, good friend," said the dentist laughing. "The shadow goes with the jackass, that's understood."

"Now by Jason! That is *not* understood," shouted the jackass man quite defiantly. "The ass is one thing, his shadow another. You rented the ass from me for so and so much. If you had wished to rent the shadow in addition, then you should have said so. In a word, sir, get up and get on with your journey, or pay me for the ass's shadow, as is fair!"

"What? cried the dentist, "I've paid for the ass and now I'm supposed to pay for its shadow, too? Now, you can call me a triple ass if I do that. The jackass is mine for this entire day, and that's simply how it is, and I'm going to sit down in its shadow as often as I like and stay sitting there as long as I like, you may rest assured of that!"

"Do you mean that seriously?" asked the other with the complete deliberatenes of an Abderite donkey driver.

"Quite seriously," replied Struthion.

"Then sir, let's go straight back to Abdera right now before the authorities," said the other. "There we'll see which of the two of us is going to be right. As truly as Priapus[5] has mercy on me and my jackass, I'll just see who's going to bully me against my will out of my ass's shadow."

The dentist was really minded to let the donkey driver properly feel the strength of his arm. He was already clenching his fist, his stubby arm was already raised. But when he eyed his man more closely, he found it better to let his raised arm sink again and to make another try with gentler representations. But in doing so he ran out of breath. The uncouth man insisted that he wished to be paid for the shadow of his ass. And since Struthion remained just as obstinate in not wanting to pay, there was no other way left but to return to Abdera and to begin legal action before the city magistrate.

Chapter Two

Hearing before the municipal judge Philippides.

The municipal judge *Philippides,* who had original jurisdiction in all disputes of this kind, was man of many good qualities; an upright, sober man who administered his office assiduously, who listened to everyone with great patience, amiably gave people the information they wished, and, in general, had the reputation of being incorruptible. He was, moreover, a good musician, collected natural curiosities, had produced a few plays which, since they catered to the taste of the city, had been *quite popular,* and he was almost certain to become the *nomophylax* when that office would next fall vacant.

With all these merits the good Philippides had only one single small failing, and that was that whenever two parties came before him, it always appeared to him that whoever had spoken last was right. The Abderites were not so stupid as not to have noticed that; but they believed one could surely pardon a man possessing so many good qualities *one single flaw.* "Yes," they said, "if Philippides didn't have *this* failing, he would be the best city magistrate Abdera has ever seen!"

Meanwhile, the circumstance that both parties always appeared to the honorable man to be right, naturally had the good consequence that nothing was more important to him than to settle *amicably* the disputes that were brought before him. And thus the good Philippides' timidity would have been a true blessing for Abdera, had the vigilance of the *sycophants,*[6] who were ill served by his peaceable disposition, not found means to thwart its effects in all cases.

And so the *dentist Struthion* and the *donkey driver Anthrax* came running in great agitation before this worthy city magistrate, and both at the same time preferred charges with a great deal of shouting. He listened to them with his customary patience, and when they finished or were tired of shouting, he shrugged his shoulders, and the dispute appeared to him one of the most confused of all that had ever come before him. "Now just which of the two of you is really the *plaintiff?*" he asked.

"I am charging the *jackass man,*" answered *Struthion,* "with breaking our contract."

"And *I,*" said the other, "am charging the *dentist* with having gratuitously arrogated to himself a thing which I had not hired out to him."

"Here we have two plaintiffs," said the city magistrate, "and where is the *defendant?* A strange dispute. Tell me the whole thing once more with all the circumstances, but one after the other, for it is impossible to make head or tail of it if both are shouting at once."

"Your Worship," said the dentist. "I rented from him the use of the ass for one day. It is true that in all that there was no mention of the ass's shadow. But who has ever heard of a clause about the shadow being inserted in such a rental agreement? By Hercules, this is, after all, not the first ass to be hired out in Abdera."

"There you are right, sir," said the magistrate.

"The ass and his shadow go together," *Struthion* continued, "and why should the one who has rented the ass himself not also enjoy the use of his shadow?"

"The shadow is an accessory, that is clear," replied the magistrate.

"Your Worship," shouted the donkey driver. "I am only a common man and don't understand your fancy words, but my four senses tell me that I am not obligated to let my ass stand in the sun for nothing so that somebody can sit down in his shadow. I hired the ass out to this man, and he paid me half in advance, that I admit; but the ass is one thing, his *shadow* another."

"That's true, too," murmured the city magistrate.

"If he wants *that,* half of what he paid for the ass himself will do; for I'm asking for nothing but what is fair, and I beg you to help me get justice."

"The best you can both do in this matter," said *Philippides,* "is to come amicably to terms. You, honorable man, include the shadow in the rent because it is, after all, only a shadow; and you, Mr. Struthion, give him half a drachma for it, so both parties can be satisfied."

"I won't give the fourth part of a farthing,[7]" shouted the dentist, "I want my rights!"

"And I," shouted his counterpart, "insist on mine. If the ass is mine, then his shadow is mine, too, and I can do with it as I like, since it's my property; and because this man here doesn't want to hear anything about justice and fairness, I'm going to ask twice as much now; and I'm just going to see whether there's any justice left in Abdera!"

The judge was in a state of great perplexity. "Just where is the ass?" he asked finally, since in his anxiety nothing else had occurred to him in order to gain some time.

"He's down on the street in front of the door, your Worship!"

"Bring him into the yard!" said Philippides.

The owner of the jackass was glad to obey, for he considered it a good sign that the magistrate wished to see the leading character in the play. The jackass was brought in. Too bad that he could not also give his opinion on the matter. But he stood there quite calm, looking first with raised ears at the two gentlemen and then at his master, screwed up his mouth, let his ears sink again, and said not a word.

"There, see for yourself now, your Worship," shouted Anthrax, "whether the shadow of such a fine, splendid jackass isn't a real bargain at two drachmas, all the more on a day as hot as it is today."

The city magistrate tried using kindliness once more, and the parties were already beginning to incline towards a settlement when, unfortunately, *Physignatus* and *Polyphonus*,[8] two of the most notable sycophants in Abdera, happened along, and, after they had heard what was being discussed, suddenly gave the matter a new turn.

"Mr. Struthion has justice entirely on his side," said *Physignatus*, who knew the dentist to be a well-to-do man, and hot-headed and stubborn as well. The other sycophant, although a bit vexed that his colleague had so speedily stolen a march on him, cast a side glance at the jackass, which appeared to him to be a fine, well-fed animal, and immediately declared himself most emphatically in favor of the donkey driver. Now both parties wished to hear no word of a settlement, and the worthy Philippides found himself compelled to set the date for a trial. They left after that, each with his sycophant, for home. The ass, however, with his shadow, as the object of the legal dispute, was led off, pending the settlement of the affair, to the community stables of Abdera.

Chapter Three

How the factions seek support at a higher level.

According to the municipal laws of the Abderites, all disputes regarding mine and thine which arose among the common citizenry were settled before a court of twenty worthies who gathered three times a week in the portico of the Temple of *Nemesis.*[9] Everything, out of fair consideration for the sustenance of the sycophants, was transacted *in writing* before this court, and because the course of *Abderite justice* described a kind of *snail's shell spiral* and progressed, too, with the *speed* of a snail, all the more as the sycophants were not bound to make their concluding remarks until they had no more to say, so the *writing up of complaints* commonly lasted as long as the means of the disputing parties could, in all probability, last. However, this time so many special motives met to give the affair greater impetus that one should not be astonished that the proceedings about the ass's shadow had in less than four months got so well under way that now the *final judgment* was to be rendered the next time the court would be in session.

A lawsuit about an ass's shadow would without doubt have attracted attention in any city in the world. Just imagine, therefore, what kind of effect it had to have in *Abdera!*

Hardly had the rumor about it got out, when from that very hour all other topics of conversation were dropped, and everyone spoke with so much *concern* for this lawsuit as if he had something big to win or lose by it. Some declared themselves for the dentist, the others for the donkey driver. Indeed, even the jackass himself had his friends who contended that he would be quite well justified in intervening as a third party, since he was obviously *injured* most by the unreasonable demand to allow the dentist to sit in his shadow while he stood in the burning heat of the sun. In a word, the aforesaid jackass had cast his shadow on all of Abdera, and the affair was carried on with a liveliness, a zeal, and an interest that could scarcely have been greater if the welfare of the city and Republic had been at stake.

Although this way of doing things will now surprise no one at all who has become acquainted with the citizens of Abdera in the preceding true historical account, we believe all the same that we are performing no unpleasant service for such readers as believe they know the real facts about a story only if they are shown the action of the wheels and main springs with the entire relation of causes and effects of an event, if we tell them in somewhat greater detail how it happened that this lawsuit, originally only between people of small importance and about an extremely insignificant object, could become important enough finally to draw the whole Republic into its whirlpool.

The entire citizenry of Abdera was (as from time immemorial most of the cities in the world) divided into *guilds,* and by virtue of an old custom the dentist Struthion belonged to the *guild of the cobblers.* The reason for this was, as all the Abderites' reasons were wont to be, awfully subtle. For in the first era of the Republic this guild had included only the shoemakers and cobblers. Later on all kinds of *menders* were added as well, and so it came about that in the course of time the surgeons, as *menders of men,* and finally (*ob paritatem rationis*[10]) the dentists, too, were assigned to the shoemakers' guild. Accordingly, with the single exception of the physicians, with whom he always was on very bad terms, Struthion had the entire laudable guild of shoemakers, and especially all the cobblers, on his side who (as you will still remember) made up a very considerable part of the citizenry of Abdera. Naturally, therefore, the dentist turned immediately to his superior, the guild master *Pfriem*[11]; and this man, whose patriotic zeal for the freedoms of the Republic is unknown to no one, explained immediately with his customary irascibility that he would rather stab himself with his own shoemaker's awl than allow the rights and freedoms of Abdera to be thus grossly encroached upon in the person of a brother guild member.

"Fairness," he said, *"is the highest justice.* What, however, can be fairer than that he who has planted a tree, even though it was actually done with the *fruit* in mind, should incidentally also enjoy the *shade* of the tree? And why should what holds good of a tree not also be just as true for an ass? Where the devil is *our freedom* coming to if a guild man of Abdera can't even sit down in the shadow of an ass if he wants to? Just as if an ass's shadow were more exclusive than the shadow of the town hall or of the Temple of Jason, in which whoever wishes may stand, sit, or lie. A shadow is a shadow, no matter whether of a tree or a statue, of an ass or of his Grace, the archon himself! In a word," master Pfriem added, "rely on me, Mr. Struthion; that coarse fellow is going to let you have not only the shadow but leave you the ass in the bargain for

your proper "saxfation," or there would be neither freedom nor private property in Abdera any more; and by heavens, things are just not going to go that far as long as my name is guild master Pfriem."

During the time in which the dentist had assured himself of the favor of such an important man, the donkey driver Anthrax, for his part, didn't spare any pains either in seeking a protector who could at least counterbalance the former. Anthrax was actually not a citizen of Abdera, but rather a freedman who stayed in the precincts of the Temple of Jason; and, as a person enjoying its protection, he was under the immediate jurisdiction of the *archpriest* of this hero[12] who, as is well known, was worshipped in Abdera as divine. Naturally, therefore, his first thought was of how he might succeed in getting the archpriest *Agathyrsus*[13] to assist him energetically. However, the archpriest of Jason was a very important person in Abdera, and a donkey driver could scarcely hope to gain access to a gentleman of this rank without a special channel.

After many deliberations with his most intimate friends, the following way was at last favored. His wife, named *Krobyle*,[14] was acquainted with a *woman who made finery,* whose *brother* was the most favored lover of the *chambermaid* of a certain *Milesian*[15] *dancer* who (so rumor had it) was in the good graces of the archpriest. Not as if he perhaps—the way things go——especially because the priests of Jason had to be unmarried—in brief, how suspicious the world is; to be sure, people said all kinds of things. But the truth of the matter is: the archpriest *Agathyrsus* was a great admirer of pantomimic solo dances, and because, so as not to give offense, he did not want to have the dancer come to him during the day, he therefore had no other choice but—with the necessary prudence—to have her led at night through a small garden gate to his room. Now, since certain people had once seen a heavily veiled person emerge again at dawn, a murmuring started to the effect that it had been the dancer and that the archpriest had pressed a special friendship upon this person who, in fact, would have been capable of arousing something substantially more in anybody else but an archpriest. Now, whatever the truth about all that was, enough, the donkey driver spoke to *his wife, the wife, Krobyle,* to the *maker of finery,* she to *her brother,* the brother to *the chambermaid;* and because the chambermaid had her way completely with *the dancer,* about whom it was taken for granted that she could do anything with the *archpriest,* who could bring *the magnates of Abdera* and—*their wives* to do anything he wanted,

Anthrax doubted not a moment that he had laid his cause into the best hands in the world.

But unfortunately it turned out that the dancer's favorite had taken a vow to hire out her power to do everything no more *free of charge* than Anthrax the shadow of his jackass. She had a kind of *scale of fees* according to which the smallest service demanded of her presupposed an acknowledgment of *four drachmas;* and in the present case she could be so much the less expected to reduce her price by even only half a drachma since she was expected to do such great violence to her modesty as to recommend a matter in which an ass was the central figure. Briefly, *Iris* insisted on four drachmas, which was just twice as much as the poor man could win with his lawsuit at best. He therefore found himself again in his former predicament. For how could a simple donkey driver hope, without a stronger support than the mere justice of his case, to stand his ground against an opponent who was supported by an entire guild and boasted everywhere that victory was already in his hands?

Finally, honest Anthrax hit upon a way in which he might, perhaps, get the archpriest over to his side without the intervention of the dancer and her chambermaid. The best part of this, he thought, was the fact that he did not need to look very far for it. Without much ado—he had a daughter named Gorgo who, in the hope of finding employment in one way or other in the theater, had learned how to sing quite passably and to play the lyre. The girl was not exactly one of the most beautiful. But a slim figure, a pair of big black eyes, and the fresh bloom of youth made up amply (so he thought) for what her face lacked; and in fact, when she had washed thoroughly she looked, in her holiday finery with her long pitch-black braids and with a bouquet of flowers at her bosom, rather like *Anacreon's wild Thracian girl.*[16] Since now, after more detailed inquiries, it turned out that the archpriest Agathyrsus was also an admirer of lyre playing and of *little songs,* a great number of which young Gorgo knew how to sing not at all badly, Anthrax and Krobyle had great hopes of attaining their goal in the shortest way through the talent and figure of their daughter.

Anthrax, therefore, turned to the archpriest's valet, and Krobyle meanwhile instructed the girl how to behave in order, if possible, to cut out the dancer and to remain the exclusive master of the little garden gate.

The thing came off as desired. The valet, who was not seldom hard pressed through the proclivity of his master to the *new* and *varied,* seized this fine opportunity with both hands, and for a beginner young Gorgo played her role masterfully. Agathyrsus found in her a certain blend of innocence and mischievousness and kind of wild grace, which he found charming because it was new to him. In a word, she had hardly sung two or three times in his room, when Anthrax already heard from a reliable source that Agathyrsus had recommended his just cause to various judges and had intimated quite emphatically how he was of no mind to abandon even the least of those enjoying the protection of the Temple of Jason to the chicanery of the sycophant Physignatus and to the party prejudice of guild master Pfriem.

Chapter Four

Trial. Judicial opinion of the assistant judge Miltias. Verdict and what ensues therefrom.

Meanwhile the day of the trial had arrived when this strange dispute was to be decided by legal verdict. The sycophants had made their concluding statements, and the records were turned over to an official adviser to the court named *Miltias,* against whose impartiality the people who wished the dentist ill made various objections. For it was not to be denied that he was very well acquainted with the sycophant Physignatus; and, what is more, there was loud talk to the effect that Madame Struthion* (who passed for one of the pretty women in her class) had at various times recommended to him in person her husband's just cause. However, since these objections had no valid grounds and it now came to be Miltias' *turn,* things proceeded as had been planned.

Miltias presented the history of the dispute so ingenuously and in such detail in both the arguments against and those in support of his conclusions that his listeners did not notice for a long time what he was really driving at. He did not deny that both parties had much *for* and *against* them. "On the one side nothing appears clearer," he said, "than that the person who rented the ass as the principal object also tacitly included the accessory, the ass's shadow, in the bargain; or (in case one might not wish to admit such a silent agreement either) that the shadow follows its body *by itself,* and therefore he, who has acquired the usufruct of the ass,

---

*We know very well that this has not been expressed in the Greek fashion; but Madame Struthion is like Mrs. Damon in our comedies; and of just what importance is it to the reader what the actual name of the dentist's wife may have been?

is entitled to as much use of the shadow as he likes without further remonstrance; all the more, as not the least thing is taken thereby from the essential nature of the ass himself. Whereas, on the other side, it seems not less evident that, although the shadow can be regarded neither as an essential nor an inessential part of the ass, consequently, it could not by any means be surmised by the renter of the latter that he *wanted* to rent silently the former with the latter; nevertheless, since the shadow under discussion can by no means exist independently of the aforesaid ass, and an *ass's shadow* is basically nothing but a *shadow ass,* the owner of the *real ass* can with justice be regarded, too, as owner of the *shadow ass* emanating from the former, and hence he cannot by any means be stopped from letting the renter of the former have the latter free of charge. Moreover, and even if one wanted to admit that the shadow is an accessory of the several times aforementioned ass, still no right to the same could accrue thereby to the renter, in that he did not acquire through the rental agreement *any use* of the same but rather only that without which the intention of the contract, namely his planned journey, could not be attained. However, since among the laws of Abdera none is to be found in which the present case is clearly and plainly included, and since the verdict, therefore, must be drawn solely from the nature of the matter, things thus depend chiefly on a point to which the sycophants on both sides have paid no heed or have touched upon only superficially, namely upon the question whether *what is called a shadow* is to be counted among *the common things* to which everyone has the same right, or among *the special ones* to which individual persons can have and acquire an exclusive right. Since now, in the absence of a positive law, the agreement and general custom of humanity, as a true oracle of nature itself, has with reason the force of a positive law, by virtue of this general custom, however, the shadows of things (also those things belonging specifically not only to individual persons but also to entire communities, indeed even to the immortal gods themselves) have up until now everywhere been free to everyone, whoever he may be, it is thus evident that *ex consensu et consuetudine generis humani*[17] the abovementioned *shadows,* just like *free air, wind and weather, flowing water, day and night, moonlight, dawn,* and so forth are to be classed with the *common things* whose use is free to everyone and to which—so far as the abovementioned use possibly under certain circumstances carries with it some element of exclusion—the first man who gets control of them has obtained a momentary right of ownership. Having laid down this proposition (for the corroboration of which sharp-witted

Miltias advanced a large number of inductions, which we want to spare our readers)—this proposition as his basis, he could, therefore, so he said, do nothing else but to cast his vote to the effect that the shadow of all the asses in Thrace, consequently also that one which had directly given rise to the present lawsuit, could just as little constitute a part of the property of an individual as the shadow of Mount Athos or of the city tower of Abdera, consequently the several times aforementioned shadow could neither be inherited nor bought, nor be given as a present *inter vivos*[18] or *mortis causa,*[19] nor hired out, nor made in any other way into the subject of a civil contract, and that, therefore, for this and other reasons which have been adduced in the matter of the donkey driver Anthrax, plaintiff, party of the first part, versus the dentist Struthion, defendant, party of the second part, with respect to the ass's shadow appropriated to himself by the defendant to the alleged jeopardy and detriment of the plaintiff (*salvis tamen melioribus*[20]) let the decision be: that the defendant was well within his rights in making use of and benefiting from the above mentioned shadow; the plaintiff, however, objections notwithstanding, is not only to be dismissed with his unauthorized claims but also sentenced to pay, after a previous reduction as determined by the court, all costs as well as full compensation for all losses and damages suffered by the defendant.

According to the Law."

We leave it to the gentle reader with experience in legal matters who is so inclined to entertain whatever reflections he may wish on this adjudication of the sharp-witted Miltias which we have, to be sure, given in part only. And since we have decided not to presume to have an opinion in this matter but rather to act merely as an impartial historian, we are contented to report that it had from time immemorial been the custom of the courts in Abdera to confirm the expert opinion of the official adviser every time, whatever it was like, either unanimously or, in any case, with a large majority of the votes. At least, for more than a hundred years no example of the contrary had been seen. Under the circumstances it was unlikely that things could be any different. For in the course of the recital, which generally lasted a very long time, the associate magistrates were accustomed to do anything but pay attention to the *rationes dubitandi et decidendi*[21] of the official adviser. Most of them stood up, looked out of the window or went off to breakfast on cakes or small fried sausages, or they paid a flying visit to the home of a good lady friend; and the few who remained seated and appeared to be somewhat interested in the matter had something to whisper to their neighbor every few moments or even dropped off to sleep while listening. In short, there prevailed a kind of silent *compromise* with regard to the official adviser, and merely for the sake of form it happened that a few minutes before he came to his actual conclusion, everyone returned to his seat in order to help endorse the formulated judgment.

This is the way things were done till now, even with quite important disputes. However, the trial about the ass's shadow had the unprecedented honor of the entire court's remaining together and (except for three to four associate justices who had already promised their votes to the dentist and did not wish to cede their right of sleeping while the court was in session) of everyone's listening with all the attention worthy of such a marvelous trial. And when the votes were counted, it was found that the judgment was endorsed with only a majority of twelve to eight.

Immediately after the results were made public, Polyphonus, the plaintiff's sycophant, did not fail to raise his voice and to appeal to the *Great Council of Abdera* against this judgment as unjust, biased, and encumbered with irreparable nullities. Now, since the trial concerned a matter which the plaintiff himself had valued no higher than two drachmas, and this (even with the reasonably modest costs and damages included) was far from a *Summa appella-bilis*,[22] a great din was raised about it in court. The *minority* affirmed that the important thing here was not at all the sum but a *general legal question* which concerned property and had as yet been determined by no law in Abdera. Consequently, by virtue of the nature of the matter, it had to be taken before the law-giver himself as the person who alone in doubtful cases of this kind has the right of pronouncing the verdict. How it happened that the official adviser, with all his sympathy for the defendant's cause, had not foreseen that those who wished the opposition well would use this pretext to manage getting the case before the Great Council, for this we cannot give any other reason than *that he was an Abderite* and, in keeping with the general, traditional habit of his compatriots, was accustomed to see everything from one side only, and even then only rather superficially. But perhaps he can still be excused by the fact that he had spent a part of the previous night at a great banquet and, when he got home, still had to grant a rather long audience to *Dame Struthion* and, therefore, presumably had not had enough sleep. Enough, after long quarreling and noise-making the city magistrate Philippides finally declared that, in view of the circumstances, he could not help but bring before the *Senate* the question whether the appeal entered by the plaintiff's party would take place.

With this he stood up. The court adjourned with considerable tumult, and both parties hastened to deliberate with their friends, well-wishers, and sycophants about what they might do now in this matter.

Chapter Five

Political attitudes in the Senate. The virtue of beautiful Gorgo and its effects. The priest Strobylus enters, and things get more serious.

The trial about the ass's shadow, which in the beginning had merely amused the citizens of Abdera by its absurdity, now began to turn into an affair in which the prerogatives, the supposed honor, and all kinds of passions and interests of various, in part important, members of the Republic became involved.

Guild master *Pfriem* had wagered his head on the victory of his brother guild member; and since mostly every evening he turned up at places where the common citizens forgathered, he had already brought nearly half of the people over to his side, and the number of his adherents was growing daily.

The *archpriest,* on the other hand, had until now not considered the affair sufficiently important to bring his entire prestige to bear in favor of the person under his protection. However, since matters between him and beautiful *Gorgo* began to get more serious because she, instead of a certain docility which he had hoped to find in her, put up a resistance that was not to be suspected in someone of her origin and upbringing, indeed had even declared how she had misgivings about once more exposing *her virtue* to the danger of a visit through the small garden gate, it was quite natural for him to delay no longer in acquiring, through the zeal with which he began to support the cause of her father, a more specific claim on the gratitude of the daughter.

The new clamor which the ass's trial provoked in the city through the appeal to the Great Council gave him an opportunity to talk off the record with a few of the most prominent councillors. "However ridiculous this affair may be *per se,*" he said, "it can, after all, not be permitted that a poor man under the protection of Jason suffer oppression from what is *obviously a plot.* The *cause,* which for the most important events is often very slight, doesn't matter, but rather *the spirit in which the thing is done* and *the secret intentions* one may have *in mind.* The insolence of the sycophant *Physigna-tus,* who is really to blame for this whole *row,* has to be chastised, and reins must be applied in good time to the tyrannical, foolish *demagogue Pfriem* before he succeeds in overthrowing the *aristocracy* entirely," and so on.

For the sake of the truth we must say that in the beginning there were various councillors who saw the affair approximately for what it was and who blamed the city magistrate Philippides very much for not having had sufficient prudence to throttle such an absurd dispute right at birth. However, people's views changed imperceptibly, and the giddiness that had turned a part of the citizenry topsy-turvy finally seized the greater part of the councillors, too. Some began to view the matter as more important because a man like the archpriest Agathyrsus appeared to be taking such a serious interest in it. Others grew uneasy about the danger to the *aristocracy* which might arise from the projects of guild master Pfriem. Various people sided with the donkey driver's party merely to be contrary, others because they really felt he was suffering injustice, and still others declared themselves for the dentist because certain persons, with whom they wished never to agree, had expressed their support of his adversary.

With all of that, this trivial affair, however much the Abderites— were Abderites, would nevertheless have never caused such a violent fermentation in their community had not the evil demon of this Republic also stirred up *the priest Strobylus* to get involved without any more cogent reason than his restless spirit and his hatred for the archpriest Agathyrsus.

In order to make this more comprehensible to the gentle reader we will have to start the thing (like that ancient poet his *Iliad*) *ab ovo,*[23] so much the more as certain passages in our story about the adventure with Euripides and certain expressions directed against Democritus which escaped the priest Strobylus will also be put thereby into the proper light.

Chapter Six

Relation of the Temple of Latona to the Temple of Jason. Contrast in the characters of the high priest Strobylus and the archpriest Agathyrsus. Strobylus declares himself for the party in opposition to the latter and is supported by Salabanda, who begins to play an important role in the affair.

The service of *Latona*[24] was (as Strobylus had assured Euripides) as old in Abdera as the transplantation of the Lycian colony; and the utmost simplicity of the style of her small temple could be regarded as an adequate confirmation of this tradition. As plain as the Temple of Latona was, so small also was the *donated* income of its priests. However, as want is inventive, these gentlemen had long ago found means, in partial compensation for the scantiness of their regular income, to tax the superstition of the Abderites; and since even this would not suffice, they finally induced the *Senate* (because it would not in any case hear of an *increase in pay*) to earmark certain revenues for the maintenance of the sacred frog ditch, the greater part of which the unassuming and fair-minded frogs left to their *providers.*

Things were entirely different with the Temple of *Jason*, this famous leader of the *Argonauts* who had the honor in Abdera of being elevated to the status of a god and being worshipped publicly, without our being able to advance any other reason for this than that some of the oldest and richest families in Abdera traced their lineage from this *hero.* One of his grandsons had, according to tradition, settled in this city and become the common ancestor of various families, some of whom were still in their prime in the days of our present history. In the beginning, following an ancient custom, they had established only a small private chapel to the memory of the hero from whom they were descended. After a long time it had developed into a kind of public temple which the piety of the descendants of Jason gradually had provided with many goods and revenues. Finally, when through trade and fortunate accidents, Abdera had become one of the richest cities in Thrace, *the Jasonites* decided to build for their deified ancestor a temple the beauty of which could do honor in posterity to the Republic and to themselves. The new Temple of Jason became a splendid work and, with its buildings, gardens, living quarters of the priests, officials, and protected persons, constituted an entire district of the city. Its archpriest always had to be *from the oldest line of the Jasonites;* and since he, with very considerable revenues, also had jurisdiction over the persons and goods belonging to the temple, it is easy to imagine that the high priests of Latona could not look upon these advantages with indifferent eyes, and that between these two prelates a jealousy had to prevail which was inherited by their successors and was manifested in their conduct on every occasion.

The high priest of Latona was, to be sure, regarded as the head of the entire Abderite priesthood; however, the archpriest of Jason with his subordinates constituted a special council which was indeed under the protection of the city of Abdera, but was free of any dependence of whatever name. The feasts of the Temple of Latona were, it is true, the actual great holidays of the *Republic*. However, since its moderate revenues permitted no special extravagance, the Feast of Jason, which was celebrated with extraordinary pomp and solemnity, was in the eyes of the people, if not the most distinguished, at least the one it looked forward to the most. And all the respect people had for the antiquity of the service of Latona and the great faith of the populace in its high priest and its holy frogs could, after all, not prevent *the greater figure* cut by the *archpriest* from enjoying a higher degree of *respect and authority*. And although *the common people* in general liked the priest of Latona more, this advantage was in turn outweighed by the fact that the priest of Jason had connections with the *aristocratic houses,* giving him so much influence that it would have been easy for an ambitious man in this position to act like a small *tyrant of Abdera.*

In addition to so many reasons for the traditional jealousy and dislike between the two princes of the Abderite clergy there was, besides, a *personal antipathy* which *Strobylus* and *Agathyrsus* felt toward one another that was a natural result of the contrast in their mentality.

Agathyrsus, more man of the world than priest, had in fact little more of the latter about him than his garments. The love of pleasure and amusement was his ruling passion. For although he was not lacking in haughtiness, it cannot be said about anyone that he is ambitious as long as his ambition allows another passion to exist at the same time. He loved the arts and intimate association with virtuosos of all kinds, and he had the reputation of being one of those priests who have little faith in their own gods. At least it cannot be denied that he often quite freely made fun *of the frogs of Latona;* and somebody wanted to affirm on oath that he had heard from his own mouth the words: "the frogs of this goddess had long ago been transformed into wretched poets and Abderite singers." That he was on quite good terms with *Democritus* was not very likely to corroborate his orthodoxy either. In brief, Agathyrsus was a man of gay temperament, he was clearheaded, and he led a rather free life, was popular among the Abderite nobility, more popular still among the members of the fair sex and, because of his liberality and his Jason-like form, popular even among the lowest classes of the people.

Now, nature could not have brought forth in her drollest minute a more complete antipode of all that *Agathyrsus* was than the priest

Strobylus. This man had found out (like many people such as he) that a wrinkled countenance and a stiff bearing are infallible means for one's being taken for a wise and irreproachable man among *hoi polloi.* Since by nature he looked rather sullen, it had cost him little effort to make a habit of this *gravity* which, with most people, proves nothing but *the ponderousness of their wit and their uncouth manners.* Without any sense for the great and the beautiful, he was a born despiser of all talents and arts which presuppose this sense, and his hatred for philosophy was merely a mask for the natural resentment of a blockhead toward all who understand and know more than he. He was wrong and one-sided in his judgments, stubborn in his views, heated and rude in contradiction, and extremely vindictive whenever he thought someone had offended either his own person or the frogs of Latona; but he was, nevertheless, pliant to the point of meanness as soon as he could not succeed without the help of a person he hated in a matter he considered important. Moreover, there were some grounds for his reputation of being ready, upon receiving the proper box of *Darics and Philips,*[25] to do anything in the world, which was not entirely incompatible with the overt aspects of his character.

From such contrary dispositions and from the many occasions for envy and jealousy on the side of the priest Strobylus there arose of necessity in both a mutual hatred which bore with difficulty the constraint imposed on them by their rank and position and differed only in the fact that Agathyrsus *had* too much *contempt* for the high priest to hate him very much, and the *latter envied* the former too much to be able to hold him as cordially in contempt as he might well have wished.

There was, in addition to all this, the circumstance that *Agathyrsus,* by virtue of his birth and his situation, was *for the aristocracy; Strobylus,* on the contrary, in spite of his relations with a few councillors, was a *declared friend of democracy,* and, next to guild master Pfriem, was the one who through his character, his dignity, his fanatic ardor, and a certain popular kind of eloquence, had the most influence on the rabble.

It can now easily be foreseen that the affair about the ass's shadow or shadow ass necessarily had to take a serious turn as soon as a couple of men like the two high priests of Abdera got involved in it.

As long as the trial was going on *before the city magistrates, Strobylus* had taken no part in it other than to declare occasionally that, had he been in the dentist's place, he would have done the same thing. But hardly did he learn from Madame *Salabanda,* his niece, that *Agathyrsus* had espoused the cause of the man under his protection who had been found guilty in the court of original jurisdiction, when he suddenly felt called upon to join those at the head of the defendant's party and to support the intrigue of the guild master with all the authority he enjoyed among the councillors as well as among the people.

Salabanda was too much accustomed to having her hand in all Abderite quarrels for her to have been among the last who took sides in the present one. Besides her relationship to the priest Strobylus, she had an additional, special motive for being on his side, a reason no less weighty for her keeping it to herself. We have mentioned on another occasion that this lady, be it now for merely political purposes, or that perhaps a little coquetry—and who knows whether or not occasionally, too, what is called in the language of the more modern French world of refinement *the heart* of a lady was inclined to interfere as well. Enough, it was a fact that she always had at hand a number of submissive slaves among whom (so people thought) the one or the other at least always had to know *what he was serving for.* The secret chronicle of Abdera related that the archpriest Agathyrsus had for a long time had the honor of being one of the latter; and, as a matter of fact, a great many circumstances came together indicating why one could consider this rumor as something more than mere conjecture. So much is certain, that the most intimate friendship had existed between them for a long time when *the Milesian dancer* came to Abdera, and soon the fickle *descendant of Jason* found her so remarkable that Salabanda could no longer help considering herself sacrificed.

Agathyrsus, to be sure, still paid visits at her house on the footing of an old acquaintance, and the lady was too politic to allow the slightest change to show through in her outward behavior toward him; but her heart was seething with revenge. She forgot nothing that could involve him in the affair ever more deeply and get him more and more inflamed. Secretly, however, she had his every step and all the large and small front and back doors that could lead *to his room* watched so closely that she quite soon discovered his intrigue with young *Gorgo* and could make it possible for the priest Strobylus to put the zeal of the archpriest for the donkey driver's cause in a light just as *odious* as she herself was clandestinely striving to make it appear ridiculous.

Agathyrsus, as little as it cost him to sacrifice political advantages and aspirations to the interest of his pleasures, nevertheless had moments in which the smallest resistance, in a matter basically of no importance to him at all, incited all his pride to revolt; and as often as this happened, his animation would generally lead him infinitely further than he would have gone if he had deigned to consider the matter coolly. The reason why he meddled with this absurd affair in the first place was now in fact no longer relevant, for beautiful *Gorgo* had, in spite of the instructions of her mother Krobyle, either not had sufficient skill or enough endurance to adhere properly to the initially outlined plan of defense against such a dangerous and experienced besieger; however, he was now involved in the matter; his honor was concerned here; daily and hourly he received news of how indecently the guild master and the priest Strobylus were, with their followers, inveighing against him, how they threatened, how insolently they hoped to succeed in their endeavor, and so forth, and this was more than was necessary to get him to the point of deciding to apply his entire power in order to knock down opponents whom he so very much disdained and to punish them for the temerity of having opposed him. In spite of the intrigues of Madame Salabanda (which were not spun finely enough to remain concealed from him for long), the greatest part of the Senate was on his side; and although his opponents failed to do nothing that could embitter the people against him, he nevertheless had a following of rough, sturdy fellows, especially among the guilds of the tanners, butchers, and bakers, who were just as hot-headed as they were strong and were ready at any sign, as might be necessary, to shout or lay on for him and his party.

Chapter Seven

All of Abdera divides into two parties. The case comes before the Council.

Things were in this ferment when suddenly the names *Shadows* and *Asses* were heard in Abdera and in a short time were generally used to designate the two parties.

We have no reliable information about the true origin of these nicknames. Presumably, because parties can, after all, not long exist without names, the adherents of the dentist Struthion among the rabble had begun to call *themselves* the *Shadows* because they were fighting for his right to the *ass's shadow,* and *their opponents* in derision and scorn the *Asses* because they wanted, as it were, to turn the shadow *into the ass itself.* Since now the supporters of the archpriest could not prevent their being called by this name, they had without really noticing (as such things generally go) become accustomed to using it themselves, although at first only in jest, only with the difference that they turned the spear around and linked the *contemptible* with the *shadow* and the *honorable* with the *ass*. "If it's going to be one of the two," they said, "then every honest fellow will, after all, at any time prefer to be a real living ass with all that comes with him rather than the mere shadow of an ass."

However that may have happened; enough, in a few days all of Abdera was divided into these two parties; and as soon as they had a *name*, the *zeal* on both sides increased so swiftly and violently that being neutral was no longer permitted at all. *"Are you a Shadow or an Ass?"* was always the first question which the common citizens directed at one another if they met in the street or in a tavern; and if a *Shadow* just had the misfortune to be the only one of his kind among a number of *Asses* at such a place, then, if he didn't manage right off to escape, he could do nothing but *apostatize* on the spot or suffer a severe beating and get thrown out through the door. The many and great disorders that were hence bound to break out can be imagined without our assistance. In a short time the animosity grew to such proportions that a *Shadow* would have preferred to waste away to a real phantom from being hungry than to buy three farthings worth of bread from a baker of the other party.

The women, too, as can easily be imagined, took sides, and certainly not with the least ardor. For the first *blood* which was shed on the occasion of this strange civil war came from the nails of two *huckstresses* who had attacked one another's physiognomies in the public market. It was meanwhile noticed that by far the greater part of *the Abderite women* declared their support of *the archpriest;* and in a house where the husband was a *Shadow,* one could be sure that the wife was a *she-Ass,* and commonly such a heated and intractable she-Ass as can be imagined. Among a great number of partly terrible, partly ridiculous consequences of this factious spirit which came over the women of Abdera, none of the least was the fact that many a love affair was suddenly broken off by it because the obstinate *Seladon*[26] preferred to give up his claims rather than his party; just as, on the contrary, many a man who for years had been courting the favor of a beautiful woman in vain and had been able to overcome her antipathy toward him through nothing which is generally tried by an unlucky lover, now suddenly needed no other title in order to become happy than to convince his lady that he was—an Ass.

Meanwhile the *question of a preliminary hearing,* whether the appeal to the *Great Council* filed by the plaintiff would take place or not, was brought before the *Senate*. Although this was the first time that the case about the ass was discussed before this venerable body, it was soon noticeable, however, that everyone had already chosen sides. The archon *Onolaus* was the only one who appeared in a dilemma as to how he might be able to give the matter a tolerable color. For it was noticed that he spoke much more softly than usual, and at the close of his statement he broke out into the remarkable and *ominous* words: he feared very much that the ass's shadow, about which people were quarreling with so much heat, *might obscure the fame of the Republic for many centuries*. It was his opinion that it would be best to reject as inadmissible the appeal that had been filed, to confirm the ruling of the municipal court (save the matter of costs, which could cancel one another out), and to impose everlasting silence on both parties. However, he nevertheless added: if the majority found that the laws of Abdera did not suffice to settle such a trivial lawsuit, then he would have to consent to the Great Council's rendering its verdict on the matter; still, he wanted to propose in this regard that someone search in the archives to see whether by chance such unusual cases had not come up in older times and how they were dealt with.

This restraint on the part of the *archon,* which will unanimously be credited to him by an impartially judging posterity as proof of a true sovereign's wisdom, was at that time, when the factious spirit had blinded all eyes, interpreted as weakness and phlegmatic indifference. Various senators of the archpriest's party declared verbosely and with great zeal that one could call nothing *trivial* which concerned the rights and freedoms of the Abderites; where there was no law, no legal proceedings took place either, and the first example of the judges' being allowed to decide a case on grounds of *an arbitrary equity* would be the end of freedom in Abdera. Even if the quarrel concerned something still more unimportant, it was not a matter of *how much or little it was worth,* but rather *which of the two parties was right;* and since no law existed which might decide in the present case whether the ass's shadow was tacitly included in the rent or not, then neither the lower court nor the Senate itself could, without the most manifest tyranny, presume to award to the renter something to which the owner had at least just as much right or even an incomparably better one, since it by no means *necessarily follows* from the nature of their contract that it had been the intention of the latter to hire out the shadow of his ass to the other man, and so on. One of these gentlemen went so far that in his excitement he blurted out that he had always been an enthusiastic patriot; but before he would allow one of his fellow citizens to presume to deny *arbitrarily* to another only *the shadow of a hollow nut,* he would sooner see all of Abdera on fire and in flames.

Now guild master Pfriem lost his patience entirely. The fire, he said, with which the whole city is being threatened with such temerity, ought to be ignited with that man who dares to speak in this way. "I am not an educated man," he continued, "but by all the gods, I'm not going to let somebody sell me mouse droppings for pepper! You've got to have lost your mind to want to make a healthy person believe that a special law is needed when it is a question of whether somebody might sit down on the shadow of an ass who has purchased with cash the right to sit on the ass itself. It is altogether a shame and mockery that so many serious and intelligent men are cudgeling their brains about an affair which any child would have settled on the spot. When in the world did anybody ever hear that shadows are among the things which people rent out to one another?"

"Sir," the councillor *Buphranor*[27] interrupted the guild master, "you are hitting yourself in the mouth when you maintain that. For if the ass's shadow *could* not *be* rented out, then it is clear that it hasn't *been* rented out; for *a non posse ad non esse valet consequentia.*[28] The dentist can, therefore, according to your own principle, have no right to the shadow, and the verdict is *in itself* null and void."

The guild master was taken aback, and because it did not come to him right away what answer might be given to this fine argument, he began to shout all the louder and called on heaven and earth to be his witnesses that he would sooner pluck out his gray beard hair by hair than have somebody make an Ass of him in his old days. The men of his party supported him with all their might; but they were outvoted, and all they could achieve with the aid of the archon and the councillor who always trod lightly was that the case should remain for the time being in *statu quo* until someone had checked in the archives to see whether a *precedent* could be found by which this affair could be settled without greater complicating difficulties.

Chapter Eight

Good order in the secretariat of Abdera. Precedential decisions that do not matter. The people want to storm the town hall and are calmed down by Agathyrsus. The Senate decides to turn the case over to the Great Council.

The secretariat of the city of Abdera—because, after all, the opportunity is offered here to mention it with a couple of words—was in general as well appointed and tended as will be expected of such a wise republic. For all that, it nevertheless had two defects in common with many other secretariats, about which there had been almost daily complaints for centuries without anyone's having hit upon the idea of whether it might not just be possible in one way or another to correct what was at fault.

That the documents and records were kept lying in some very musty and damp vaults where, for lack of air, they got moldy, rotted, were eaten by cockroaches and worms and gradually became wholly unusable, was one of these defects; the other that, in spite of all the searching, nothing could be found in it. As often as this happened, some patriotic councillor or other would make the comment, mostly with the approval of the whole Senate, "the trouble is merely *that no one keeps the secretariat in order.*" As a matter of fact, a hypothesis could scarcely be conceived by means of which this phenomenon could be explained in an easier and more comprehensible way. That was the reason now why almost every time when it was decided in the Council that someone ought to go and check in the secretariat, everybody knew beforehand and mostly counted as certain *that nothing would be found.* And that was also the reason why the usual explanation which ensued at the next session of the Council, "in spite of all the searching nothing was found in the secretariat," was received with the frostiest composure as a thing that had been expected and was a matter of course.

This had now also been the case when the secretariat had received the order to look into the older records and see whether a *precedent* could not be found which could serve as a torch for the wisdom of the Senate in coming to a decision about the extremely difficult lawsuit concerning the ass's shadow. *Nothing was found* in spite of the fact that various gentlemen in the last session gave their quite positive assurance that *innumerable* similar cases had to exist. Meanwhile the zeal of a councillor from the party *of the Asses* had all the same dredged up the records of two old lawsuits that at one time had made a lot of noise in Abdera and appeared to have some similarity to the present one.

The one concerned a quarrel between the owners of two pieces of land in the fields within the city about the right of ownership to a small hill situated between both which amounted to approximately five or six paces in circumference and may have, in the course of time, originated from some molehills that had come together. A thousand small accessory circumstances had gradually aroused such vehement animosity between the two quarreling families that each party had made up its mind to prefer losing house and home to losing its alleged right to this molehill. Abderite justice was thereby all the more embarrassed, since evidence and counterevidence depended upon such an enormous combination of infinitely small, doubtful and insoluble circumstances that, after a trial of twenty-five years, the case not only did not come one step closer to a decision, but to the contrary had become just twenty-five times more confused than in the beginning. Probably it would never have come to an end either if both parties had not seen themselves compelled finally to make over to their sycophants for the court costs and lawyers fees the *plots of land* between which lay the object of litigation, with all appurtenances, prerogatives, and all claims, among which there was also the right to the molehill. Then, at this stage, the sycophants came amicably to an agreement, still on the same day, to dedicate this little hill to great *Themis*,[29] to plant a fig tree on it, and to have someone set up under that the statue of the aforementioned goddess out of good pine, painted so as to resemble stone, the costs to be defrayed jointly. It was also stipulated, with the guarantee of the Senate of Abdera, that the owners of both plots of land would for all time be obliged to pay jointly for the maintenance of the aforementioned statue together with the fig tree. And so it came about that the two of them, in eternal remembrance of this remarkable lawsuit, were still to be seen in the time of the present one, and the fig tree, in fact, in a very imposing condition; the statue, however, was dilapidated and worm-eaten.

The other trial appeared to have a still closer relationship to the present one. An Abderite named *Pamphus* possessed an estate the principal amenity of which consisted in its having on its southwest side a magnificent view over a beautiful valley that ran along between two wooded hills, became narrower and narrower in the distance, and finally disappeared into the Aegean Sea. Pamphus often used to say that he would not sell this view for one hundred Attic talents; and he had so much the more cause to value it so highly since the estate *per se* was so inconsiderable that no one looking for mere utility would have given him five talents for it. Unfortunately, a quite prosperous Abderite peasant who was his neighbor on just this southwest side had reason to have a barn built which deprived good Pamphus of such a large part of his view that his little country estate, according to his calculations, depreciated because of that by eighty talents. Pamphus brought everything possible to bear, earnestly but amicably, to prevent his neighbor from putting up such an odious structure. The peasant, however, insisted on his right of building on his inherited land wherever and however he pleased. Consequently, a trial was the result. Pamphus, to be sure, could not prove that the view in dispute was a necessary and essential appurtenance of his estate, or that the new structure deprived him of air and light, or that his grandfather, who had acquired the estate for his family by buying it, had paid only one drachma more for the sake of the aforementioned view than the estate was in itself worth according to the prices of that time, nor yet that his neighbor, the peasant, was dependent on him because of some kind of lien on his property by virtue of which he might have the right to pull down his structure; however, his *sycophant* maintained that the bases for making a decision in this matter lay much deeper and would have to be derived directly from the primary, original source of all rights to property. "If air were not a transparent substance," said the sycophant, "then Elysium and Olympus itself might be situated across from my master's estate, and still he would have got to see as little of it as if a wall that reached up to the sky were standing in front of his windows. The *transparent nature* and property *of air* is, therefore, the first and true primary cause of the beautiful view which blesses my client's estate. Now, however, free, transparent air, as everybody knows, is one of the *common things* to which originally all have an equal right, and precisely for that reason every portion of it, of which no one has yet taken possession, is to be regarded as no one's property, as a thing which does not yet specifically belong to anybody and hence becomes the property of the first person to seize it. From time immemorial my client's ancestors have possessed, owned, and enjoyed as part of this estate the now disputed view, unhindered and undisputed by all and sundry. They therefore occupied *with their eyes* the portion of air necessary for that, and through this occupation as well as through uninterrupted possession from time immemorial it has become a proper part of the estate mentioned several times before, of which not the least can be taken away without overturning the fundamental laws of all civil order and security."—The Senate of Abdera found these arguments quite dubious; there was a long debate pro and con with great subtlety, and since Pamphus some time later was elected to the Council, the matter appeared to become so much the more complicated and his arguments from time to time ever *more dubious*. The peasant died without living to see the outcome of the affair, and his heirs, who ultimately noticed that common peasant folk like them could win nothing against such a big man who was a councillor of Abdera, finally allowed themselves to be persuaded by their sycophant to make a settlement by virtue of which they paid the court costs and all the more refrained from building the disputed barn since they— had no more money to do that, and the trial had eaten away so much of their inheritance that they no longer had any need of a new barn in order to store the little fruit which remained for them to cultivate.

Now, to be sure, it was quite clear that these two lawsuits could offer very little light for coming to a decision about the present one, especially as in neither of the two a *definite* judgment resulted, but rather both had ended with an amicable settlement; however, the councillor who produced them appeared not to want to make any other use of them either than to show the Senate that these two disputes, which, with respect to the *importance of the subject as well as the subtlety of the legal arguments,* appeared to have much similarity to the donkey trial, had been carried on and tried before the *Small* Council of Abdera for so many years without its occurring to anyone to take the case before the *Great* Council or only to doubt whether the *small one* was indeed competent to make decisions in matters of this kind.

All of the Asses supported the opinion of their fellow party member with so much greater zeal since they had the majority of the votes if the case had been disposed of before the Council. However, precisely for that reason the *Shadows* persisted all the more stubbornly in their opposition.

The entire morning was spent in quarreling and shouting, and the gentlemen would finally (as used to happen to them often) have dispersed when it was time to eat without having achieved their object, if a great number of common citizens from the *Shadow party* who had assembled in front of the town hall as arranged by guild master Pfriem and reinforced by a crowd of riffraff of the lowest sort had not finally settled the matter. The party of the archpriest subsequently charged the guild master with having deliberately stepped to the window and given the people signals inciting them to riot. However, the opposing party denied this charge absolutely and maintained that the unseemly cries which a *few Asses* had suddenly set up gave the citizens assembled below the idea that their leaders were being attacked, and this mistake had caused all the noise.

Whatever the facts of the case were, all of a sudden a bellowing clamor resounded up to the windows of the town hall: *"Freedom, freedom! Long live guild master Pfriem! Away with the Asses! Away with the Jasonites!"* and so forth.

The *archon* came to the window and commanded the rioters to be quiet. But their shouting increased, and a few of the most insolent threatened to set fire to the town hall then and there if the gentlemen wouldn't disperse immediately and turn the case over to the Great Council and to the people. Some dissolute knaves and female herring vendors actually forced their way into the neighboring houses, tore firebrands from the hearths, and returned with them in order to show the fine gentlemen that their threats were being made in earnest.

Meanwhile, the tumult caused thereby had summoned a number of *Asses* who wanted to come to the aid of the leaders of their party with clubs, tongs, hammers, carving knives, pitchforks, and the first thing that had come into their hands; and although they were *outnumbered* by far by the *Shadows,* their courage and the contempt with which they regarded the party of the *Shadows* drove them to answer the insulting words with such strong blows and punches that heads were bloodied, and in a few moments everybody was fighting.

Since things had taken such a turn, there was, of course, nothing left to do in the Council chamber but to resolve *unanimously* that, solely for the love of peace and for the common good, no precedent being set herewith, one could permit the case about the ass's shadow to be brought before the Great Council and decided by it.

In the meanwhile, the good councillors began to feel so uneasy that, as soon as they had agreed (although in a very tumultuous way) upon this conclusion, they asked guild master Pfriem with hands raised imploringly to go down and calm the furious people. The guild master, who felt mightily good at seeing the proud patricians so deeply humbled under the power of the shoemaker's stirrup, did not, to be sure, hesitate to give them this proof of his good will and of his standing with the people, but the tumult was already so great that his voice, although one of the best beer voices in all of Abdera, was heard just as little as the shouting of a cabin boy up in the crow's nest in the roaring and howling of a storm and the rush of crashing waves. In the first fury into which the rabble flared up when they saw him (they did not recognize him right away) he would even have been uncertain of his own life if, fortunately, the archpriest *Agathyrsus,* who considered this chance tumult the most opportune moment for attacking the opposing party in the flank, had not come along at precisely this moment, *his gilded fleece* on a staff before him and his entire priesthood following after him, to put a stop to the riot by assuring the mob that their demands would be met and that he himself was the first to urge that the case be settled before the Great Council.

This public assurance of the prelate and his condescension and affability, in addition to the respect which the Abderite people customarily had for the *golden fleece,* had such a good effect that in a few moments all was quiet again, and the entire marketplace resounded with a loud "Long live the archpriest Agathyrsus." The wounded went off homewards quietly and unobtrusively in order to have their heads bound up; the remaining troop of hangers-on streamed along behind the returning archpriest. The guild master, however, suffered the annoyance of seeing that a great part of his otherwise so faithful and devoted Shadows, affected by the contagion of the rest of the crowd, helped to magnify the triumph of his adversary and, in this moment of frenzy, could easily have been brought to the point of venting on their own friends, *the Shadows,* the mischief which a short time before they were ready to direct against their alleged enemies, *the Asses.*

Chapter Nine

The politics of both parties. The archpriest follows up his attained advantage. The Shadows retreat. The decisive day is fixed.

This unexpected advantage which the archpriest won over the Shadows hurt the *latter* so much the more grievously as he stunted not only the joy and honor of the victory they had won in the Senate, but weakened their party itself perceptibly and in general showed them how little they might rely on the support of the thoughtless mob which is tossed by any wind to another side and seldom really knows what it wants, let alone what those wish to do with the mob whose leadership it accepts.

Agathyrsus, who was now *the declared leader of the Asses,* had learned through his emissaries that the opposing party had made gains among the common citizenry through nothing more than through the resistance which the protectors of the donkey driver initially put up when the case was to be maneuvered before the Great Council.

Since this Council was made up of *four hundred men* who were regarded as the *representatives* of the entire *citizenry of Abdera* and of which half were really mere small shopkeepers and artisans, every commoner, therefore, considered himself personally insulted by the supposed intention of wishing to restrict its prerogatives; and guild master Pfriem's pretense that the objective was a total overthrow of their *democratic constitution* was accepted all the more readily.

As a matter of fact, what appeared to be *democratic* in the government of Abdera was also mere shadow play and political legerdemain. For the *Small Council,* two-thirds of which consisted of *old families,* actually did whatever it pleased; and the cases where the *Four Hundred* had to be convened were left as so uncertain in the constitution of Abdera that it depended almost entirely upon the decision of the Small Council when and how often they wanted to convene the *Four Hundred* so that the latter might give their faithful and obedient assent to whatever the former had already decided. For generally, this was all that was expected of these worthy people who (according to a reasonable assumption) were much too occupied with their own affairs to cudgel their brains with legislative and administrative matters. But precisely because this prerogative of the Abderite commons had little significance, they were so much the more jealous of it, and it was so much the more necessary to conceal from the people the strings by which they were being led while they thought they were walking unaided.

It was a truly masterful coup of the archpriest that he, all at once and at a moment when its effect had to be sudden and decisive, now declared he would support the will of the people in a matter to which it attached so much importance. And since he, instead of risking something in this, effected thereby on the contrary a large breach in the plan of the opposition, the *latter* now had every reason to think of new ways and means for depriving the archpriest and his followers again of their advantage and of how they might extinguish the favorable impression which he had made on the common people.

The leaders of the *Shadows* assembled still on the same evening in the house of Dame *Salabanda* and decided that, instead of urging the *archon* to set an early date for convening the *Four Hundred,* they would use their influence rather (in case it should be necessary) to bring about a delay in order to give the people time to cool down again. Meanwhile they wished to try to persuade the citizenry secretly and with all imperturbability how foolish they were to allow the archpriest and his *fellow Asses* to credit them with something as being meritorious which was, after all, nothing less than good will, but rather merely a result of their weakness. If the *Asses* had had the power to tear the case from the hands of the Great Council they would have done so and troubled themselves little about whether the people liked it or not. This sudden departure from their former well-known political behavior in the affairs of the city was all too rude a stratagem for *dividing* the People's Party to deceive anybody. There was, rather, so much the more reason to be on one's guard, since it was obviously their intention to lull the people to sleep with sweet words and to bring them unawares to the point of unwittingly becoming a tool of their own oppression.

The high priest Strobylus, who was present at this conference, approved indeed of everything one might be able to do to diminish his rival's standing with the citizens and to render his intentions suspect. "However, I doubt very much," he added, "that we will witness the expected fruits of this. But I'm preparing a different and more corrosive caustic solution for him which will be all the more effective because we are going to pour it over his head quite unexpectedly. It is not yet time for me to speak more plainly. Just leave it all in my hands. Let him flatter himself for a while with the hope of dragging the priest Strobylus along behind him in triumph. That pleasure is going to be spoiled for him very properly, you may rest assured of that. Meanwhile, if we (as I hope) deal with one another honorably, and if we are in earnest about gaining a victory over our enemies, we must keep silent about what I have revealed to you about my secret plot and what I will disclose about it in due course. Agathyrsus must be made to feel secure. He must believe that we will attack with only one flank and that all our hope rests on our confidence in being able to predominate in the Great Council."

Everybody thought that the high priest had handled the matter properly, and the gathering broke up very curious about what kind of plot it might be which he had prepared against the archpriest, but also quite convinced that, if its aim was the downfall of the latter, the business could be put into no better hands than those of the priest Strobylus.

Meanwhile *Agathyrsus* did not fail to draw every possible advantage from the small victory he had gained over his opponent at such an opportune time through his peculiar presence of mind. He had bread and wine passed out to the common people who accompanied him as far as the forecourt of the archpriest's palace before, (with an earnest admonition to be quiet) he had them leave again for home, where they now overflowed with praise for his person, his affability, and generosity toward his neighbors and acquaintances. However, although he was acquainted with the spirit of republics too well *to have no regard for the favor of the mob,* he well knew, after all, that with that he had still *not* gained very *much.* The most necessary thing was his completely assuring himself of the good will of the greatest part of the *Four Hundred,* partly because now everything depended on the latter, partly because one could boast more about them than about the rest of the people. Among them he already had a considerable following indeed, but besides a number of declared and zealous *Shadows* with whom he wished to have nothing to do, there were still very many, and they were mostly from the most prosperous and distinguished part of the citizenry, who had either not at all declared themselves or leaned toward the party of the Shadows only because the leaders of the opposition had been described to them as tyrannical, violent people who had hatched this whole silly *ass's shadow-war* only to cause confusion in the city and to use the disturbances of which they were themselves the cause as a pretext and implement for their ambitious purposes.

To bring these people over to his side now seemed to him as easy as it was decisive for the triumph of his party. Still on that very same evening he invited them all to be his guests. Most of them came, and the archpriest, who had a special gift for coating his politics with a varnish of candor and straightforwardness, did not conceal from them that he had invited them in order, with the help of such honest and sensible men, to dispel the prejudices which (so he heard) people had been spreading about him among the populace. That people, he said, in the affair between a *donkey driver* and a *dentist,* and in an affair concerning merely the *shadow of an ass,* wished to make a man of his rank the leader of a party appeared to him to be altogether too silly for it ever to occur to him to refute such a foolish charge. However, poor *Anthrax* was under the protection of the Temple of Jason, and therefore he could not refuse him his assistance to the degree that justice required. Without the flaring rage of guild master Pfriem who inopportunely set himself up as the advocate of the dentist, not because the latter was in the right, but rather merely because he belonged to the shoemaker's guild, such an insignficant matter could not possibly have achieved such dimensions. If, however, someone has lighted a fire, people can always be found who profit from blowing on it and feeding it. He, for his part, had always made it a rule not to meddle in what was not his business. That he used his influence, however, in putting a stop, through his interference and friendly persuasion, to the dangerous tumult which was provoked this morning by the guild master's adherents in front of the town hall would not, so he hoped, be taken by any fair-minded person for an unseemly presumptuousness, but rather for the deed of a good citizen and patriot, especially as it was always more proper to the *character of a priest* to bring about peace and to prevent disorders than to pour oil into the fire, as was known about some people he didn't need to name. For the rest, he did not deny that, since the business about the ass's shadow had, as happens to be the case, been botched in the court of original jurisdiction and had developed into a legal dispute in which all of Abdera saw itself compelled, as it were, to take part, he had always wished that the case would be brought, the sooner the better, before the Great Council; not only so that poor *Anthrax* might obtain the satisfaction due him (although it was not to be doubted that such could not accrue to him from this high court), but that limits might sometime be set, finally, to the unbridled mischievousness of the sycophants through some kind of appropriate law, and that such base quarrels, which did not redound to the honor of the city of Abdera, might in the future be prevented as far as possible.

Agathyrsus expressed all this with so much composure and restraint that his guests could not be sufficiently astonished at the injustice of those people who would have wished to represent such a right-minded gentleman as the principal instigator of these disturbances. They were now all fully convinced of the contrary, and in a few hours he succeeded in making these good people, without their noticing it themselves and while they still believed they were completely impartial, into as good *Asses* as there were perhaps in all of Abdera; particularly after the excellent wines with which he besprinkled them at the evening meal had removed every shadow of suspicion and made each soul receptive to all the impressions he wanted to give them.

It can easily be imagined that this step of Agathyrsus caused the opposition not a little uneasiness. Since the revolution effected thereby in that part of the citizenry which had until now remained indifferent soon started to become very considerable and all the batteries arrayed against it with redoubled zeal did not remain without effect but rather had just the opposite effect and made the evilmindedness of the *Shadows,* compared with the moderation and the patriotic way of thinking of the prelate, only so much the more striking, the aforesaid Shadows would have been extremely at a loss as to how to proceed in giving their almost completely foundered party renewed vitality if the priest Strobylus had not kept up their courage and assured them that, as soon as the date of the trial was set, he would bring a storm thundering down on *little*

Jason (as he was accustomed to call him) which, with all his cleverness, he certainly didn't expect and through which the affair would immediately take on a quite different complexion.

The *Shadows* now appeared to keep so still that Agathyrsus and his adherents could ascribe this despondency of their spirits very probably to the small hope left them after the double advantage secured by the opposition. Therefore, they redoubled their efforts to have the *archon Onolaus* (whose son was an intimate friend of the archpriest and one of the most hot-tempered Asses) schedule *a day in the near future* for convening the Great Council; and by means of their impetuous urging they finally got this ceremony set for the sixth day after the last meeting of the Council.

Those people who are wont to pass judgment on the wisdom of a plan or measure according to the *success* achieved will perhaps find in the archpriest's confidence in the face of the sudden inactivity of the opposition a lack of shrewdness and caution, of which we cannot, to be sure, entirely absolve him. Quite certainly it would have been more wary of him to ascribe this inactivity rather to some important scheme which they were secretly hatching than to their crushed spirits. But it was one of the flaws of this Jasonite that, from a much too spirited feeling of his own strength, he always disdained his opponents more than prudence allows. He almost always acted like someone who does not consider it worth the trouble to determine what injuries his enemies can do him because he is, in general, conscious that he will never lack the means to fend off the worst they can do him. However, we can, in the present case, presume that a thousand others in his place, and with things appearing to be so favorable, would have thought just as he did and believed they were doing the right thing by making the most of the good will of their new friends before it cooled again, and allowed their enemies no time to recover.

That his success was not commensurate with his expectations resulted from a stroke by the priest Strobylus which, with all his cleverness, he could not foresee and which, however much it might be based on the character of this man, was nevertheless so constituted that only by direct experience could one be brought to the point of considering him capable of doing it.

Chapter Ten

The kind of mine the priest Strobylus has exploded against his colleague. The convening of the Council of Ten. The archpriest is subpoenaed, but he finds means very much to his advantage for getting out of the difficulty.

For several weeks the trial concerning the ass's shadow had constantly stirred up extensive disturbances in the unfortunate city of Abdera. On the day before this matter was to be brought to a decision before the Great Council, the high priest *Strobylus,* with two other priests of Latona and various persons from among the people, came early in the morning with aroused emotions and in haste to the *archon Onolaus* in order to report to his Grace a *miraculous sign* which (as there was the best reason to fear) threatened the Republic with some sort of great misfortune.

He reported that two or three nights ago a few persons from the Temple of Latona thought they heard *the frogs of the* Sacred Pond uttering, insted of the usual wreckeckeck koax koax, which they otherwise had in common with all other natural frogs and even with those in the *stygian swamps* (as can be seen in Aristophanes), quite common lamentable sounds; although the people mentioned did not care to approach closely enough to be able to distinguish these with any accuracy. On the basis of the report which had been made to him, the high priest, on the previous evening, had found the matter to be of sufficient importance to spend the entire night with his subordinates at the Sacred Pond. Until near midnight the profoundest quiet prevailed on it; but at the time mentioned, gloomy sounds prophesying disaster had suddenly arisen from the pond, and when they went closer they were able one and all to make out quite clearly the sounds: *Woe! Woe! Pheu! Pheu! Eleleleleu!* This wailing lasted for a whole hour and had been heard, besides by the priests, by all of the people he had brought along to be witnesses of such an unprecedented and extremely disquieting miracle. Since it was now not to be doubted that the goddess, by means of this threatening and wonderful *omen,* had wished to warn the city of Abdera, which she had loved until now, of some sort of impending great misfortune or perhaps to exhort the citizens to investigate and punish some sort of not-yet-discovered crime which could draw down the anger of the gods on the whole city, he, by virtue of his office and in Latona's name, wished accordingly to request his grace herewith to have the venerable *Council of Ten* convened without delay, so that the matter could be considered in a way suitable to its seriousness, and so that the further measures could be taken which such an occurrence required.

The *archon,* who had the reputation of inclining rather strongly toward the liberal opinions of *Democritus* with regard to the sacred frogs, shook his head when he heard what the high priest was saying and left the priests without an answer for quite a while. However, the earnestness with which these gentlemen expressed the matter, and the strange impression which it appeared already to have made on the persons present who were of the people, allowed him readily to foresee that in a few hours the whole city might be full of this alleged miracle and be having frightening presentiments, a state of affairs which would not allow him to remain indifferent. Therefore, there was nothing left for him to do but to give the order immediately in the presence of the priests that the *Council of Ten* should assemble within an hour in the Temple of Latona because of an extraordinary incident.

Meanwhile, through an arrangement of the high priest, the rumor of the dreadful, miraculous omen which had been heard for three nights in the Grove of Latona had already spread through all of Abdera. The friends of the archpriest Agathyrsus, who were not so simple as to be taken in by such hocus-pocus, were embittered thereby because they did not doubt that some evil plot or other against their party was at the bottom of it. Various young patrician gentlemen and ladies made a show of scoffing at the alleged miracle and arranged parties for going out during the following night to listen to the new-fangled dirges in the frog pond. But on the common folk and on a great part of the more refined who, in matters of this sort, are everywhere in the habit of being *common people,* the invention of the high priest was completely effective. The *Pheu! Pheu! Eleleleleleu!* of the frogs of Latona suddenly interrupted all civic and domestic pursuits. Old and young, women and children ran together in the streets and inquired after the details of the miracle with frightened faces. And since almost everybody claimed he had heard about it from the first witnesses' own mouths, and the impression which such stories are seen to have on the listeners is usually a natural stimulus for the teller always to add something that makes the matter more interesting, so in less than an hour the miracle was padded with such frightful particulars that simply hearing about it made their hair stand on end. Some people gave their assurance that *the frogs,* when they began to break out into their dreadful singing, *had raised human heads out of the pond;* others, *that they had quite fiery eyes the size of a walnut;* still others, *that people had at precisely that time seen all kinds of ghosts emitting monstrous howling sounds while flitting about in the grove;* again others, *that with not a cloud in the sky there were frightful thunderclaps and bolts of lightning over the pond;* and finally, *a few auricular witnesses* gave their assurance that repeatedly they had been able to distinguish quite plainly the words:

Woe unto you, Abdera! In brief, the miracle (as usual) grew bigger and bigger the further it rolled on and was all the more believed the more absurd, contradictory, and unbelievable the reports were which people made about it. And since soon thereafter the *Ten Magistrates,* at an unusual time and with purposeful expressions on their faces, were seen proceeding in great haste to the Temple of Latona, no one any longer doubted that events of the greatest importance were being mixed in the cup of Abdera's fate, and the whole city was suspended in trembling expectation of things that were to come.

The Council of the Ten Magistrates was made up of the archon, the four eldest senators, the two eldest guild masters, the high priest of Latona, and two directors of the Sacred Pond and represented the most venerable of all the tribunals in Abdera. All matters directly concerning the religion of Abdera were under its jurisdiction, and its prestige was almost unlimited.

It is an old observation that intelligent people usually grow wiser with age and fools, with the years, get sillier and sillier. An *Abderite Nestor*[30] had, therefore, seldom gained much from having seen two or three new generations; and thus it could without any danger be assumed that the *Ten Magistrates of Abdera* constituted, on the average, the committee of the most foolish minds in the entire Republic. These good people were so ready to accept the high priest's story as a *fact* to which there could be no objection at all that they appeared to regard the interrogation of the witnesses as a mere *formality* to be got through as quickly as possible. Now, since Strobylus found the gentlemen so well convinced in advance that the miracle was true, he accordingly believed he was risking so much less if, without losing any time, he advanced to the matter because of which he had taken the trouble to invent this entire fiction.

"From the very first moment," he said, "when my own ears were witnesses of this miraculous sign, which (as I surely can say) has never had its like in the annals of Abdera, the thought arose in me that it could be a *warning of the goddess* against the consequences of her vengeance which might be hovering over our heads because of some secret unpunished crime; and this made it necessary for me to induce his grace, the archon, to call the present meeting of the very venerable Council of Ten. What formerly was mere conjecture has cleared up into certainty in the single hour just past. The evil-doer has already been discovered, and the crime can be proved through eyewitnesses, against whose veracity some doubt prevails all the less since the perpetrator is a man of too great authority for something less than fear of the gods to induce people of low estate to appear against him as a witness. Should you ever have considered it possible, esteemed gentlemen, that someone in our midst could be bold enough to *show contempt* for our anciet religious service and its customs and sacred objects bequeathed to us by the first founders of our city and preserved immaculate through so many centuries and, with respect neither for the laws nor for the commonly held faith and the customs of our city, to abuse wantonly what is sacred and venerable to us all? In a word, can you believe that there is a man living in the middle of Abdera who, in defiance of the letter of the law, *is keeping storks in his garden which are daily feeding on frogs from the Pond of Latona?*"

Amazement and horror were expressed on each face at these words. The archon, at least, had to pretend to be just as thunder-struck as his remaining colleagues really were so as not to be the only exception. "Is it possible?" three or four of the eldest cried out at the same time, "and who can be the scoundrel who has committed such a crime?"

"Pardon me," replied Strobylus, "if I ask you to soften this hard expression. I, for my part, prefer to believe that not impiety, but rather mere frivolity and what one, these days, especially since *Democritus* scattered his weeds among us, is accustomed to call *philosophy* is the source of this apparent contempt for our hallowed customs and dispositions. I want to and have to believe this all the more since the man who can be proved guilty of the aforesaid sacrilege through the unanimous testimony of more than seven reliable persons, even a man of sanctified profession, even a priest, in a word, since it—is *the Jasonite Agathyrsus*."

"*Agathyrsus?*" the astonished Ten Magistrates cried out as if from one mouth. Three or four of them turned pale and appeared to be embarrassed at seeing a man of such importance, and with whose house they had always been on good terms, involved in such a grave affair.

Strobylus left them no time to recover. He gave orders for the witnesses to be called in. They were interrogated one after the other, and the upshot of it was that Agathyrsus had for some time, to be sure, been keeping two *storks* in his gardens, that they were often seen hovering over the Sacred Pond and that actually one of its croaking denizens, who was just about to sun himself on the shore, had been devoured by one of the same.

Although now the truth of the accusation appeared hereby to be put beyond any doubt, the archon Onolaus nevertheless believed that for the prevention of unpleasant consequences prudence required that a man like the archpriest of Jason be dealt with carefully. He therefore moved that they should be satisfied with advising him in a friendly way that the Ten Magistrates were inclined this time to believe that the matter about which a complaint was being made, took place *without his knowledge;* however, relying on his well-known reasonable way of thinking, they were hoping that he would not for a moment hesitate to turn the criminal storks over to the directors of the Sacred Pond and to give therewith to the Ten Magistrates as well as to the entire city agreeable proof of his respect for the laws and religious rites of his native city.

Three votes out of nine supported the archon's motion; but Strobylus and the rest opposed it with great zeal. They maintained, moreover, that they could in no wise approve using such excessive lenience toward a citizen of Abdera who has been proved guilty of a crime of such gravity. Then, too, the rules of the court required that he not be sentenced before his answer to the charges had been heard. Accordingly, Strobylus moved that the archpriest be summoned to appear forthwith before the Ten Magistrates and to answer the charge brought against him; and this motion, all objections of the minority notwithstanding, passed with six votes to four. The archpriest was, therefore, summoned with all the formalities which are customary in such cases.

Agathyrsus was not unprepared when the deputies of the Ten Magistrates appeared in his house. After he had allowed them to wait over an hour, they were finally led into a large room where the archpriest, sitting on a raised armchair of ivory and in full array, listened with great composure to the stuttered words of their spokesman. When they had finished, he signaled with his hand to a servant who was standing to one side behind his chair. "Lead these gentlemen," he said to him, "into the gardens and show them the *storks* that people have been talking about so that they can tell their masters that they have seen them with their own eyes; after that bring them back here again."

The deputies stared with wide-open eyes. But their respect for the archpriest restrained their tongues, and they followed the servant silently like people who did not feel quite right about what they were doing. When they had again returned, Agathyrsus asked them whether they had seen the storks, and since they had all together answered with yes, he continued: "Well, then go and pay my compliments to the very venerable Court of the Ten Magistrates and tell them who have sent you that I am letting them know that these storks, like everything else living within the confines of the Temple of Jason, are also *under Jason's protection,* and that I find the presumptuousness of summoning an archpriest of this temple and of wishing to judge him under the laws of Abdera very ridiculous." And with that he motioned to them to depart.

This answer—which the Ten Magistrates should have expected all the more as it could not have been unknown to them that the Temple of Jason was completely exempt from the jurisdiction of the city of Abdera—caused them indescribable embarrassment, and the chief priest *Strobylus* got worked up over it into such a violent fit of anger that in his rage he did not know any more at all what he was saying, and finally he finished by threatening the entire Republic with ruin if this intolerable pride of a little puffed up cleric, who (as he said) could not even be regarded as a *public* priest, were not humbled and the fullest satisfaction given to the offended *Latona*.

However, the archon and his three senators declared that Latona (for whose frogs, after all, they had all due respect) had nothing to do with the Ten Magistrates' having exceeded the limits of their jurisdiction. "I told you beforehand," said the archon, "but you didn't want to listen. Had my motion been passed, I am certain the archpriest would have given us a polite and complaisant answer; for a kind word is never lost. But the venerable chief priest thought he had found an opportunity for giving vent to his old resentment of the archpriest, and now it turns out that he and those who allowed themselves to be carried away by his unseasonable zeal have brought upon the Court of the Ten Magistrates a stain of disgrace which all the water of *Hebrus* and *Nestus*[31] will not wash away again in a hundred years. I admit," he added with a fury not perceived in him in many years, "that I'm getting tired of being the head of a Republic that is allowing itself to be destroyed by *asses' shadows* and *frogs,* and I very much am minded to resign my office before morning; but for as long as I'm still holding it, Reverend Chief Priest, you're going to have to answer to me for every disorder which from this moment on will occur on the streets of Abdera." And with these words, which were accompanied by a very serious glance at *Strobylus,* who was perplexed, the *archon* went off with his three adherents and left the rest behind in speechless consternation.

The chief priest, who began to be not a little alarmed by the turn which the mechanism of his invention had taken contrary to all expectation, finally said, "What are we going to do now, what are we to do now, gentlemen?"

"That we don't know," said both guild masters and the fourth senator and likewise departed, so that *Strobylus* and the two directors of the Sacred Pond were alone and, after all three had spoken at the same time for a while without themselves quite knowing what they were saying, finally agreed that before anything else, at the house of one of the directors, they would—eat their noon meal and then deliberate with their friends and supporters as to how they might now go about turning the agitation of the people that morning toward an end which could determine the victory of their party.

Chapter Eleven

Agathyrsus calls together his supporters. The substance of his speech to them. He invites them to a great sacrifice. The archon Onolaus wishes to resign his office. Anxiety of the archpriest's party regarding this intention. By what kind of strategy they thwart it.

Meanwhile, as soon as the deputies from the *Ten Magistrates* had left, *Agathyrsus* immediately invited to his residence, in addition to all the *Jasonites,* the most prominent of his supporters in the Council and among the citizenry. He related to them what he had just encountered at the instigation of the priest *Strobylus* and the Ten Magistrates, and he pointed out to them how necessary it now was for the repute of their party as well as for the honor and even for the preservation of the city of Abdera to thwart the designs of this scheming man and to give the populace, which he had alarmed by means of the ridiculous tall tale about the lamentations of the Frogs of Latona, a push in the opposite direction. It was obvious to everyone, he explained, that *Strobylus* had invented this wretched cock-and-bull story for no other reason but *to prepare* the likewise absurd charge, which he had brought against him, the archpriest, before the Ten Magistrates and wished to make out of it a matter concerning the welfare of the whole Republic, and which was all the more dangerous because of the superstitious prejudices of the people. But also this business about the welfare of the Republic was basically, after all, only a means he had seized upon in desperation in order to help put his collapsing party back on its feet and in the impending decision of the case about the ass's shadow to take advantage of the commotions which had thereby been stirred up in the city. Now because for precisely this reason it was easy to foresee that the nervous priest would take new material out of what had happened that morning with regard to the Ten Magistrates in order to make him, the archpriest, hated by the people and, in an

emergency, probably to stir up even a renewed, still more dangerous insurrection, so, he assured them, he had considered it necessary to put his and the community's most reliable friends in a
position to be able to give to the people and to all who might be
in need thereof more accurate notions about the events of the day
and their possible consequences. As for the *storks,* they had come
by themselves without his help and had built a nest in a tree in his
garden. He did not think he had the right to prevent their doing so,
partly because from times immemorial among all civilized peoples
storks had enjoyed a kind of sacred right to hospitality, and partly
because the freedom of the Temple of Jason and the protection of
this god applied to all living and lifeless things within the confines
of its walls. The law by which the Ten Magistrates had banished
storks from the domain of Abdera some years ago did not concern
him, since the jurisdiction of this tribunal extended only to what
concerned the worship of Latona and its rites. And he added that
it was, after all, common knowledge that the Temple of Jason was
associated with the Republic only to the extent that, on the occasion of the former's founding, the latter had promised to protect
the Temple against all violent undertakings of domestic or foreign
enemies; otherwise however, it was completely and forever free
from the jurisdiction of the Abderite courts. Therefore, by rejecting
the unauthorized summons he had done nothing but what his office
required of him. The Ten Magistrates, on the contrary, had, by this
ill-advised step to which the majority of them had been misled by
the priest *Strobylus,* placed him in the position of having to demand
from the Republic in the name of Jason and all the Jasonites the
strictest and most complete satisfaction because of such a gross
violation of his prerogatives as archpriest. The affair had more
serous consequences than the supporters of guild master *Pfriem*
and *Strobylus* and his frog tenders perhaps imagined. The *Golden
Fleece,* which the Jasonites preserved in this temple as their most
important patrimony, had for centuries been regarded and revered
as the *palladium of Abdera.* The citizens of Abdera had, therefore,
better not take, nor allow to be taken, any steps by which they
could, perhaps through their own fault, be robbed of the thing to
which, according to an ancient belief that had become a part of
their religion, the fate and the preservation of their Republic was
bound.

After this lecture, the archpriest received from all present the
strongest assurances of their zeal, for the common cause as well as
for the rights and liberties of the Temple of Jason. They discussed

the various measures they wished to take in order to stregthen the favorable attitude of the citizenry and to win back those people who might have become bewildered by the alleged miraculous sign about the frogs of Latona or stirred up against the archpriest's storks. Thereupon the meeting broke up, and everyone went to his post after Agathyrsus had invited them all to a solemn offering which he intended to make to Jason that evening in his temple.

While this was taking place in the archpriest's palace, the archon, extremely displeased over the not all too honorable role which he had had to play against his will, had arrived at home and had sent for all his relatives, brothers, brothers-in-law, sons, sons-in-law, nephews and cousins in order to announce to them that he had firmly resolved to give up his office before the Great Council on the next day and to retire to an estate which he had bought a few years ago on the Island of Thasos.[32] His eldest son and some members of his family were not present at this family convention because a half hour earlier they had been asked to the archpriest's. Now, since the rest saw that Onolaus, all their entreaties and expostulations notwithstanding, remained firm in his intention, one of their number stole away to report it to the meeting in the Temple of Jason and to call upon the people there for their support in opposing such an unexpected inimical step.

He arrived just when the people at the meeting were at the point of leaving. Those who had for a long time been acquainted with the archon's character found the matter more disquieting than appeared to most of them at first glance. "In ten years," they said, "this is perhaps the first time that the archon has come to a decision *all by himself.* Certainly it did not come to him all of a sudden! He has been brooding over it for a long time, and today's event merely burst open the shell which would have had to break sooner or later anyway. In short, this resolution is *his own doing;* it can, therefore, surely be depended on that it will not be so easy to dissuade him from it."

The entire gathering got uneasy about it. They thought that this turn, at such a precarious moment as the present one, could become very deterimental for the entire party and for the Republic itself. It was, therefore, unanimously decided that they would indeed have to allow as much about this intention of the archon to get out among the people as was necessary to frighten them and to keep them on tenterhooks; at the same time, however, they also wanted to manage, still prior to the sacrifice in the Temple of Jason, to have the most distinguished of the councillors and citizens of both parties go to the archon and implore him in the name of all Abdera not to abandon the helm of the Republic in the middle of a storm when they were most in need of *such a wise pilot.*

The idea of uniting the most distinguished people of both parties in this became necessary because it was foreseen that without this expedient all their work on the archon would be fruitless. For although from his youth he had been ardently devoted to the *aristocracy,* he had made it a principle *to avoid being known for this;* and his *popular appeal,* which he had been cultivating to this end for such a long time that it finally seemed quite natural to him, was precisely what had made him so much of a favorite with the people as few of his ancestors had ever been. Especially since the city was divided into the two parties of the *Asses* and the *Shadows,* he had made it a regular point of honor so to conduct himself that he might give neither of the parties cause to consider him one of them; and although almost all of his friends and relatives were out-and-out *Asses,* the *Shadows* nevertheless remained convinced that they were thereby at no disadvantage with him and that the Asses were at the same time not the gainers; the latter were compelled to hide all their steps from him, and with each advantage which they gained over the Shadows, they could rely on his inclining toward the side of their opponents in order to get matters back into equilibrium, although he did not like a single one of them personally.

The announcement of the archon's decision had the expected effect. The people became alarmed about it. Most of them said that there was no further need for investigating what the lament of the sacred frogs portended; if the archon were forsaking the Republic in the sorry condition it was in, then everything was lost.

The priest Strobylus and guild master Pfriem got the news about the great sacrifice organized by the archpriest at the same time as they heard the rumor about the archon's decision to resign his office. At one glance they foresaw the implications of this double coup and hurried to *reply* to the one and to *anticipate* the other. Strobylus had the people invited to an *expiation* rite which was to be put on that evening in the Temple of Latona with great ceremonies in order *to purify* the city of *secret crimes* and to ward off the evil omen of the *eleleleleleu* of the sacred frogs. On the other hand, Master Pfriem went out to look for the councillors, guild masters, and the most esteemed citizens of his party and to confer with them about how the archon might be persuaded to change his mind. Most of them had already been prepared by the secret agents of the other party who had been whispering about *as a great secret* that it was known to be quite certain that the Asses were doing everything possible secretly to strengthen the archon in his resolve. The Shadows were convinced thereby that their opponents were thinking of raising someone from their midst to the highest office in the Republic and, therefore, already seemed to be quite certain of having a majority in the Great Council, the body responsible for the election. This notion so greatly alarmed them that, with a crowd of people trailing behind them, they hurried over to *Onolaus's* house and, while the rabble's cheers for the archon resounded again and again, went up to beseech his Grace in the name of all the citizens to give up the unfortunate idea of resigning and never to forsake them, and least of all at a time when his wisdom was indispensable for pacifying the city.

The *archon* appeared to be very pleased about this public proof of the love and confidence *of his worthy fellow citizens*. He did not hide from them that barely a quarter of an hour earlier the greatest part of the councillors, of the Jasonites, and of all the rest of the old families of Abdera had come to him and had made the same request of him in just such gracious and urgent terms. He added that, although he had compelling reasons for being tired of the heavy burden of governing and for wishing that it might be put on stronger shoulders than his own, he did not have the heart to resist this so vividly expressed trust of both parties. He considered, he said, this unanimity of theirs with regard to his person and his office as a favorable augury for the early restoration of general peace and would, for his part, contribute to that end with pleasure.

When the archon had finished this fine speech, the *Shadows* looked at one another with wide-open eyes and were suddenly, much to their displeasure, more clever by half than before; for they now perceived that they had been tricked by the *Asses* and misled into making a false move. Believing that they *alone* were taking this step, they had hoped to draw the archon by that means entirely to their side, and now it turned out that he was under just as much obligation to their opponents as to them, which amounted to exactly the same as if to them he were under none at all. But this was not yet the worst. The deceitful behavior of the Asses was manifest proof of how important it was to them that the position of archon would *not* be vacated. Now *the person of Onolaus*, however could not matter much to them, for he had never done the least thing for their party. If, therefore, they so ardently wished that he might keep his position, then that could happen for no other reason than that they felt sure the *Shadows* would win the election of the new archon. These considerations, which now came to them at a glimpse, were of such an annoying kind that the poor *Shadows* had a world of trouble in concealing their indignation, and then they left quite hastily to the great pleasure of the archon, to whom it would not have occurred to be surprised by that or to notice the change in their faces.

That had been a great day for the wise and quite corpulent *Onolaus,* and he was now again completely reconciled with Abdera. He therefore commanded that his door be locked, he retired to the women's quarters, threw himself into his armchair, chatted with his wife and his daughters, ate his dinner, went early to bed and slept, well-consoled and unconcerned about the fate of Abdera, until the bright hours of the next morning.

Chapter Twelve

The day of decision. The measures of both parties. The Four Hundred assemble, and the trial begins. Philanthropic-patriotic dreams of the editor of this remarkable history.

The body politic of Abdera, while appearing to have the greatest inner agitation, was caused—by the jolts it had received in opposing directions from the various machines which had been allowed to run all day long on both sides—to waver in a sort of horizontal swaying, by virtue of which, at the time when the *Four Hundred* convened to come to a decision about the *case of the ass's shadow,* everything was in approximately the same state as a few days before, that is, that the Asses had on their side the greatest part of the Council, the patricians and the most notable and wealthiest of the citizens, the *Shadows,* on the other hand, drew most of their strength from the *greater number;* for, since the solemn procession around the frog pond of Latona which Strobylus had put on the evening before and which had been very devoutly attended by all the Shadows with the nomophylax *Gryllus* and guild master Pfriem at their head, the rabble had again declared for the latter party.

On the occasion of this procession it would have been an easy matter for the priest Strobylus and the other leaders of his party to cause much mischief in Abdera on the very same evening through their authority over a fanatical crowd of people who, for the greater part, had more to gain than to lose in the total ruin of the Republic. However—besides the fact that the chief priest had once again been most emphatically ordered in the name of the archon to keep the rabble in proper order and to see to it that the Temple and all the entrances to the Sacred Pond be locked before sundown—they, too, were themselves far away from carrying the thing to extremes without any really urgent cause or wishing to immerse the entire city in blood or to set it on fire; and, in spite of their *abderidity* in most respects, they were nevertheless intelligent enough to perceive that, if once the rabble had torn the reins from their hands, they would no longer be able to restrain again the violent rage of such a blindly rapacious animal. The guild master, therefore, since the procession was over and the doors of the Temple were being locked, contented himself with saying to the scattering crowd of people that he hoped all honest Abderites would turn up the next day at nine o'clock in the market place to hear the finding of the court about the affair of their fellow citizen Struthion and, as many of them as were going to be there, would help to see that his just cause might come off victorious.

This invitation was, of course, in spite of the mild and (in his opinion) very cautious expressions he used in stating it, not much better than an utmost illegal action of a seditious guild master who, in the last resort, wished to compel the judges by means of the immediate danger of a tumult to render the verdict he wished; however, it was just this that the *Shadows* had firmly resolved to risk bringing off; and since the other party was thoroughly convinced of this, they, on their part, had taken all possible measures to be prepared for the worst that could happen.

As soon as the trial began, the archpriest had all the entrances to the Temple of Jason guarded by a band of stalwart tanners and butchers who were furnished with stout clubs and knives; and in the houses of the most distinguished *Asses,* people had put themselves into a frame of mind as if they were thinking of holding out against a siege. The *Asses* themselves appeared at the place of the trial with daggers under their long garments; and some of those who talked the loudest had had the foresight even to wear armor under their doublets in order to be able to oppose their patriotic breasts with so much the greater security to the blows from the enemies of the good cause.

The ninth hour was now approaching. All Abdera was atremble in expectation of the outcome which such an unprecedented lawsuit would have; no one had eaten a proper breakfast, although everyone had been on his feet by daybreak. *The Four Hundred* assembled on the raised court in front of the Temple of Apollo and Diana (the customary place for the meetings of the Great Council in the open air) across from the big market place from which a broad flight of stairs with fourteen steps led up to the terrace. The plaintiff and the defendant had also already arrived with their closest relatives and their two sycophants and taken their proper places, while the entire market place filled up with a crowd of people whose views were plainly enough revealed by a noisy cheer whenever a councillor or guild master from the Shadow's party came by.

Everybody was now waiting for the *nomophylax* who, following the customs of the city of Abdera, presided whenever the meeting of the Great Council did not directly concern public affairs. The *Asses* had indeed done everything to persuade the archon Onolaus to occupy with his own venerable person the ivory arm chair (placed for the president three steps over the councillors' benches) because, after all, this would be a matter of a new law; but he declared that he would prefer to die rather than agree to preside over an ass's-shadow-court. Therefore, they saw themselves forced to yield to his sense of propriety.

The nomophylax—as a great devotee of etiquette and accustomed on such occasions to have people wait for him—had seen to it that in the interim the meeting would be entertained by music of his own composition and (as he put it) be prepared for such a solemn action. This inspiration, although it was an innovation, was, nevertheless, very favorably received and had a very good effect (against the intentions of the nomophylax, who wished therewith to inspire his party with greater courage and zeal). For the music gave members of the archpriest's party cause for making a great many facetious remarks about which, from time to time, there was much laughter. One said: "This *allegro* sounds like a battle song, don't you know"—"*for a fight between quail,*" another chimed in. "But then," said a third, "the *adagio* sounds as if it were to be sung at the funeral of the toothbreaker Struthion and Master *Cobbler,* his protector."—"All of the music," said a fourth, "deserves to be made by Shadows and heard by Asses," and so on. Now, however chilling these jokes were, with such a jovial and easily infected small nation nothing more was needed, though, to bring the entire assembly, without anyone's noticing it, round to its natural, comic mood; a mood which imperceptibly detoxicated the partisan frenzy of which they were no longer possessed and contributed more perhaps than anything else to the preservation of the city at this crucial moment.

Finally the nomophylax appeared with his bodyguard of poor emaciated and infirm workmen who, armed with dull halberds[33] and a pacifistic kind of rusty swords, had more of the appearance of the ridiculous figures with which one frightens birds from the garden than of warriors who were, in the eyes of the rabble, to lend the court dignity and to inspire fear. Meanwhile, here's to the Republic that for the protection of its gates and its internal security has need of no other heroes than these!

The sight of these grotesque militiamen and the clumsy, droll way they behaved in the martial attire in which they had, not without effort, been disguised, awakened among the spectators a new attack of merriment so that the herald had a lot of trouble getting the people finally to be tolerably quiet and to show the respect which they owed to the highest court.

Now the president opened the session with a short speech, the herald ordered all to be silent again, and the sycophants of both sides were called upon individually to present their indictment and defense.

For the sycophants, who were considered great masters of their kind, the opportunity alone to display their art on the *shadow of an ass* had in itself to be very encouraging. It can, therefore, easily be imagined how thoroughly they must have pulled themselves together, since this ass's shadow had become an object in which the entire Republic was interested and on account of which it had split into two parties, each of which had made the cause of one of the clients its own. From the time an Abdera had been in the world, no one had yet seen a lawsuit that was so ridiculous in itself and so serious in the way it was treated. A sycophant would really have had no genius and no *sycophant-sense* at all who, on such an occasion, would not have surpassed himself.

So much the more must it be deplored that the notorious ravages of time, which so many other great works of genius and wit could not escape nor, alas, will escape in the future, did not spare the originals of these two famous speeches either—at least, so far as we know. For who knows whether a future *Fourmont, Seven,* or *Villoison*[34] who is bent on discovering old manuscripts may not some day succeed in tracking down a copy of the same in some dusty corner or other in an old monastery library? Or, if this could not be hoped for, who can say whether or not in the sequence of ages Thrace itself will fall again into the hands of Christian princes who will consider it an honor to be great patrons of the sciences, to establish academies, to have buried cities excavated, and so on. Who knows if this present history of Abdera itself (as incomplete as it is)—translated into the language of this *better Thrace* of the future, will not have the honor of causing such a *new-Thracian leader of the Muses* to get the idea suddenly of evoking the city of Abdera from out of its ruins?—since then, without a doubt, also the office of the city clerk and the archives of this famous Republic will again be found, and in the same, all the original documents of the trial about the ass's shadow along with the speeches, the loss of which we are deploring. At least it is pleasant to soar into the future on the wings of such *patriotic-philanthropic dreams* and to anticipate one's share of the bliss in store for our descendants; bliss obviously guaranteed by the ever greater perfection of the sciences and the arts and, what is flowing from them over all mortals, the enlightenment, embellishment, and sublimation of one's way of thinking, of taste, and of morals.

Meanwhile, it affords us some consolation, after all, that from the papers out of which the present fragments of the history of Abdera have been taken, we can furnish at least an excerpt of these speeches whose authenticity is so much the more trustworthy since no reader who has a nose will mistake the *scent of abderidity* arising therefrom. An inner argument which, when all is said and done, always appears to be the best after all that can be given for the work of any mortal, be he now an *Ossian*[35] or an *Abderite fig speaker.*[36]

Chapter Thirteen

The speech of the sycophant Physignatus.

The sycophant Physignatus who, as counsel of the dentist *Struthion,* spoke first, was a man of medium height, strong muscles, and mighty lungs. He took pride in the fact that he had been a pupil of the famous *Gorgias*[37] and claimed to be one of the greatest orators of his time. But in this respect, as in many others, he was a manifest Abderite. His greatest art consisted in his jumping around like a squirrel from one interval to another in the range of one and one-half octaves in order to give more vivacity and expression to his verbose speech by means of the varied modulation of his voice and making, besides, so many faces and gestures as if his audience could understand him only through pantomime.

Still, we do not want to deny him the merit of knowing how to use pretty dexterously all the tricks with which one predisposes judges in one's favor, confuses their mind, makes one's opponent hated, and in general can make a thing appear better than it is; also, on occasion, he knew how to create no mean *pictures,* as the perspicacious reader will best gather from his speech itself without our reminder.

Physignatus behaved with all the impudence of a sycophant who relies on having Abderites as his audience, and therefore he began:

"Noble, honorable, and wise men. High and mighty members of the Four Hundred!

"If ever there was a day on which the excellence of the constitution of our Republic was revealed in its greatest resplendence, and if I have ever appeared among you with the feeling of what it is to be a citizen of Abdera, then it is on this great day when, before this highest court, before this expectant and sympathetic crowd of people, before this imposing confluence of foreigners, crowds of whom have been attracted by the renown of such an extraordinary spectacle, a lawsuit is to be brought to a head which, in a less free, less well organized state, which even in a Thebes, Athens, or Sparta would not have been considered important enough to occupy the proud administrators of the commonwealth for one moment. Noble, praiseworthy, thrice fortunate Abdera! You alone enjoy under the protection of legislation to which even the least, even the most dubious and most subtle rights and claims of the citizens are sacred, you alone enjoy the existence of a security and freedom, of which other republics (whatever the advantages may otherwise be which their patriotic vanity boasts of possessing) have only the shadow as their share.

"Or, tell me, in which other republic would a lawsuit between a common citizen and one of the lowest from among the people, a lawsuit which at first glance amounts to barely two or three drachmas, about an object that appears to be so insignificant that the laws have completely forgotten it in the designation of things which can be accounted as property, a lawsuit about something whose name as a thing a subtle logician could even dispute—in a word, a quarrel about the shadow of an ass—tell me, in which other republic would *such* a lawsuit have become the object of general interest, become everyone's concern and, therefore, if I may say so, the concern of the entire state? In what other republic are the laws of property so clearly stated, the mutual rights of the citizens so guaranteed against any arbitrary action on the part of persons in authority, the most trivial claims or demands of even the poorest man considered so momentous and important in the eyes of the government that the highest court of the republic itself does not deem it beneath its dignity to assemble with pomp and ceremony in order to render a judgment on the dubious seeming right *to an ass's shadow.*

"Woe betide the man who at these words could turn up his nose and, on account of silly, childish concepts of what is great or small, could look with the uncomprehending smile of contempt upon what constitutes the highest honor of our laws, the glory of our government, the triumph of the entire Abderite way of life and of each good citizen! Woe betide the man, I repeat for the second and third time, who would not have the sense to feel this. And hail to the republic in which, the instant the prerogatives of the citizens, some doubt about mine and thine, the foundation of all civic security, are concerned, an ass's shadow is no small thing either.

"But while, to such a degree, I feel and recognize on the one hand with all the warmth of a patriot, with all the just pride of a real Abderite, what glorious testimony the present trial will give to our furthest posterity of the splendid constitution of our Republic as well as of the impartial firmness and the solicitude overlooking nothing with which our most praiseworthy ruling authorities are handling the balance of justice, how much must I deplore, on the other hand, the diminution of that guileless simplicity of our forefathers, the disappearance of that civic-minded and neighborly disposition, of that mutual diligence, of that voluntary inclination, out of love and friendship, because of a good heart, or at least for the sake of peace, to give up some of our supposed, strict rights— how much, in a word, must I deplore the decline of the good old ways of Abdera, which is the true and only source of the degrading and shameful lawsuit in which we are entangled today! How will I be able to speak frankly without much blushing? Oh once so famous honesty and goodheartedness of our old people, have things come to *such a pass* with you that Abderite citizens—they who on every occasion ought to be ready, out of patriotic loyalty and neighborly friendship, to exchange their hearts with one another— are so selfish, so stingy, so unkind, what am I saying, so inhuman as to deny to one another even the shadow of an ass?

"Yet—I beg your pardon, worthy fellow citizens, I erred in using that word—pardon my uttering an unintentional insult. He who was capable of such a low, such a coarse and barbaric turn of mind is not one of our fellow citizens. He is only a tolerated inhabitant of our city, one who merely enjoys the protection of the Temple of Jason, a man from the crassest scum of the rabble, a man from whose birth, upbringing, and way of life nothing better could be expected, in a word, *a donkey driver*—who, except for the same soil and the common air which he breathes, has nothing more in common with us than the wildest peoples of the Hyperborean wastes.[38] His shame adheres to him alone; it cannot besmirch *us*. An Abderite citizen, I venture to say, could not have made himself guilty of such an outrage.

"However—am I, perhaps, using too strong a term for this

deed?—Put yourself, I beg you, in the place of your good fellow citizen *Struthion*—and feel!

"He is traveling on business from Abdera to Gerania. The business of his noble art is concerned solely with the lessening of the suffering of his fellow human beings. It is one of the most sultry days of summer. The severest heat of the sun appears to have transformed the entire horizon into the hollow belly of a glowing oven. No little cloud that might subdue its scorching rays. No breath of air to refresh the wanderer parched with thirst. The sun blazes over his head, sucks the blood from his veins, the marrow from his bones. Athirst, his dry tongue cleaving to his palate, his dim eyes being blinded by heat and glare, he looks about him for a shady spot, for any single compassionate tree under whose shade he might be able to take a rest, breathe in a mouthful of fresh air, be safe for a moment from the fiery arrows of inexorable Apollo.

"In vain! You all know the country between Abdera and Gerania. For two hours, let it be said to the shame of all Thrace! no tree, no shrub which could rest the eye of the wanderer in this dreadful expanse of meager fields, some with grain and others lying fallow, or give him refuge from the noonday sun.

"Finally, poor Struthion sank from his animal. Nature could hold out no longer. He had the ass halt, and he sat down in its shadow. Weak, wretched means to get a rest. But as little as it was, it was something nevertheless.

"And what a monster the unfeeling, stonyhearted churl had to be who could withhold from his suffering fellow man in such circumstances the shadow of an ass! Would the existence of such a man be credible if we didn't see him before us with our own eyes?— But here he stands, and—what is almost even worse, even more unbelievable than the deed itself—he freely admits it, appears to boast of his shame; and so that he might leave to nobody like him who may be born sometime in the future any possibility of matching his shameless impudence, he is carrying it so far, after having already been found guilty by the venerable municipal court of original jurisdiction, as to maintain, even before the majesty of this highest court of law, the Four Hundred, *that he was right in doing so.*—'I did not deny him the ass's shadow,' he says, 'although by strict rights I wasn't bound to let him sit in it; I only asked him for a fair token of gratitude for letting him now also have the shadow in addition to the ass I had rented out to him.'—Wretched, shameful excuse! What would we think of the man who would want to prevent a half-dead wanderer from sitting down free of charge in the shadow of his tree? Or what would we call the man who would not allow a stranger dying of thirst to revive from the water flowing on his own property?

"Remember, oh men of Abdera, that this alone and no other was the crime of those *Lycian peasants*[39] whom the father of gods and men, in vengeance for a similar cruelty which these wretches perpetrated on his beloved *Latona* and her children, transformed into frogs as a frightful example for all future times. A horrible miracle, whose truth and memory are kept alive, immortalized and, as it were, renewed daily in our midst in the Sacred Grove and Pond of Latona, the revered tutelary goddess of our city. And you, *Anthrax,* you, an inhabitant of the city in which this fearful monument of the wrath of the gods at humaneness refused is an object of the public faith and worship, you were not afraid to draw their vengeance down upon you through a similar crime?

"But you stubbornly insist on your property rights. 'Whoever justly avails himself of his rights does no one an injustice. I owe somebody else no more than he deserves from me. If the ass is my property, then his shadow is, too.'

"Is that what you say? And do you think, or does the sharp-witted and eloquent legal adviser, into whose hands you have placed the worst case which ever came before a court of gods or men, does he think, with all the sorcery of his eloquence or with all the cobwebs of sophistic fallacies, that he can so overwhelm and ensnare our minds that we might be persuaded to regard a shadow as something real, let alone as somehing to which someone could have a direct and exclusive right?

"I would be abusing your patience, high and mighty gentlemen, and offending your wisdom, if I wished here to repeat all the arguments with which I demonstrated in the court of original jurisdiction, as can be read in the records, the nullity of our opponents' sophistries. I will for now content myself, as is required by necessity, with saying only this little about it. A *shadow* cannot, to speak precisely, be classed with real things. For what makes it into a shadow is nothing real and positive, but rather just the opposite, namely the withdrawal of that light which is on the other things surrounding the shadow. In the present case, the oblique position of the sun and the *opacity* of the ass (a property which does not adhere to him in so far as he is an ass, but rather inasmuch as he is *a dense and opaque body*) are the sole, true cause of the shadow which the ass appears to cast, and which any other body in his place would cast; for the form of the shadow is irrelevant here. Therefore, my client did not sit down, strictly speaking, in the shadow *of an ass,* but rather in the shadow *of a body;* and the circumstance that this body was an ass, and the ass a housemate of a certain Anthrax of the Temple of Jason in Abdera, concerned him no more than it was pertinent. For, as I have said, not the *asininity* (if I may so put it) but rather the corporeality and opacity of the frequently mentioned ass is the cause of the shadow he appears to cast.

"However, even if we unnecessarily admit that the shadow belongs among *things,* then from countless examples it is clear and known the world over that it is to be ranked among the *common things* to which everyone has as much right as another and to which he acquires the most direct right who first takes possession of it.

"But I will do still more; I will even admit that the ass's shadow is an *appurtenance* of the ass as much as his ears are; what will our opponents gain with that? *Struthion* had rented the ass, hence also his shadow. For with every lease it is understood that the lessor turns over to the lessee for the latter's use the thing under discussion with all its appurtenances and with its entire usufruct. With what shadow of a claim could *Anthrax,* therefore, demand of Struthion an additional, special payment for the shadow of the ass? The dilemma is beyond all contradiction; either the shadow of the ass is an appurtenance of the ass or not. If it is not, then Struthion and everybody else has just as much right to it as Anthrax. But if it is, then Anthrax, by renting out the ass, had also rented out the shadow; and his demand is just as absurd as if someone had sold me his lyre and then insisted, if I wished to play on it, I would have to pay him for its *sound* besides.

"However, why so many arguments in a matter which is so clear to common sense that one need only to hear about it in order to see on which side justice lies? What is an ass's shadow? What impudence of this Anthrax, in so far as he has no just claim, to usurp it to practice usury! And if the shadow was really his, what meanness to deny such a small thing, the least that can be named or imagined, something completely useless in a thousand other cases, to a man, a neighbor, and a friend in that single instance where it is indispensable to him.

"Do not allow, noble and high and mighty men of the Four Hundred, do not allow it to be said of Abdera that such malice, that such a crime had found refuge in a court before which (as before that famous *Areopagus* at *Athens*)[40] gods themselves would not blush to have their quarrel arbitrated. The dismissal of the plaintiff with his inadmissible, unjust and ridiculous suit and appeal, a judgment against him for all costs and damages which he caused the innocent defendant to have through his unauthorized behavior in this affair, that is now the least that I can ask in the name of my client. The incompetent plaintiff is also under obligation to render satisfaction, and enormous satisfaction indeed, if it is to be commensurate with the magnitude of his crime. Satisfaction to the defendant, whose domestic peace and quiet, business, honor, and reputation have been disturbed and attacked in countless ways by the plaintiff and his protectors during the course of this trial. Satisfaction to the venerable municipal court, from whose just decision, without cause, he appealed to this high tribunal. Satisfaction to this highest court itself which he has maliciously dared to importune with such a contemptible lawsuit. Satisfaction, finally, to the entire city and Republic of Abdera which, on this occasion, he disturbed, divided, and placed in danger.

"Do I ask too much, high and mighty gentlemen? Do I ask something unjust? Look here at all of Abdera which throngs in countless numbers to the steps of this high court and, in the name of a meritorious but grievously wronged fellow citizen, indeed in the name of the Republic itself, *expects* satisfaction, *demands* satisfaction. If respect binds their tongues, then, nevertheless, this just demand is sparkling from every eye, a demand that cannot be refused. The confidence of the citizens, the security of their prerogatives, the restoration of our private and public peace and quiet, the establishment of the same for the future, in a word, the welfare of our entire state depends on the verdict that you will render, on the fulfillment of a just and general expectation. And if, in the first ages of the world, when the Titans made a sudden attack at night, an *ass* could take the credit for rousing up the slumbering gods with his braying and thereby saving Olympus itself from devastation and destruction[41]—then may *the shadow of an ass* now be the occasion and this day the happy epoch in which this ancient city and Republic, after so many dangerous convulsions, is again pacified, in which the bond between authorities and citizens is tightly drawn together again, in which all past dissensions are cast into the abyss of oblivion, in which, through the just conviction of a single criminal donkey driver, the entire state is saved and its flourishing prosperity secured for all time."

Chapter Fourteen

Answer of the sycophant Polyphonus.
As soon as Physignatus had stopped speaking, the people, or

rather the rabble, who filled the market place, indicated their approval with loud shouting which was so vehement and incessant that the judges finally began to fear that the entire procedure might thereby be interrupted. The party of the archpriest got visibly embarrassed. The *Shadows,* on the other hand, although they constituted the minority in the Great Council, took new heart and expected a favorable outcome from the impression that this prelude would have to make on the Asses.

In the meantime, the guild masters did not fail to let the people know through signals that they should be quiet, and after the herald had finally restored a general quiet by calling out three times, Polyphonus, the donkey driver's sycophant, a thick-set, sturdy man with short, curly hair and thick, jet-black eyebrows, raised his bass voice that resounded all over the market place and spoke as follows.

"High and mighty men of the Four Hundred!

"Truth and light are superior to all other things in the world by virtue of their needing no extraneous help in order to be seen. I willingly leave to my adversary all the advantages he thought he was drawing from his oratorical tricks. It befits him who is in the wrong to hoodwink children and fools through figures of speech and locutions and feints and all the legerdemain of school rhetoric. Intelligent people do not allow themselves to be deceived by these things. I have no intention of inquiring into how much honor and posthumous fame the Republic of Abdera will gain with this lawsuit about an ass's shadow. I will seek neither to corrupt the judges with crude flattery nor to frighten them with veiled threats. Still much less do I intend with seditious speeches to give to the people the signal for making noise and for rioting. I know why I am here and to whom I am speaking. In short, I will be satisfied with proving that the donkey driver Anthrax is *in the right* or, to express myself more precisely and fairly than could be required of an advocate, is *less in the wrong* than his indefensible adversary. The judge will then certainly know what his office requires of him without my needing to remind him of it."

At this point a few of the rabble who were standing close to the steps of the terrace began to interrupt the speaker with shouts, abusive remarks, and threats. Since, however, the nomophylax arose from his ivory throne, the herald once again gave the order for silence, and the militiamen who were posted at the steps raised their long spears, everything was suddenly quiet once more, and the speaker, who was not so easily disconcerted, continued thus:

"High and mighty gentlemen, I am not standing here as the advocate of the donkey driver Anthrax, but as the authorized representative of the Temple of Jason and on behalf of the illustrious and very reverend *Agathyrsus,* its present archpriest and head, Guardian of the true Golden Fleece, highest court authority over all its foundations, estates, courts and jurisdictions, and leader of the most noble race of Jasonites, in order to ask in the name of Jason and his Temple that satisfaction be given the donkey driver Anthrax, *because actually he is, after all, most in the right;* and that he is I hope to prove so clearly and audibly that the blind will see the point and the deaf hear it in spite of all the subterfuges which my opponent boasts of having learned from his master *Gorgias.* So, with no further introduction, let's get down to brass tacks.

"Anthrax rented out his ass to the dentist Struthion for one day, not to use just as he might wish, but to bear him, the dentist with his portmanteau, halfway to Gerania which, as everyone knows, is eight long miles from here.

"Naturally, when the ass was being rented out, neither of the two thought of its shadow. But when the dentist dismounted in the middle of the field and forced the ass, which had truly suffered more from the heat than he, to stand in the sun so that he could sit down in its shadow, it was quite natural that the master and owner of the ass did not stay indifferent while that was going on.

"I do not wish to deny that Anthrax did something silly and asinine when he asked the toothbreaker to pay him for the ass's *shadow* for the reason that he had not rented out to him the *shadow* as well. But then, too, he is merely a donkey driver by heritage, that is, a man who, precisely because he grew up among nothing but asses and lives more among asses than among honest people, has inherited and acquired a kind of right to be not much better than an ass himself. When all is said and done, it was merely—the joke of a donkey driver.

"But into what class of brute are we to place the man who took such a joke in bad part? If Mr. Struthion had acted like an intelligent man, he need only have said to the rude fellow: good friend, we're not going to have a quarrel about an ass's shadow. Because I did not rent the ass from you to sit down in its shadow but to ride on it to Gerania, it is in any case only fair for me to compensate you for the few minutes of lost time caused you by my dismounting, particularly since the ass has to stand in the heat all the longer and isn't improved thereby. Here, brother, is half a drachma for you; let me catch my breath here for a moment, and then we will, in the name of all frogs, set out again.

"Had the dentist taken this tone, he would have been talking like an honest and reasonable man. The donkey driver would even have said to him for the half drachma 'May God reward you for it!', and the city of Abdera would have been spared the uncertain posthumous fame which my counterpart promises it from this ass's trial, and all the disturbances that had to develop therefrom as soon as so many great, notable gentlemen and ladies interfered in the matter. Instead of that, the man gets up on his own high ass, insists on his unlimited right, on the strength of his lease, to sit down in the ass's shadow as often and as long as he may want, and by so doing gets the donkey driver into such a rage that he goes running to the municipal judge and makes a charge which is as fatuous as the defendant's answer.

"Now I just wonder if, as an instructive example, it were not a good thing to crop the ears of the sycophant Physignatus, my most worthy colleague, to whose agitation, don't you see, we must quite exclusively attribute the toothbreaker's not agreeing to the fair settlement proposed by the venerable judge Philippides, and, for the service he has rendered with all this to the Abderite commonwealth, to fasten in their place, as an eternal souvenir perhaps, a pair of ass's ears; likewise, the kind of a public reward the venerable guild master Pfriem and the other gentlemen who, with their patriotic zeal, threw oil into the fire, might have earned for their trouble, the illustrious archpriest, my employer, leaves to the special, discerning judgment of the highest court, the Four Hundred. He, for his part, as hereditary sovereign and judge of the donkey driver Anthrax, will not fail to have twenty-five strokes with a stick counted to him immediately after the end of the trial as a well-deserved reward for the stupidity he displayed in this lawsuit. However, since therefore the right of the often-mentioned donkey driver to demand satisfaction nevertheless continues in full force because of the abuse he suffered at the hands of the dentist Struthion, because of the latter's misuse of his ass, and because of the refusal of fair indemnification for the lost time involved and for the deterioration of his beast of burden, the illustrious archpriest desires and expects of the justice of this high court that, without further delay, the proper, most complete compensation and satisfaction be rendered his subject.

"To you, however" (he added, turning toward the people) "I am to announce in Jason's name that all of you who, in an improper and seditious way, sympathized with the evil cause of the toothbreaker are to be and will remain excluded from the charities which the Temple of Jason bestows every month on the poor citizens until such time as proper compensation for that will have been made."

Chapter Fifteen

*Stir caused by the speech of Polyphonus. Supplementary state-
ment made by the sycophant Physignatus. Embarrassment of the
judges.*

For a few moments this short and unexpected speech brought
forth a deep silence. To be sure, the sycophant *Physignatus* appeared to wish very much to speak ardently about the passage
that had concerned him personally; however, when he noticed the
dejection which the content of his opponent's last sentence seemed
to have caused among the common people, he was satisfied with
keeping to himself *quaevis competentia*[42] he might have said
against the libellous passage about cutting off ears and other innu-
endoes, shrugged his shoulders, and said nothing.

The light in which the sycophant *Polyphonus* had placed the true
state of the controversy had such a good effect that there were
hardly twenty men among all of the Four Hundred who did not,
according to Abderite habit, give their assurance *that from the very
beginning this had been their view of the matter, too;* and there
was some talk in quite vivid terms against those who were to blame
that such a simple matter had been stirred up into such difficulties.
Most of them appeared to be proposing not only that the archpriest
be awarded the compensation and satisfaction demanded for his
subject, but also that a committee from the Great Council ought
to be appointed to investigate stringently just who were the first
instigators and inciters of this affair.

This proposal suddenly again enraged the guild master and those
who had sided with him in advance before there was any hope for
success. The sycophant Physignatus, who drew new courage from
that, asked the nomophylax to be allowed to speak once again
because he had something new to say with regard to his counterpart's speech; and since by rights this could not be refused him,
he expressed himself as follows:

"If the well-deserved trust in such a venerable court as this one
deserves the odious name of corrupting flattery, which my counterpart did not hesitate to call it, then I must resign myself to allowing
blame to rest on me which I cannot avoid; and I believe, in any
event, that I am sinning less by having a far too high opinion of
you, high and mighty gentlemen, than my adversary by imagining
he can capture your righteousness and discernment in so rude a
snare as he has set for you. The semblance of common sense with

which he has coated his coarse notions of the matter, and a tone which he seems to have borrowed from his client can at best cause a momentary surprise; but that they could have the power to overturn completely the wisdom of the highest council of Abdera would be blasphemy of me to fear and was nonsense for him to hope.

"How is that? Polyphonus, instead of defending the just cause of his client as he did before the venerable municipal court, and up until now always stubbornly, now suddenly himself admits that the donkey driver was unjust and unreasonable in basing his charge against the dentist Struthion on his supposed proprietary right to the ass's shadow; he publicly admits that the plaintiff made an incompetent, unfounded, frivolous charge, and he dares to prate about a right of indemnification and, in the defiant tone of a donkey driver, *to demand satisfaction*? What new unprecedented kind of jurisprudence, if the party in the wrong, when he no longer knew any other way out, could scrape through by admitting in the end that he was at fault and, with twenty-five strokes of a stick, which he would accept for that and which a fellow like Anthrax can take across his back all right, could acquire a right to compensation and satisfaction in addition! Supposing, too, that the donkey driver's fault consisted merely in *his not initiating the proper action;* of what concern is that to his innocent opponent or to the judge? The former must make his answer conform to the charge, and the latter renders a judgment on the case, not as it could appear perhaps in another light and from a different point of view, but as it was presented to him. I hope, therefore, in the name of my client that, despite the opposition's beating of the air, the present case will be adjudicated, not according to the new direction which Polyphonus tried to give it and which runs counter to all the trials held until now, but according to the nature of the charge and of the evidence. The point in question in the present litigation is not the loss of time or the deterioration of the ass, but *the ass's shadow.* The plaintiff maintained that his proprietary rights to the ass also extended to its shadow, and he has *not proved it*. The defendant maintained that he had as much right to the ass's shadow as the owner, or that he had acquired, through the lease, whatever part of it could perhaps be sold; and he has *proved* his contention.

"Therefore, high and mighty gentlemen, here I stand and demand a judicial verdict on what has until now constituted the subject of the dispute. On that account alone the present highest court was convened. This alone now constitutes the issue on which it has to pass judgment! And I venture to say before all these people listening to me—either there is no longer any justice in Abdera, or my demand is lawful, and the rights of every citizen are involved in my client's being awarded his."

The sycophant stopped talking, the judges were taken aback, the people began murmuring anew and started to become restless, and the Shadows tossed their heads again.

"Now," said the nomophylax while he turned to Polyphonus, "what does the counsel for the plaintiff wish to bring forward regarding this?"

"Highly esteemed Chief Justice," answered Polyphonus, "nothing—but everything word for word what I have already said. The trial about the ass's shadow is such a bad lawsuit that it cannot be settled soon enough. The plaintiff was in the wrong in this, the defendant was in the wrong, the counselors were in the wrong, the judge of the court of original jurisdiction was in the wrong, all of Abdera was in the wrong! It would seem that an evil wind had blown at us all, and we were not quite as right in the head as might possibly be wished. If it were absolutely important for us to prostitute ourselves any longer, then I would probably not lack the breath either to give a speech in support of my client's right to his ass's shadow which would take from sunrise to sunset. But, as I have said, if the comedy we have been playing still can be excused as long as it remained comedy merely, it would, after all, in no wise be right, it seems to me, to continue playing it any longer before such a venerable court as the High Council of Abdera. At least I have no mandate to do so, and therefore I leave it to you, high and mighty gentlemen, while repeating once again everything I rightly demanded in the name of the illustrious and right reverend archpriest, to arrive at a decision about this case and to settle it—as the gods will inspire you."

The judges were very much at a loss, and it is hard to say of what expedient they would finally have availed themselves in order to get out of the affair with honor if chance, which at all times has been the great tutelary god of all Abderites, had not looked after them and given to this fine *middle-class drama* an evolution that a moment before no one expected, nor could expect.

Chapter Sixteen

Unforeseen evolution of the entire comedy and restoration of peace and quiet in Abdera.

The ass, whose shadow had (according to the words of the archon Onolaus) until now caused such a strange eclipse in the crani-

ums of the Abderites, had been led off to the public stable of the
Republic, where it was to stay until the conclusion of the trial. It
had been fed poorly there ever since, and the best that can be said
about it is that it had grown no fatter.

Now on this morning the stable hands of the Republic, who knew
that the lawsuit was about to end, suddenly got the idea that the
ass, who, so to speak, was playing a central figure in the case,
ought in fairness to be in on it, too, after all. They had, therefore,
curried him, decorated him with wreaths of flowers and with rib-
bons, and were now leading him up in great pomp in the company
of innumerable urchins cheering after them. Chance would have it
that they got into the next street which ran into the market place
just as Polyphonus had finished his supplementary remarks and
the poor judges were entirely at their wit's end, whereas the people
wavered in an uncertain and ill-humored kind of agitation between
fear of the archpriest and the new impulse given them by the second speech of the sycophant Physignatus. The noise made by the
above-mentioned urchins around the ass drew everyone's eyes toward the side it was coming from. People were taken aback and
crowded around. "Ha," a man from the mob finally cried out, "here
comes the *ass* himself."—"It probably wants to help the judges
come to a decision," said another. "That damned ass," shouted a
third, "he's been the ruination of us all! I wish the wolves had eaten
him before he got us saddled with this ungodly lawsuit."—"Hey!"
shouted *a tinker* who had always been one of the most enthusiastic
Shadows, "*whoever is a good Abderite, have at the ass!* He's going
to pay the piper for us! Don't leave one hair out of his shabby tail
remain of him!"

In one moment the whole crowd pounced upon the poor animal,
and in a few moments it was torn into a thousand pieces. Everyone
wanted to have a bit of it, too. They ripped, beat, tugged, scratched,
scuffled, and tussled for it with an incomparable rage. The fury of
some went so far that they devoured their share on the spot, raw
and bloody; most of them, however, ran home with what they had
carried away; and since each one had a crowd chasing along behind
him that attempted to snatch his booty away from him with great
clamor, the entire market place got as empty in a few minutes as
at midnight.

On the spur of the moment the men of the Four Hundred were
so greatly alarmed by this uproar, the cause of which they could
not see right away, that all of them, without themselves knowing
what they were doing, drew forth the murderous weapons they
were carrying concealed under their cloaks, and the gentlemen

looked at one another with no small degree of astonishment when suddenly, from the nomophylax down to the lowest member of the court, there was a bare dagger glistening in each hand. When they finally saw and heard what it was all about, however, they quickly put up their knives again and, to a man, like the gods in the first book of the *Iliad,* they all burst out in inextinguishable laughter.

"Thank heaven!" the *nomophylax* finally cried out laughing after the very venerable gentlemen had once again recovered their senses, "with all our wisdom we could not have given the case a more suitable outcome. Why did we wish to cudgel our brains any longer? The ass, the innocent cause of this confounded affair, has (as things usually go) become its victim; the mob vented its anger on it, and now all that matters is a good decision on our part, and then this day, which but a little while ago looked as if it would come to a melancholy end, can become a day of joy and restoration of general peace. Since the ass itself no longer exists, what good would it do to keep arguing about its *shadow?* I therefore make a motion that this entire *ass's case* be herewith publicly accepted as terminated and settled, that an eternal silence be imposed on both parties, *whose costs and damages will be reimbursed from the funds in the city treasury,* that a *statue,* however, paid for out of the public funds of the city, be erected to the poor ass to serve both us and our descendants as an everlasting reminder *of how easily a great and flourishing republic could have been ruined by nothing more than an ass's shadow.*"

Everyone applauded the motion of the nomophylax as the most clever and equitable way out that could be taken under the circumstances. Both parties could be satisfied with it, and the Republic was still buying its pacification and the prevention of greater ignominy and mischief cheaply enough. The resolution was, therefore, drawn up unanimously by the Four Hundred in accordance with this statement, although it cost some effort to get guild master Pfriem not to play odd man out; and the Great Council, with its warlike militia making up the van and the rear, accompanied the nomophylax back to his residence, where he invited his colleagues one and all for the evening to a great concert with which, in consolidation of re-established concord, he wished to oblige them.

The archpriest Agathyrsus not only let off the donkey driver from receiving the promised twenty-five strokes with a stick, but in addition made him a present of three fine mules from his own stable with the explicit prohibition not to accept any indemnification from the municipal funds of Abdera. On the following day he gave all the *Shadows* in the Small and Great Council a splendid banquet, and in the evening, among the common citizens of all the guilds, he had half a drachma handed out to each man, so that they could with that drink to his health and to the health of all good Abderites. This generosity suddenly won him all hearts again, and since anyway the Abderites were people (as we know) whom it cost nothing to go from one extreme to the other, it is not surprising, in view of such noble conduct on the part of the man who, until now, had been the leader of the stronger party, that shortly the names of Asses and Shadows were no longer heard at all.

The Abderites themselves now laughed at their folly as a seizure of feverish madness which was, thank goodness, over now. One of their ballad mongers (of whom they had very many and very bad ones) hurried as fast as he could to put the entire story into the form of a *popular song* that was immediately sung on all the streets, and the maker of dramas *Thlaps* did not fail within a few weeks to put together even a comedy out of it, for which the nomophylax composed the music with his own hand.

This fine piece was performed in public to great applause, and both of the former parties found so much in it to laugh at as if the subject had not at all concerned them.

Democritus, who had allowed himself to be persuaded by the archpriest to go along to this play, said when he left: "*This* similarity to the *Athenians* must at least be admitted to the Abderites, they can laugh quite ingenuously at their own foolish tricks. For that reason they get no wiser, I admit, but a lot has always been gained when a nation can bear to have honest people make fun of its follies, and when it laughs, too, instead of getting spiteful about it like the apes."

It was the last Abderite comedy to which Democritus ever went in his life; for soon thereafter he moved with bag and baggage away from the region of Abdera without telling anybody where he was going; and from that time on we have no further word of him.

Fifth Book:
The Frogs of Latona

Chapter One

Initial source of the evil that finally brought on the decline of the Abderite Republic. Policy of the archpriest Agathyrsus. He has his own public frog pond constructed. More immediate and more remote consequences of this new institution.

For a few years after the dangerous commotions caused by the ass's shadow had, thanks to the city's benign genius, come to a fortunate conclusion, the Republic of Abdera enjoyed the most perfect peace and quiet in both its internal and external affairs. And if it were possible in the natural course of things for Abderites to feel well for long, then apparently, one should have promised their prosperity the longest duration. But unfortunately for them, a cause hidden from them all, a secret enemy that was all the more dangerous because they carried it around in their own breast, was working covertly toward their decline.

From time immemorial, as we know, the Abderites had been venerating *Latona* as their tutelary goddess.

However much can justly be said in objection to the cult of Latona, it was, after all, the popular and state religion they had inherited from their ancestors. And in this respect they were no worse off than all the rest of the Greek peoples. Whether they worshipped *Minerva* like the Athenians, or *Juno* like the people of Samos, or *Diana* like the Ephesians, or the *Graces* like the inhabitants of Orchomenos,[1] or whether they worshipped *Latona,* that did not matter. They had to have some religion, and, for lack of a better one, any religion was better than none at all.

But the service of Latona could also have existed without the Frog Pond. Why did they find it necessary to prop up the simple faith of the old Teians, their ancestors, with such a dangerous adjunct? Why the *frogs* of Latona, when they had Latona herself?

Or, if indeed they had need of a visible memorial of that marvel-

256

ous transformation of the Lycian peasants to nourish their Abderite faith, would not a half dozen stuffed frog skins, set up with a beautiful golden inscription in a chapel of the Temple of Latona, covered with a brocaded veil, and displayed every year to the people with the requisite solemnities, have performed the same services for their imagination?

Democritus, their good fellow citizen—but unfortunately a man who could not be believed because he had the evil reputation of believing nothing himself—had occasionally, while he was still living among them, now and then dropped a word to the effect *that it was easy to do too much of a good thing, especially where frogs are involved.* And since his ears, after his absence of twenty years, were not so accustomed to the lovely *wreckeckeck koax koax* that jarred his ears in Abdera day and night as were the somewhat thick ears of his compatriots, he had several times remonstrated with them vigorously against their *deisibatrachy,*[2] as he called it, and often predicted to them, sometimes jokingly, sometimes seriously, that if they did not take preventive measures in good time, their croaking fellow citizens would finally croak them right out of Abdera. The more eminent people could tolerate jokes about this matter very well, for they, at least, did not want to be taken for people who believed more in the frogs of Latona than Democritus himself. But the calamity was his being able neither in jest nor in earnest to persuade them to consider the matter from a reasonable point of view. If he joked about it, they did, too; if he talked seriously, then they laughed at him for being able to treat *something like that* seriously. And so then things stayed, as always in all things in Abdera—the way they *customarily* had been, objections notwithstanding.

All the same, people claimed that already in the times of Democritus they perceived a certain *lukewarm attitude* toward the *frogs* among the aristocratic young people of Abdera. At least the priest *Strobylus* often intoned great laments about the fact that most of the good families were imperceptibly allowing the frog ditches they had maintained from olden times in their gardens to deteriorate, and that the common man was almost the only one who, in this respect, was still sticking to the old commendable custom and showing his reverence for the Hallowed Pond by means of voluntary gifts.

Who, now, as things stood, should have imagined that just that person among all the Abderites, on whom suspicion that he was suffering from deisibatrachy could least fall—that the archpriest

Agathyrus was the man who, soon after the conclusion of the feud between the *Asses* and *Shadows,* gave renewed life to the cooled-off zeal of the Abderites for the frogs?

For all that, it is impossible to exculpate him from this odd contradiction between his inner conviction and his outward behavior; and if we were not already informed about his way of thinking, the latter could hardly be explained. But we know this priest to be a very ambitious man. During the recent troubles he had seen himself at the head of a powerful party and had no desire to exchange this pleasure for a lesser equivalent than a continuing influence on the entire, now pacified, Republic; something that he could by this time obtain through no more certain means than through a great *popularity* and a complaisance toward the prejudices of the people that cost him so much the less since he, like so many of his kind, regarded religion merely as a *political machine* and was, at bottom, extremely indifferent about whether it be frogs, or owls, or sheepskins that accorded him the freest and most certain gratification of his favorite passions.

In conformity with this, therefore, and in order *in the cheapest way* to maintain his authority over and influence on the people, he not only banned the *storks,* about which the *Frog Guardians* had complained, from all jurisdictions and areas of the Temple of Jason soon after the shadow war, but he carried his complaisance toward his new friends so far that he had a pond dug out in the middle of an esplanade that one of his forebears had turned into a public promenade, and for the stocking of the same he requested of the chief priest Strobylus in a very courteous way a few barrels with frog spawn from the Hallowed Pond. After a solemn sacrifice had been made to Latona, these were then brought him, too, accompanied, with much pomp, by the entire rabble of Abdera.

From this day on, *Agathyrsus* was the idol of the people, and a frog pond constructed at the right time procured for him what he would otherwise never have attained with all his politics, eloquence, and generosity. Without ever entering the Council Chamber, he ruled as absolutely in Abdera as a king; and because he invited councilmen and guild masters two or three times each week to eat with him and never insinuated his orders to them in any other way than in full goblets of Chian wine, nobody had any objections to such an amiable tyrant. Nevertheless, at the city hall these gentlemen thought they were expressing their own opinions, although their votes were only an echo of the resolutions that were drawn up the day before in the banqueting hall of the archpriest.

Agathyrsus was the first who, among intimate friends, made fun of his new frog pond. But the people heard nothing about that. And since his example had a greater effect on the nobles of Abdera than his jokes, one should have seen the rivalry with which they, likewise to give proofs of their popularity, either repaired the dried-up frog ponds in their gardens or constructed new ones where there had not yet been any.

Since in Abdera all follies were contagious, no one remained free of this one either. At first it was a mere *fashion,* a thing that belonged to good form. A citizen of some means would have accounted it to his shame to fall short of his more genteel neighbor in this. But imperceptibly it became a requisite of a good citizen; and whoever could not produce at least a little frog pit within the four corners of his property would have been proclaimed an enemy of Latona and a traitor to his country.

With such warm zeal on the part of private persons, it is easy to imagine that the Senate, the guilds, and other boards were not the last to give Latona similar proofs of their devotion. Every guild had its own frog pit dug out. In every public square in the city, yes, even in front of the city hall, where the women selling herbs and eggs were already making enough noise, large water containers with borders of reeds and grass were laid out. And from the walks with which Abdera was surrounded, that commission that was principally responsible for *embellishing the city* finally even got the idea of having narrow canals dug on both sides of them and having these canals stocked with frogs. The project was brought before the Council and passed without opposition, even though, in order to provide these canals and the rest of the public frog ponds with the necessary water, they found themselves compelled to have the Nestus River almost entirely drained. Neither the costs with which the city treasury was burdened by all these operations nor the various disadvantages that resulted from draining the river were in the least taken into consideration. And when a young councillor mentioned merely in passing that the Nestus was close to drying up, one of the *Frog Guardians* cried: "All the better! So we have one great frog ditch more without its costing the Republic a farthing."

The people who enjoyed most this enthusiasm *for the embellishment of the city with its frog pits,* possible only in Abdera, to be sure, were the priests of the Temple of Latona. For, in spite of their selling the spawn from the Holy Pond very cheaply, namely an Abderite *Kyathos*[3] (that might amount approximately to a pint in our measure) for only two drachmae, someone, nevertheless, claimed to have calculated that in the first two to three years, when the rage was at its height, they made a profit of five thousand *darics* from it. For all that, this sum seems to us to be too high an estimate, although it cannot be denied that for the spawn they delivered *to the Republic* they had had themselves paid double from the fund for public works.

Moreover, in all of Abdera nobody thought of the consequences of these fine arrangements. The consequences came, as usual, of their own accord. However, because they did not appear all at once, it not only took ample time for people to notice them, but since they finally became conspicuous enough not to be overlooked any longer, even by Abderites, the latter were not able to discover their source, in spite of their well-known sagacity. The Abderite physicians racked their brains in guessing what might be causing head colds, fluxes, and skin diseases of all kinds to be spreading from year to year so mightily and becoming so chronic that they defied all their art and all of the hellebore from Anticyra.[4] In short, Abdera with the entire surrouding region was almost converted into a general, vast frog pond before it occurred to one of their political pointed heads to raise the question: could a limitless increase of the *quantity of frogs,* perhaps, not damage the state more than the advantages that were expected from it were ever capable of compensating?

Chapter Two

Character of the philosopher Korax. Information about the Academy of Sciences in Abdera. Korax raises a captious question in it with regard to the frogs of Latona and sets himself up as the head of the Antifroggers. Conduct of the priests of Latona against this sect and how they were induced to regard it as harmless.

The remarkable thinker who first perceived that the quantity of frogs in Abdera was indeed excessive and wholly out of proportion to the number and need of the two-legged, unfeathered inhabitants was called *Korax.*[5] He was a young man from a good family who had lived for some years in *Athens* and in the Academy (as the school of philosophy founded by *Plato* was called, as is well known). There he had absorbed certain principles that were not all too favorable to the frogs of Latona. To tell the truth,*Latona herself* had lost so much of her influence on him through his sojourn in Athens that it was no wonder if he could not regard her frogs with all the reverence that was required of an orthodox Abderite. "Every beautiful woman is a goddess," he used to say, "at least a goddess of hearts; and Latona was doubtless a very beautiful woman. But of what concern is that to *the frogs*? And—merely looking at the matter humanly and in the light of reason—of what concern, after all, are the frogs to *Latona*? Supposing, too, however, that the goddess—for whom, by the way, I have all the reverence that is due a beautiful woman and a goddess—supposing that she had taken the frogs, in preference to all the little animals and vermin in the world, under her special protection; does it then follow therefrom that one could *never have too many of the frogs*?"

Korax was, when he began splitting hairs like that, a member of the Academy that had been founded in Abdera in imitation of the one in Athens. This Academy was a small forest with portions cleared out for walks, very near the city. And since it was under the protection of the Senate and had been laid out at the public expense of the city, the *gentlemen of the commission of embellishment* had not failed to provide it amply with *frog pits*. The members of the Academy, to be sure, were not seldom disturbed in their profound meditations by the monotonous choral song of these *croaking Philomelas*. However, since this would have been the case just as well at any other place in and around the city, they had always resigned themselves to it patiently; or, to speak more correctly, people were so accustomed to the singing of frogs in Abdera that they heard it no more than did the people living near *Katadupa*,[6] the great waterfall of the Nile, in the neighborhood of which they live, or the dwellers near any other waterfall in the world.

But with Korax, whose ears had regained during his stay in Athens the sensitivity natural to all sound, human ears, it was another matter. It will, therefore, not be thought strange that, right in the first meeting he attended, he made the pointed comment that he believed the little owl of Athena[7] was uncommonly better qualified to be a special member of the Academy than the frogs of Latona. "I do not know, gentlemen, how *you* regard the matter," he added, "but to me it seems that the frogs in Abdera have been proliferating for some years in a quite incomprehensible way."

The Abderites were a dull-minded little nation, as we all know; and there was, perhaps, no other in the world (one single famous nation excepted in any event) that could have contended with them in the odd attribute *of not being able to see the forest for the trees*. But they had to be given credit for the fact that, as soon as it occurred to one among them to make a remark that *everyone* could have made just as well as he, although *no one* had done so before him, they one and all appeared to awaken suddenly from a long sleep, suddenly saw—what was lying under their nose, marveled at the discovery that had been made, and believed they were much obliged to the one who had helped them see it. "Indeed," the gentlemen of the Academy answered, "the frogs have been increasing for some time in a quite incomprehensible way."

"When I said in a quite *incomprehensible* way," Korax replied, "I wanted by no means to imply that there was anything supernatural involved. There is, after all, nothing more comprehensible than that frogs have to increase in a place where such *facilities* for their accommodation are provided as in Abdera. What is incomprehensible, in my modest opinion, is merely that the Abderites can be foolish enough to provide these facilities."

All the members of the Academy were taken aback at the liberty of this speech, looked at one another, and appeared to be at a loss about what they should think of the matter.

"I am merely talking from the human point of view," *Korax* said.

"We don't doubt that," replied the *President of the Academy*, who was a councillor and a member of the *Council of Ten*, "but up until now the Academy has made it a rule to prefer not to touch upon such slippery subjects at all on which reason can so easily lose its footing—"

"The Academy in *Athens* has made no such rule," Korax interrupted him. "If one is not allowed to philosophize *about everything*, then it would be just as well to philosophize about—*nothing at all*."

"About everything," the President and member of the Council of Ten said with a grave countenance, "only not about *Latona and*—"

"*Her frogs?*" *Korax* added smiling. Indeed, it really was this that the President had wanted to say. But at the little word *and* a kind of anxiety came over him, as if he felt involuntarily that he was about to say something foolish. And so he suddenly stopped with his mouth open and left it to Korax to finish the sentence.

"Each thing can be examined from many different sides and under various lights," Korax continued. "And to do this, it seems to me, is precisely what befits the philosopher and what distinguishes him from the stupid, unthinking rabble. Our frogs, for example, can be considered *simply as frogs* and *as frogs of Latona*. For, inasmuch as they are simply frogs, they are neither more nor less frogs than others. Their relation to the Abderites is *to that extent* approximately the same as the relation of all remaining frogs to all remaining human beings; and *to that extent* nothing can be more innocent than to inquire whether *the quantity of frogs* in a state stands in a suitable relation to the *number of people* or not—

and if it were found that the state would have to feed a great number of frogs more than would be necessary, to propose the most suitable means by which their excessive quantity could be reduced."

"What Korax says is intelligent," said *a few young academicians.*

"I'm merely speaking of the matter from the human point of view," *Korax* said.

"I would prefer that we had not begun discussing it at all," the *President* said.

This was the first spark that Korax threw into the giddy heads of a few impertinent young Abderites. Imperceptibly he became the head and spokesman of a sect about whose principles and views people did not speak all too favorably in Abdera. They were accused, not without reason, of maintaining, not only among themselves but even in large social gatherings and on the public promenades, that it could not be proved with one single cogent argument that the frogs of Latona were something better than common frogs. The legend that they were descendants of the Milisian *frog peasants* or *peasant frogs* was a silly popular tale, and even the tradition that Jupiter had transformed the aforesaid peasants for not being willing to allow Latona and her twins to drink from their pond was something about which, in any event, one could have one's doubts without, just for that reason, sinning against Jupiter or Latona. However that might be, it was absurd to make the entire city and Republic of Abdera into a frog puddle out of devotion for beautiful Latona—and whatever more assertions of this kind there were, which, as simple and reasonable as they may even appear to us these days, were in Abdera, however, found to be very *evil sounding,* especially in the ears of the priests of Latona, and brought upon the philosopher Korax and his adherents the odious name *Batrachomachetas* or "Antifroggers," a title of which they were so much the less ashamed because they had succeeded in infecting almost all of the *young* and *fashionable* people with their liberal views.

The priests of the Temple of Latona and the noble board of the Frog Guardians did not fail to show at every opportunity their displeasure with the roguish wit of the Antifroggers. And the chief priest *Stilbon,* with this inducement, augmented his book *Concerning the Antiquities of the Temple of Latona* with a large chapter "On the Nature of the Frogs of Latona." Meanwhile, they had a very important motive for letting the matter rest there; and this was that, in spite of the freethinking turn of mind concerning the frogs that Korax had made *a fashion* in Abdera, there was not a single frog pit less to be seen in and about the city than before.

Korax and his followers had been sly enough to notice that they could not buy themselves the freedom *to think too loudly* whatever they *wished* about the frogs any more cheaply than if, so far as *practice* was concerned, they did exactly what all other people were doing. Indeed, wise Korax, as the one to whom people paid the most attention and who considered it safer to do rather too much than too little, had, right after his admission to the Academy, laid out on the land he had inherited one of the finest frog pits in all of Abdera and stocked it with a considerable quantity of fine, fat frogs from the Hallowed Pond, for each of which he paid the priests four drachmae. This was a courtesy for which these gentlemen, as little as they might otherwise consider themselves obliged to him for it, nevertheless could not help *appearing* to be grateful for the sake of the good example; all the more since this same action of the so-called philosopher gave sufficient pretext to persuade those people who would have been inclined to be annoyed by his liberal views and witty ideas *that he was not serious about it.* "His tongue is worse than his mind," they used to say. "He wants people to think he's got too much wit to think as other people do; but at bottom it's just affectation. If he were not convinced of something better *in his heart,* would he be likely to contradict his freethinking views with his actions? You must not judge such people by what they say, but by what they do."

With all that it cannot be denied that Korax was secretly occupied with a plot no less modest than, like a new Hercules, Theseus, or Harmodious,[8] *to free his native country from the frogs;* by which, as he was accustomed to say, it was being threatened with greater harm than all the monsters, robbers, and tyrants had ever caused in all of Greece, of which it was freed by those heroes.

Chapter Three

An unfortunate accident compels the Senate to take notice of the excessive quantity of frogs in Abdera. Imprudence of the councillor Meidias. The majority decides to ask the Academy for its opinion. The nomophylax Hypsiboas protests against this resolution and hastens to stir up the chief priest Stilbon against it.

The adversity that the Abderites endured because of the enormous increase of their holy frogs became more oppressive from day to day, but the archon of that time, *Onokradias,* son of the famous *Onolaus's* sister and, to tell the truth, the most frivolous steersman ever to reel at the helm of Abdera, could not manage to bring the matter before the Senate—until, on the occasion of a great solemn observance when the Council and the entire citizenry had to walk in procession through the main streets, it happened accidentally that a few dozen frogs that had ventured too far from their pits were trampled underfoot by the throng and, in spite of all the help that was swiftly provided, perished miserably.

This incident appeared to be so serious that the archon found himself obliged to have a special session of the Council called to consider what kind of reparation the city would have to make to Latona for this—although unintentional but nevertheless most unfortunate—*sacrilege* and by what measures a similar misfortune could be prevented in the future.

After many Abderite platitudes about the matter had been expressed for a good while, the councillor *Meidias,* a relative and adherent of the philospher Korax, finally blurted out: "I don't understand why you gentlemen care to make such a fuss about thirty frogs more or less. Everyone is convinced that the thing was merely an accident that Latona cannot possibly hold against us. And, because fate, that rules over gods, men, and frogs, did now wish to ordain the destruction of a few croaking creatures, it might, you see, just as well have been many myriads instead of twenty-four!"

Among all the councillors there were perhaps not five who had not complained a thousand times in their home or in private gatherings (at least since *Korax* had first made his *discovery*) about the much too great increase of frogs. However, since it had never come up for discussion in the full Senate before, everybody was startled by the boldness of councillor Meidias just as if he had seized Latona herself by the throat. A few old gentlemen looked so frightened as if they expected their colleague to be turned into a frog for this audacious speech.

"I have all due respect for the Hallowed Pond," *Meidias,* who noticed everything very well, continued quite calmly, "but I appeal to the inner conviction of all human beings whose common sense is not yet completely dried up. Can anybody among us deny that the quantity of frogs is monstrous?"

The councillors had meanwhile recovered from their initial alarm, and they saw that Meidias was still sitting there in his human form and had been allowed to say with impunity what they all, in reality, felt to be the truth. And so one after the other began admitting, and after a while it appeared that the entire Senate was unanimously of the opinion, that: *it would be desirable to have fewer frogs in Abdera.*

"You're not safe against them any longer in your own house," one of them said. "You can't cross the street without running the risk of crushing one or a few of them with each step," said another. "Right from the beginning limits should have been set to the freedom of constructing frog pits," a third said. "If I had been in the Senate when it was decided to establish the public frog ponds, I would never have cast my vote for it," said a fourth. "But just who would have thought that the frogs would multiply so extraordinarily in just a few years?" said a fifth. "I dare say I saw it coming," said the *President of the Academy,* "but I have made it a rule to live in peace with the priests of Latona."

"I, too," Meidias said, "but our circumstances are not improved with that."

"Well, gentlemen, just what do you suggest we do, things being as they are?" the archon Onokradias finally asked in his usual nasal tone.

"There's the rub!" answered the councillors in one voice. "If only somebody would say what is to be done!"

"What's to be done?" *Meidias* cried hastily and suddenly fell silent again.

There followed a general stillness in the Council Chamber. The wise men let their heads fall to their breast and appeared to reflect—with all their facial muscles straining—on *what was to be done.*

"But what do we have an Academy of Sciences for in Abdera anyhow?" the *archon* cried after a while to the general surprise of all those present. For since he had been elected archon, he had never yet been heard to express his opinion with a rhetorical question.

"Your High Wisdom's idea cannot be improved," the councillor *Meidias* replied. "Let us charge the Academy to give us its opinion on the means—"

"That's just what I mean," the *archon* interrupted him, "what do we have an Academy for if we're supposed to rack our brains with subtle questions of that kind?"

"Splendid!" exclaimed a crowd of fat councillors while at the same time all of them drew the flat of their hand across their low brows. "The Academy, let's have the Academy give us its opinion!"

"I beg you, gentlemen," shouted *Hypsiboas,*[9] one of the leaders of the Republic, for he was now the *nomophylax, first Frog Guardian, and a member of the venerable Council of Ten.* In spite of all these offices, there was scarcely a man living in Abdera who, in his heart, sympathized less with Latona and her frogs than he. But because in the last election for archon the *Jasonite Onokradias* had been preferred to him, he had made it a principle always to be against the new archon in everything. For that reason he was not unfairly accused by the *Jasonites* and their friends of being an unstable person and of being preoccupied with nothing less than the formation in the Council of a party that was to oppose all the aims and resolutions of the Jasonites, who, to be sure, had for a long time been playing the role of master in the city.—"I beg you, gentlemen, do not be in too great a hurry," Hypsiboas shouted, "this is not a matter for the Academy; it should come before the Board of the *Frog Guardians*. It would be contrary to all good order and would have to be considered the grossest insult by the priests of Latona if you wished to charge the Academy with a question of this nature and importance!"

"It does not, however, concern merely the *matter of frogs*, Sir Nomophylax," *Meidias* said with his usual sarcastic composure. "Thanks to the fine arrangements in effect for the last few years, it is, unfortunately, a *matter of state*—"

"And perhaps the most important one that has ever made necessary a general uniting of all patriotic people," *Stentor*[10] interrupted him; Stentor, one of the hottest heads in the city, who had much power in the Senate on account of his rumbling voice. The Jasonites had brought him over to their side, even though he was only a *plebeian,* by getting him married to a natural daughter of the deceased archpriest Agathyrsus, and they were usually accustomed to make use of his good voice whenever they found it necessary to carry their point against *Hypsiboas,* who had a voice just as strong, although not as rumbling, as *Stentor.*

This time it was fortunate that, because of the eternal *koax koax* of their frogs, the ears of the Abderite councillors had become a little thick skinned; they would otherwise have been in danger on this occasion of becoming completely deaf. But people were already accustomed to such civility in the city hall of Abdera and allowed the two mighty bawlers, therefore, to bellow at one another like two jealous bulls for so long until—they were too hoarse to shout any longer.

Since from this moment on it was no longer worth listening to them, the archon asked the city clerk what time it was. And having received the assurance that noontime was approaching, he immediately proceeded to poll the members.

The reader should please remember here that whenever a resolution was drawn up in Abdera, no great importance was ever attached to weighing coldbloodedly against one another the reasons that had been expressed for or against a view and to inclining to the side of the person who had advanced *the best ones;* but one rather sided either with the one who had shouted the longest and loudest or with the person whose party one supported. To be sure, in ordinary matters the party of the archon was usually the stronger one; however, this time, since, to speak with the President of the Academy, such a *slippery* subject was concerned, Onokradias would hardly have got the upper hand if *Stentor* had not quite extraordinarily exhausted his lungs. With twenty-eight votes to twenty-two, it was, therefore, resolved that an opinion was to be demanded of the Academy on the ways and means by which the excessive propagation of frogs in and about Abdera could be checked, without prejudice in any way, however, to the reverence due Latona and to the rights of her Temple.

The councillor Meidias had this clause expressly inserted in order to leave the party of the nomophylax without any pretext for stirring up the people against the majority. But Hypsiboas and his followers gave their assurance that they were not so simple as to allow themselves to be fooled with clauses. They asked that their protest be included in the minutes, had an extract given them in a form suitable for their records, and went off in a procession to the chief priest *Stilbon*[11] in order to give His Reverence a report of this unheard-of encroachment upon the rights of the Frog Guardians and of the Temple of Latona and to agree with him on measures that would most promptly have to be taken to maintain their authority.

Chapter Four

The character and mode of living of the chief priest Stilbon. Negotiations between the priests of Latona and the councillors of the minority. Stilbon looks at the affair from his own point of view and goes to remonstrate with the archon himself. Remarkable conversation between those who remained behind.

The chief priest *Stilbon* was already the third who had followed the venerable *Strobylus* (may his ashes rest in peace!) in this office. Except for their zeal about the concerns of their order, there was otherwise little similarity in the characters of these two men. From his youth, *Stilbon* had loved solitude and had been occupied in the most inaccessible tracts of the Grove of Latona or in the remotest nooks of her Temple with speculations that had all the greater attraction for his mind the further they appeared to rise above the limits of human understanding, or (to speak more correctly) the less the least practical use could be made of them to the advantage of human life. Like a tireless spider, he sat at the center of his web of thoughts and words, perpetually busy with spinning out the small stock of ideas that, while leading such a secluded life, he had been able to acquire in the narrow compass of the Temple of Latona, into such clear and thin strands that, with them, he could cover over and over as with tapestry all the innumerable empty cells of his brain.

Besides these metaphysical speculations, he had busied himself mostly with the *antiquities* of Abdera, Thrace, and Greece, especially with the history of all continents, islands, and peninsulas which, according to ancient traditions, had *once existed* but from time immemorial *had no longer been in existence*. The honest man knew not a word about what had been going on in the world during his own time and even less about what had taken place fifty years *before* his time. Even the city of Abdera, at one end of which he was living, was less familiar to him than Memphis or Persepolis.[12] In return, however, he was all the more at home in the old land of the Pelasgians,[13] knew exactly the name of every people, every city, and each little hamlet before they got the name they bear now, knew who built each temple that is now lying in ruins, and ticked off on his fingers the lines of all the kings who sat under the gates of their small cities *before the deluge of Deucalion*[14] and dispensed justice to everyone—who was not able to procure it for himself. The famous island of *Atlantis* was so familiar to him as if he had seen all of its splendid palaces, temples, market places, gymnasia, amphitheaters, and so on, with his own eyes. And he would have been inconsolable if someone could have shown him the smallest inaccuracy in his thick book *On the Peregrinations of the Island of Delos*,[15] or in any other of the thick books that he had published on equally interesting materials.

With all this knowledge, Stilbon was, of course, a very learned, but despite that, also a very limited man; and in all matters concerning practical life he was extraordinarily simple-minded. His notions about human affairs were almost useless because they rarely or never were suitable to the situations to which he applied them. The judgments he made about whatever was standing right in front of him were always askew, he always drew correct conclusions from false premises, always wondered at the most natural occurrences, and always expected a happy outcome from expedients that necessarily had to thwart his aims. His head was and remained, as long as he lived, a depository of all popular prejudices.

The silliest little old woman in Abdera was no more credulous than he; and as absurd as it will seem to many of our readers, so it is certain that he was, perhaps, the only man in Abdera who in all seriousness believed in the frogs of Latona.

With all that, the chief priest Stilbon was universally considered a *well-meaning* and *peace-loving* man—and insofar as he was given full credit for the *negative virtues* that were a necessary consequence of his mode of life, his class, and his inclination to a speculative life, it was possible, to be sure, to consider him better and wiser than any of his fellow Abderites. The latter took him for a man without passions because they saw that nothing of all that customarily arouses the appetites of other people had any power over him. But they did not think about his attaching no importance to any of these things—either because he was not acquainted with them, or because, by being for a long time in the habit of living in mere speculations, he had incurred an aversion to and an incompetence in everything that presupposes other habits.

Nevertheless, good *Stilbon,* without knowing it himself, had a passion that was, in itself, sufficient to cause as much trouble in Abdera as all the rest that he did *not* have; and that was the passion *for his opinions.* Most completely persuaded of their truth himself, he could not comprehend how anyone, even if he had nothing but his mere five senses and the barest common sense, could have any notion other than his own about something. Therefore, when such a thing happened, he did not know how to account for its possibility otherwise than with the alternative: that either such a person must *not be in his right mind*—or that he must be a *malicious, deliberate, and obdurate enemy of truth,* and, hence, an entirely abominable human being. With this turn of mind, the chief priest *Stilbon,* with all of his erudition and all of his negative virtues, was a dangerous man in Abdera and would even have been a great deal more so if his indolence and his decided inclination toward solitude had not removed everything that happened around him so far away that it seldom appeared significant enough to him to take the slightest notice of it.

"I have never heard that there could be a reason for complaining about a much too great quantity of frogs," Stilbon said quite calmly when the *nomophylax* had come to the end of his statement.

"That's not what we're talking about now, Sir Chief Priest," the former replied. "The Senate is pretty much of one mind about this point, and, I think, the entire city, too. But that *the Academy* has been charged with proposing ways and means by which the excessive quantity of frogs could most suitably be remedied, that's what we can never allow."

"Did the Senate give the Academy such a charge?" *Stilbon* asked.

"You're hearing about it," *Hypsiboas* cried somewhat impatiently, "that's just what I told you and why we're here."

"Then the Senate has taken a step at which its customary wisdom entirely abandoned it," the chief priest replied just as deliberately as before. "Do you have the resolution of the Council with you?"

"Here is a copy of it!"

"Hm, hm," said Stilbon and shook his head after he had read through it very warily once or twice, "there are really almost as many absurdities as words here! First, it still remains to be proved that there are *too many* frogs in Abdera; or rather, this *cannot* ever be proved. For, in order to be able to determine what is *too much,* one must first know what *enough* is; and it is just this that is impossible for us to know, unless Delphic Apollo or his mother Latona herself wished to inform us about it by means of an oracle. The matter is *as clear as daylight.* For, since the frogs are under the direct protection and influence of the goddess, it is absurd to say that there are ever more of them than pleases the goddess. And, therefore, the matter does not only *need* no investigation at all, but rather *it also admits* of no investigation. Second, supposing that there actually were too many of the frogs, then it is, after all, absurd to speak of ways and means by which their number could be reduced. For there are no such ways and means, at least none that are at our discretion, which is as much as if there were none at all. Third, it is absurd to give the *Academy* such a charge. For the Academy not only has no right to make decisions about issues of this importance, it also consists for the greatest part, so I hear, of would-be wits and shallow people who do not understand anything about such things at all. And, as clear proof that they do not understand anything about them, they are said, so I hear, to be *foolish* enough to engage in jests and mockery about them. I credit these poor people with doing this *out of stupidity.* For, if they had carefully read my book *Concerning the Antiquities of the Temple of Latona,* then they would either have to be deprived of all their senses or be obvious miscreants if they could oppose the truth that I have expounded in it as clear as daylight. The *resolution of the Council* is, therefore, as I have said, quite absurd and can, consequently, be of no effect, since an absurd proposition is tantamount to no proposition at all. Tell that to our gracious gentlemen in the next session, highly respected Sir Nomophylax! Our gracious gentlemen will surely think better of it; and in that case it will be best for us *to let* the matter *rest*."

"Sir Chief Priest," *Hypsiboas* answered, "you are a most scholarly man, we all know that. But, don't take it amiss, Your Reverence does not understand worldly affairs and matters of state well. The *majority* in the Senate has adopted a resolution that is prejudicial to the prerogatives of the *Frog Guardians*. Nevertheless, according to the rules, this resolution of the Council continues to be in effect, and the archon will have carried it out before I could have presented your logical objections in the next session, even if I wished to assume the burden of doing so."

"But in such speculative matters, don't you see, things don't depend on the *majora*,[16] but on the *saniora*,"[17] *Stilbon* said.

"Splendid, Sir Chief Priest," the *nomophylax* replied. "That is some word! the *saniora*! The saniora *are* unquestionably right. The question is, therefore, now only what we have to do so that they *carry* their point, too. We have to devise some swift means of stopping the execution of the Council's resolution."

"I will immediately send His Grace, the archon, my book on the antiquities of the Temple of Latona. He must not have read it yet. For, in the chapter *on the frogs*, everything that is to be said about this subject is made clear."

"The archon has never read a book in his life, Sir Chief Priest," said one of the councillors laughing. "This expedient will not have any effect on him, I guarantee it!"

"All the worse!" *Stilbon* replied. "What kind of times are we living in if that is true? If the head of state gives an example like that—Yet, it is impossible for me to believe that things have already gone that far with Abdera."

"You really are entirely too innocent, Sir Chief Priest," the nomophylax said. "But let's leave it at that! Things would still be good enough if that were the archon's greatest failing."

"I see only one thing to do in this matter," said one of the priests named *Pamphagus*.[18] "The very praiseworthy Council of Ten is superior to the Senate—consequently—"

"Pardon," a *councillor* interrupted him, "not *superior* to the Senate, but rather only—"

"You didn't let me finish," said the priest somewhat heatedly. "The Ten are not *superior to* the Senate in matters concerning justice, the state, and administration. But since all matters in which the Temple of Latona is concerned come before the Council of Ten and there can be no appeal from their decision, it is then clear that—"

"The Council of Ten is *not superior* to the Senate," the former interrupted him, "for the Senate does not at all saddle itself with *Latona matters* and can, therefore, never come into collision with the Ten."

"So much the better for the Senate," the priest said. "But if then the people in the Senate were sometime to take it into their heads to make decisions about an issue that is at least very closely related to the service of Latona, as is now actually the case, then I see no other remedy but to have the Council of Ten convened."

"Only the *archon* can do that," Hypsiboas objected, "and naturally he will refuse to do so."

"He *cannot* refuse if he gets requests about it from the entire priesthood," *Pamphagus* said.

"I don't share your opinion, colleague," the chief priest interrupted. "It would violate the dignity of the Council of Ten and even violate good order if in the present case we wished to insist on its convocation. The Ten can and must meet if religion actually has been offended. Where, however, is the offense here? The Senate has drafted an absurd resolution, that's all. It is bad, but not bad *enough*. You would have to be able to prove then that the Ten are there to *reprimand* the Senate when it passes absurd resolutions."

The priest *Pamphagus* bit his lips together, turned around to the nomophylax's seat, and murmured something into his left ear.

Stilbon, without paying any attention to that, continued: "I will immediately go to the archon myself. I will take him my book on the antiquities of the Temple of Latona. I'll have him read the chapter about the frogs! It is impossible for him not to be convinced right away of the absurdity of the resolution."

"So go then and try your luck," the nomophylax replied. The chief priest left without delay.

"What a brain that is!" the priest *Pamphagus* said after he had gone.

"He is a very learned man," the councillor *Bucephalus*[19] replied, "but—"

"A learned man?" the former interrupted. "What do you call learned? Learned in all kinds of stuff nobody wants to know!"

"You're a better judge of that, Your Reverence, than people like us," the councillor answered. "I understand nothing about it. But it has always seemed incomprehensible to me that in matters of business such a learned man can be as simple as a small child."

"It is unfortunate for the Temple of Latona," another priest said.
"And for the entire state," a third added.

"I just don't know," the *nomophylax* said with a hypercritical sneer, "but let's stick to the point. You gentlemen all seem to me to be of the opinion that the Council of Ten would have to be convoked—"

"All the more," said one of the councillors, "because we are certain to have a *majority* against the archon."

"If we can't hit on something better," the nomophylax continued, "then well and good. But ought we not to be able to do better for ourselves in a matter in which Latona and her priesthood are on our side? Don't we constitute almost half of the Council? We lost by merely six votes, and we will stick together firmly—"

"That we will," the councillors shouted loudly.

"I have a plan, gentlemen; but I have to allow it to mature some. Choose two or three from your midst with whom I could discuss its details this evening in my summerhouse. Meanwhile we'll find out how far the chief priest got with the archon Onokradias."

"I'll bet my head against a melon," the priest *Charox* said, "that he's going to make what's bad worse."

"All the better," the nomophylax replied.

Chapter Five

What took place between the chief priest and the archon—one of the most instructive chapters in this entire history.

While this was being discussed in the chief priest's vestibule, the latter personally went to see the archon and insisted on an audience about a matter "which is of great importance to the archon."

"Oh, that will quite certainly concern the frogs," said the councillor *Meidias,* who just happened to be alone with the archon and had reported to him that the nomophylax with all his followers had been seen going to the Temple of Latona.

"Hang all the frogs anyway—may Latona forgive me!" *Onokradias* cried impatiently. "Here that peevish cleric is going to prate my ears so full of *wherefores* and *therefores* that in the end I'll not know where my head is. Save me, I beg you, from this ghastly old fellow!"

Meidias laughed at the archon's straits. "Just keep listening to him," he said, but *maintain your authority,* and adhere to the principle *that necessity knows no law.* We can truly not allow ourselves, after all, to be eaten up by frogs. And if things were to continue as they have up to now, then Latona might just as well turn us all together into frogs. It would still be the most fortunate thing that could happen to us if we are not helped soon in some other way. In any event, it can't hurt either if Your Grace gives the priest to understand that *Jason,* too, has a temple in Abdera, and that gods are gods only insofar as they do good."

"Fine, fine," the archon said. "If only I could remember everything as you said it to me. But I'll pull myself together all right. Just let the priest come!—Meanwhile, go into my private chamber Meidias. You'll find a goodly number *of little pieces by Parrhasius*[20] in there that you don't see everywhere—But don't tell my wife anything about it. You understand me, don't you?"

Meidias slipped into the chamber. The archon put himself on guard, and Stilbon was shown in.

"Gracious Sir Archon," he said. "I come to give Your Grace a good piece of advice because I have a high opinion of your wisdom and would very much like to prevent trouble."

"I thank you for both, Sir Chief Priest! Good advice is, as you know, never lost. What is the nature of your complaint?"

"The Senate," Stilbon continued, "so I hear, has made itself guilty of passing a rash resolution about matters concerning the frogs of Latona—"

"Sir Chief Priest!— —"

"I'm not saying that you did it out of ill will. Human beings sin only because they are ignorant. Here I'm bringing Your Grace a book in which you can inform yourself about the circumstances connected with our frogs. It cost me a lot of effort and many vigils. From it you can learn that the Academy, which is a new institution without experience, can have no right to make decisions about frogs that are as old as the divinity of Latona. The frogs in Abdera are, as we all should know, quite different from the frogs in other places in the world. They belong to Latona. They are the witnesses that will never die out and living documents of her divinity. It is nonsense to say that there could be too many of them and a sacrilege to speak of means by which their number is to be reduced."

"A sacrilege, Sir Chief Priest?"

"I would not merit being chief priest if I were to keep silent about such things. For, if sometime we had permitted the number of Latona frogs to be reduced, then our still worse descendants might well degenerate so far as to wish to exterminate them entirely. As I said, in this book Your Grace will find everything that is to be believed about the subject. See to it that copies of it are made and that each house is supplied with one. When this has been done, then the surest thing will be not to argue about the matter any longer at all. Otherwise the Academy may give opinions on whatever it wishes. All of nature lies open before it. It can discuss subjects from the elephant to the plant louse, from the eagle to the water moth, from the whale to the loach, and from the cedar to the lycopodium; but about *the frogs* it is to be silent."

"Sir Chief Priest," the archon said, "may the gods keep me from ever getting the idea of inquiring into the circumstances connected with your frogs. I am the archon in order to leave everything in Abdera as I found it. Nevertheless, it is clear that we can no longer budge because of having nothing but frogs; and this nuisance must be checked. For our situation must not get worse, you see that yourself. Our ancestors were satisfied with maintaining the Hallowed Pond, and whoever wished, was free to have his own frog pit. We should have let it go at that. Since, however, things have now gone so far with us that we will soon be in danger of being eaten dead or alive by frogs, Your Reverence will surely not expect us to risk such an eventuality. For, if a person were eaten by frogs, it would surely be small consolation for him to keep in mind that they are no common frogs. In short, Sir Chief Priest, the Academy is to give its opinion because it has been charged to do so by the Senate; and—with all the respect I owe Your Reverence, I will *not* read your book. And I'm going to have it settled once and for all whether the frogs are here for the sake of the Abderites, or the Abderites for the sake of the frogs. For, as soon as the Republic is endangered by the frogs, you see, it becomes a matter of state, and then the priests of Latona have to keep from meddling in it, as you know. For necessity knows no law, and—in a word, Sir Chief Priest, we don't want to allow your frogs to eat us. Should you, however, contrary to our hopes, insist on it, then I would feel sorry to have to tell you that the Temple of Latona is not the only one in Abdera, and the Golden Fleece, the custody of which the gods have entrusted to my family, could possibly manifest a virtue unknown until now and suddenly—free Abdera of its entire predicament. I don't wish to say any more. But do bear in mind, Sir Chief Priest! The pitcher goes to the well until it breaks."

The good chief priest did not know whether he was awake or dreaming, when he heard the archon, whom he had always considered a right-thinking and exemplary regent, using such language. He stood there without being able to utter a word; not because he did *not* know what to say, but rather because he had *so much* to say that he did not know where to begin.—"I would never have considered it possible," he finally began, "that I should live to see the time when the chief priest of Latona would have to hear from the mouth of an archon what I have heard!"

The archon began to grow uneasy at these words. For, because he himself no longer really knew what he had said to the chief priest, he started to fear he might have said more than was proper. With some embarrassment he looked over at the door of his private chamber as if he would gladly have called for help from his privy councillor Meidias. Since this time, however, he had no one but himself to give him help, he alternately tugged on his nose and his beard, coughed, cleared his throat, and finally gave his reply to the chief priest with all the dignity he could muster in haste: "I don't know how I am supposed to take what you just said to me. But this I know; if you believe you heard something that you were not supposed to hear, then you must have understood me quite incorrectly. You are a very learned man, and I have all possible respect for your person and your office—"

"You want to read my book then?" Stilbon asked.

"Not exactly; however—if you insist on it—if you believe that it is absolutely—"

"You should not force the good on anybody," the priest said with a touchiness over which he had no control. "I'll leave it here for you. Read it or not! So much the worse for you if you are indifferent to whether you think correctly or incorrectly—"

"Sir Chief Priest," the archon, who was also finally getting heated, interrupted him, "you are a touchy man, as I see. I do not blame you, to be sure, for attaching great importance to the frogs, for that's why you are the chief priest. You, however, should also consider that I am the archon of Abdera and not of a frog pond. Stay in your temple and rule there as you wish and can; let *us* rule at the city hall. The Academy is to give its opinion on the frogs, you have my word on it!—and it will be communicated to you before the Senate drafts a resolution about it, you can depend on that, too!"

The chief priest swallowed his indignation at the unexpected, bad outcome of his visit as well as he could, made a bow, and withdrew with the assurance that he was thoroughly convinced the Senate would not take any steps regarding these matters without first coming to an agreement with the priests of the Temple of Latona. In return, the archon assured him that the rights of the Temple of Latona were as holy to him as the rights of the Senate and the best interests of the city of Abdera. And thus, according to the circumstances, they parted on still fairly polite terms.

"That priest made things unpleasant for me," the archon said to the councillor Meidias while wiping his brow with his handkerchief.

"But you also bravely stood your ground," the councillor replied.

"That little priest will be seething with rage and malice. But his lightning flashes are only artificial. Merely keep from entering into his distinctions and syllogisms, then he's defeated and doesn't know what to do next."

"Yes, if the *nomophylax* were not sticking behind him," replied the archon. "I wish I hadn't spoken so openly. But what an unreasonable expectation that is, too, to read that thick book on which the hollow-eyed old fellow worked until he got blind from writing. Who would not have become impatient?"

"Don't worry, Sir Archon! We have the Academy with us, and in a few days the laughers in all of Abdera are going to be on our side, too. I will scatter little songs and popular ballads among the people. I'm going to have the ballad writer *Lelex* compose a ballad on the story of the Lycian frog peasants about which the people are going to laugh themselves sick. We must make the gentlemen with their frogs ridiculous. In a subtle way, it goes without saying; but blow upon blow, ballad after ballad! Your Grace will see how this means takes effect."

"I cordially hope that it will," the archon said. "For you can hardly imagine how throughout this wet summer the confounded frogs made a mess of my garden! I can't stand to look at that calamity any longer at all. All we need is for a dry year to come soon and besides to send down on our neck an army of field mice and moles."

"First, let us get rid of the frogs," Meidias replied. "For the mice that are still to come there will also be remedies."

"But what the deuce am I supposed to do with that thick book the chief priest left for me?" the archon asked.—"Surely you don't expect me to read it!"

"Jason and Medea forbid, Sir Archon," Meidias replied. "Give it to *me*. I'll take it to my cousin *Korax,* who without a doubt will be charged with drawing up the Academy's opinion. He'll make good use of it, I guarantee you that."

"There's likely some fine rubbish in it," the archon said.

"If we cannot use it for anything else," the councillor replied, "then we'll reduce it to powder and feed it to the rats, who, according to Your Grace's prophecy, are still to come. It will be splendid rat poison."

Chapter Six

What the chief priest Stilbon did after he had returned home.
As soon as the chief priest Stilbon had again arrived in his cell,

he sat down at his desk and took to hand his work *Concerning the Antiquities of the Temple of Latona* with the intention of rereading the chapter "On the Frogs," which was the longest chapter in the entire book, and, indeed, as he flattered himself, with all the impartiality of a judge who has no other interest in the subject than the discovery of the truth. For, however convinced he was of the results of his investigations, he nevertheless considered it just and necessary, before he ventured further, to examine once again his entire system and its proofs point by point with the intention of being able, if it should prove to be true even after this new and severe examination, to maintain it all the more confidently against all the attacks of the wit and the fashionable philosophy of his time.

Poor Stilbon! If you were *honest,* as I prefer to believe rather than not, what a deceptive thing a human being's *reason* is! And what a slippery, seductive serpent is the arch-sorceress *egotism!*

Stilbon read through his chapter on the frogs with all the impartiality of which he was capable. He examined every sentence, every proof, and every syllogism with the cold-bloodedness of an *Arcesilas,*[21] and—found: *that one had either to renounce common sense or be convinced of his system.*

That cannot be possible, you say? I beg your pardon, that can be very possible, for it happened and still happens every day. Nothing is more natural. That good man loved his system like his own flesh and blood. He had generated it out of his own self. For him it took the place of wife and child, of all possessions, honors, and pleasures of the world, which he had renounced upon entering the Temple of Latona; it was more to him than anything else. As he sat down to examine it anew, he was already so completely convinced of its truth and beauty as of his own existence. It was, naturally, just the same with him as if he had sat down to investigate with all the cold-bloodedness in the world whether the snow on the summit of the Haemus Range[22] was white or black.

"That the Milisian peasants who prevented thirsting Latona from drinking out of their pond were changed into frogs," Stilbon said in his book, "*that is a fact.*

"That a number of these frogs were transported to Abdera and placed in the pond of the Grove of Latona, in the way tradition reports, *is a fact.*

"Both *facts* are based on what is the basis of all historical truth, on human belief in human testimony. And, as long as Abdera has existed, no reasonable person has taken it into his head to contradict the general belief of the Abderites in these facts. For whoever wished to deny them would have to prove their *impossibility;* and where in the world is the man who could do this?

"However, whether the frogs that are in the Hallowed Pond today, in our own time, are precisely the ones that were transformed
into frogs by Latona, or, what amounts to the same thing, by Jupiter at Latona's request, about that there have up to now been various opinions.

"Our scholars have, for the greatest part, held that the maintenance of the Hallowed Pond was to be regarded with due honor as
a mere institution of our forefathers and the frogs kept therein as
mere mementoes of the might of our tutelary goddess.

"The common people, on the other hand, have always spoken
and thought of these frogs as if they were the same ones to whom
the well-known miracle had happened.

"And I—Stilbon, at present through Jupiter's and Latona's
mercy the chief priest of Abdera, have, after mature consideration
of the matter, found that this popular belief rests on irrefutable
arguments; and here is my proof!"

It is hardly likely that the gentle reader would find himself edified
if we wished to give him this proof to read in all the prolixity with
which it is expounded in the aforesaid book of the chief priest
Stilbon; all the more, since we are all at least just as completely
convinced *in advance* of its lack of foundation as good Stilbon was
of its solidity. We are content, therefore, to say, in a word or two,
that his entire system about the aforementioned frogs hinged on a
hypothesis that is very common nowadays, but at that time, at
least in Abdera, was quite new and, according to Stilbon's express
assurance, was discovered by himself; namely, it hinged on the
theory "that all procreation is nothing but the development of original seeds." When Stilbon first made this discovery, he found it so
splendid and knew how to support it with so many dialectic and
moral arguments, for physics was not his special concern, that with
each day it appeared more probable to him.

Finally he believed that he had carried it to the *highest degree
of probability.* Now, since from the latter to *certainty* it is necessary
to take only a small leap, is it any wonder that such an ingenious,
such a subtle, such a probable hypothesis—a hypothesis that he
had discovered himself, worked out with so much effort, connected
with all his own ideas, and made into the foundation of a new
thoroughly reasoned system about the frogs of Latona—finally
seemed to him just as certain, clear, and beyond question as any
theorem in Euclid?

"When the Milisian peasants were transformed," Stilbon said,
"they carried within them the *seeds* of all the peasants and non-
peasants who could and should spring from them, from that time

up until today, and from today until the end of days in the regular course of nature, in an equally large number of seeds telescoped into one another. And at the moment when the aforesaid Milisian peasants became frogs, all the *human seeds* that each individual carried within him were changed into *frog seeds*. "For," he said, "either these seeds were *destroyed,* or they were *ranified,*[23] or they were *left as they were. The first* is impossible, because something can become nothing no more than nothing, something. The *third* cannot be imagined either; for, if the aforesaid seeds had remained *human seeds,* then the Milisian Ανθρωποβατραχοι, or *men-frogs,* would have to have produced *real human beings,* which is against historical truth and in every way absurd in itself. Therefore, only *the second* remains, namely, they were *ranified,* that is, *changed into frog seeds.* And one can say, therefore, with complete accuracy that the frogs that are in the Hallowed Pond on this very day, and all the rest whose descent from them is demonstrable, consequently all the frogs in Abdera, are precisely the ones that were transformed into frogs by Latona; that is to say, insofar as they were at that time present *in the seed* within the peasants that were becoming frogs and were transformed at the same time *uno eodemque actu*[24] with them."

With this having once and for all been assumed as demonstrated truth, nothing seemed to honest Stilbon *clearer than daylight,* as he was in the habit of saying, than the conclusions that flowed therefrom, as it were, of their own accord. "As, for example, an oak struck by lightning is regarded with awe and shuddering as a *res sacra,*[25] as belonging to the Thunderer Zeus and hallowed, just so," he said, "the men-frogs transformed by Latona and Jupiter together with all their descendants that were changed with them in the seed, down to the thousandth and ten thousandth generation, must be considered *intermediate beings* of a wonderful kind belonging to Latona and must, therefore, also be treated and honored as such. To be sure, they are, as regards their exterior, like other frogs. For, since by birth and nature they had been human beings, and everything we are by nature and birth gives us an inextinguishable character, they are not frogs as much as *frog-human beings,* and thus, in a certain sense, they are still *of our race,* our brothers, our brothers who met with misfortune, marked as a warning to us with the dread stamp of the vengeance of the gods, but just for that reason worthy of our most tender *sympathy.* Yet not only of our sympathy," Stilbon added, "but also of our *veneration,* since they are enduring, inviolable memorials of the might of our goddess that one cannot violate without violating her herself; since their preservation over so many centuries is the most eloquent proof that she wants them to be preserved."

The good chief priest—a man who would not seem quite so contemptible to our readers as he presumably appears to them if they knew how to project their minds into his soul—had spent the entire evening reading through and examining his chapter on the frogs and had become so absorbed in the attempt to strengthen his system with new arguments that his promise to give the nomophylax a report of the success of his book with the archon had slipped completely from his mind. He did not remember it until he heard the door of his cell opening, towards dusk, and saw this gentleman in person standing before him.

"I don't have much that is consoling to report to you," he burst out. "We are in worse hands than I had ever supposed. The archon refused to read my book, perhaps because he cannot read *at all*."

"I wouldn't guarantee that," Hypsiboas said.

"And he spoke in a tone that I would never have expected from the head of the Republic."

"Just what did he say?"

"Thank heaven that I have again forgotten most of what he said. Enough, he insisted that the Academy would have to give its opinion—"

"I should say it will have to leave that alone," the nomophylax interrupted him. "The Antifroggers are going to find more opposition than they will expect. However, so that no one might be able to accuse us of proceeding with violence before we have tried more gentle means, the entire minority is determined to remonstrate immediately with the Senate in writing, provided that the priesthood of Latona is inclined to make common cause with us."

"With the greatest of pleasure," Stilbon said, "I will compose the letter of remonstrance myself. I will prove to them—"

"For the present," the nomophylax interrupted him, "a short *memorandum* that I have already drafted *sub spe rati et grati*[26] can suffice. We have to hold such a learned pen as yours in reserve for the ultimate emergency."

The chief priest, it is true, did allow himself to be set right; he resolved, however, to work during the coming night on a little treatise, in which he wanted to present his system on the frogs of Latona in a new light and, in a way still more subtle than in his work on the antiquities of the Temple of Latona, to anticipate all the objections that the philosopher Korax could make against it. "Arrows seen coming are all the less dangerous," he said to himself. "I will put the matter down so clearly and distinctly that even the simplest people will be convinced. There would surely have to be something truly strange about it if the *truth* were to have lost its natural power over the human intellect in only just this instance."

Chapter Seven

Excerpts from the opinion of the Academy. A word about the intentions Korax had in this, with an apology, in which Stilbon and Korax can share their interest equally.

Meanwhile, in the course of all this commotion among the Senate minority and among the priests of Latona, the Academy had received an order to submit to the Senate within seven days its opinion on the question: *"By what suitable means can the excessive quantity of frogs* (without prejudice to the prerogatives of Latona) *be checked with the greatest haste?"*

The Academy did not fail to hold a meeting on the following morning. Since the *Antifrogmen* for the time being constituted the greatest part of it, the philosopher *Korax* was charged with drawing up the opinion; however, with the explicit reminder from the President that he should take the greatest care not to get the Academy involved in any nasty quarrels with the Temple of Latona.

Korax promised he would summon all of his wisdom to say the truth in an inoffensive way if possible. "For, as you know, highly honored gentlemen, no one is, in any case, obliged to do the *impossible.*"

"You are right there," the President replied, "I merely meant that you should be as careful *as possible.* For the Academy, of course, may—*as much as possible*—not compromise the *truth.*"

"That's what I always say," Korax replied.

"Into what a strange situation an honest man can really get as soon as he has the misfortune of being an Abderite," *Korax* said to himself as he prepared to write down the Academy's opinion on the matter of the frogs. "In which other city on earth would anyone take it into his head to submit such a question to an academy of sciences? And yet, the Senate is to be credited for still having so much intelligence and courage as to ask the Academy. There are cities in the world where such a thing is not left up to the Academy. It must be admitted that the Abderites, out of sheer folly, occasionally hit upon a good idea!"

So Korax sat down at his desk and so put his heart and soul into the task at hand that he finished writing his opinion before sunset.

Since we have given the gentle reader an adequate if not detailed report on the chief priest Stilbon's system, impartiality, as the first duty of the historian, demands that we also impart to him at least as much of the content of this academic opinion as appears to be necessary for him to understand this remarkable history.

"The noble Senate," Korax said in the introduction of his document, "in the esteemed resolution which it has sent to the Academy, presupposes that the *number of frogs* in Abdera at present surpasses the *number of its inhabitants* to an excessive degree, and thereby it spares the Academy the disagreeable task of having first *to prove* something that, as a fact known to the city and the world, is there for all to see.

"Consequently, it looks as if the Academy, such being the case, would only have to propose *the means* whereby this dreadful state of things could be remedied most promptly.

"However, since the frogs in Abdera, by virtue of an institution and the faith of our forefathers that have become ancient and venerable, have acquired prerogatives, to disturb them in the possession of which may seem objectionable to many, and to some even unlawful; and since, by virtue of the nature of the matter, it could easily happen that the only suitable remedies that the Academy has to propose in the present extreme emergency of the community could appear to be prejudicial to those real or supposed privileges of the Abderite frogs, it will be quite as appropriate as unavoidable to give as a preface an historical-pragmatical elucidation of the question: what special circumstances are connected with our aforesaid frogs?

"The Academy, therefore, in this theoretical part of its opinion— which is open to correction—asks so much the more for the well-disposed attention of all the most and right honorable members of the noble Senate, as the happy outcome of this entire matter that is of such great importance to the Republic depends solely upon the emendation of the preliminary question: whether and to what extent the frogs of Abdera are to be regarded as *real frogs* or not."

This emendation itself takes up more than two-thirds of the entire opinion. The sly philosopher, surely mindful of what he had promised the wary President, mentions the transformation of the Milisian peasants only in passing and with all the deference owed an old folk tale. He presupposes it, with reference to the book of the chief priest Stilbon, as a matter exposed to no more doubt than the transformation of *Narcissus* into a flower, of *Cycnus* into a swan, of *Daphne* into a laurel tree,[27] or any other transformation that rests on equally firm ground. Even if it were not inadmissible and improper to wish to deny such old legends, it would be, he thinks, injudicious. For, since on the one hand it is impossible to annul their credibility by means of *historical evidence,* and on the other, no naturalist in the world is in a position to prove their *absolute impossibility,* every sensible person will prefer all the more to refrain from doubting them, since he could, after all, say nothing further against them than the common platitudes: *it is incredible, it is contrary to the course of nature,* and formulas of that kind, that at first glance would have to occur just as well to even the dullest mind. Therefore, he considers the transformation of the Milisian peasants into frogs *a matter to be dropped.* However, he maintains that its truth in the present question is a matter of complete *indifference.* For surely no one will wish to deny, after all, that these Milisian *men-frogs* have already been dead and disposed of for at least a few thousand years. Supposing, too, however, that the *Abderite frogs* could satisfactorily prove their descent from them, then they would surely have proved with this nothing further than that, from time immemorial, from father to son, they have been born true, genuine *frogs.* For, as soon as the aforementioned Milisian peasants, by their transformation and from the moment of their "enfrogment," would have ceased to be human beings, they would also from this moment on have been able to procreate nothing else but their kind, namely true, natural frogs. In a word, *frogs are frogs,* and the circumstance that their first ancestors *before their transformation* had been Milisian peasants changes no more in their present frog-nature than a beggar descended from thirty-two ancestors is regarded as a prince, although it would be demonstrable that the first beggar in his family tree had sprung in a direct line from *Ninus and Semiramis.*[28] The adherents of the opposed view even appeared to realize this so well themselves that, in order to explain the ostensible higher nature of the Abderite frogs, they had to have recourse to a hypothesis whose mere presentation makes all refutation superfluous.

The sagacious reader, and it goes without saying that a work like this can have no other readers, will immediately, and without our having reminded him, have noticed that Korax wanted with this turn to arrive at the chief priest Stilbon's *system of the seeds* which—before he dared to venture bringing up his proposal with regard to the reduction of the frogs—he had either *to refute* or *to ridicule.*

Since of these two courses the latter was also the most convenient and the one most appropriate to the capacity of the noble and most wise members of the Senate with whom he was dealing, Korax contented himself with carrying what is incomprehensible in this hypothesis to the point of preposterousness by means of a comical calculation of the infinitesimal size of the alleged seeds.

"We will assume," he said, "in order not to tire out the attention of the noble Senate with arithmetical subtleties, that, in his condition as a seed, the son of the biggest and fattest of the frogs that had been Milisians stood in relation to his father as one to a hundred million. We will assume so merely for the sake of the round number, although it could be proved without much trouble that the largest among all the little beings is, as a seed, at least ten times still smaller than I have indicated. Now, according to the view of the priest Stilbon, there is inside of this seed, reduced by the same proportion, the seed of the grandson, in the seed of the grandson the seed of the great-grandson, and so on in each succeeding descendant down to the ten thousandth generation, always a hundred million times smaller at each stage, the seed of the one immediately following; so that the seed of a now-living Abderite frog, even supposing he were only removed in the fortieth degree from his ancestor, the Milisian man-frog, at the time when he was still within the aforesaid ancestor as a seed, would have been by so many millions of billions, of trillions, and so on, smaller than a cheese mite that the quickest scribe the noble Senate of Abdera has in its secretariat could in his entire life scarcely manage all the zeroes that he would have to write to denote this number, and the entire area of this praiseworthy Republic, as much of it, namely, as has not yet been changed into frog pits, would hardly have space enough for the paper or parchment that would be big enough to hold this colossal number. The Academy leaves it to the judgment of the Senate whether the very tiniest of all the small animalcules in the world are tiny enough for a person to get an idea of such an inexpressible smallness, and whether, therefore, one can believe anything else but that the reverend chief priest must have made a mistake when he hit upon the hypothesis of the seeds in order to give the alleged sacredness of the Abderite frogs a not very plausible, but yet at least a very obscure and incomprehensible, foundation.

"The Academy has with all diligence not wished to strain unduly the imagination of the illustrious fathers of our country. If one considers, however, how short the natural life of a frog is, and that our present frogs, according to our presupposition, are descended at least in the five hundredth degree from the Milisian peasants, then the hypothesis of the very reverend chief priest disappears in such an abyss of smallness that it would be absurd and *cruel* to say a word more about it.

"*Nature,* as the famous inscription in Sais[29] reads, *is all that is,*

that was, and that will be, and *no mortal has ever lifted its veil.*
The Academy, imbued with this great truth more profoundly than
anyone else, is far from claiming some special and more accurate
insight into mysteries that are to remain unfathomable. It believes
that it is of no avail to wish to know more about the way organic
beings originate than what the senses discover with persistent attention. And if indeed it considers it *permissible* to indulge the
inborn urge of the human mind—by means of *hypotheses* to wish
to make everything comprehensible for oneself—it still finds *that*
the most natural one by virtue of which the seeds of organic bodies
are not formed through the secret forces of nature until it really
has need of them. According to this way of explaining things, the
seed of every croaking creature now living in all the bogs and frog
pits of Abdera is no older than the moment of its procreation and
has nothing more in common with the individual frog that was
croaking at the time of the Trojan War, and from which the frog
living now is descended in a straight line, than that nature has
formed them both, according to a uniform pattern, by means of
uniform organs, and for uniform ends."

The philosopher Korax, after bringing forward arguments in support of this view at length and in detail, finally draws from them
the conclusion that the Abderite frogs are just as natural, common,
everyday frogs as all the rest of the frogs in the world, and that the
odd privileges that they have been enjoying in Abdera are not based
on any superiority of their nature and their ostensible relationship
with that of human beings, but merely on a popular belief, which,
to the greatest disadvantage of the community, has much too long
been left vague and in a darkness beneath whose encouragement
the imaginations of some and the selfishness of others have had
free play to engage in a kind of mischief with these frogs, the like
of which can scarcely be found in the world outside of Egypt.

"The antiquities of Abdera," he continues, "in spite of all the
light that the reverend and learned Stilbon has so copiously shed
on them, still lie, like the antiquities of all other cities in the world,
in a mist, whose impenetrability leaves little hope to the scholar
who is eager for the truth of ever seeing his desire satisfied. But,
why would we ever have a need for knowing more about them than
we really know anyhow? Whatever the circumstances connected
with the origin of the Temple of Latona and its Hallowed Frog Pond
may be, would Latona perhaps, if we knew these circumstances, be
more or less a *goddess,* her temple, more or less a *temple,* and her
frog pond, more or less a *frog pond*? Latona is to be and must be
worshiped in her ancient temple, her ancient frog pond is and must

be duly honored. Both are an institution of our oldest ancestors, venerable owing to the greatest antiquity, strengthened by means of the custom of so many centuries, sustained by the uninterruptedly transmitted faith of our people, hallowed and made inviolable through the laws of our Republic, that have entrusted their custody and protection to the most eminent board of the state. But if Latona, or Jupiter for Latona's sake, transformed the Milisian peasants into frogs, does it follow therefrom then that *all the frogs* of Latona are holy and have to pretend to the sacerdotal prerogative of personal inviolability? And, if our worthy forefathers deemed it good to maintain a little frog pit in the precinct of the Temple of Latona, does it then follow therefrom that all of Abdera has to be changed into a frog puddle?

"The Academy knows full well the respect that is owed certain views and feelings of the people. But the superstition into which they are always ready to degenerate can, after all, be condoned only as long as it does not overstep the boundaries of harmlessness entirely too far. *Frogs can be honored; but it is unreasonable to sacrifice human beings to the frogs.* The purpose, on account of which the Abderites, our forefathers, instituted the Hallowed Frog Pond, could have been attained by means of a single frog. But never mind that an entire pondful was kept; if things had only been left at this one pond! Abdera would for that reason have been no less flourishing, powerful, and fortunate. Only the strange delusion that there could not be enough frogs and frogponds carried matters to the point that we are now really left with no other choice but either to rid ourselves of these most troublesome and much too fertile fellow citizens immediately, or to walk, all of us together with uncovered heads and feet, to the Temple of Latona and, by asking the goddess on our knees, persist in our request to her until she renews the old miracle with us and, as many of us as there are, *transforms us into frogs, too.*

"The Academy would have to sin very grossly against the leaders and fathers of our country if it were to doubt for a moment that the remedy that it has been called upon to propose in such a desperate situation—the only remedy it is capable of proposing—were not to be grasped with both hands. This remedy has all of the attributes called for by the noble Senate. It is in our power; it is suitable and of immediate effect; it is not only connected with no expenditure but even with a considerable saving; and neither Latona nor her priests can, with proper limitations, have any objections to make against it."

And now, gentle reader, guess what kind of a remedy that could

possibly be.—It is, not to detain you long, the simplest remedy in
the world. It is something that has been very common in Europe
from times long ago until the present day; a thing about which no
one in all Christendom has the least scruples and at which, however, as this passage of the opinion was read in the Senate of Abdera, the hair of half the councillors was standing on end. In a
word, the remedy that the Academy of Abdera proposed in order
to get rid of the surplus frogs in a good way was—*to eat them.*"

The author of the opinion asserted that on his journeys to Athens
and Megara, in Corinth, in Arcadia, and in a hundred other places,
he had seen people eating frogs' legs and had eaten them himself.
He gave his assurance that it was a very wholesome, nourishing,
and very tasty dish, whether served fried, fricasseed, or in small
pasties. He calculated that in this way the excessive number of
frogs would in a short time be brought down to a very moderate
quantity and the common man and the middle-class man provided,
in these bad times, with no small relief with this new food. And
although the advantage accruing from that would have to decrease
by virtue of the nature of the matter, the loss, on the other hand,
would be all the more abundantly compensated by their gradually
being able to drain several thousand frogponds and pits and to
cultivate them again; a circumstance whereby at least the fourth
part of the land belonging to Abdera would be reclaimed and be of
benefit to the inhabitants. "The Academy," he added, "has considered the matter from all possible points of view and cannot con-
ceive how the least objection to it could be made on the part of
Latona or her priests. For, as far as the goddess herself is concerned, she would, without a doubt, feel very offended through
the mere suspicion that she cared more for the frogs than for the
Abderites. It is, however, to be expected of the priests that they
are much too good citizens and patriots to oppose a proposal,
through which what, up until now, has been the greatest evil and
hardship of the Abderite community, would be transformed, merely
by means of an adroit change, into its greatest benefit. Since, however, it is not more than fair not to affect them, the priests, adversely for the sake of the community's best interests, the
Academy humbly suggests that the inviolability of the ancient Frog
Pond near the Temple of Latona be not only guaranteed them anew,
but that an ordinance be made that, from the moment the Abderite
frogs' legs would be declared a permissible food, a tax of one or
two *oboli* from every hundred of them would have to be paid to
the Temple of Latona. A tax which, according to a very modest
estimate, would in a short time yield a sum of thirty to forty thou-

sand drachmae and, therefore, abundantly compensate the Temple of Latona on account of all the other small advantages that ceased owing to the new arrangement."

Finally, the philosopher Korax concluded his opinion with these remarkable words: "The Academy believes that through this recommendation, which is as public-spirited as it was dictated by necessity, it has done its duty. Regarding the outcome, it is quite unperturbed, since it is withal no more affected than all the rest of the citizens of Abdera. But since it is convinced that only quite professed *frog worshipers* could be capable of opposing such an unavoidable reformation, it hopes that the praiseworthy fathers of the country would not permit such a ridiculous sect to gain the upper hand and to sully the name of Abdera in the eyes of all Greeks and barbarians with a stain that no time would erase."

It is *difficult* to judge a man's *intentions* by his *actions* and *harsh* to suspect bad intentions merely because a deed *could* have proceeded just as easily from an evil as from a good motive; but to consider everyone a *bad* man whose way of thinking is not our own is unjust and unreasonable. So although we cannot say for certain how *pure* the intentions of the philosopher *Korax* might have been when he wrote this opinion, we cannot help believing that the priest Stilbon went too far in his passion when he declared the aforesaid Korax, on account of his opinion, to be an *evident enemy of the gods and of men* and accused him of having an obvious intention to overthrow all religion. However persuaded of *his* view the chief priest Stilbon possibly was, it was, nevertheless, not impossible, with the great and involuntary diversity in ways of thinking that prevails among poor mortals, that Korax was just as honestly convinced of the truth of his own; that, at his heart's core, he considered the Abderite frogs nothing more than mere natural frogs and believed that by means of his proposal he was really rendering his country an important service. However, the writer of this history quite willingly concedes that for us who are living now, and considering that the principles generally accepted in Europe are little favorable to the frogs, it is an extremely delicate matter to make a completely impartial judgment on this point.

However the *morality* of the philosopher Korax's intentions may have been constituted, so much, at least, is certain: he was just as little without passions as the chief priest, and he much too zealously made it his business to increase the number of his adherents not to arouse the suspicion that the vanity of being the head of a party, the eagerness to win a victory over Stilbon, and the proud thought of some day cutting a figure in the annals of Abdera had contributed at least as much to his great activity in this matter of the frogs as his *virtue*. But that everything he did was done *merely to satisfy his craving for delicacies* we consider a defamation by weak-minded and vehement people, of which there is no lack on such occasions, particularly in small republics, as everyone knows.

Korax had taken the steps necessary for his opinion to be approved unanimously in the second meeting of the Academy. For, the President, and three or four honorary members who did not want to commit themselves, had taken a trip out to the country the day before.

Chapter Eight

The opinion is read before the Senate, and after various violent debates, it is unanimously resolved that it should be communicated to the priests of Latona.

The opinion was handed over to the *archon* in the specified time and read at the next meeting of the Senate by the city clerk *Pyrops*,[30] a declared *Antifrogman*, at the top of his voice and with uncommonly precise attention to all commas and other marks of punctuation.

The *minority*, of course, had meanwhile been very active in trying to persuade the *archon* to postpone the execution of the resolution and, in a special meeting of the Senate, to take a chance once again on getting a majority to decide whether they ought not to bypass the Academy and turn the matter over to the *Council of Ten. Onokradias* had also accepted this proposal with the proviso that he have time to think it over, but, in spite of the daily urging by the opposition, had postponed his answer all the more, since he had been assured that the opinion was to be finished by the day the Senate was to have its next regular meeting.

The nomophylax *Hypsiboas* and his adherents, therefore, felt not a little offended when, after terminating the regular business, the archon drew a large pamphlet from under his cloak and told the Senate that it was the opinion which, owing to the last resolution of the Council, the Academy had been charged with drawing up in the well-known *unpleasant matter of the frogs.* They all suddenly stood up raging, accused the archon of having acted underhandedly, and declared that they would never permit the reading of the opinion.

Onokradias, who, among his other small flaws of character, had the habit of always being heated where he should have been indifferent, and indifferent where he should have been heated, would have given a very heated answer if the councillor *Meidias* had not asked him to be still and to allow the gentlemen to do their shouting. "When they have said everything," he whispered to him, "they'll have nothing more to say, and then they will surely have to stop of their own accord."

And this is what happened, too. The gentlemen made a lot of noise, crowed, and gesticulated until they were tired out; and since they finally noticed that no one was listening to them, they sat down again grumbling, wiped the perspiration from their brows, and—the opinion was read.

We know the way the Abderites had of passing, as quickly as turning a hand, from the tragic to the comic and, because of the smallest occasion for laughter, of completely losing sight of a matter's serious aspect. The third part of the opinion had hardly been read, when the effect of this jovial frame of mind already appeared even among those who shortly before had shouted so loudly against it. "That's what I call really giving proof," one of the councillors said to his neighbor while Pyrops paused in order, as was the custom in those days, to take a pinch of hellebore.—"You have to admit," another said, "that thing is written in a masterful way."—"I'm looking forward," a third said, "to what objection anybody's going to be able to make to the proof that in the end the frogs are, after all, only frogs."—"I've been noticing something like that for a long time," a fourth said with a sly look; "but it's pleasant, you know, to see that learned people share our opinion."

"Just go on," Meidias said to the city clerk, "for the best is yet to come."

Pyrops continued reading. The councillors laughed so hard at the calculation of the smallness of the priest Stilbon's seeds that they had to hold their sides. But they suddenly got serious again when the sad alternative appeared, and they imagined what a pity it would be if, with the ruling archon at their head, they had to proceed in a body to the Temple of Latona and, in addition, consider it a special favor to be changed into frogs. They craned their fat necks and gasped for air at the mere thought of how they would feel in the event of such a catastrophe, and they were heartily inclined to approve any means whereby such a misfortune could be prevented.

But now, when the secret was out, when they heard that the Academy had no other remedy to propose than *to eat* the frogs which a moment before they had wished to be rid of at any price— which tongue could describe the mixture of astonishment, shock, and vexation on account of their disappointed expectation that suddenly appeared on the distorted faces of the old councillors, who made up almost half of the Senate. These people looked no different than if they had been expected to allow their own children to be chopped into little pasties. Overwhelmed suddenly by the inexplicable might of prejudice, they all started up in horror and declared that they wished to hear nothing more, and that they had never expected such ungodliness from the Academy.

"But you do hear, don't you, that it is only common, natural frogs that we are to eat," shouted councillor Meidias. "After all, we eat peacocks and doves and geese despite the former's being sacred to Juno and Venus, and the latter to Priapus[31] himself. Does beef then agree with us less, possibly, because Jupiter transformed himself into a bull and the princess *Io* into a cow? Or do we have the least misgivings about eating all kinds of fish, although they are under the protection of all the water gods?"

"But we are talking about neither geese nor fish, but about frogs," the old councillors and guild masters shouted; "that is something quite different. Just gods! To eat the frogs of Latona! How can a man of sound mind get an idea like that?

"Do pull yourselves together, gentlemen," the councillor *Stentor* shouted towards them; you surely will not wish to be such *frog worshipers*—"

"Rather *frog worshipers* than *frog eaters*," cried the *nomophylax,* who did not want to let this lucky moment for setting himself up as the head of a party escape, on whose shoulders he hoped in a short time to be raised to the *office of archon.*

"Rather anything else in the world but *frog eaters*," shouted the minority councillors and a few graybearded guild masters who sided with them.

"Gentlemen," the archon Onokradias said while jumping up with some heat from his ivory chair, since the frog worshipers began shouting so loudly that he began to be anxious about his sense of hearing—"a proposal of the Academy is still no resolution. Please sit down and listen to reason, if you can. I hope there is no one here who imagines that it matters so much to me to eat frogs. I will also surely still know how to find ways and means of preventing their eating me. But the Academy, which consists of the most learned people in Abdera, must surely, after all, know what it is talking about—" ("Not always," *Meidias* muttered through his teeth.) "And since the best interests of the community come before all else, and it is not reasonable that the frogs are sacrificed to the human beings—that the human beings, I say, are sacrificed to the

frogs, as the Academy has very well proved, it is my suggestion—
that the opinion, without further ado—be communicated to the
reverend priests of Latona. If you can make a better proposal, I
will be the first to second it. For I, for my part, have nothing against
the frogs, to the extent that they do no damage."

Since the proposal of the archon was nothing other than what
both parties would have had to propose anyhow, the communica-
tion of the opinion was, of course, unanimously approved. But the
peace and quiet in the Senate were not thereby restored, and from
this hour the poor city of Abdera found itself divided again, under
other names, into *Asses* and *Shadows*.

Chapter Nine

*The chief priest Stilbon writes a very thick book against the
Academy. It is read by no one; otherwise, however, everything, for
the time being, stays as it was.*

Everyone believed that the chief priest would be spitting fire in
his anger about the Academy's opinion, and people were not a
little astonished when, to all appearances, he then remained so
composed as if the affair did not concern him at all.

"What wretched brains!" he said shaking his head while he was
looking over the opinion cursorily. "And yet one should think they
would have to read my book on the antiquities, in which everything
is set forth so obviously. It is inconceivable how anybody with five
sound senses can be so *ignorant*. But perhaps I am still going to
open their minds to understanding. I am going to write a book—a
book that I dare all the academies in the world to refute, if they
can!"

And *Stilbon*, the chief priest, sat down and wrote a book that
was three times as thick as the first one that the archon Onokradias
did not want to read, and in it he proved: that the author of the
opinion had no common sense; that he was an ignoramus who had
not even learned that there is nothing great or small in nature; who
did not know that matter could be divided ad infinitum, and that
the infinite smallness of the seeds (even if they were assumed to be
infinitely smaller still than Korax had done in his quite ridiculously
exaggerated calculation) did not prove the least thing against their
being possible. He supported the foundations of his system of the
Abderite frogs with new arguments and answered with great accuracy and elaborateness all possible objections that he made against
them himself. While he was writing, his conceit and his rancor

imperceptibly got so heated that he indulged in very bitter attacks against his opponents, accused them of a deliberate and obdurate hatred of truth, and rather clearly intimated that such people ought *not at all* to be *tolerated* in a well-ordered state.

The Senate of Abdera was startled when, after several months (for Stilbon, although he wrote day and night, had not been able to get his book finished any sooner) the archon brought before the Senate the chief priest's refutation, which was so voluminous that, to make the thing more amusing, he had it hauled in on a litter by two of the most broad-shouldered sack-heavers of Abdera and deposited on the large table of the Senate. The gentlemen found that there was no possibility of having such an extensive work read. Therefore, it was resolved by a majority of the votes to send it to the philosopher *Korax* at once, with the charge of addressing in writing to the ruling archon as soon as possible whatever comments he might possibly have against it.

Korax was just standing in the midst of a crowd of cheeky young Abderites in the vestibule of his house when the sack-heavers arrived at his place with their erudite load. When he now had learned from the courier—whom the Senate had sent along—what this was all about, such an immoderate laughter broke out among all those present that it could be heard in the Senate Chamber three or four blocks away. "The priest Stilbon has a sly genius," Korax said. "He has availed himself of precisely the most infallible means for not getting refuted. But he shall find himself deceived after all! We're going to show him that a book can be refuted without having been read."

"Where should we unload?" asked the sack-heavers, who had already been standing there a good while with their litter and did not understand any of the humorous remarks made by the learned gentlemen.

"There's no room in my little house for such a big book," Korax said.

"Do you know what?" one of the young philosophers interrupted him, "because the book is, after all, written *not* to be read, donate it to the *Senate Library*. It will be safe there, and, under the protection of an incrustation of dust as thick as your finger, it will reach remote posterity unread and in good condition."

"That's an excellent idea," Korax said. "Good friends," he continued turning to the sack-heavers, "here are two drachmae for your trouble. Carry your load over to the Senate Library, and don't be concerned about anything further. I'll take the responsibility for the entire business."

So the bearers, accompanied by a crowd of street urchins, marched over to the Senate Library. And one of the young gentlemen hastened to turn the entire story into a song that was sung in all the streets of Abdera by the next night.

Stilbon, from whom the fate of a book that had cost him so much time and effort could not long remain concealed, was so astonished and furious that he knew neither what to think nor say. "Great Latona," he exclaimed again and again, "what times we are living in! What can you do with people who don't want to listen? But let it be so! I have done all I can. If they don't wish to listen, then they may leave it alone! I will not take up my pen again nor move a finger any more for such an ungrateful, uncouth, and unreasonable people."

Such were his thoughts in his initial ill humor. But the good priest deceived himself because of this apparent composure. His egotism was much too offended for him to stay that calm. The more he thought the matter over, and all night he could think of nothing else, the more strongly he felt convinced that he was not allowed to do nothing for the good cause in the face of such a blatant challenge.

The nomophylax and the remaining enemies of the archon Onokradias did not fail to inflame his zeal completely by their agitation. Meetings were held almost daily in order to deliberate on the measures that would have to be taken to put a stop to the spreading current of disorder and profligacy, as Stilbon called it.

But the times had really changed very much. Stilbon was no *Strobylus.* The people knew him little, and he had none of the talents by which his aforementioned predecessor had assumed, with infinitely less erudition, such airs of importance in Abdera. Almost all of the young people of both sexes were infected *by the principles of the philosopher Korax.* The greater part of the councillors and distinguished citizens was inclined, *without principles,* to the side where there was the most to laugh about. And even among the common people, *the street ballads* with which a few of the *versemongers* among Korax's followers had filled the city had been so effective that, for the present, there was little hope of stirring up the rabble as easily as formerly. But, what was still the very worst thing, there was reason to believe that this one and that one *among the priests themselves* maintained secret contacts with the *Antifrogmen.* It was, in fact, more than mere suspicion that the priest *Pamphagus* was hatching a plot to take advantage of the present circumstances and do dislodge honest Stilbon from a position, to which, as Pamphagus underhandedly intimated, he was in no wise equal in such a serious *crisis* because of his total inexperience.

In all of this, however, the *frog worshipers* made up a considerable party, and Hypsiboas had skill enough always to keep them in an agitated state that more than once could have led to dangerous eruptions, if the opposition—satisfied with the victories they had achieved and disinclined to endanger the preponderance they possessed, had not remained so inactive and carefully avoided everything that could have occasioned an unusual stir. For, although they did not appear exactly to decline the name of *frogeaters,* and the frogs of Latona yielded the most usual material for mirth in their social gatherings, they let it go at that, in true Abderite fashion, and the frogs, in spite of the Academy's opinion and the jokes of the philosopher Korax, still remained, undisturbed and uneaten, in the possession of the city and region of Abdera.

Chapter Ten

Strange development of this entire tragi-comical farce.

In all probability the frogs of Latona would still have enjoyed this security for a long time if, as it happened, an endless host of *mice* and *rats* of all colors had not in the next summer suddenly flooded the fields of the unfortunate Republic and thereby unexpectedly fulfilled the quite harmless and casual prediction of the archon *Onokradias.*

To be eaten up by frogs and mice at the same time was too much all at once for the poor Abderites. The matter came to be serious.

The *Antifroggers* now insisted without further ado on the necessity of implementing the Academy's proposal immediately.

The *frog worshipers* cried that the yellow, green, blue, red, and flea-colored mice, who in a few days had caused the most dreadful devastation on the Abderite fields, were a visible punishment of the frog eaters' impiety and were obviously sent directly by Latona to destroy entirely the city that had made itself unworthy of the protection of the goddess.

The Academy proved in vain that yellow, green, and flea-colored mice were not, for all that, *mousier mice* than others; that what was going on with these mice was quite natural; that similar examples could be found in the annals of all peoples; and that by this time, since the aforesaid mice appeared to be determined to leave the Abderites nothing else to eat anyhow, it was all the more necessary to indemnify oneself for the damage that both kinds of common enemies of the Republic caused with at least the edible half of them, namely with the frogs.

The priest *Pamphagus* intervened to no avail by proposing that in the future they convert the frogs into regular *sacrificial animals* and, after the head and entrails have been sacrificed to the goddess, eat the legs as *sacrificial meat* in her honor.

The people, perplexed by a natural calamity that they could not visualize otherwise than with the image of a *judgment* by angry gods, and roused to indignation by the leaders of the frog party, ran in mobs to the city hall and threatened to leave none of the gentlemen's bones unbroken if they did not immediately find the means to save the city from ruin.

Never yet had good counsel been so hard to come by in the city hall of Abdera as now. The councillors broke out in a cold sweat. They struck their foreheads, but the echo was hollow. The more they reflected, the less they hit on what might be done. The people did not want to be refused and swore they would break the necks of both *Profroggers* and *Antifroggers* if they did not find a way out.

Finally, the archon *Onokradias* suddenly jumped up from his chair as if inspired. *"Follow me,"* he said to the councillors and walked with big steps out onto a marble rostrum that was intended for public addresses to the people. His eyes sparkled with an unusual brightness, he looked taller by a head than otherwise, and his entire figure had something more majestic about it than had ever been seen in an Abderite. The councillors followed him silently and full of expectation.

"Hear me, *you men of Abdera*," *Onokradias* said with a voice that was not his own. *"Jason,* my great ancestor, has descended from the seat of the gods and is at this moment inspiring me with the means by which we can all save ourselves. Go, each one of you, to your house, pack up all of your implements and belongings, and appear tomorrow at sunrise with your wives and children, your horses and asses, your cattle and sheep, in short, with bag and baggage in front of the Temple of Jason. From there, with the *Golden Fleece* at our head, we are going to set out, turn our backs to these walls that are scorned by the gods, and seek in the broad plains of fertile *Macedonia* another place to live until the anger of the gods will have subsided and it is again granted to us, or to our children, to return with auspicious portents to beautiful Abdera. The pernicious mice, when they find nothing more to exist on, will eat one another up, and as far as the frogs are concerned—may Latona be merciful to them! Go, my children, and make ready!

Tomorrow, with the rising of the sun, all of our hardships will come to an end."

All the people jubilantly shouted their approval at the inspired archon, and in a moment only one soul was again breathing in all the Abderites. Their volatile imagination was suddenly in full flame. New prospects, new scenes of happiness and joys danced in their minds. The broad plains of fortunate Macedonia lay spread before their eyes like a fruitful paradise. They were already breathing the milder breezes and yearning with indescribable impatience to get out of the close, frog-swampy atmosphere of their disgusting native city. Everyone made haste to get ready for an exodus, of which, a few moments before, no one had had the slightest intimation.

On the following morning all the people of Abdera were ready to start their journey. All of their belongings that they could not take along they left behind without regret in their houses; they were that impatient to move to a place where they would no longer be plagued by either frogs or mice.

On the fourth morning of their emigration, King *Kassander*[32] met them. The din of their column could be heard from afar, and the dust they raised darkened the daylight. *Kassander* ordered his men to halt and sent somebody out to inquire what this might be.

"Most gracious lord," the returning scout said, "it is the *Abderites* who, because of frogs and mice, did not know how they could stay in Abdera any longer and are seeking a new place to live."

"If this is the case, then I am sure it is the *Abderites,*" Kassander said.

In the meanwhile, *Onokradias* appeared at the head of a deputation of councillors and citizens to submit their request to the King.

The affair seemed so hilarious to Kassander and his courtiers that, with all of their courtesy, they could not help laughing boisterously in the Abderites' faces. And the Abderites, when they saw the entire court laughing, *considered it their obligation to laugh, too.*

Kassander promised them his protection and allotted them a site at the borders of Macedonia where they could live until they found the means to reach an equitable settlement with the frogs and mice of their fatherland.

From this time on we know little more than nothing about the *Abderites* and their *affairs.* Yet, it is certain that a few years after this odd emigration (the historical certainty of which is placed beyond all doubt by the testimony of the historian *Trogus Pompeius,* book 15, chapter 2, cited in an excerpt by *Justinus*[33]) they moved back to Abdera. Presumably they had to have left behind in Macedonia the *rats in their minds* that usually had always caused more of a hubbub therein than all of the rats and frogs in their city and region. For, *from this epoch on,* history says nothing further about them but that, under the protection of the Macedonian kings and the Romans, they led a quiet and peaceful life through several centuries, and, since they had neither more wit nor were more stupid than other city dwellers of their kind, they gave historians no opportunity to write anything bad or good about them.

In order to give our gentle readers consummate proof of our candor, we are not going to conceal from them that—insofar as *Pliny* the Elder and his stated informant *Varro*[34] deserved credence in this matter—*Abdera* had not been the only city in the world to be snatched away from its natural inhabitants by such insignificant enemies as frogs and mice. For *Varro* is said to mention not only a city in *Spain* that was destroyed by *rabbits* and another one, by *moles,* but also a city in *Gaul,* whose inhabitants, like the Abderites, had had to give way to the frogs. However, since *Pliny* gives neither the name of the city to which this misfortune is supposed to have happened nor says explicitly from which of the countless works of the learned *Varro* he took this anecdote, we believe we are not questioning the deference owed this great man if we suspect that his memory, on the accuracy of which he did not seldom rely too much, had foisted Gaul on him for *Thrace,* and that the city that *Varro* mentions was none other than our Abdera itself.

And with this then, let the apex be set on the monument to this republic, once so famous and now forgotten again for so many centuries, which we have been impelled to erect, no doubt, by a demon concerned about its fame, not without the hope, despite its being composed of such slight materials as the odd whims and jovial follies of the Abderites, that it will last so long until our nation will have reached that fortunate time when this history will no longer be of concern to anyone, will no longer entertain anyone, will no longer serve to annoy anyone or amuse him; in a word, when the Abderites *resemble no one any longer* and, therefore, their affairs will be just as incomprehensible to us as stories from another planet; a time that can no longer be far off, if the boys of the first generation of the nineteenth century *will be wiser* only by as much as the boys in the last quarter of the eighteenth *fancy* themselves wiser than the men of the previous one—or if all the books on pedagogy, with which we have, for twenty years, been so richly endowed and which are still presented to us daily, have only one-twentieth of the splendid effect that their well-meaning authors lead us to hope.

The Key to the History of the Abderites, 1781

When the *Homeric poems* had become known, the Greeks, the people—who in many things are wont to see more accurately with their plain common sense than the gentlemen with spectacles— had just enough wit to see that in these great, heroic stories, in spite of the marvelous, the fantastic, and the incredible elements with which they are abundantly interwoven, there is more wisdom and instruction for practical life than in all of the Milesian Tales[1]; and we see from Horace's letter to Lollius,[2] and from the use that Plutarch[3] makes, and teaches how to make of those poems, that, still many centuries after Homer, the most intelligent men of the world among the Greeks and Romans were of the opinion that one could learn what is right and useful, what is unjust and harmful, and how much a man is capable of through virtue and wisdom from Homer's stories as well as and even better than from the most subtle and most eloquent moralists. It was left to *old* childish minds (for the young were taught better) to stick to the *material* component of the poems; intelligent people felt and perceived the *spirit* informing this corpus and did not take it into their heads to wish to sever what the *Muse* had joined inseparably, the *true* under the cover of the *marvelous,* and the *useful,* by means of an art of blending that has not been revealed to all, brought into harmony with the *beautiful* and the *agreeable.*

As happens in all human affairs, so things went here, too. Not satisfied with finding admonishing and encouraging *examples* and an instructive *mirror of human life* in the diverse classes, circumstances, and scenes in Homer's poems, the scholars of later times wanted to penetrate *still more deeply,* see *still more* than their ancestors; and so they discovered (for, what does one not discover if one has once taken it into his head to discover something?) *allegory* in what was only an *example,* a *mystical meaning* in everything, even in the mere apparatus and settings of the poetic scene. Finally, they found in every character, depiction, and little story, God knows what secrets of *Hermetic, Orphic,*[4] and *magic philoso-*

phies, of which the good poet certainly had no more thought that Vergil did that, twelve hundred years after his death, evil spirits would be exorcised with his verses.[5]

Meanwhile, it imperceptibly grew into an essential requirement of an *epic poem* (as the larger and heroic poetic stories are customarily called) that, besides the *natural* meaning and the moral that it presented at first glance, it had to have an additional *secret* and *allegorical* one. At least among the *Italians* and *Spaniards,* this fad won the upper hand; and it is more than ridiculous to see what pains the commentators, or even perhaps the poets themselves, take to spin out of an *Amadis* and *Orlando,* out of Trissino's *Liberated Italy* or Camoëns' *Lusiads,* indeed even out of Marino's *Adonis,*[6] all kinds of metaphysical, political, moral, physical, and theological allegories.

Now since it was not the readers' concern to penetrate on their own into these secrets, it was necessary, if they were not to be deprived of such splendid treasures, to provide them with a *key* for these, and this, you see, was the exposition of the allegorical and mystical meaning, although the poet commonly did not think about what hidden similarities and relationships could possibly be puzzled out of his poem until he had completed it.

What in many poets was merely complaissance toward a prevailing fashion that they did not dare to disregard, became for others the real *intent* and *main feature.* The famous *Zodiac of Life* of the so-called Palingenius, Barclay's *Argenis,* Spenser's *The Faerie Queene,* Dame Manley's *New Atlantis,* the *Malabarian Princesses,* the *Tale of the Tub,* the history of *John Bull,*[7] and a great many other works of this kind, of which especially the sixteenth and seventeenth centuries were very productive, were by their nature and intention *allegorical* and could, therefore, not be understood without a key, although a few of them, for example, Spenser's *Faerie Queene* and the allegorical satires of *Dr. Swift* are so constituted that any intelligent and experienced person can find the key to them in his own head without anyone else's assistance.

This short discussion will be more than adequate to make comprehensible to those who, until now, have never thought about how it happened that imperceptibly a kind of common prejudice and probable opinion has established itself in most minds to the effect that every book that resembles a *satirical novel* is endowed with a hidden meaning and, therefore, requires a *key.*

That is also the reason, then, that the editor of the present history—as he became aware of the fact that most people, among the great number of readers that his work has had the honor of finding, were firmly convinced that there had to be more to it than the words appear to be saying at first glance and, therefore, wished to obtain a *key* to the *History of the Abderites* as an indispensable requirement for the complete understanding of the book—did not allow this desire of his readers, which he often heard, to disturb him in the least. On the contrary, he considered it, rather, a courtesy that he owed them to satisfy this desire, as important as it was, and to impart to them, *as a key* or *in place* of the *desired* key, which actually amounts to the same thing, everything that can contribute to a more thorough understanding and a profitable use of this work that was written to entertain all intelligent people and to admonish and chastise all fools.

To this end, he finds it necessary to inform them, first of all, about the history of its genesis, candidly, and in the author's own words, a writer little known, to be sure, but much read since the year 1753.[8]

"It was (so runs his account)—it was a beautiful evening in the autumn of the year 177–. I was alone in the upper story of my house, and (why should I be ashamed of admitting to human shortcomings?) out of *sheer boredom,* I was looking out of the window, for my genius had abandoned me entirely for many weeks. I could neither think nor read. All the fire of my spirit seemed extinguished, all of my fancy, like a volatile salt, to have evaporated. I was, or at least felt, *stupid;* but, alas, without partaking of the *bliss of stupidity,* without a single grain of this proud self-satisfaction, this imperturbable conviction that assures certain people that everything they think, say, dream, and talk in their sleep is true, witty, wise, and is worthy of being engraved in marble—a conviction that, like a birthmark, makes the genuine son of the great goddess recognizable and turns him into the happiest of human beings. In short, I *was aware* of my condition, and it weighed heavily upon me. I shook myself in vain, and things (as I have said) had gone so far with me that I was looking through a rather inconvenient little window out into the world without knowing what I saw, or seeing something that would have been worth knowing or seeing.

"Suddenly it seemed to me as if I were hearing a *voice*—whether it was truth or illusion, I do not wish to decide—that called out to me: *'Sit down and write the history of the Abderites!'*

"And suddenly my mind was illuminated. 'Yes indeed,' I thought, 'the *Abderites.* What can be more natural? I will write the history of the Abderites! Just how was it possible for me not to get such a simple idea long ago?' And now I sat down immediately and wrote, looked things up, made compilations, arranged my materials, and continued writing; and it was a pleasure to see how quickly my work progressed.

"While I was now engaged in writing at my best (our author continues in his candid account), there came to me in a strange mood or in a *whim,* or whatever one wishes to call it otherwise, the idea of giving my imagination free rein and carrying things just as far as they could go. 'It applies only to the *Abderites,*' I thought, 'and there is no sinning against the Abderites; indeed, they are, after all, nothing but a pack of fools. The absurdities with which history charges them are great enough to justify the most preposterous things you can ascribe to them.'

"I confess frankly, therefore—and if it was unjust, may Heaven forgive me!—I strained all of my powers of invention to the bursting point in order to have the *Abderites* think, talk, and behave as foolishly as at all possible. 'It is, indeed, over two thousand years since they have, all of them, been dead and buried,' I said to myself. 'It can harm neither them nor their descendants, for, of the latter there are no mortal remains left either.'

"In addition to all this came another idea that attracted me by a certain semblance of *kindheartedness.* 'The more foolish I make them,' I thought, 'the less I have to fear that the *Abderites* will be considered a *satire* and that applications of that will be made to people whom I surely, after all, cannot have meant, since their existence is not even known to me.'—But I was greatly mistaken in coming to that conclusion. The outcome proved that I had innocently created *portraits,* while I believed I was only painting *fantasies.*"

It must be admitted that this was one of the most unfortunate things that can happen to an author who has no cunning in his heart, and, without wishing to vex or grieve any soul, seeks only to banish his own and his fellow creature's boredom. However, it was this that the author of the *Abderites* encountered with the first few chapters of his little work. There is, perhaps, no city in Germany and as far as the natural boundaries of the German language go (which, in passing, is a bigger stretch of land than any other European language can boast of possessing), where the *Abderites* are not supposed to have found readers. And wherever people read the book, they claimed having seen the *originals* of the pictures in it.

"In a thousand places," the author says, "where I have neither ever been myself nor have the least acquaintance, people wondered how I knew the *Abderite men and women* and the *Abderisms* of these *places* and *everywhere* so well; and people believed I absolutely had to have a secret correspondence or a little private demon who told me anecdotes that I could not have come to know by legitimate means. Now I knew," he continued, "nothing more certain than that I had neither the former nor the latter. Consequently, it was as clear as daylight that *the ancient little nation of the Abderites* had not so entirely *died out* as I had imagined."

This discovery induced the author to engage in research, which he had considered unnecessary as long as he had consulted his own imagination and caprice in the writing of his work more than history or documents. He rummaged through some large and small books without any particular success, until he finally found in the sixth decade of the famous *Hafen Slawkenbergius,*[9] p. 864, the following passage that appeared to give him some information about these unexpected incidents.

"The good city of *Abdera* in Thrace," says *Slawkenbergius* in the passage already cited, "formerly a great, populous, and flourishing city of commerce, the Thracian *Athens,* the native town of Protagoras and Democritus, the paradise of fools and frogs, this good, beautiful city—is no more. We look for it in vain on the maps and in the descriptions of present-day Thrace. Even the place where it formerly stood is unknown, or at least can be indicated only by conjectures.

"But not so the *Abderites!* They still continue living and being active, although the original place where they used to live has long ago disappeared from the earth. They are an *indestructible, immortal* tribe. Without their having a firm abode anywhere, they are found *everywhere;* and although they live dispersed among all other people, they have nevertheless kept themselves pure and unmixed and remain so true to their old ways that one only needs to see and hear an *Abderite* for a moment, wherever one meets him, in order just as certainly *to see* and *hear* that he is an *Abderite,* as in Frankfurt and Leipzig, Constantinople, and Aleppo, one sees in a Jew that he is a Jew.

"The strangest thing, however, and a circumstance in which they differ essentially from the Israelites, Bedouins, Armenians, and all other unmixed peoples, is that, *without the least danger* to their *Abderidity,* they *intermarry* with all the rest of the earth's inhabitants, and, although everywhere they speak the language of the country where they live and have in common with *non-Abderites* their constitution, religion, and customs, also eat and drink, trade and travel, dress and groom themselves, dress their hair and use perfume, have themselves purged and clysterized, in short, that they do everything that belongs to the necessities of human life in approximately the same way—as other people. Nevertheless, I say, in all things that make them into Abderites they *remain so constantly like themselves* as if, from time immemorial, they had been isolated by a wall of diamond, three times as high and thick as the walls of ancient Babylon, from the sensible creatures on our planet. All other races of mankind change through transplantation, and two different ones produce a third through intermarriage. But it has never been possible to perceive the least essential alteration in the *Abderites,* wherever they were transplanted and however much they mixed with other peoples. Everywhere they are still the same fools they were two thousand years ago in *Abdera.* And although it has not been possible for a long time to say, see, *here is Abdera,* or *there is Abdera,* there is, nevertheless, in Europe, Asia, Africa, and America, as far as these great parts of the earth are civilized, no city, no market town, village, nor hamlet, where one might not meet a few members of this *invisible association.*" So far the aforesaid *Hafen Slawkenbergius.*

"After I had read this passage," our author continues, "I now suddenly had *the key* to the aforementioned experiences that had seemed at first glance so inexplicable. And as the *Slawkenbergian account* made comprehensible what I had encountered in the Abderites, so the latter, on the other hand, confirmed the credibility of the former. The Abderites had, therefore, left behind a seed that had shot up in all lands and spread into a numerous progeny; and since almost everywhere the characters and doings of the *ancient* Abderites were regarded as copies of and anecdotes about the *modern ones,* there was proved thereby as well the strange attribute of *uniformity* and *invariability,* which differentiates this people, according to the testimony cited, from other people on the continents and the islands of the sea.

"The reports that came to me about this from all over were a great comfort to me for two reasons: first, because I now suddenly found myself relieved of all inner reproach for *having,* perhaps, *treated* the Abderites *too badly;* and second, because I learned that my work was being read with pleasure (even by the Abderites themselves) and that especially the striking *similarity* between the *ancient* and *new ones* was being admired, which had to be very flattering to the latter, to be sure, as obvious proof of the authenticity of their derivation. The few who are said to have complained of having been depicted with *too much resemblance* do not come into consideration compared with the multitude of those who are content; and even these few would, perhaps, do better if they accepted the matter otherwise. For since, as it appears, they do not care to be taken for what they are, and have, for that reason, slipped into the skin of a more noble animal, prudence demands they themselves do not stick up their ears in order to arouse the attention of others, which can but redound to their disadvantage.

"On the other hand, however, I also allowed the circumstance that I wrote the history of the *ancient* Abderites, as it were, *under the eyes of the modern ones,* to serve as a motive for holding my imagination, that I had initially left merely to its own caprice, with a tighter rein, for guarding carefully against producing caricatures, and for doing strictest justice to the Abderites in everything that I related about them. For now I saw myself as the historian *of the antiquities of a family that is continuing to flourish,* that would be justified in taking umbrage at someone's laying something or other to the charge of its ancestors without reason and in contradiction to the truth.

"*The History of the Abderites* can, therefore, justly be regarded as one of the truest and most reliable mirrors, and, just for that reason, a faithful one, in which the moderns can look at their countenance, and, if only they wish to be honest with themselves, can discover in what respect they resemble their ancestors. It would be superfluous to make much ado about the usefulness this work can and must have in this regard as long as there are still going to be Abderites—and this will presumably be long enough. Therefore, we are only mentioning that it could, incidentally, even have the usefulness, too, of making the *descendants of the ancient Germans* among us more cautious to be on their guard against whatever could arouse the suspicion that they either were of Abderite blood or wished, from an exaggerated admiration for *Abderite nature and art*[10] and a mania for imitation springing therefrom, to pass themselves off as having similarities to this people, in which for divers reasons, they would have little to gain.[11]

And this, worthy readers, would, therefore, be the promised *key* to this remarkable original work, with the attached assurance that there is in it not the smallest secret drawer that you ought not to be able to unlock with this key; and if someone wished to whisper in your ear that there is still *more* concealed in it, you can certainly believe that he either does not know what he is talking about or is up to some mischief.

—Sapientia prima est stultitia caruisse—[11]

End of the History of the Abderites

Notes

Introduction

1. Eric A. Blackall, *The Emergence of German as a Literary Language 1700–1775*, 2d ed. (Ithaca and London: Cornell University Press, 1978).
2. *Dreiundsechzigster Literaturbrief.*
3. So, e.g., Friedrich Sengle, *Wieland* (Stuttgart: Metzler, 1949), 90–92.
4. See John A. McCarthy, "Wielands Metamorphose," in *Deutsche Vierteljahrschrift für Literaturwissenschaft und Geistesgeschichte* 49 (1975) Sonderheft: "18. Jahrhundert": 149–67.
5. Sengle, 134–35.
6. John A. McCarthy, *Christoph Martin Wieland* (Boston: Twayne, 1979), 68.
7. *Hamburgische Dramaturgie*, 69. Stück.
8. Fritz Martini, "Nachwort," in Christoph Martin Wieland, *Werke*, ed. Fritz Martini and Hans Werner Seiffert, 5 vols. (Munich: Hanser, 1966), 2:847.
9. Sengle, 267.
10. Sengle, 269–70.
11. Sengle, 408.
12. Cf. Christoph Martin Wieland, *Agathon* (Leipzig: Weidmanns Erben und Reich, 1773), 4:n.p.
13. McCarthy, *Wieland,* 127.
14. Hans Werner Seiffert, "Nachwort," in Christoph Martin Wieland, *Werke,* ed. Fritz Martini and H. W. Seiffert, 5 vols. (Munich: Hanser, 1966), 5:869.
15. Max Dufner, "The Tragedy of Laïs in Wieland's *Aristipp,*" *Monatshefte* 52 (1960): 63–70.
16. Sengle, 532.
17. Walter H. Bruford, *Culture and Society in Classical Weimar, 1775–1806* ([London]: Cambridge University Press, 1962), 295.
18. Martini, "Nachwort," 855.
19. As translated into English in the present volume. All further references to this version of Wieland's *History of the Abderites* will be made in the text of the Introduction by page number only.
20. K. W. Böttiger, ed., *Literarische Zustände und Zeitgenossen, in Schilderungen aus Karl Aug. Böttigers handschriftlichem Nachlasse* (1838; reprint, Frankfurt a. M.: Athenäum, 1972), 1:179.
21. Böttiger, 1:166–67.
22. As is noted by W. E. Yuill, "Abderites and Abderitism, some reflections on a novel by Wieland," *Essays in German Literature,* ed. F. Norman (London: University of London Institute of Germanic Studies, 1965), 1:84ff.
23. This was discussed and called Wieland's "negative point" by Marga Barthel, *Das "Gespräch" bei Wieland. Untersuchungen über Wesen und Form seiner*

Dichtung, Frankfurter Quellen und Forschungen zur germanischen und romanischen Philologie 26 (1939; reprint, Hildesheim: Gerstenberg, 1973): 40–43.

24. Anthony, Earl of Shaftesbury, *Characteristics,* ed. and with notes by John M. Robertson and an introduction by Stanley Grean (Indianapolis: Bobbs-Merrill, 1964), 2:252–53.

25. Yuill, 82.

26. Wieland's relationship with J. J. Winckelmann, whose tract on the imitation of the Greeks (1755) had set off this trend in Germany, is taken up in two informative articles by William H. Clark: "Wieland and Winckelmann: Saul and the Prophet," *Modern Language Quarterly* 17 (1956): 1–16; and "Wieland *Contra* Winckelmann?", *The Germanic Review* 34 (1959): 4–13.

27. Aristophanes, *The Frogs and other Plays,* trans. and intro. David Barrett (Baltimore: Penguin, 1966), 45.

28. No. 460, Ὄνου σκιά, "Pars quinta, Fabulae Graecae," in *Aesopica,* ed. Ben Edwin Perry (Urbana: University of Illinois Press, 1952), 1:503.

29. No. 460, "The Shadow of the Ass," *Aesop Without Morals,* trans. and ed. Lloyd W. Daly (New York: Thomas Yoseloff, 1961), 246.

30. Kuno Francke, *A History of German Literature as Determined by Social Forces* (New York: Henry Holt, 1931), 261.

31. Three of these are listed in a note by Fritz Martini, "Wieland. Geschichte der Abderiten," in *Der deutsche Roman,* ed. Benno von Wiese (Düsseldorf: Bagel, 1963), 415: A. von Kotzebue, *Des Esels Schatten oder der Process in Krähwinkel, Eine Posse,* 1810; Ludwig Fulda, *Des Esels Schatten, Lustspiel,* 1920; and Friedrich Dürrenmatt, *Der Prozeß um des Esels Schatten. Ein Hörspiel* (nach Wieland—aber nicht sehr), 1958. Martini also lists W. Schlippe, *Die Narren und der Weise,* Ein Hörspiel, broadcast by SWF in Baden-Baden on 5 May 1960. It is not clear whether this is an adaptation of the Fourth Book, the entire novel, or one of its other parts. I have not seen the script.

Two other plays I have found are: Sammy Gronemann, *Der Prozess um des Esels Schatten,* Komödie in 4 Akten und einem Vorspiel, frei nach Wielands "Abderiten" (Tel-Aviv: Moadim: Palestinian Play Publishers, 1945; and Kurt Wassermann, *Der Prozeß um des Esels Schatten,* ein Lustspiel in vier Bildern nach Wielands berühmtem Roman "Die Abderiten" (Graz: Verlag Spiel und Fest, [1969]).

I am indebted to Hansjörg Schelle of The University of Michigan for pointing out that Gero von Wilpert mentions two additional versions in his study *Der verlorene Schatten* (Stuttgart: Kröner, 1978), 14–15 and 19–20. The first of these is an operetta-like work written at the suggestion of Joseph Gregor, the librettist of the composer Richard Strauss, as an entertainment for the pupils at the Benedictine Monastery at Ettal. The libretto begun by Gregor was finished by Hans Adler. Strauss's music was completed after his death (in 1949) by P. S. Schaller and K. Haussner. This work was performed in Ettal in 1964 to celebrate the centennial of Strauss's birth, then in Naples in 1967, and again in the Badische Staatstheater in Karlsruhe four years later. The other work is the Turkish play *Esegin Gölgesi (The Ass's Shadow)* by Haldun Taner, which was performed in both Istanbul and Ankara in 1965. There appears to be no published version of either.

And finally, in his Wieland bibliography published serially in the *Lessing Yearbook,* Schelle lists in 21 (1989), 208, the version written by Christian Gurzeler and entitled *Der Prozeß um des Esels Schatten. Ein Spiel in drei Akten.* Its first edition appeared in 1962, and the sixth was published in [1983] in Aarau by Sauerländer. Apparently this was written for performance at a secondary school.

Preface

1. Pierre Bayle (1647–1706) published the first volume of his *Dictionnaire historique et critique (Historical and Critical Dictionary)* in 1697. Wieland, as well as many of his German contemporaries, was thoroughly familiar with this French philosopher's monumentally erudite compendium of enlightened, skeptical, and critical scholarship directed, with satire and even sarcasm, against superstition, unsupported notions, preconceived ideas and theories, and the fallacious in general.

2. Lucian of Samosata (ca. A.D. 115–ca. 200), whose works Wieland translated in six volumes (1788–89), wrote a *True History,* a witty satire of Hellenistic tales of travel that involves both a flight to the moon and a voyage in the belly of a whale. At one time Wieland considered writing something in the same manner. See also Introduction, p. 21.

3. Representatives of the individual Greek peoples in the Amphictyony, a religious association of those Greeks who worshipped at the shrine of the same god, e.g., at Delphi. The literal meaning of the Greek term is "they who dwell around," or "next neighbors."

4. Members of the highest Athenian court, the Areopagus, before which cases of murder and other capital crimes were tried.

5. Roman magistrates of various kinds. A commission of literally "ten men," the most famous being the composers of the so-called "Twelve Tables," published in 451–450 B.C., and the commission which consulted and interpreted the oracular books of the Sibyl.

6. Centumviri: in ancient Rome a college of judges chosen annually for civil suits, especially such as related to inheritances; literally "a hundred men." Ducentumviri: Wieland's humorous enhancement of the two previous Latin compounds.

7. Melusine: a fairy who periodically reverts to her shape as part woman, part serpent (in later versions as a mermaid). She is the principal figure in a fourteenth-century French romance by Jean d'Arras and has been the subject of numerous European literary works written since then.

8. Marie Catherine le Jumel de Barneville de la Motte, Baronne d'Aulnoy (1650–1705) published the three volumes of her fairy tales in 1698. Wieland was well acquainted with this French collection and drew themes and plots from it for his own tales.

First Book: Democritus among the Abderites

1. The Latinized name of Claude Saumaise (1588–1653), a celebrated French classical scholar who studied at Heidelberg and held a professorship at Leiden. At the invitation of Queen Christina he visited Sweden in 1650. Wieland had a very high regard for his knowledge of ancient Greek.

2. In Laurence Sterne's novel *Tristram Shandy* (1760–68), one character begins five times in succession to relate *The History of the King of Bohemia who had Seven Castles,* but his listener's impatience prevents him from doing so.

3. Aristides of Miletus (2d century B.C.) wrote a collection of erotic short

stories (some of which were translated into Latin by Cornelius Sisenna in the 1st century B.C.) regarded generally as the forerunners of Boccaccio's *Decameron* and the *Heptameron* of Marguerite of Navarre.

4. Joshua Barnes (1654–1712), eminent English scholar of Greek, who published an edition of Euripides in 1694, of Homer in 1711, and of Anacreon in 1705.

5. Poem by Anacreon, a famous lyric poet of the 6th century B.C., born in Teos but said to have gone to Abdera, and perhaps he died there. The poem, in Edmonds' translation, begins: "Pray, why do you look askance at me, Thracian filly, and shun me so resolutely as though I knew nothing of my art?" Cf. *Lyra Graeca,* ed. and trans. J. M. Edmonds (London: Heinemann, 1931), 2:181. Wieland mentions this poem again in his Fourth Book.

6. Marcus Junianus Justinus (2d or 3d century A.D.) abridged the Latin history of the world written in forty-four books by Trogus Pompeius in the time of Augustus Caesar. The abbreviation by Justinus constitutes most of what we still have of the larger work.

7. The croaking sounds made by the chorus of frogs in Aristophanes' comedy *The Frogs.*

8. King Henry IV of France, born in 1553.

9. Literally, "little man" or "manikin," apparently intended here as a metaphor for *fetus* as it is also used by Laurence Sterne in *Tristram Shandy* (London: Lehmann, 1948), 60.

10. Latin: "who as a companion governs the star of birth," from Horace, *Epistles,* 2.2.187.

11. Ancient Greek term (combining *kalos,* "beautiful," and *agathos,* "good") expressing the ideal of education achieved by the cultivation of the physical as well as the moral and spiritual aspects of the human being.

12. Greek name: Leto. A Greek goddess, daughter of the Titans Coeus and Phoebe, whose twin children, fathered by Zeus and born on Delos, were Artemis and Apollo. It is not clear why Wieland chose to use the Latin name of the tutelary goddess of his Abdera.

13. In ancient Athens the *archon* was the term used to designate the real head of state, the first of the nine chief magistrates. Wieland uses the term in this novel to mean something like "Lord Mayor."

14. A pupil of Plato who became an Athenian general and statesman. He was a dour opponent of Demosthenes and a contemporary of Philip II of Macedonia and Alexander the Great. The Athenians charged him with treason and condemned him to death in 318 B.C. when he was 80 years old. In Plutarch's Life of *Phocion* we are told that his countenance was so composed that he was hardly ever seen by any Athenian either laughing or in tears.

15. γνωθι σεαυτον ("Know thyself!").

16. Claude Adrien Helvétius (1715–1771), French utilitarian philosopher.

17. Laïs of Corinth was one of the most famous and beautiful courtesans of ancient Greece. Wieland recreated her as one of the principal characters in his last major novel, *Aristipp and a Few of His Contemporaries* (1800–1801).

18. Apollonius of Tyana, born ca. 4 B.C., a wandering Pythagorean mystic and philosopher who acquired considerable fame as a worker of wonders. His life was written by Philostratus, and Wieland wrote a novel about him entitled *Agathodämon* (1799). See also Introduction, pp. 20–21.

19. Ancient Greek author (2d century A.D.) who wrote a ten-part guidebook *Hellados Periegesis (Description of Hellas)* about what he had seen on his travels through the Greek world.

20. Daniel Solander, eighteenth-century Swedish botanist who was a pupil of the celebrated Carl von Linné (Linnaeus).

21. An Indian people from whom silk was first brought to Greece.

22. A people in North Africa between Carthage and Ethiopia according to the account in the *Natural History,* 5.8.3 by Pliny the Elder (ca. A.D. 23–79).

23. Reference to one of the paradoxes used by Zeno of Elea (5th century B.C.) to discredit belief in plurality and motion. If the tortoise starts off first, Achilles will never catch up with it; for, while he traverses the distance from his own starting point to that of the tortoise, the tortoise goes on farther, and while Achilles covers this distance, it goes on still farther, and so on ad infinitum.

24. Constructed by the god of the forge to catch his wife, the goddess Aphrodite, in dalliance with the god Mars. This story is sung by the bard Demodokos in book 7 of Homer's *Odyssey.*

25. King Agamemnon's having to return his prize, Chryseis of the fair cheeks, daughter of the priest of Apollo, leads to the incident that arouses the wrath of Achilles in book 1 of Homer's *Iliad.*

26. Probably the greatest statesman (500–429 B.C.) of Athens and its first citizen in the period preceding the Peloponnesian War until his death.

27. In his dialogue *Gorgias* (482) Plato has Socrates swear "by the dog the god of Egypt." To the Greeks and Romans the jackal-headed Egyptian god Anubis, who conducted the souls of the dead to the underworld, looked like a dog.

28. Two cities in ancient Egypt.

29. Athenian tragic poet of the late 5th century B.C. Only fragments of his creations are still extant. His house is the setting of Plato's *Symposium.*

30. Typical of the names Wieland gives many of the characters in this novel, Gryllus (Greek γρύλλος) means "pig."

31. In Homer's *Iliad* this aged leader of the warriors from Pylos has seen two generations perish and keeps telling members of the third at the camp before the walls of Troy that in his time he saw much better men than they. Cf. *Iliad* 1. 247ff.

32. Allusion to the *Batrachomyomachia* (Greek for *Battle of the Frogs and Mice*), a parody of an epic poem that was believed by the ancients to have been a work by Homer. William Cowper wrote an English translation. That Abdera ever went to war with Lemnos appears to be Wieland's invention.

33. This name is the Greek word for "senseless," "foolish," or "silly." The situation described here appears based on the Athenians' sending Alcibiades as one of the three Athenian commanders of the ill-fated attempt at the conquest of Sicily in 415 B.C.

34. The Greek word meaning "young dog," "whelp," or "puppy." Wieland's nomophylax is thus named Pig, the son of Whelp.

35. These famous gardens of Alcinous, King of the Phaeacians on Scheria, are described in book 7 of Homer's *Odyssey.*

36. Wieland has named this cobbler after a tool of his trade, for the German word *Pfriem* means "awl."

37. Celebrated Greek painter (5th century B.C.) who had great skill in producing illusion in his works of art.

38. Another famous Greek painter. He is said to have defeated Zeuxis, his contemporary, in a contest of painting illusions.

39. That is, the ninth of these philosophers, Daemonax.

40. Francis Bacon (1561–1626), English essayist, statesman, and philosopher, author of *The New Organon or True Directions Concerning the Interpretation of Nature,* is generally considered the founder of modern empirical science.

41. Olaus (actually Olaf Claudii) Borrichius (1626–90), an extremely learned Danish scholar who was professor of philosophy, poetry, botany, chemistry, and medicine.

42. Pater Martin Antonio Del Rio (1551–1608), a Jesuit professor of philosophy and theology who taught at Liège, Louvain, Graz, and Salamanca. His best-known work, *Disquisitionum magicarum libri VI* (3 vols., 1599), was said to have promoted the use of torture in witch trials.

43. The southernmost and smallest province in Portugal; at one time a kingdom.

44. Technique or art of discovering character traits and temperament from external features such as the face, shape of the head, etc. Wieland's friend and correspondent J. C. Lavater (1741–1801), a well-known clergyman in Zürich, wrote the work *Physiognomische Fragmente (Physiognomical Fragments)*, 4 vols., 1775–78, the first part of which Wieland reviewed in *The German Mercury* in 1775.

45. Literally: "little Greeks." Wieland found this Roman word in Juvenal's *Satires* 1.3.78. It expresses both sarcasm and envy and refers to a Greek bel esprit and know-all.

46. A French physician who became a professor of medicine in Pavia. He was one of the modern revivers of atomism and wrote *Democritus reviviscens sive vita et philosophia Democrati* (Pavia, 1646).

47. Greek: "lawgiver."

48. Friedrich von Hagedorn (1708–54), a German poet. He wrote the short piece called "The Blind Man." The sense of the poem is that a blind husband is easily persuaded of his wife's faithfulness. Wieland himself used this theme in his romantic epic *Oberon* of 1780.

49. Orpheus, the legendary Thracian poet and musician, went down to Hades to recover his dead wife Eurydice. With his music he persuaded Persephone, queen of the lower world, to let her go. But he forgot the condition not to look back at his wife, who then disappeared forever. Later he was torn to shreds by Thracian Maenads, "mad women," the devotees of the god Dionysus, either because he interfered with their rites or because, since he had lost Eurydice, he had become a hater of women.

50. Pliny the Elder.

51. Aulus Gellius (ca. A.D. 130–180), Roman author and grammarian, whose only work, *Noctes Atticae (Attic Nights)*, is of interest today because it is a compendium of all kinds of information about life in its author's time and contains excerpts from the works of authors no longer extant.

Second Book: Hippocrates in Abdera

1. Marcus Vitruvius Pollio (1st century B.C.), author of a treatise in ten books *De Architectura*.

2. See note 45 in First Book.

3. Hermes Trismegistus ("thrice great") was the name given by the Neoplatonists, mystics, and alchemists to the Egyptian god Toth, regarded as more or less identical with the Greek Hermes. Zoroaster (ca. 628–ca. 551 B.C.), Persian religious teacher and prophet who founded Zoroastrianism. Zoroaster is the Greek form of his Persian name: Zarathustra. In this context Wieland is referring to Orpheus as the founder of the Orphic Mysteries or Orphism, a religious cult of

ancient Greece. Orpheus was the legendary author of the sacred poems from which the Orphic doctrines were derived. Pythagoras (ca. 582–ca.507 B.C.), the pre-Socratic philosopher who founded the Pythagorean school. Although born on the island of Samos, he established himself at Crotona, a Greek settlement in southern Italy. Here he founded an ascetic religious and philosophical brotherhood that believed in the transmigration of souls (an affinity with Orphism) and that the explanation of the universe was to be found not in matter, but in number and numerical relations. The Pythagoreans had a significant influence on mathematics and astronomy.

4. At best a vague designation. However, in this context, Wieland probably means those philosophers who taught in Alexandria in the 1st century B.C. and the 1st century A.D. such as, perhaps, Philo Judaeus (fl. A.D. 39), who, among other things, wrote allegorical interpretations of the Old Testament. Quite generally, these thinkers have been characterized as eclectic, and their teachings included Neo-Pythagoreanism as well as Neoplatonism. Gradually oriental mysticism played an increasingly important role in their doctrines synthesizing elements from Plato, the Stoics, and Aristotle.

5. See note 14 in First Book.

6. Marcus Porcius Cato, "Cato the Censor," (234–149 B.C.), criticized the lax morals of the wealthy and noble Romans.

7. Lucius Annaeus Seneca (ca. 4 B.C.–A.D. 65), born at Corduba in Spain, was a Roman philosopher, a voluminous author, and writer of nine (or ten) plays that were to have a great influence on modern drama in England as well as in Italy. Wieland found the passage by Seneca that follows here in chapter 15 of his dialogue *De Tranquillitate Animi*.

8. Heraclitus of Ephesus, a Greek philosopher (fl. ca. 500 B.C.), whose melancholy suggested to others a comparison with Democritus, "the laughing philosopher."

9. Latin: "unless he is troubled with a cold in the head." But the text of Horace, *Epistles* 1.1.108 actually says: "nisi cum pituita molesta est."

10. Cf. end of book 1 of *The Iliad*.

11. Origines (A.D. 185 or 186–ca. 254), probably the most prolific author as well as the most distinguished theologian—with the possible exception of St. Augustine—of early Christianity, he succeeded Clement as head of the Christian school at Alexandria. To escape temptations of the flesh he castrated himself. Wieland wrote a verse tale, *Kombabus* (1771), based on a theme from Lucian, in which the hero castrates himself so that he will not violate Queen Astarte, who has been entrusted to his care by the king.

12. According to the *OED:* "a person superstitiously or extravagantly reverenced, or otherwise likened to a heathen deity; an idol."

13. Quintus Septimius Florens Tertullian (ca. A.D. 150–ca. 240), a Christian writer in Latin. Wieland is quoting from his *Apologeticus* 46.11. Cf. trans. by T. R. Glover in Loeb Classics (New York: Putnam, 1931).

14. See note 26 in First Book.

15. Solon (ca. 640–558 B.C.), first Attic poet and wise archon of Athens, whose laws he reformed. Anaxagoras of Clazomenae in Ionia, a Greek philosopher (born ca. 500 B.C.). He went to Athens where he became a friend of Pericles. Both Euripides and Thucydides were his pupils.

16. Johannes Stobaeus (ca. A.D. 500) wrote an anthology in four books of excerpts from Greek writers on a number of subjects. Sextus Empiricus (fl. ca. A.D. 190), a physician and philosopher, whose writings in Greek constitute the

chief source of our information on the philosophy of the Skeptics. Censorinus was a Roman grammarian and astrologer of the third century A.D. Still extant is his work *De die natali.*

17. Latin: "He is the greatest in trifles."

18. See p. 48 in First Book for an explanation of this term.

19. The largest river in ancient Thrace, east of Abdera.

20. Important city on the southeastern coast of Sicily, originally a colony of Corinth.

21. Dionysius I, ruler of Syracuse (404–367 B.C.).

22. Georges-Louis Leclerc, comte de Buffon (1707–88), French naturalist and author of the monumental *Histoire naturelle* (44 vols., 1749–1804).

23. Greek writer of comedies (ca. 372–270 B.C.). He is supposed to have written 245 plays, of which only fragments have survived.

24. Greek grammarian and sophist (fl. ca. 200 B.C.), author of the *Deipnosophistae* (in 15 books), which might be rendered in English: *The Company of Learned Diners.* Here we find in dialogue form all manner of subjects having to do with domestic and social life. It contains quotations from some 1500 other Greek authors whose works are no longer extant.

25. Latin: "a certain person" or "somebody."

26. A city in India southwest of New Delhi.

27. A character from the novel *Le sopha* (1742) by the French author Claude-Prosper Jolyot Crébillon (1707–77).

28. omrah—(Hindi *umrā,* from Arabic *umarā,* pl. of *amir:* ruler, commander) a lord or grandee of a Muslim court in India. Wieland also uses this word in his novel *The Golden Mirror,* 1772.

29. Title given Persian prime ministers from the seventeenth century on. Again a title Wieland uses in *The Golden Mirror.*

30. Eminent Greeks living ca. 620–550 B.C. who were considered wise. The generally accepted list includes the names of Bias, Chilon, Cleobulus, Periander, Pittacus, Solon, and Thales. However in his Protagoras (343), Plato lists Myson the Chenian instead of Periander.

31. The relationship between the literal meaning of this term ("person who shows figs") and the sense in which it came to be used ("a common informer, a false accuser") is by no means clear. In any case, the Greek verb συκοφαντέω means "to be an informer, to inform against, accuse falsely," and "extort." Wieland's *sycophants* are clearly intended to perform the function of lawyers in Abdera, and he makes them and litigiousness the objects of his satire throughout this novel. His sycophants, in fact, behave in such a way that the meaning of the term in modern English, namely "servile self-seeking flatterer," is not far off the mark here.

32. A medicinal herb, of which two varieties are mentioned by the ancients: *niger* (black), used as a purgative, and *albus* (white), as an emetic. The first variety, apparently with some kind of admixture, was also used as a remedy for madness. According to Strabo, the best was to be obtained in Anticyra, a city in Phokis. Thus the expression: "You need Anticyra," and "Let him sail to Anticyra."

33. The famous Greek physician born on the island of Cos, ca. 460 B.C. We know very little about his life. He died in Larissa (ca. 356 B.C.). While many writings were attributed to him, only a few have been found to be genuine. He is perhaps best known today for his *Aphorisms.*

34. In the northern Aegean Sea not far off the coast of Thrace, south and a bit west of Abdera.

35. City in Thessaly, presumably the home of Hippocrates.

36. The Molossians were Hellenic and settled in Epirus. However, they mixed so readily with foreign peoples that other Greeks considered them half barbarian.

37. In Greek mythology the son of Apollo and the god of medicine. He learned his art from the wise Centaur Chiron.

38. From the city of Miletus on the coast of Asia Minor.

39. The very accomplished and celebrated hetaera or courtesan from Miletus who was the lifelong companion of Pericles.

40. See Introduction, p. 30.

41. My translation of the German word *Mückenseiger,* a term Wieland may well have taken from Luther's translation of Matt. 23.24, where the expression is used to convey "those who strain at a gnat."

42. Orestes avenged the murder of his father, the great king Agamemnon, by killing his mother, Clytemnestra. His cousin, Pylades, was his faithful and resourceful friend. Both figures appear in the play *Iphigenia in Tauris* by Euripides and in Sophocles' *Electra,* although in the latter play Pylades does not have a speaking role.

43. See note 32 above in this Book.

44. Region in Asia Minor between Phrygia and Cappadocia.

45. That is, the Oracle of Apollo.

46. A philosopher and historian who accompanied Alexander the Great.

47. Armed with a helmet from Pluto to make him invisible, with wings on his feet from Hermes, and with a shining mirror from Athena, Perseus went forth to bring back the head of Medusa, one of the three terrible Gorgons. Because he could look at her indirectly with the mirror, he was not turned into stone, and so he cut off her head and took it with him. Later he changed a monster into stone by showing it Medusa's head. He then managed to free the beautiful Andromeda who had been chained to a rock because her mother had offended the Nereïds. He married Andromeda, but he had to fight off another suitor, Phineus, whom he turned to stone with all his men by showing them the head of Medusa.

48. Literally: *Dios kouroi,* "the sons of Zeus," Castor and Polydeuces (Pollux in Latin), were the twin sons of Zeus and Leda, and thus they were the brothers of Helen (of Troy). Later legends place them both among the stars as the constellation Gemini ("the Twins").

49. The literal equivalent of the term *Zahnbrecher* in the original German with which Wieland may be translating the comical Latin word *dentifrangibulus* meaning "toothbreaker" or "one who knocks out teeth." Cf. the *Bacchides* 4.2.23 of Plautus.

50. One of the Greeks at Troy, about whom Homer tells us in book 5 of *The Iliad* that he could shout in a voice as great as fifty other men shouting together.

51. The Greeks did mark the middle of the day, but since they divided the time between sunrise and sunset into twelve hours, the middle of the day, or noon, could not have been the twelfth hour as here. This anachronism—among the many others in this novel—is a deliberate bit of humor. This scene, no doubt, reflects the behavior of Wieland's fellow citizens at a meeting of the town council in Biberach.

Third Book: Euripides among the Abderites

1. The basis of this opposition is the famous quarrel in seventeenth-century France between the faction of the Ancients, led by Boileau, whose ideal of beauty in art was based on the imitation of the ancients, and that of the Moderns, led by

Perrault, whose concerns were rather aimed at a future achieved through rationalism and progress.

2. In the Hanser Edition, edited by F. Martini and H. W. Seiffert, 2:243, this expression appears, probably correctly, as *quid pro quo,* which means "something for something" (i.e., "an exchange").

3. We are supposed to understand that this homegrown Abderite play is the exact opposite of the excellent tragedy *Antigone* written by Sophocles in 442 B.C. However, we are given no clue as to whether Physignatus wrote his play about the Erigone who hanged herself when she found the grave of her slain father Icarius, or about Erigone, the daughter of Clytemnestra and Aegisthus.

4. Greek: "living pleasantly."

5. Greek: "evil genius."

6. Quoted from Horace's *Epistles* 1.7.94: ". . . by the guardian spirit, the right hand, and the family deities. . . ."

7. In the decade before Wieland began writing his *History of the Abderites,* the establishment of standing theaters was seriously discussed and considered in various parts of Germany. The existence of the *Comédie-Française* in Paris suggested that such a theater in Germany should be a "National Theater." This was first accomplished in Hamburg, where Lessing served as critic. Other such theaters were then established in Vienna (1776), Mannheim (1779), and Berlin (1786). See W. H. Bruford, *Theatre, Drama, and Audience in Goethe's Germany* (London: Routledge, 1957), 102–7. Wieland's personal experiences with the National Theater at Mannheim, founded by Karl Theodor, Elector of the Palatinate, are said to have suggested many of the incidents in the Third Book of this novel.

8. Minerva was the Roman goddess identified with the Greek Athena, patroness of Athens. Accordingly Wieland means Athens here. With this, however, he is parodying the proclivity of many of his German contemporaries to find admirable whatever has come from Paris.

9. Wieland is poking fun here at the national subject matter that the young, noisy poets of the "Storm and Stress" movement (ca. 1769–78) thought appropriate for German writers.

10. Latin: "treasury."

11. Quoted from Horace's *Epistles* 2.1.117: "Whether learned or not, we write poetry at random."

12. Wieland has made up this name from Greek *onos,* "ass," and *laos,* "people."

13. A tragedy. The Greek word τραγῳδία is thought to have meant "goat song."

14. Just why Wieland has these young men sitting on the women's laps rather than the other way around is not clear.

15. Latin: "King Midas has the ears of an ass." According to an ancient story, this semi-legendary Phrygian ruler judged Pan's flute playing better than Apollo's. For this Apollo gave him the ears of an ass as a sign of his stupidity. Midas did his best to hide his peculiar ears under his cap. His barber, however, discovered the secret. Since he was not permitted to tell anyone but was also unable to keep the secret, he dug a hole and into it whispered the words: "King Midas has the ears of an ass." But when reeds grew up in that place, they repeated the words of the barber whenever the wind blew, and that is how the world learned about the ears of Midas.

16. Either in *Iphigenia in Aulis* or in *Iphigenia in Tauris,* both of them extant plays by Euripides (ca. 480–406 B.C.).

17. Either in *The Trojan Women* or *Andromache,* also extant plays by Euripides.

18. This deliberate anachronism was necessary to Wieland's parody of certain

situations at the National Theater at Mannheim. Ancient Greek actors were men, who played even the female roles.

19. Two writers of tragedy in Athens, father and son, bore this name. Both wrote in the fourth century B.C., and especially the elder is said to have been a prolific author with more than 200 plays attributed to him. None of their plays are extant; we only know some of their titles.

20. Terms for the first two stanzas of a lyric triad in Greek poetry.

21. See note 34 in First Book.

22. These plays by Gryllus had famous models, for Euripides had written a play about each of these three women.

23. By Asiatic Greece is meant the areas to the east of the Aegean Sea which were settled by Greeks in what is Turkey today.

24. Damon was an Attic theoretician of music in the second half of the fifth century B.C. He was one of Pericles' teachers.

25. Wieland apparently constructed this name from the Greek verb *thláō* which means "crush" or "bruise," but also "bray."

26. Meaning, presumably, that they deserved to be flayed as was the flute-playing Phrygian satyr Marsyas, who challenged Apollo to a musical contest and lost.

27. All five were celebrated Greek poets. Anacreon (sixth century B.C.) wrote elegies, epigrams, and light and playful songs about love and wine. Alcaeus (seventh to sixth century B.C.) was a lyric poet whose name is associated with the Alcaic stanza. Pindar (ca. 522–ca. 442 B.C.), the greatest of the Greek lyric poets, was especially gifted as a writer of odes. Aeschylus (525–456 B.C.) was the writer of great tragedies, among them the trilogy known as the *Oresteia*. Aristophanes (ca. 448–ca. 380 B.C.), the great Athenian comic poet; his plays include *The Clouds, The Wasps,* and *The Frogs.*

28. A favorite theme of Greek art and literature was the pitiful story of Niobe, the daughter of Tantalus. She boasted to the goddess Leto of her superiority, for she had six (or seven) sons and six (or seven) daughters, the number seems uncertain, while Leto had only two children, Apollo and Artemis. Angered by Niobe's boasting, Apollo and Artemis killed all of her children with their arrows. She was petrified by her grief and remains a large stone on Sipylus, a Lydian mountain. Wieland's mention of a play about Niobe in this context could be a jab at the Storm and Stress author Friedrich ("Maler") Müller, who wrote a lyrical drama *Niobe* in 1778, but Wieland denied that this had been his intention.

29. These syllables are conventional interjections used by Greek tragic poets.

30. Greek poet (ca. 342–292 B.C.), most famous writer of New Comedy. Although we have only a few fragments of his plays, his influence survives in the comedies of Plautus, Terence, and Molière.

31. Latin: "in a pure state of nature" (i.e., "as they really were").

32. See note 10 above in Third Book.

33. Quotation from the Bible: Deut. 25.4.

34. Most of Wieland's German-speaking readers, except the Swiss and Alsatians, were inhabitants of the Holy Roman Empire of the German Nation, which was not dissolved until 1806.

35. Latin: "without burdening the public."

36. Latin: "to each one" (i.e., "per person").

37. Originally a Persian measure of weight, the talent, as adopted by Athens and Corinth, was a monetary unit representing about fifty-eight lbs. of silver. Presumably its worth was approximately the same in Abdera.

38. Produced in 412 B.C. Only a few fragments of it remain, but they suggest its beauty.

39. See note 49 in First Book.

40. Another of Wieland's names based on Greek words. This one means "she of the fair bosom."

41. City on the Corinthian Gulf and just west of Corinth. Polyclitus, creator of the well-known statue called the *Doryphorus (Spear Bearer)*, founded the school of sculpture in Sicyon. If they were associates of this renowned master, the artists there surely had good taste.

42. See note 27 in First Book.

43. Andromeda's mother was Cassiopeia. The woman in the audience means that Eukolpis should have been given the role of "a more mature" woman.

44. See Wieland's note at the bottom of p. 70.

45. In Elis, where the Olympian Festival provided poets and orators opportunity to recite from their works. The games, of course, constituted the main feature of these events.

46. One of the labors imposed by Eurystheus on Heracles was the slaying of the Hydra, a huge serpent that lived in the marshes of Lerna near Argos. Whenever one of its numerous heads was cut off, others grew in its place.

47. See note 44 in First Book.

48. Greek form of the name EURIPIDES.

49. Latin: "Singers like to drink." Wieland gives us no clue as to why a Thracian Greek should be quoting a Latin adage.

50. Ruled 413–399 B.C.

51. Greek: "supernatural things," or "demons," or "the spirit world."

52. See note 1 in Preface.

53. Great Greek lyric poet (ca. 556–ca. 468 B.C.) whose moral sayings were often quoted.

54. A great huntress in Greek mythology. Her suitors had to defeat her in a race on foot, but Hippomenes dropped three golden apples in her path. She stopped to pick them up and so lost the race.

55. Like wealthy young men of the eighteenth century, among whom it was fashionable to make the "grand tour" of Paris, London, and Rome.

56. This is an obvious error, for the Ionian Sea lies west of the Greek mainland, not to the east. Wieland means the Aegean Sea.

57. Son of Cecrops II and Metiadusa, the sister of Daedalus, he became ruler of Megara after having been expelled from Athens. He reconquered Attica and divided the land among his four sons—probably before the sixth century B.C.

58. Ancient name for the Thracian river flowing south into the Thracian Sea just west of Abdera.

59. Cyrus the Great, founder of the Persian Empire. He died in 528 or 529 B.C.

60. But in the King James Bible this expression is rendered with the word *superstition,* and Luther used the German word *abergläubig,* which also means "superstitious."

61. The guild master means "principle."

62. The guild master's Latin, too, leaves much to be desired. He means, of course, *Vox populi, vox Dei,"* "the voice of the people is the voice of God."

63. Latin: "that which is single," or "simple." Here Pfriem has stumbled once again, for it appears likely he meant to use the Greek word συμβουλή, "counsel."

64. Latin: "by closing the eyes," or "pretending not to notice."

65. Latin: "without consequence" (i.e., "without establishing a precedent").

66. Cf. in Homer's *Iliad* 5.859ff.

67. Theater perspective was introduced in the late sixteenth century by the Italians Palladio and Scomozzi in the Renaissance theater of the Olympian Academy at Vicenza. Further developments were achieved at Parma in the second decade of the seventeenth century in the Teatro Farnese, which has been called the first modern theater. Wieland, of course, expected his readers to appreciate this anachronism.

68. See note 37 in First Book.

69. Johann Georg Forster, *Johann Reinhold Forsters Reise um die Welt*, 2 vols. (1778–80). A version in English had already been published in 2 vols. in 1777 entitled *A Voyage towards the South Pole and round the World*.

70. *A Sentimental Journey through France and Italy by Mr. Yorick* (1768), a work making fun of travel books, was written by Laurence Sterne, the author of *Tristram Shandy*.

71. The material quoted here by Wieland from Sterne has not been translated from his German. Instead, the actual text is reproduced here, with Wieland's cuts as indicated, from the chapter "A Fragment" in Sterne's *A Sentimental Journey*, ed. Ian Jack (London: Oxford University Press, 1968), 34–35.

72. See note 15 above in Third Book.

73. Oh Eros, you, Lord of gods and men!
    Either do not teach us that foul is fair,
    Or help the poor lovers you created to bear
        to good issue as they toil,
    The toils you have imposed on them, etc.

74. See note 2 in Preface.

75. The phrase *the German Garrick* is apparently to be read as being in apposition with *Schröter*. Johann F. H. Brockmann (1745–1812) was a German actor who won fame in the role of Hamlet. Schröter = Friedrich Ludwig Schröder (1744–1816), the distinguished theater manager in Hamburg and so famous an actor of Shakespearean roles that he was compared to David Garrick (1716–79), probably the greatest actor on the English stage in the eighteenth century.

76. After the death of Alexander the Great, this general became first the governor and then the king of Thrace. He died in 282 or 281 B.C.

77. Italian: "If it is not the truth, it is a clever invention."

Fourth Book: The Trial Concerning the Ass's Shadow

1. Latin: "the form of the deed" (i.e., "the kind of thing done").

2. Expression used by Laurence Sterne in passage quoted in Third Book, p. 185.

3. Wieland depicts the destruction of Abdera by frogs, rats, and mice in the Fifth Book.

4. City on the Saronic Gulf facing the island of Salamis.

5. Considered a god of fertility, especially in Asia Minor, this son of Aphrodite once killed a favorite ass of Dionysus, which may have given rise to the practice of sacrificing asses to this minor deity.

6. See note 31 in Second Book.

7. Perhaps *farthing*, a former monetary unit in Britain worth one-fourth of a

penny, best translates the German *Blaffert,* a small coin once used in southwest Germany.

8. Two further examples of the humorous names Wieland gives his characters. The first means "puff-jaw," the second "loud-crier" or "big-talker", and both are the names of frogs in the pseudo-Homeric *Batrachomyomachia.* Cf. Hesiod, *The Homeric Hymns and Homerica* (London: Heinemann, 1977), 553 and 557, respectively.

9. The goddess who, originally, allotted to human beings the share of both fortune and misfortune that they deserved. Later on she was thought to be the goddess who punished overweening pride, especially such as was insolent to the gods.

10. Latin: "on account of likeness of procedure," or "because of similarity of intellect."

11. See note 36 in First Book.

12. It turns out that a temple to Jason in Abdera was not Wieland's invention for, among his other sources, Pierre Bayle mentions this in the article on Abdera in his *Dictionnaire historique et critique,* 4me éd. par Des Maizeaux (1730) 1:15.

13. One of the sons of Heracles was named Agathyrsus (cf. Herodotus 4:10), but this appears to have no significance so far as Wieland's archpriest is concerned.

14. In a dialogue by Lucian of Samosata a mother named Krobyle urges her daughter to become a courtesan. See *Lucian* (London: Heinemann, 1961), 7:386ff.

15. From Miletus in Asia Minor.

16. See note 5 in First Book.

17. Latin: "from the agreement and general custom of mankind."

18. Latin: "between living persons."

19. Latin: "because of death."

20. Latin: "yet without prejudice to better interpretations."

21. Latin: "reasons for deliberating and coming to a decision."

22. Latin: "a sum high enough to warrant review by an appellate court."

23. Latin: "from the egg" (i.e., "from the very beginning"). This expression is found in the *Ars poetica* of Horace, line 147. The real point is that Horace is praising Homer for *not* beginning his *Iliad* from the "two eggs" of Leda. In the translation of Francis Howes in *The Art of Poetry,* ed. A. S. Cook (New York: Stechert, 1926), 11, the pertinent lines run as follows: "Nor does he run his subject out of breath / In dry detail from Meleager's death / To Diomed's return; nor yet begins / The Trojan War from Leda and her twins; / But posting onwards, brooking no delay, / To the mid-theme he boldly bursts his way." We can only conclude that Wieland is joking with those of his readers who knew their Horace well.

24. See note 12 in First Book and chapter 9 of Third Book, 172ff., where Strobylus relates to Euripides the history of the frogs of Latona.

25. Persian and Macedonian gold coins from the time of Darius I of Persia and Philip II of Macedonia.

26. Céladon is the name of a sentimental lover in the pastoral novel *L'Astrée* by the French writer Honoré d'Urfé (1568–1625).

27. Still another of Wieland's humorous names. It is compounded from the Greek word meaning "ox" plus that meaning "understanding" or "mind," and so adds up, in German, to *Ochsenkopf,* "head of an ox," which is as much as to say "blockhead" in English.

28. Latin: "it is proper to conclude that if a thing cannot be, it is not."

29. Greek goddess personifying justice.

30. See note 31 in First Book.

31. The ancient names of two Thracian rivers. The Hebrus is to the east of Abdera, the Nestus just to the west.

32. See note 34 in Second Book.

33. Weapons used mostly in the fifteenth and sixteenth centuries A.D. Wieland uses this word to convey that the weapons were far out of date.

34. Three prominent French scholars. Étienne Fourmont (1683–1745) and François Sevin were Orientalists, and Jean Baptiste Gaspar D'ansse de Villoison (1750–1805) was a renowned scholar of Greek, particularly of Homer's *Iliad*. In the early 1780s the latter visited Weimar, where Wieland was one of his greatest admirers.

35. The Scottish poet James Macpherson (1736–96), a teacher by profession, published *Fragments of Ancient Poetry collected in the Highlands of Scotland* in 1760 and the prose epic *Fingal* in 1762, followed by *Temora* in 1763. These he passed off as translations from the Gaelic by the blind Gaelic bard Ossian. Among those on the Continent who were taken in by these claims were both Goethe and Herder. The latter's *Extract from Correspondence on Ossian and the Songs of Ancient Peoples* of 1773 helped lay the theoretical foundations of the Storm and Stress movement in German literature.

36. Wieland is here playing in German *(Feigenredner)* with the translation of the Greek word *sycophantes,* that literally means "a person who shows figs." See also note 31 in Second Book.

37. A sophist and teacher of rhetoric from Leontini in Sicily who lived from ca. 485 to 375 B.C. and was noted for his beautiful, rhythmic expression and the short, symmetrical clauses in his sentences. The turgid prose Wieland puts into the mouth of Physignatus is supposed to create a humorous contrast to the style of this sycophant's teacher, a joke that Wieland surely expected the Greek scholars among his readers to understand and appreciate.

38. According to Greek legend, the lands beyond Boreas ("the north wind") peopled by worshipers of Apollo.

39. See chapter 9 of Third Book, p. 172.

40. At first a term applied to the "Hill of Ares" in ancient Athens. It was on this hill that, according to legend, Orestes was tried for avenging his father's murder by killing his mother Clytemnestra. This name was later applied to the distinguished judicial body itself that sat on this hill.

41. An incident like this occurs in Wieland's own humorous verse tale *Die Titanomachie (The Battle of the Titans)* of 1775, in which, in lines 80–83, the ass of Silenus alerts the Olympian gods with his braying.

42. Latin: "whatever appropriate."

Fifth Book: The Frogs of Latona

1. Orchomenos, city of the Minyai, adjoining the land of the Boeotians, not Orchomenos north of Mantinea in Arcadia.

2. Wieland's humorous construction in analogy with his use in the Third Book, p. 176, of the Greek word *deisidaemonia,* which he translates as "fear of the gods." Since the Greek word *batrachos* means "frog," *deisibatrachy* would mean "reverence for frogs."

3. Greek word meaning simply "cup," but it was also a unit of liquid measure

which was the equivalent of 0.0456 liter. Obviously, the Abderite *kyathos* held more.

4. See note 32 in Second Book.
5. Greek: "crow" or "raven."
6. From the Greek *Katádoupoi*, "the Cataracts" of the Nile.
7. The owl was one of the attributes of Athena, Greek goddess of wisdom, and symbolized the sharpness of her vision.
8. As is recounted in Thucydides (6:54–59), Harmodius, together with his friend Aristogiton, conspired in 514 B.C. to rid Athens of the tyrannical Peisistratidae.
9. Greek: "loud shouter." This, again, is the name of a frog in the pseudo-Homeric *Batrachomyomachia*.
10. See note 50 in Second Book.
11. The Greek verb στίλβω means metaphorically "shine" or "be bright." Wieland evidently so named Stilbon because he was, as the Germans say, *eine große Leuchte seines Fachs,* "a great light in his field."
12. Memphis was the capital of ancient Egypt through most of its early history. Persepolis was the capital of ancient Persia proper, although the kings resided mostly in Babylon or Ecbatana.
13. The people inhabiting Greece before the invasion from the north of the tribes that introduced Indo-European speech, ca. end of the third or beginning of the second millenium B.C.
14. The ancient Greek parallel to the story of Noah and the flood in the Old Testament. The crimes among men having become altogether too great, Zeus decided to destroy mankind with a flood. But Prometheus warned Deucalion, who built a ship for himself and his wife Pyrrha. When the water subsided, they landed on Mt. Parnassus.
15. Delos, the birthplace of both Apollo and Artemis, is a tiny Aegean island that, according to legend, floated about in the sea until Apollo fastened it into place between the islands Mykonos and Rhenea.
16. Latin: "majority."
17. Latin: "those sounder in mind."
18. This name is based on two Greek words which, in combination, mean "eater of everything."
19. Greek: "bullheaded."
20. This distinguished Greek painter (fl. ca. 400 B.C.) is said to have produced, among many other works, a number of erotica.
21. Skeptical Greek philosopher (ca. 315–240 B.C.).
22. Range of mountains in ancient northern Thrace. They are known today as the Balkan Mountains.
23. Translation of Wieland's German word *ranifiziert,* based on the Latin word for "frog," *rana.*
24. Latin: "in one and the same act."
25. Latin: "holy object."
26. Latin: "in hope of approval and appreciation."
27. As related by the Roman poet Ovid (43 B.C.–A.D. 18) in his *Metamorphoses* 3:339ff.; 12:64ff; and 1:452ff. respectively.
28. Ninus, according to Greek legend, was the founder of the Assyrian Empire, and the beautiful and wise Semiramis was his queen. When he died, she ruled in his stead for forty-two years.

NOTES

29. In "Isis and Osiris" in Book 5 of Plutarch's *Moralia,* trans. F. C. Babbit (London: Heinemann, 1936), 25, we read: "In Saïs, the statue of Athena, whom they believe to be Isis, bore the inscription: 'I am all that has been, and is, and shall be, and my robe no mortal has yet uncovered.'"

30. This city clerk's name literally means "fire-eye." Could he, like his modern counterpart, Wieland, who was the city clerk in Biberach, have been up all night writing verses? Perhaps this is why he now appears with bloodshot eyes before the Council of Abdera.

31. See note 5 in Fourth Book.

32. Son of Antipater, Kassander ruled impetuously and tyrannically in Macedonia from 318 to 297 B.C.

33. See note 6 in First Book.

34. Marcus Terentius Varro (116–27 B.C.) was a poet, grammarian, geographer, jurist, historian, philosopher, and—very probably the most learned of the Romans. Very little of all he wrote (in more than 600 volumes) has survived. The information from Varro, of which Wieland speaks here, is conveyed by Pliny the Elder in his *Naturalis Historia* 8:43.

The Key to the History of the Abderites, 1781

1. Wieland actually says *Ammenmärchen,* "old wives' tales." For *Milesian tales* see note 3 in First Book.

2. Horace *Epistles* 1.2. Horace holds up Odysseus as being particularly worthy of emulation.

3. Wieland is referring here to the essay "How the Young Man Should Study Poetry" in Book 1 of Plutarch's *Moralia.*

4. Hermetic beliefs were associated with Toth, the Egyptian god of wisdom whose name was sometimes translated into Greek as Hermes Trismegistus and was, therefore, equated with the Greek god Hermes. On the term *Orphic,* see note 49 in First Book and note 3 in Second Book.

5. The notion that the Roman poet Vergil, author of *The Aeneid,* was a magician was widespread in the medieval world, when many people regarded him with superstitious reverence. One of the earliest pieces of written evidence of such belief in his magical powers is a letter, dated 1194, of the imperial chancellor of the Holy Roman Empire.

6. *Amadis de Gaula (Amadis of Gaul),* a famous chivalric romance, survives only in a Castilian text. Its date, author, and original language are unknown, but it is claimed by both Spain and Portugal. While the oldest known edition is dated 1508, this epic is undoubtedly older.

Orlando furioso (The Frenzy of Roland), begun in 1503 as a continuation of the epic *Orlando Innamorato (Roland in Love)* by Matteo Maria Boiardo, was first published in 1516, and in an expanded version (forty-six cantos) one year before the death of its author, Ludovico Ariosto (1474–1533).

Italia liberata dai Goti (Italy Liberated from the Goths) is an Italian epic poem written by Gian Giorgio Trissino (1478–1550).

The great epic of the Portuguese is *Os Lusiadas (The Lusiads)* of 1572, the most celebrated work of Luis de Camoëns (ca. 1524–80). Its central theme is a voyage to India by Vasco da Gama.

Adone, a long allegorical poem, was first published in Paris in 1623. Its Italian author, Giambattista Marino (1569–1625), wrote in an elaborate and florid style, much admired and imitated in his time, which came to be known as "Marinismo."

7. *Zodiacus vitae,* a didactic poem in Latin, was published at Basel in 1543. Its author, Pier Angelo Manzolli, called "Marcellus Palingenius," was born near Ferrara around the end of the fifteenth century.

John Barclay (1582–1621), a Scottish satirist and Latin poet, wrote the Latin romance *Argenis.* It was printed in Paris in 1621. Most of the editions are supplied with a key to the characters and names.

Edmund Spenser (ca. 1552–99), using as his models the great poems of the Italians Ariosto and Tasso, wrote a very long, although uncompleted, allegory *The Faerie Queene* (1590–95).

Marie de la Rivière Manley (ca. 1663–1724), one of the first women to earn a living by writing, wrote the scandalous narrative *Secret Memoirs . . . of Several Persons of Quality from the New Atlantis, an Island in the Mediterranean,* 1709.

Les Princesses malabaras, ou Le Célibat philosophique (The Malabarian Princesses or the Philosophical Bachelor), a satirical romance directed against the Jesuits, appeared anonymously in 1743 with the fictitious Andrinople as the place of publication. Its author has been thought to be either Louis Pierre de Longue or the Abbé Dufresnoy.

Jonathan Swift (1667–1745), dean of St. Patrick's in Dublin, wrote *A Tale of a Tub,* 1704.

John Arbuthnot (1667–1735), British physician and author, a close friend of both Jonathan Swift and Alexander Pope, wrote a satirical work consisting of five tracts, of which the first appeared in 1712, and they were published together, in two parts, in 1727 under the title *History of John Bull.*

8. By the end of 1753, Wieland's twentieth year, he had already produced a number of literary works including the didactic poem *Die Natur der Dinge (The Nature of Things);* the poem on a subject from the Bible, *Der gepryfte Abraham (The Testing of Abraham);* and *Briefe von Verstorbenen an hinterlassene Freunde (Epistles from the Dead to Surviving Friends),* a series of poems in hexameters.

9. What follows at this point in the novel is a fictitious quotation from the learned work of the equally fictitious German scholar Hafen Slawkenbergius, the fanciful creation of Laurence Sterne in his novel *Tristram Shandy.* Slawkenbergius has spent most of his life on a vast philosophical treatise *De Nasis (On Noses).* Sterne offers three bilingual double-pages as a sample from this great work under the title "Slawkenbergii Fabella" ("Slawkenbergius's Tale"), wherein we read of Nosarians and Antinosarians, a party division bound to have appealed to Wieland.

10. An unmistakably sharp jab at the Storm and Stress writers. They accepted as their literary program the ideas set forth in the tract *Von deutscher Art und Kunst (On German Nature and Art),* 1773, that contained, among other things, essays by Herder on *Ossian and the Songs of Ancient Peoples* and on *Shakespeare,* and a piece by Goethe in praise of Gothic art. The work generally emphasized indigenous art and culture in preference to the rational and cosmopolitan.

11. Latin: "To have eschewed folly is the beginning of wisdom." This is quoted from Horace's *Epistles* 1.1.41–42, and the entire passage reads: "Virtus est vitium fugere et sapientia prima stultitia caruisse." ("To flee from vice is the beginning of virtue and to have eschewed folly is the beginning of wisdom.")

Select Bibliography on Wieland and on His Novel *History of the Abderites*

In English:

Abbé, Derek M. van. *Christoph Martin Wieland (1733–1813). A Literary Biography.* London: Harrap, 1961.

Blackall, Eric A. *The Emergence of German as a Literary Language 1700–1775.* 2d ed. with a new bibliographical essay. Ithaca and London: Cornell University Press, 1978.

Bruford, Walter H. *Culture and Society in Classical Weimar, 1775–1806.* [London]: Cambridge University Press, 1962.

——. *Germany in the Eighteenth Century: The Social Background of the Literary Revival.* Cambridge [Eng.]: At the University Press, 1965.

Kurth-Voigt, Lieselotte E. "The Reception of C. M. Wieland in America." In *The German Contribution to the Building of the Americas: Studies in Honor of Karl J. R. Arndt,* 97–133, edited by Gerhard K. Friesen and Walter Schatzberg. Hanover, N. H.: Clark University Press, 1977.

McCarthy, John A. *Christoph Martin Wieland.* Boston: Twayne, 1979.

Yuill, W. E. "Abderites and Abderitism, some reflections on a Novel by Wieland." In *Essays in German Literature,* edited by F. Norman, 1:72–91. London: University of London Institute of Germanic Studies, 1965.

In German and English:

Kurth, Lieselotte E. and John A. McCarthy, eds. *German Issue:* "Christoph Martin Wieland, 1733–1813." *Modern Language Notes* 99 (April 1984): 421–706. (Contains fourteen articles in German, three in English.)

Schelle, Hansjörg, ed. *Christoph Martin Wieland, North American Scholarly Contributions on the 250th Anniversary of his Birth 1983.* Tübingen: Max Niemeyer, 1984. (Contains thirteen articles in German, eleven in English.)

In German:

Edelstein, Ludwig. *Wielands "Abderiten" und der deutsche Humanismus.* University of California Publications in Modern Philology, vol. 26, no. 5. Berkeley and Los Angeles, 1950.

Günther, Gottfried, and Heidi Zeilinger, eds. *Wieland-Bibliographie.* Berlin and Weimar: Aufbau Verlag, 1983.

326

Jakobs, Jürgen. *Wielands Romane*. Bern and Munich: Francke, 1969.

Martini, Fritz. "Wieland. Geschichte der Abderiten." In *Der deutsche Roman,* edited by Benno von Wiese 1:64–94. Düsseldorf: Bagel, 1963.

Schelle, Hansjörg, ed. *Christoph Martin Wieland*. Wege der Forschung, no. 421. Darmstadt: Wissenschaftliche Buchgesellschaft, 1981.

Sengle, Friedrich. *Wieland*. Stuttgart: Metzler, 1949.

Sommer, Cornelius. *Christoph Martin Wieland*. Sammlung Metzler, no. 95. Stuttgart: Metzler, 1971.

Starnes, Thomas C. *Christoph Martin Wieland. Leben und Werk*. Aus zeitgenössischen Werken chronologisch dargestellt. 3 vols. Sigmaringen: Thorbecke, 1987.

Wolffheim, Hans. *Wielands Begriff der Humanität*. Hamburg: Hoffmann und Campe, 1949.